T0000280

ADVANCE PRAISE

"To read this book is to explore a gentle, thriving garden. Myriad kinds of identity and love blossom in different colors, shapes and sizes, every aroma beautifully distinct. Story-vines weave throughout, interconnecting petal-layers of meaning, truths springing from deep roots and opening toward the sun."

—RoAnna Sylver, author of *Chameleon Moon*

"Through a deep world, lush prose, and delightfully crafted characters, Cochrane employs fairy tales within fairy tales to explore queerness and self-realization with a delicate and honest touch. *The Story of the Hundred Promises* is a beautiful tale of trust and love that will dig its roots deep within you and never let go."

—Claudie Arseneault, author of *Baker Thief*

"Neil Cochrane's *The Story of the Hundred Promises* is set in a world where folktales can come true, where magic can change lives, where a quest undertaken with a pure heart just might succeed. His cast of characters sweeps you along, but they quest not for treasure or sacred objects—they quest for wisdom and knowledge, for renewal and connection. Cochrane has a gift for describing the sublime moments of natural beauty we see when we slow down enough to live in the moment. Amongst the many layers of this complex and deftly woven novel are both a love song to the restorative powers of nature, and a cautionary tale about the perils of commodifying natural resources. *The Story of the Hundred Promises* is an affirmation of the myriad ways of being a human, and of the many forms that love takes when loosed from the confining bonds of a binary culture. Cochrane's novel offers the hope that, if we do the work on ourselves and our relationships to heal the traumas of the past, we can and do rise to our best selves, and to our highest ideals of kindness and inclusiveness."

—Stevan Allred, author of *The Alehouse at the End of the World*

"I absolutely love Neil's latest book! The lush writing, the adventure, the lyrical fairytale bent to the prose. This book is gorgeous! It's a wondrous look at finding one's true self and what that means when presented with a challenging past."

—Annie Carl, bookseller, The Neverending Bookshop

"*The Story of the Hundred Promises* is a rosebud of a story, with fairy-tale petals tightly wound around the characters at its core. As the tale unfurls, the reader is drawn deeper into the world as it explores the nature of love in its many forms, and you can't help but feel enchanted by the last page."

—Lish McBride, author of *Curses*

"In a world of alternatives, love of all sorts weaves throughout this fantastic tale like rose vines. But it is self-acceptance and love for one's own being that rings true throughout all realities."

—Jonah Barrett, author of *Moss Covered Claws*

"A lush and evocative fantasy that explores the quiet places of generational trauma with true gentleness, through the eyes of characters who feel so honest and true you can't help but cling to optimism even in the face of fear. A fairy tale every bit as new as it is familiar, this book is a triumph."

—Emmie Mears, author of the Stonebreaker series

Praise for *The Longing and the Lack*

"Combines ancient curses and stolen kisses effortlessly, bringing a progressive passion to the paranormal."

—William Ritter, author of the
New York Times-best-selling *Jackaby* series

"Gothic curses, deadly love affairs, and vengeful ghosts combine to make this paranormal mystery a compelling page-turner."

—Tina Connolly, Nebula-nominated author of *Ironskin*

THE STORY OF
THE HUNDRED PROMISES

THE STORY OF THE HUNDRED PROMISES

a novel

NEIL COCHRANE

FOREST AVENUE PRESS
Portland, Oregon

This is a work of fiction. Any resemblance these characters have to actual persons, living or dead, is entirely coincidental.

© 2022 by Neil Cochrane

All rights reserved. No portion of this publication may be reproduced in any form, with the exception of reviewers quoting short passages, without the written permission of the publisher.

Library of Congress Cataloging-in-Publication Data

Names: Cochrane, Neil, 1989- author.
Title: The story of the hundred promises : a novel / Neil Cochrane.
Description: Portland, Oregon : Forest Avenue Press, [2022] | Summary: "Trans sailor Darragh Thorn has made a comfortable life for himself among people who love and accept him. Ten years after his exile from home, though, his sister asks him to reconcile with their ailing father. Determined to resolve his feelings rather than just survive them, Darragh sets off on a quest to find the one person who can heal a half-dead man: the mysterious enchanter who once gave him the magic he needed to become his true self. But so far as anyone knows, no one but Darragh has seen the enchanter for a century, and the fairy tales that survive about em give more cause for fear than hope. In lush and evocative prose, and populated with magical trees and a wise fox, The Story of the Hundred Promises is a big-hearted fantasy suffused with queer optimism"-- Provided by publisher.
Identifiers: LCCN 2022010438 (print) | LCCN 2022010439 (ebook) | ISBN 9781942436515 (paperback) | ISBN 9781942436522 (epub)
Subjects: LCGFT: Fantasy fiction. | Novels.
Classification: LCC PS3603.O29326 S76 2022 (print) | LCC PS3603.O29326 (ebook) | DDC 813/.6--dc23/eng/20220308
LC record available at https://lccn.loc.gov/2022010438
LC ebook record available at https://lccn.loc.gov/2022010439

Distributed by Publishers Group West

Published in the United States of America
by Forest Avenue Press LLC
Portland, Oregon

Printed in the United States

Forest Avenue Press LLC
P.O. Box 80134
Portland, OR 97280
forestavenuepress.com

1 2 3 4 5 6 7 8 9

To Ori, Lydia, Elisabeth, and Bree

PRINCIPAL CHARACTERS

Darragh, a sailor

Vesta, his sister

Jovan, their father

Sidra, captain of the merchant ship *Augustina*

Janne, Sidra's committed partner

Gabin of Iarom, a sorcerer

Earrin, captain of the river barge *Celestino*

Amon, oar-hand on the *Celestino*

Berin, innkeeper in Iarom

Frederick, guardian of the forest

Aurelia of Cathal, a baker's daughter

Branwen of Iarom, a blacksmith

Breda, Gabin's apprentice

Fionn, a surveyor's apprentice

Merrigan, the Enchanter

ABOUT THE PRONOUNS

IN THIS BOOK, SINGULAR they/them pronouns are used to refer to a person whose gender is unknown; this is done in the absence of salutations or worn symbols that indicate to others how the person wants to be identified.

Many characters in this book are agender or nonbinary; they use the pronouns e/em, also known as the Spivak pronouns.

subject: e
object: em
possessive (adjective): eir
possessive: eirs
reflexive: emself

Example: I looked at em as e opened eir eyes; while mine looked outward, eirs seemed to turn in on emself.

PART I

1
A FAMILY MEAL

HER LAUGHING VOICE, SO long unheard and yet instantly recognized, cut through the noise of the port. But Darragh did not pay heed to it. The brisk spring air was hazy and bright with layers of color, sunlight bouncing off the deep cove's water, the weathered gray piers, the verdant cliffs above the harbor. His eyes settled into their well-used squint as he let his awareness diffuse into the shouts of sailors and merchants and tax collectors, into the creaking of the great wooden ships and the squeaking of damp rope, the cries of gulls and the slap of water upon the piers. Comforting noises all, the sound of home; and a happy one it was, though it smelled of rot and refuse when there was not a strong gale from over the water. He reached for its cacophony, enough to unsettle many a mainland heart, and wished with all *his* heart that it would work its talismanic power on the source of that voice, erase Vesta and her words from the salt-sharp air.

This was what she had said, amid her too-familiar chuckle: "I cannot call you Beauty anymore, can I?"

There was work to be done. Darragh caught a barrel, rolling

off the plank, and sent it on down making no accommodation for Vesta, a deliberate choice though the motion was as deep in him as the grain of the barrel's wood was in it. She moved out of its way, still laughing, and called to him again, this time by the name he'd been given at his birth.

He knew his crewmates listened, their ears as tuned as his to unusual sounds and unfamiliar voices, to unexpected sights. His sister was all three, with her untanned beige skin, the swish of her bright silks, the high notes of her speech. Had she come even three years ago, he might have answered to that name, if only to stop her using it with noticeable volume. But he was ten years away from that name now.

Was it possible Vesta had forgotten his name? Had she received his letters, read them? She had ever been their father's child, and their father had sworn to erase him from the family. Perhaps she had been loyal to that edict and consigned his missives to the fireplace.

The last barrel came down. Darragh caught it, sent it on, then perched upon a crate, wiping his face of sweat with his kerchief, still careful not to look at his sister while he rolled his stiff neck. No, she must have read his letters, for he had changed ships several times since he'd left home. For her to have found him there, she must have known both his name and the name of the ship on which he served, known whence it came and the day of its arrival. He knotted the kerchief round his neck once more, tugging too tightly as he schooled his frustration. Must he ever be seeking reasons for his family's unkindnesses, to explain and excuse their behavior? If ten years of exile had not wrung this impulse from him, what would?

It was a different matter to have her there beside him than away at home and he at sea; that he would concede. He could see the hem of her dress, pristine from her carriage ride, at the edge of his vision; he could smell the ambergris she used for scent and wondered if it had been delivered by his own ship at its last docking. No; of course it had come from her own merchants.

He could hear her indignant sigh, and the tightness in that birdsong voice when she said, at last, "Darragh?"

He faced her then, though what his face showed, he could not guess, for he was torn between two impulses. The first, his custom, was to look neutral whenever he was not happy, rather than to show his displeasure and invite argument; the second, to let his triumph shine and blind her, to revel that she was required to submit to his terms, call him by his name, before he would acknowledge her. She was his elder by three years, and thus he had been always ordered to respect her without question. Though it might be considered dishonorable, it gave him pleasure now to have the advantage. His ten years as a sailor had done much to roughen him.

Whatever she saw, it chastened her, and the sad tightening of her brow dampened the light of Darragh's small victory; he knew her coming signaled something very grave indeed, and though he might rail privately at himself for the feeling, he regretted causing Vesta more pain than she already carried. He took her hand, the fine fabric of her glove catching on his calluses, and stretched himself enough to kiss her cheek.

"Sister," he said. "Come, let me return you to your carriage. Go and wait for me at the Maiden's Lantern, and I shall join you when my duties are discharged."

She pulled her hand away from his and said, looking down at him, "I made it down here well enough on my own; I have no need of your escort. Come quickly. Time is short."

Sidra, his captain and a truer sister than the one whose retreating back threatened to recall other shunnings, came alongside him, still buttoning her shore clothes over her flat, blue-black chest.

"Well, Thorn," she said. "I do not know what one such as you might have done to warrant the attention of a silk-swathed lady, but best go change your shirt and follow after her. Seems to me a woman like that ought not be kept waiting."

Darragh gave her a wry smile, the privilege of a longtime friend, for he and Sidra had sailed together before ever she wore a captain's belt. "This one can wait awhile," he said.

FOR ALL HIS TEASING with Sidra, though, Darragh did as she suggested, and changed into the linen shirt he kept in a tarred chest in his bunk. The shirt was his finest possession, purchased on his fifteenth birthday. The rest of that first suit succumbed to wear and to the changing body of its owner, but the shirt he cared for above all things, and it had lasted these ten years. He had never worn it since that birthday, except on the day Sidra was given her captaincy and he made second mate. When he put it on to meet his sister, it was soft with age, but the seams were all firm. He buttoned his waistcoat over it, a hand-down from Sidra that Darragh had resized himself.

Though it was unseemly, he left his coat on the ship, for it was a ragged sailor's thing, and the evening was mild.

The Maiden's Lantern sat midway up the hill above the wharf. A comfortable, middling sort of tavern, it served business and pleasure and would accommodate both Vesta in her finery and Darragh in his threads. The wood of it was warped but clean, shaved down and polished smooth so that the doors never stuck, and it had heavy curtains at the windows and the doors to block the sea drafts. Its sconces were polished brass, which gave the rooms an amber glow once the candles were lit, even on the stormiest nights.

When he entered the place, a person he did not recognize was tending to the bar. He went to them, inquired after Vesta, and was duly directed to the private booth she had secured at the back of the room. These booths had shutters on the outside, were paneled all around and curtained inside, with a table and benches protected from both ears and eyes. Such seating was suitable for secret rendezvous of all kinds, and Darragh wondered why such privacy might be required for a sister to speak to her brother. Perhaps she simply did not want to be seen with him, in service to his continued erasure.

He rapped on the first booth, the one he had been told contained his sister, and said, "It's Darragh."

"Come in."

When the curtains were firmly shut behind him, he looked at her. She had dressed for the evening, he noted with amusement and the smallest spark of fondness; he was not usually afforded such ceremony. She looked very well in her off-the-shoulder gown, which he assumed must be the latest fashion. A gown for transitional seasons, like the spring that wreathed Cathal in perfume. Here, above the wharf, Darragh could almost smell the fragrant step-orchards, which would be just flowering now.

Her gray eyes flitted over him, narrowing at the lack of coat, observing the muddled edges of the waistcoat, his unstarched cuffs and collar. If she recognized the shirt, she gave no sign. Well, there was no reason she should know it from any other.

A pitcher of wine was on the table already, with two goblets. She poured him one and said, "I've already ordered the meal."

Oh, how many choice things he could have said in reply—but he held his tongue and only nodded.

"I'm sorry. I thought I had prepared myself, but . . . I was rude to you, on the dock," Vesta said.

Darragh could not stop a small, disbelieving laugh. He wanted to be civil, but he would not be dishonest, and she seemed determined to offend him. "I can forgive your first greeting according to that apology, and I do," he replied. "But you cannot think I'll so easily forgive the name."

Her goblet stopped on its course to her lips. "Really, Darragh, I don't remember a propensity for petty grudges in you."

Her tone was light, but her mouth was pinched, so he only stared at her, willing her to linger in her embarrassment, to feel the absurdity of her words. Could he rely on his hope that the sensitivity, the intelligence he remembered, still prevailed in her? A name was no small thing. Names were identity, or at least the herald of it in the world, for a name could travel ahead of a person and linger behind them. A name given to a person by their parents signaled the hopes and predictions of those parents, and for one such as Darragh, it was no different, save that it encompassed his hopes for himself. In that way it was even more precious than that which a parent might give, and the offense of denial that much greater. Darragh leveled his unamused stare at Vesta as she sipped her wine with small, tense movements, and knew she knew her error. It should have been relieving, but it only saddened him that she let her pride rule her.

"It was a lapse. I'm just so used—well, Father still calls you that," she said.

"He still speaks of me?"

Vesta looked away. "From time to time."

"Well. I am surprised you took the trouble of finding my berth but did not practice hailing me by my own name," he said.

"It was a lapse!" she said again. "And I am sorry."

He wanted to press her on it—to make her apologize further, for minimizing the denial of his name as a mere *lapse*, for siding with his father, for not writing to him, for so many things—but they had no time, and he had no stomach for it, truly. He'd thrown out his list of hurts years ago; only their impressions, the ghostly scratching of the quill, flooded him now. He sipped the wine and was surprised it was unwatered. Did she fear the water this far down the hill? Or was she fortifying herself?

"Then I forgive you," he said, with a sharp look that warned it would not be offered twice.

"You do look very rough," she said.

He laughed. When last she'd seen him, he'd been a stripling of fifteen, from a wealthy family, all soft and dewy and smooth. Now his brown hair was brittle and blond, bleached by the sun, the wind, the salt, and he kept it cropped short to keep away the matting and make the lice easier to kill. His skin, once beige like hers, was tanned to such a degree it would never be pale again; his face and back and chest were mottled with scars, from the work and from the years of peeling and burning and chafing. His chin, under his beard, was marginally less scored, for once he'd been able to grow a beard, he'd let it reign while at sea rather than waste water shaving. And he knew he looked older than five and twenty, thanks to the lines around his eyes from squinting against the sun's reflection off the water.

Rough indeed! He was surprised she'd recognized him at all.

"Rough. But strong," she said. Then she smiled a little, and said, "It's just as well those old-fashioned shirts are made so large, or it'd not have lasted you so long."

He returned the smile, then quickly drank of his wine again to hide the unexpected rush of fondness, and the confusion that followed it. "I do shave when we make land, but I had an urgent meeting that could not be put off." Turning serious again, he asked, "What's brought you to me now, Vesta?"

A tap at the shutters prevented her answering, and dinner was delivered—two steaming pots of stew with a serving of asparagus on the side, a very modern addition. Darragh noticed that she had ordered white bread to go with their meal; this was set on the table arranged on a china platter, unlike their pewter bowls, and it was served with butter and sugar besides. His mouth watered; and he could not stop his eyes from widening when another platter appeared, this piled high with fruit and yet more sugar in a small bowl with a delicate spoon. He reached for an orange, only to have Vesta arch her eyebrows and say, "That is for dessert."

He withdrew his hand, but slowly, and said, "It's been four years since I had an orange." Vesta made a noise of surprise, so he added, "We take spoonfuls of concentrated lime juice aboard ship."

"Even officers?" She had seen his belt.

"When the owner spends less on the officers, each person on the crew gets paid more," Darragh replied. "We're none of us pampered on the *Augustina*."

"It seems to me a bit of fruit is hardly pampering," Vesta said.

Since she would not let him have the fruit to start, he set to his stew. It was too hot to eat yet, so he tore a bit of bread off the loaf and dipped it in the broth. It quickly turned to mush, dissolving into the liquid; he stuffed the whole piece in his mouth. Vesta raised her eyebrows again and spread her bread with butter, then sprinkled sugar on it, but said nothing of his uncouth display.

"Would you rather salt for the bread?" she asked.

"I get my fill of salt; I daresay I'm a good portion salt myself by now," he replied. "It's Father, isn't it?"

"He did not send me," Vesta said.

"But you are here on his behalf."

"He's dying."

Darragh set his spoon down and leaned away from her. His face was hot from being so close to the candelabra on the table; that must have been the reason, for the rest of him had gone cold.

"Darragh?"

"What happened?" he asked.

"He fell ill. Stomach pains. He has been confined to his bed for several months now. A few weeks ago he began to find it difficult to speak." Her spoon dipped in and out of her stew, turning the pieces of meat, the dumplings, without any move toward lifting them. "So I began to look for you."

He could not stop himself from asking, "And was it a hard search?"

"I read your letters," she replied. "I read them to him, too, though I had to wait until he was bedridden and dependent on me. I knew the name of your ship, but that damned Newlin, he always *forgets* to file the routes and manifests until after the ship's come in. The man is a crook, and you'd do well to leave his service."

"What, and work for you?" Darragh asked.

Vesta frowned at him but said nothing. Even if she offered him something, he'd not take it. The hurt of not knowing whether she'd read his letters was now supplanted by other hurts. His first few letters had been full of pain and indignity, his first duties under cruel quartermasters—and those hard to find, for he'd been hardly strong enough to push a barrel up a plank and didn't look likely to get stronger. He had begged in more than one letter for a place on one of his father's ships, said he would go by another name, that no one would recognize him. These pleas had earned no response.

If Vesta should offer him even a captaincy now, he did not think he could suppress the laughter. But she was wiser than that.

He tucked into his stew, having held off long enough. It mattered little that his gut was churning; he'd had more than enough practice at swallowing his gorge. Soon it would be time for him to leave Vesta, and he did not want to lose the fine meal, even if he had to snatch the fruit and run.

"Will you come home with me?" she asked.

Darragh swallowed the half-chewed beef and drained the bowl of broth, setting it empty on the table. Vesta's stew looked untouched. "He did not bid you come for me; he does not want to see me," he replied.

"I think he does, he's just too proud to say it."

"And what of my pride?" He paused and lowered his voice; he did not want to shout at her. "This is no lingering adolescent stubbornness, Vesta. I gave up too much of my pride just to survive after he cast me out, and now that I have regained some dignity, I'm in no mood to offer it up to him to shatter again."

She pressed her lips together. "He's an old man, Darragh—"

"Not so old. He chooses to indulge in old prejudices. He chose to wield them against his only son." He stood; the bench thudded into the paneling behind him. "I can give you some money. For a doctor."

"The doctors have been," Vesta said quietly. "There's nothing left for them to do."

"Then I hope his last breath comes swiftly, for your sake and mine . . . and his," Darragh said. He lifted his gaze to smile at her, but she did not look at him. "Write to me, if it is in your heart to do so."

He opened the curtains and had pushed the shutters apart when she said, "Darragh, wait." Turning, he saw that she was holding out an orange.

It was so perfect, round and dimpled, the very color of the sun as it plummeted toward the horizon he had spent ten years watching. He remembered the flavor, because he had eaten the last one with painstaking slowness, determined to commit the experience to memory, and it almost seemed to him that he could smell the bright, insistent juice contained inside that orb. His mouth and eyes both watered, for opposing reasons. For all the fullness of her cupped hand, the gesture was empty; the juice would be bitter.

He shook his head and left.

THE STORY OF
BEAUTY AND THE THORN

nce upon a time, there was a child who was called Beauty.

The child was much beloved by all who knew her, for she was quiet and gentle and sweet. She loved nothing better than to spend her days in the meadows beyond her father's house, pretending she was at sea, as he was. She built herself a little captain's cabin, and when her nanny scolded her for playing while it stormed, she replied, "Out on the ship, Father has naught for protection but a cabin, and I am quite as sturdy as he is." The family had laughed at that story for many a year and called her adventurous.

In her twelfth year, the red flower came to her and filled her with pain and dread, for she had an older sister and had learned its terrible truth along with her. It had not seemed so bad at first, and indeed, her nanny and Vesta had been happy when the blood came to Vesta. The blood, Beauty did not mind, for she bled often enough in exploring her meadow. 'Twas what came after that was frightful—for Vesta had grown great heavy flesh on her chest, and been given gowns of ever greater girth in service of fashion, and she lifted nothing for herself anymore, but asked the stable-hands to do it, for she seemed to grow ever more fragile with the accumulating years of bleeding, as if she were slowly dying.

One night, Beauty woke with a cry, for she had rolled onto her chest and the soreness shocked her out of sleep. She knew then that it was come for her; she imagined great bosoms like Vesta's growing upon her and found she could not breathe. She ran with all haste to her meadow and crawled weeping into her cabin.

She knew not how long she sat in sorrow, but at length she slept again, and woke to a whisper beyond the fallen branch that served her for a door.

"Why do you weep, child?" asked the voice.

Beauty thought she must still be sleeping, so she answered, "I do not want to grow breasts, and there is nothing I can do to stop it."

"Do you fear to grow up?"

"No," Beauty said. "That is, I—must all girls have such things upon their chest?"

The voice was quiet for a moment, then said, "No. But they will grow on yours if they are not stopped."

Fresh tears spilled from Beauty's eyes. "I know. I feel them coming, and there's nothing I can do."

"Why do you fear them?"

"I do not fear them," she said. "But I do not want them on *me*."

Again the voice said nothing for several moments, while Beauty strove to master her feelings. She would be brave, and face the breasts. Perhaps, she comforted herself, they would not be so large as Vesta's; perhaps she could continue to dress as she did, in plain gowns and in trousers. Perhaps she could bear it.

"Will you join me? The sun is rising," said the voice.

It no longer felt like a dream, and Beauty hesitated—but the voice was kind, and the night was over. She pushed the branch aside and crawled out. There she saw a person seated amid the tall meadow grass, a cloak draped over their head. They smiled at her, and though it seemed to her their look was a little sad, she smiled back, and hers was a little sad, too, though she knew it not.

The person put one brown hand on the ground beside them, and Beauty settled there, facing east with them and watching the sky slowly lighten over her home.

"You do not have to be what they say you are," the person said.

"Father says we are what we are, and it is abominable to change that," Beauty said.

"He is right. But then who decides what we are?" asked the person.

"Our parents?" Beauty said.

"Do they know your every thought and feeling?" The person looked at Beauty slyly. "Will you tell them what you have told me?" Beauty frowned, and the person laughed softly. "Then how can they know what you are?"

She shivered, though she was not cold. "If I told them . . ." She shook her head. "Father would never allow me to see the physicians, not for this. He dismissed our cook when she took her daughter to them."

"You have considered this already."

"When the blood came," she said. "I thought perhaps that was all that would come."

The sun was a red orb, hovering, obscured by the mist yet clinging to the ground. Together, Beauty and the stranger watched it rise. The stranger's gaze was steady and unmoving, but Beauty's often drifted to their profile. Their skin shone ever warmer, its tones changing from blue-tinged sand to dusky rose. She knew the moment when the sun broke from the mist, because the stranger's skin turned gold. They smiled and faced her with a look that said they had felt her gaze all the while; then they reached into the sleeve of their cloak, and withdrew a thorn nearly as long as Beauty's hand.

"Prick yourself with this thorn and draw three drops of blood; flick each into either a fire or water," said the stranger. "Do this every day for three months, then every three weeks for three years, then every three months for the rest of your life, and you shall have the form you desire."

Beauty took the thorn and held it up to the light. It did not look magic at first, but as she peered at it, it seemed to take on a kind of glow—but perhaps it was only the sunrise. She turned to thank the stranger, but they had disappeared.

Beauty then went into her little cabin, took up her flint, and set a spark to the ramshackle wood. When it was burning well, she took the thorn and pressed it to her fingertip until the blood welled. Once, twice, thrice, she gathered a bead of blood on the point and cast it into the fire.

2
STAY OR GO

HE WAS NOT DRUNK—NOT from the wine. Still, he swayed through the streets as he had the first time he returned to land after a six-month term at sea; the turns he took, the buildings he saw seemed unfamiliar to him. He stopped walking and put a hand to the pitted stone wall of a boardinghouse.

How easy it would be to slip back ten years and relive the storm of emotions that had filled him up then, to make sharp the thoughts that had been dulled with time. But it wasn't only time that had taken away the edges. Darragh had worn them down himself, purposefully, and he would not let this meeting with Vesta be a whetstone to his pain.

When he looked up, he knew the street—and his destination.

The house stood out among its fellows, fresh whitewash reflecting the street lanterns and making the buildings to either side seem dirtier. Three doors clustered together in the middle of the ground floor, and the two windows on the upper floor were shuttered for the night, and curtains drawn, if the utter lack of light was any indication. Darragh went to the middle door and jumped, scrabbling at the top of the doorframe for the key. He caught it and unlocked the door, placing the key in his pocket; he'd give it for Janne to put back emself, if e must insist on keeping it so high up. Crossing the threshold, he threw the lock behind him and went up the narrow stairs to the upper floor. When he gained the landing, he knocked on the right-hand door.

The next moment, Janne stood in the open doorway, tall, olive-skinned, and utterly at ease though e wore only a dressing gown, loosely belted, so far as Darragh could tell.

"Forgive me for intruding," Darragh said by instinct alone; his manners were ingrained enough that his newly acquired *roughness* had not gouged them out.

"It's Darragh," e said over eir shoulder; then e smiled, and let him in.

He had never been inside before, but his curiosity was at that moment very small; he noted it was a one-room apartment, whitewashed inside as out. An alchemist's light behind a pink glass shade cast a soft and romantic light, and within its glow, his gaze found Sidra. She was fastening her pants and looked at him with undisguised concern. "What's happened?" she asked. "The ship—"

"Peace, the ship is fine," Darragh said.

Sidra paused in her reach for her shirt, straightening slowly while she scrutinized him. He had never been in Janne's home before because he had promised to help Sidra preserve the brief time she got with her partner whenever they came in to port; Darragh and the first mate saw to as many of the necessary tasks as they could so that she could visit with Janne uninterrupted. He was the only one of the crew who even knew where Janne's home was. For him to come now—of course she had assumed some disaster. Guilt warmed his cheeks and clenched his gut. Had he been wrong to come?

"Who was that woman, Darragh?" Sidra asked.

"My sister. Vesta."

"Siren's balls. Love," Sidra said to Janne, "show me where you moved your tea stores. I think we shall have need of fortification."

Janne showed her, then came to Darragh and bade him sit while Sidra made a pot of tea for them all. The two of them looked silently, shyly, appraisingly at each other; it had been quite six years since they had seen each other. Janne had been a fellow seahand before the mast on Darragh and Sidra's second posting together. It was in that period that Sidra found both her gender and a committed partner in Janne, which brought an end to the platonic lovemaking Darragh and Sidra had enjoyed. But Darragh had not been sorry, for Janne was the loveliest and kindest of people, and he had come to love em quite as much as he loved Sidra. He had had some trepidation as to visiting eir house now, after the long separation—for Janne had chosen to quit sailing rather than risk being posted on a different vessel than Sidra and then never see her—but Darragh saw now that the love Janne had shown him was no more dimmed than his own for em. They reached for each other and clasped hands, and sighed into contentment.

When, to break the intimate silence, he apologized again for interrupting, Janne shook eir head. "To tell it truly, I am happy to finally see your face again!" e said with a loving but reproachful glance at Sidra.

"And it's a fine face, for a fine man, who lets me hide away up here as long as I can," the captain said from her station by the wood stove.

"I believe she has been trying to protect me from you. Apparently you are quite the seducer; I am sure she thinks that if we had more time together . . ." Janne winked at Darragh.

"Oh yes, that's how Darragh makes all his friends," Sidra said, laughing.

"I was extremely respectful, and we had a wonderful time, didn't we?" Darragh replied.

She smiled at him and said with more softness, "There you are."

He nodded to her, suddenly bashful, but her teasing had loosened his melancholy a bit, as she'd intended, and he breathed a little easier. Sidra joined them at the small table with a modest tea service. She poured tea for the three of them and set a cup in front of Darragh, her mouth softening further into seriousness. "Nine years we've known each other, and in all that time, I've never known your family to speak to you."

"You have it right." He tapped the edges of the ceramic. The tea was still too hot to drink; it seared him, even through the cup, even through his calloused fingertips.

Sidra drank of hers right away, without a wince. "What brought her now, then?"

"Shall I give you privacy for this?" Janne asked.

"No, of course you are welcome to stay," Darragh said. "I need have no secrets from you."

Janne put eir hand to eir chest and smiled warmly. Darragh returned the expression, though his heart strained inside him, caught in the twist of happiness and regret. He loved the family he had found in Sidra, on the *Augustina*, and in Janne too. Was it a reduction of that love for him to feel so anguished at the reappearance of his sister, at the news she carried? The family of his blood inspired loyalty against which he had fought for years, wallowing in his pains so that he would not excuse them or long for their company—so that he would not love them. He knew now he had but banked that love, not stamped it out. Love, of any nature, left ghosts in the soul that whispered of sweet memories and laughed at all thoughts of removal.

"My father is dying," he said at last to his patient audience. "Vesta wants me to come home. Reconcile."

"Reconcile?" Sidra echoed, eyebrows nigh to her hairline. "He sent her with this request, after ten years—"

"She came on her own. He did not send her."

"Well! That be the case, your answer must be easy. Let him end his life as he lived it, sour and sonless." Turning to Janne, Sidra explained, "Darragh's father did put him in the streets on his fifteenth birthday, when he made himself known a boy—after he had scrimped and saved his own secret earnings and bought a fine suit, the very shirt he wears now, that he might make the greedy bastard proud—"

"I'm sure it was not so tragic as that," Darragh said.

"But he did turn you out, which is tragedy enough," Sidra said. "And if he has not sent for you with the intent of apologizing, then he deserves nothing from you."

Janne gazed thoughtfully at Darragh, eir brown eyes bottomless in the dim light. "You will go, won't you," e said.

Darragh of a sudden remembered the tea, and drank of it, the perfect temperature now to warm and loosen his straining throat. Why it should strain when he screamed not, he did not know; perhaps it strained to hold something in, rather than to release, but what that *something* might be—he did not know that, either, no better than he knew the answer to Janne's question. Yet it had been no question, and he perceived that Janne knew something of how he felt.

"Oh, my soft hearts," Sidra said. "I cannot understand this masochism."

"That is because you are loved by those who promised to love you always," Janne said, eir eyes still on Darragh. "We are still taught that a parent's love is unconditional, and it breeds a kind of . . . devastating hope. Yes?"

"Yes," Darragh said, an exhalation more than a voiced syllable. He drank of his tea and spoke again. "I find that I need to know if . . ."

"If he still loves you?" Sidra asked.

"If I was right to keep my distance all these years," Darragh said. "I want to speak to him about what he did, in the way I was not able to when I was just fifteen. I want him to explain himself to me, to my face. I want to stand before him and ask if he would even now deny that I am what I say I am."

"He may do it," Janne said. "My mother did, till her last breath."

"And if he do, so be it. I will stand over him and watch life leave him, and say 'Let the old ways die with him.'"

Sidra sighed. "You will go, then."

He looked at her and saw her brows lift in surprise; then he realized that his brow was furrowed, his jaw clenched. Anger had flooded into him as he spoke, and mingled there with that hope of which Janne had spoken, as the muddy river delta meets the ocean tides. He was both hope and anger, fury and love; he was a frightened boy and a lonely, wounded man. These feelings were not a betrayal of Sidra's love; he felt that. But neither would he be complete in his new family until he had made peace with the old. That, he could not do through retrospection. Yes, he would go and meet his father as a man, and his sister too. They would find the man harder to beat down than the boy. At the very least, he would go and ask for his mother's letters.

"If my captain gives me leave," he said.

She smiled at him. "How could I not? My only regret is that I cannot go with you. We're off again in a week—is that enough time?"

"More than," Darragh replied.

THE STORY OF
THE HUNDRED PROMISES

nce upon a time, there was a young family who were happy in all things, except that they had no children. The farmer's crops never failed, the herdsman's cattle all were healthy, and the blacksmith's forge was never cold, yet they longed for a baby to raise and love, to whom they could pass on their good fortune. After a long time of trying to conceive, the farmer bade farewell to the other two and set off on a quest to find a kind witch or wizard who might help them. He wandered for a year and spoke with many people about the many methods by which they had gotten their own children. Much to his disappointment, though, these were all things he and his family had heard before and tried to no avail.

At last he went into the forest, for he had heard that there was an enchanter who dwelt there who would dispense such magic for a price. The forest was vast, and the farmer walked the whole length of it before he came to the waterfall where it was said the Enchanter could be found. He heard the rush of water and felt the cool mist, and felt as though the air of his lungs had been stolen from him, but he approached the falls, made strong by his love for the herdsman and the blacksmith.

A huge boulder stood before the waterfall, and upon this the farmer saw the Enchanter, swathed in robes the same green of the canopy above. At first, the farmer thought the Enchanter had not marked him—then e turned eir head, just so the light fell golden on the crest of eir brow.

"I seek the Enchanter," the farmer said.

"You seek magic," said the Enchanter in a melodious voice.

"I do. I wish—we are desperate for a child."

The Enchanter alighted from the boulder and held out a seed. "Plant this near your home. Every day for one hundred days, you and your family must visit the tree that grows and offer a promise to your future child. If you do this, and if every promise is sincerely and lovingly offered, your family will conceive. But heed this warning: if any of the promises are broken, the child will forsake you, and you will never see them again."

The farmer was overjoyed and accepted the seed. In return, he gave the Enchanter several seeds from his mother's garden, where the most beautiful roses in the world were grown. The farmer returned to his home and explained to his partners what they must do. Together, they planted the seed immediately, within sight of their home, and offered their first promise to the child: to always make them welcome, whenever or wherever they should meet.

Every morning from then on, the farmer, the herdsman, and the blacksmith walked together to the sapling and made a promise. They promised to listen and to guide; to laugh with their child, never at their expense; to protect them. They promised never to lie or hide the truth, and to always respect their child's thoughts and feelings. For one hundred days, the family vowed, sincerely and lovingly, to do everything in their power to ensure the child grew up happy and strong.

On the hundred and first day, the tree flowered, and the black-smith found that she was pregnant. After the usual time, she gave birth to a radiant child. The family celebrated by putting together a feast with the crops of their fields and the meat and milk of their herds, and all the village joined them to welcome their baby. And, mindful of the Enchanter's warning, the family kept all their promises to the child as the infant grew, for the family could not bear to lose the love of such a precious soul. Together, they lived happily ever after.

3
GIFTS

HE COULD HAVE RETURNED to the Lantern, acquiesced to Vesta, ridden home in the morning with her in the fine carriage that had brought her into the city and surprisingly close to the docks. Instead, Darragh spent the night on the ship, seeking the comfort and familiarity of his dark, close berth and the oddly sharp air. He woke with the sunrise, the result of ten years' training, gathered his second set of clothes, less the linen shirt, into his sack, and emerged into the chill blue morning braced against more than the ocean breeze.

It was at best a two-day walk to his family's house in the countryside, at a brisk and steady pace with few stops. Darragh was not so eager, though, and he had time, so he allowed himself to meander through the market while the orchardists and farmers and others all set out their wares. The market was a long line of stalls set up beside each other along the switchback hill road facing the sea, with gaps only for the turns—one too many stalls had been knocked off the road by riders or carriages in their hurry.

Occasionally he stopped his stroll to chat with the vendors, asking about what they had brought and what they might ask for it. He was of course primarily interested in food, but he watched curiously while a single metalsmith spread a pressed cloth over her table. She was younger than he, but not by much, and seemed to be by herself, unlike her peers in the market, most of whom were there assisting their mentors or parents. With precision, she arranged her goods, fine chains and gems wrapped in delicate metal cages and the like; she was utterly focused on her task and seemed not to notice him.

Until she turned, looked directly at him, and held out a chain. "This chain is yours, if you answer my questions."

He froze, not unlike a hare who spots a fox in the underbrush. Like a fox, she was beautiful, and possessed of a quiet, intense stillness that spoke of power. Her look, her offer, her sudden address of him, all the circumstances were surely strange; yet the strangest thing was the familiarity of her gaze. He had seen it, or something like it, before, had felt such an appraisal wash over him. It was not a perfect similitude, though. Was the cold edge he sensed to this assessment the product of his adulthood? For there could be only one memory to match this, and it was from his youth.

His curiosity roused, Darragh straightened, and walked slowly over to her.

The chain dangled from her fingers, which were so pale as to almost seem blue; the links were small and slightly flattened, and the whole of it had been finished to look black. Unclasped, it would have been quite as long as his arm. He looked from it to her and said, "I don't understand."

The metalsmith smiled, a bit unsettlingly. "What is more cruel, to harm oneself or to harm others?"

That was not the sort of question Darragh had expected, but after only a moment, he answered, "To harm oneself."

Her smile widened. "Your reason?"

"Justice may be brought against one who harms others, and if it is right, reconciliation," Darragh said. "But there can be no justice when one hurts oneself, for the punishment only compounds the original hurt, and to reconcile requires that one make peace with both one's pain and one's guilt, which is a long and lonely road."

She narrowed her eyes at him but seemed satisfied, for the look was one of appraisal and the tension in her smile had softened. "Who is deserving of love?"

Darragh frowned. "Love is not something to be deserved."

"What do you mean?"

"Love is not earned through deed or word; it is not paid for by kindness; it is not—it is not a reward. It is not given and received, exchanged like gifts shared in the bounty of midsummer or even in the scarcity of midwinter. That is generosity, but it is not love. Love is many hands weaving a blanket that warms all who lie under it. It is a ship guided through storm and calm alike by the knowledge, strength, trust, and experience of those who crew it." He shook his head. "It is curiosity instead of indignation and acceptance in place of fear."

The metalsmith listened to this speech, tilting her head as if the angle from which she saw him might impact the way she heard his words. "A very thorough answer, though it is not the one to my question," she said. "Who is . . . eligible for love?"

"Love is a garden, and any who wish to may enter it," Darragh said. "Whether they come to tend the beds, to trample them, to rest awhile, or only to pass through, is up to them."

"More metaphors," she teased. "Have you ever been in love?"

"The love I describe is not only romantic."

"Certainly not," the metalsmith said. "But have you been in love?"

"I love my family, and I love my friends," he replied. "Is that not enough to destroy me?"

She laughed. "Destroy! But love is a beautiful thing! You said so yourself."

Darragh thought of his father; he remembered Janne's words about the desperate hope inside them both. "Not always. What is your next question?"

The metalsmith considered him again and held the chain out.

"I do not need the third question now," she said. "The chain is yours."

He accepted it from her and bowed. But when he rose again with the words on his lips to ask the name of her enterprise, he was looking upon an empty stall.

Quickly, he walked away with the chain clenched in his fist. The market had blossomed while he spoke with her, but he was still able to find a seat on a stone wall along the hill edge of the road; he faced away from the market, his feet dangling over the ocean side of the wall, and he was bathed in clear morning light, for the sun had fully risen now from its salty womb.

The black chain was still cold, resisting the warmth of his skin. He ought to throw it away for that alone, for it was an ill omen at the start of a journey, even one by land. But he recalled the last time a disappearing stranger had asked him such piercing questions, and he found himself willing to wait, and see what significance the chain might bring itself. Acceptance in place of fear, he'd said.

He put the chain between his lips and pulled his seax from its sheath in his lap. With his free hand, he lifted his leather cord necklace away from his skin and sliced through it with the knife. There was no hope of unknotting it, old and dirty as it had become. Carefully he sheathed the seax and drew the cut leather necklace out from under his shirt, revealing what it bore.

A thorn, a joint longer than Darragh's longest finger, hung from the leather, threaded through a hole bored roughly into its base. He slid it off the leather with care, not because it was sharp — although it was, it would not scratch him — but because it was his most precious possession. The leather was left to tumble down the wall onto some vendor's canvas awning below, while Darragh eased the black chain through the thorn's hole. When he clasped it round his neck, the thorn rested against his sternum. He covered it with his hand, the feel of it reassuring, before tucking it below his shirt and rising from the wall. He saw to his purchases of food quickly and pragmatically, with one indulgence — a bruised orange selling at half price.

He made the orange last all the way up the hill and nearly to the edge of the city, tossing the rind aside just before he passed the last cluster of latrines outside the city walls, and set briskly down the road focused on nothing but his stride. He intended to get as far as he could before the outgoing market traffic overtook him. The weather was fine, his legs were strong, and it had been long since he could really stretch them.

At length his stomach growled, and he settled himself beside the road to eat. It was only bread and cheese, but perhaps it was as much an indulgence as the orange, for he'd bought soft goat's cheese, and soft bread to put it on—though not so soft nor so fine as that which Vesta had ordered for their dinner.

The road stretched empty before him, cutting through fields on either side, still short with that season's infant crops—wheat on one side, beans on the other, it looked like, though Darragh was no farmer. He'd helped his mother with their vegetable patch when he was a child, before she left. Or so Vesta had said, and not kindly; she had called him a changeling, a gnome their mother had found, a homunculus she had grown in that same soil. Darragh did not remember the garden; he did not remember his mother. He did remember his father constantly complaining of that vegetable patch for years afterward, wondering why she'd bothered with the effort and the expense. His merchant fleet had been established by then, and the family was becoming quite wealthy; to him, a family growing their own vegetables seemed a level of subsistence living that they had surpassed. The garden became an insult to him, and he loathed it though it was long dead, as if it had been the garden that made his wife flee.

Darragh drank of his waterskin and tried to focus on the earthy smells around him, the sound of insects, anything other than memories that might induce him to turn back. He did not want to catalog the proof that his father was closed-minded, prescriptive, and selfish, that he cared more about his own reputation than the people in his family—or did he? Would that make it easier or harder to face the man on his deathbed? Was Darragh going home to confirm his opinion of his father, or, as Vesta wanted, to reconcile, to somehow see his father in a new light? Last night, he had felt sure; he wanted justice, for himself, for his mother. Maybe for Vesta, though he was not sure she deserved it. He grimaced to himself at his own word choice—*Who is deserving of justice?*—and shook his head as if the motion could clear it.

He heard a cart on the road and watched it approach. It was a small two-wheeled affair pulled by a donkey and driven by a person wearing a cloak, despite the clear sky, still air, and the resulting heat from the unobscured sun. Both the donkey and the driver seemed tired, heads hanging, the donkey's steps slow and the reins slack; so when they were near enough, Darragh stood and said, "Hello, there! Will you share a drink with me and tell me the news?"

The driver reined the donkey to a stop, peered down at him, and said, "Now, why would a young one like you want to share a drink with an old man like me?"

Darragh smiled, recognizing the man's declaration of himself; in the south, in the cities especially, folk had grown used over the decades to not assuming a given person's gender. Once, there had been a formal script for such revelations, but the aging tradition and progressive laziness had given rise to such subtler signs. So Darragh replied, "A sailor keeps his company mainly with other sailors. 'Tis not often I have a chance to talk with those outside my trade. Though I confess I have naught but water and only one skin, I will share what I have."

The driver returned his smile then, and nodded. "All right, young sir. I'll join you." He got down from the cart with care but without difficulty, and then went to the back of it to pull something from its contents: two earthenware mugs and a bottle of wine.

"Oh, please, sir, I offered to share with you!" Darragh said.

"And so you shall; we shall share it," the driver said, chuckling. He bade Darragh sit again, and when he had, handed the mugs and wine to him before lowering himself to the grass. He unstoppered the wine and poured a small amount into the mugs, then said, "Thin it for us, for I still have a ways to go, and I think you must too."

Darragh obliged and added water to the mugs, then lifted his to the driver. They both drank. "This is a fine piece," Darragh said, for the mug was smooth and had an even color and thickness, and his and the driver's were the same size. "You are a potter?"

"Aye, these forty years," said the potter. "And my wheel was my parent's, and eir mother's before em."

"That's wonderful—you enjoy it, I hope," Darragh said.

The potter laughed. "I can hardly separate it from myself, most days; but I do love myself, so it matters little," he said. "Is sailing a family trade?"

"After a fashion," Darragh replied wryly. "My father owns a fleet of merchant ships, but I do not sail under his captains. And his parents were woodsmen, loath though he is to admit it."

"Land and sea," mused the potter. "Which do you prefer?"

Darragh considered it for a moment. "I am not prepared to say. I spent much of my childhood pretending I was at sea with my father, so I do not think I gave the meadow its proper due; and I have been the last ten years at sea whether I liked it or not."

"*Do* you like it? The sea?"

He nodded slowly. "I do. Especially the last few years, for I have had the best of captains to serve, which has made all the difference."

"Yet you travel inland now," said the potter.

"My father is ill."

The potter nodded sympathetically, and the two of them drank quietly together for some minutes. Darragh felt the impulse several times to say more on the subject, to open up to the potter and make use of the confidence between two strangers who will never see each other again, but each time, he swallowed his words; why, he could not have said. That same ineradicable speck of loyalty to blood that drove him down that inland road, perhaps.

"Have you been at the Cathal market?" Darragh asked.

"Aye, but I left early, for as you have seen, my donkey is slow, and I have had my fill of being cursed at on the road," said the potter. "Next week, perhaps I will not go. It has not been worth my time for some months now."

"But your work is so good! Are you charging the price of a family legacy, that people will not buy it?" Darragh asked.

The potter patted his hand, laughing ruefully. "You are kind. But it is all porcelain and glazing now, and I cannot give them that out of my little workshop. Do not worry for me, young sailor, I have all the work I need serving my village and our neighbors."

"I am glad to hear that. But it is a shame."

The potter shrugged. "I have no children, no apprentice. The young potters of today will learn the new methods, and change will progress as it ever has. That is no shame."

"True," Darragh said. He finished his wine, used some of his water to rinse the mug, and handed it to the potter. "Thank you for sitting with me, and for sharing your wine."

The potter accepted the mug and leveled him with a curious look. "Why do you think it is a shame that the city people no longer want earthenware?"

"It is a personal sentiment, nothing more," Darragh said. "Porcelain is beautiful, yes; but I like to find beauty in rougher things."

The potter laughed. "As do I, my young friend." He stood and went to his cart. While he replaced the mugs and the wine, Darragh joined him on his feet and prepared to say goodbye— but the potter came away from the cart holding a small but finely shaped jug, the outside painted white. Its petal-shaped mouth was the size of Darragh's palm, and its handle was in the shape of a vine winding around the neck of the jug before smoothing seamlessly into the well of it. The potter wrapped it in a soft cloth and held it out to Darragh. "For you—a little rough beauty to carry with you, if I flatter myself."

"Please, I cannot accept such a gift!" Darragh said. "It is too fine for the likes of me."

"And yet, I know you will care for it gently, which is more than I can say for this donkey," the potter said.

Darragh laughed. "Very well, I accept, and I will treasure it." He collected it, cloth and all, from the potter's hands, and ran his thumb along the frictionless lip. "Thank you, very much."

With twinkling eyes, the potter said, "You are most welcome." He climbed up onto the seat of his cart and gathered the reins. "May your path be smooth, and naught but kindness meet your ears."

"And your belly full, and all the skies above you clear," Darragh replied, to finish the blessing.

The potter snapped his reins, and the old donkey, energized by its rest, set off at a steady walk down the road. Darragh watched the cart until it disappeared over the horizon, going down a hill not far off, before he tucked the jug in the center of his sack, padded by the cloth and his clothes, put the strap over his shoulder, and set off walking again.

He expected to see the potter's cart when he crested the hill himself, but it was nowhere to be seen, though a long stretch of the road was visible. Darragh laughed softly. The old donkey must have been faster than he'd thought.

DARRAGH WALKED ON A little longer after night fell, since the sky was still clear and the paving stones even, and he remembered an inn not much farther down the road. He had many fond memories of that inn. Sometimes, he and Vesta and their nanny had stayed there on their way to the city to welcome Father back from a voyage; sometimes, they had come and met him there, to see him the rest of the way home. And it had been the place he spent his first night outcast from his family, when the innkeeper had let him stay on his own without money and without question, and fed him too. He'd not been back since that night.

The inn was where he remembered it, at the first major crossroads east of Cathal, but that keeper was gone. To the new keeper, a stout, pink-skinned person with the circle of genderlessness tattooed on eir forearm, Darragh Thorn was as anonymous as any other guest, not a prodigal son—or daughter, as the case might have been—but that was fine by Darragh. He was lucky enough to secure the last available room just as thunder rolled across the land and silenced the chatter on the tavern floor for a moment.

"Oh! That certainly doesn't sound nice, does it?" said the jolly innkeeper.

"Not at all," Darragh agreed. "And it was so clear all day."

"Just like a storm to wait for nightfall, keep everyone up all night."

"I'm only grateful the road is paved. I'm traveling by foot," Darragh said.

The innkeeper chuckled. "Then I'm grateful for you too. I remember what it was like before, so swampy after a fresh rain—and the ruts once the mud dried? As deep as my hand, I swear it." E held up eir hands to demonstrate.

"I believe it," Darragh said.

He ordered a small dinner and selected a table near the fireplace, for he was chilled despite his walking, the spring night clinging more to winter than the day had. As he waited for his food, and then as he consumed it, the tavern emptied around him while the guests all finished their ales and went up to bed. Finally, he was the only one left, save the innkeeper waiting for him to finish. He was not sleepy yet, but nevertheless he finished his ale and stood. The innkeeper likewise rose and held out a hand for his stein, but Darragh said, "Please, I can wash it; I'm sorry to have kept you up so late."

Before the innkeeper could reply, there was an urgent knock on the door. E went and opened it, and in stepped a tall, thin person drenched from the rain. They had draped their coat over what appeared to be a large tote filled to bursting with something heavy, by the way the person leaned, and so Darragh could see their pale skin shiver beneath the linen tunic and trousers that clung to their limbs. They wore good leather boots, but those squelched even with the shifting of their weight; they would need to dry by a fire if the person were to wear them tomorrow. In one hand they held a small trunk.

"A room," they said. "Please."

"I'm sorry, my good . . . ?"

"Sir," the person said.

"My good sir," the innkeeper said. "But we have no vacancies at present."

The young man's face fell, his devastated expression empha-sized by the water dripping from his ginger hair. As if to punctuate his misfortune, thunder crashed outside. The innkeeper said, "Perhaps I can find some room in the stables."

"Ah," the man said.

Though Darragh could see he was trying to be grateful, he was too exhausted to hide his disappointment. "He can have my room," Darragh said.

The young man looked at him with barely restrained relief. "That would be very kind of you, but . . ." The sound of the rain was great through the shuttered windows.

"I'm a sailor; a little rain is no bother to me," Darragh replied with a smile. "Besides, you need a fire, or you'll be ill."

"That's true enough," the innkeeper said. "Come, sir, I'll show you to your room."

The young man did not move for a moment, as if he did not quite believe them; then he held his hand out to Darragh and said, "Please, may I?" Darragh took the man's hand, which the man squeezed in gratitude; then he bent and kissed Darragh's knuckles, the handshake insufficient. "I am most grateful to you."

Darragh smiled, returned the pressure of his hand, and bade him goodnight.

There was no empty stall, for it was a small stable and some of the guests had carriage teams, but the innkeeper introduced Darragh to the inn's pony, a furry roan thing with a long forelock coyly covering one eye. The innkeeper said, "She'll be more than happy to share her stall for the night."

"Thank you. This is quite cozy," Darragh replied.

The innkeeper smiled more warmly at him than e had before, and gave him a light for his lantern before returning to the main building of the inn. Darragh gathered some fresh straw and a saddle blanket and fashioned himself a bed in the front corner of the stall. The pony watched him, her tail flicking occasionally, and her ears perked up when he went and got a brush from the shelf of supplies.

"Oh, is this something you like?" he asked. "I thought it might be. Well then, I may as well do something nice until I get tired."

DARRAGH WOKE WITH THE dawn streaming in through the walls and the pony dozing over him, feeling refreshed, though he smelled of horse and straw and travel since he had not washed the night before. He stretched and put the stall to rights, patted the pony goodbye, and went in search of the well, which he found easily. After drawing up a full bucket, he splashed the water over his bare chest, back, and face, scrubbing with his hands until he was as clean as he could make himself. He sat on the inn's porch while his skin dried. When the sounds of breakfast came from within, he put his shirt back on and went indoors.

The tavern's tables were almost fully occupied by the guests, partaking eagerly of the oatmeal and especially the bacon provided by the innkeeper and eir cook, managing the flow of food from the counter. There was small beer to drink, and for luxuries: coffee, a small bowl of dried apple and pear, and a jar of strawberry preserves to dollop into the meal. It was probably the last of their stores from the previous year's harvest; a small inn like this would not pay to get the fruit the city had, imported from the places where it was warm all year round. Darragh demurred at the dried fruit but could not resist a spoonful of preserves in his oatmeal. Though he feared to spoil his tastes for when he returned to sea, he rather thought he should enjoy the sweet treats while he could. He must take some pleasure in this trip, after all.

He ate slowly, savoring of his food, and was still eating when the young man from the night before came downstairs. He looked better, though still purple around the eyes, and his clothes bore no sign of last night's catastrophe, which meant they were likely a second set. Though the costume was clean and well-made, it looked old, and fit in a hand-down manner on the man's lanky frame. Darragh watched him with idle curiosity while he collected his food, but then the man found him among the guests and approached.

"Might I join you?" he asked.

"Of course," Darragh said.

"You are very kind." The man sat and offered Darragh his hand, as he had last night. "My name is Perrin he Gower, and I am much obliged to you for your generosity last night. You quite saved my books."

"Darragh he Thorn," he replied, taking the hand and squeezing it. Either Perrin was from the north, or he was an antiquarian, that in introducing himself he used the construction of given name, pronoun, family name. Darragh found it charming. "Is that what you were protecting with your coat?"

"Yes." Perrin smiled, a bit shyly. "Even so, the ones at the top of my bag sustained some damage. But it would have been worse for them without a drying fire."

"And for you. You've not caught cold?"

"No, thankfully."

"I'm glad," Darragh said. He smiled at Perrin, wider when a blush rose in the other man's cheeks. He seemed, by the morning light, to be perhaps Darragh's age, or a little younger. "What sort of man carries a load of books larger than his trunk?"

"A student," said Perrin. "Well—that is, I am on my way to be tutor to a family of modest means, so I suppose I am now a student in only the most philosophical of terms. But I was not sure of the family's library, and so I rather optimistically brought the bulk of my own."

They laughed at that together and ate in the companionable silence of friendship. Had they met in Cathal, Darragh might have pursued the sort of brief and passionate liaison he often sought on shore, for Perrin had an angular beauty, and his eyes and mouth both seemed responsive to Darragh's observation—but as they had met traveling, there was no time for that.

"Do you continue on the east road?" Darragh asked.

"I turn north from here, to meet the river," Perrin said.

Darragh nodded. "The river is still the best way north, then?"

"Yes. They've not taken the paving past Vicus, and I must go to Fortney yet."

He did not ask why Perrin had not taken the river from the city, where it met the sea, for he knew that to go upriver was twice as costly as to come down it, and the road was free if one could manage it. "Then I wish you well," Darragh said, as he had finished his breakfast and needed to set off.

"Wait, before you go—" Perrin reached behind him and pulled a small book out of the waist of his breeches. "Permit me to give you this as a small token of my gratitude."

Darragh smiled. "I'd rather have a kiss from you than diminish your library, after all it has been through."

"Then have a kiss." Perrin cupped the back of Darragh's head, drew him in, and kissed him with a gently open mouth that Darragh received in kind with pleasure. Then Perrin withdrew, cheeks flushed, and said, "But take this too."

Still smiling, pleased at this turn and at his own good judgment, Darragh claimed the book from Perrin's hand and said, "I shall treasure it and the memory of how it came to me." He looked at it properly; it was a cloth-bound volume about the size of his hand, and well-loved if the frayed corners and waving pages were any indication. The title, stamped into the spine in gold lettering, was *Callistan Folk Tales*.

"I thought, as a sailor, you might appreciate such a collection," Perrin said.

"You thought right," Darragh said. He looked into Perrin's eyes and, remembering another traveler's blessing, said, "For you I wish a life of light, though we now must part."

Perrin smiled, recognizing it. "What joy is yours shall be mine too, for you are in my heart."

4
HOMECOMING

THE HOUSE HAD BEEN expanded since Darragh left. Their home in his childhood had been considered large for a family of only four, but the original structure, two lower rooms and two upper, with one chimney, was now overshadowed by a modern addition. The new wing was still two stories, but with much higher ceilings, such that it was taller than the old house by half; the walls were of small, uniform bricks with white mortar between them, compared to the dry stack of the original. The old thatch roof had been replaced with slate, to match the new.

Night was near; the air was chilly on his newly bare chin, shaved clean at the fountain in the center of town. Darragh had spent the hour before reaching the town debating this action. Could his father deny his manhood with such a prodigious mask of hair upon his face? Yet was his manhood in his beard; would he concede that his manhood was made up only of those external signs? The skin of his face tingled with twofold exposure, and as he looked upon his much-changed childhood shelter, he knew not what shelter he might find there now.

No one in the town had recognized him. He had never had much access to mirrors since he'd gone to sea, so he had no real sense of how much his looks might have changed; even had he possessed a looking glass of his own, his memory of his teenage self's image was dim with both time and deliberate obscuration. He was glad of his anonymity, yet he felt, looking at the house, every inch of his profound difference from the child he had been. He was no prodigal son, who had been missed, who would be welcomed. He was a scarred, calloused sailor in thin and dirty clothing, shivering in an inland spring twilight far from the warming breezes of the southern seas, dwarfed by a pointless and private display of wealth. His forfeiture of his inheritance was not a mark of his goodness and honor, not here; here, his pride was an insult to his father's, his subsistence as offensive as his mother's had been.

Yet it was only his pride that spurred him on—he had come so far.

Bracing himself to be run off for a vagrant, Darragh went to the front door of the new construction and knocked with the heavy brass ornament fixed in the middle.

Vesta opened the door, and Darragh hardly recognized her, for she wore a plain split gown over a smock, such as he hadn't seen her wear since before the blood came to her. Her eyes were red and puffy, and they welled with fresh tears when she looked at him.

"Am I too late?" he asked.

"Too late to speak to him," she said. "He breathes yet but will not wake. The alchemists—they have provided a potion to keep him in this death-like sleep until they determine how to cure him, but . . ."

He sighed, then opened his arms; and slowly, they came together and embraced. He knew not what else to do. Such a swarm of emotions was in him that he was made dizzy by irregular breath and rushing blood, and leaning on his sister helped him to stay upright for the moment.

She led him inside. If she noted his lack of horse, she did not remark on it, and Darragh was grateful to be spared admitting he had not wanted to ride home with her. Perhaps it was better, then, that he could not speak to his father, if he was happy to avoid what by comparison would have been a simple conversation. In his travel he had kept thoughts of his destination at bay in order to keep moving toward it; and in his exile, he had not thought of his father save for the darkest and loneliest nights, when the terror of the sea made him wish his life had gone a different way. Truthfully, he had not prepared himself to confront his father. Where could he even begin? What words would better serve to redeem him in his father's eyes than the ones he'd screamed through tears the night he'd been thrust forever out the door and out of his father's heart?

Vesta brought him to the new kitchen, where a cup of tea sat on what he remembered as their formal dining table, a solid piece with minimal ornament that had been made by his mother's mother. Darragh ran his hand along its wood surface, smooth until the notch where—

"Would you like tea?" Vesta asked.

Darragh snatched his hand away. "Aye, thank you."

"It is a good thing I made a full pot," she said, pouring from a lovely earthenware teapot that made Darragh think of the potter from the road. "Almost as if I knew you were coming."

The cup she poured into was porcelain, like hers, with a saucer; the tea gave off a haze of gentle steam. "Did you?"

"I hoped." She sat and smiled wearily at him. "I know it must have been hard for you, but you have always had such a loyal nature."

"And where did I get that, I wonder?" Darragh said. "From the mother who left us both here with him, or from the father who disowned me?" Her smile flickered and died, and he felt a stab of guilt; had he not left Vesta in his turn? Was that why she had clung to their father since then, though surely she must have had opportunities to strike out on her own? Had he but lingered in the town, or sent her some message, might she have come with him?

He winced through these thoughts and continued, "I did not come to reconcile with Father. I came to face him."

"I'm glad he sleeps, then!" Vesta said. "To argue with a sick man—"

"Perhaps it is cowardly, and I wouldn't have come, except I found that after all this time I still don't understand . . ." His voice failed him, choked by sudden emotion.

"What, Darragh?" Vesta asked.

What, indeed? It was a thing that felt it should be complex, confounding, and yet was astonishingly simple. There had only ever been one question in him, one resounding echo of that night when he was chased away from the only life he'd ever known. Its answer was one that he could never discern on his own, try though he might, for how could he arrive at its result when he loved himself and believed in himself and saw himself as worthy of a life that pleased him?

"Why?" he said. "What is so wrong with who I am and what I want that he would rather erase me than love me as his son?"

The silence was thick between them. Darragh made to drink of his tea, but found his hand shook when it lifted the cup; he set it down, afraid of damaging the delicate porcelain. He could not look at Vesta.

"I think perhaps he just could never understand why *you* would want to change yourself," she said quietly, haltingly.

"Whose fault is that?" Darragh whispered. He gave a small huff. "We never spoke of it. He threw me out first."

"If you had come back sooner, you would have found him . . . calmer."

He heard the hesitation in her voice on the last word and was too astounded even to laugh. Calmer? When Darragh had appeared in his new suit and said, "Father, it's me. I am your son," his parent had taken his old cutlass off the wall and brandished it as if Darragh had been a burglar; and had the weapon not been dulled with disuse and age, he would have come away from his revelation bloodied in his flesh as well as in his heart. Instead, it was only the table that had been wounded. He could still hear Vesta's cries mingling with his own—what veil of time had fallen and persuaded her that it was Darragh who should have made the first gesture of reconciliation?

"How much calmer need he have been for me to be safe in returning?" Darragh asked. "How much calmer need he have been to write to me, or visit me himself?" He stood, unable to bear the conversation any longer. "It seems to me that you are the true loyalist here, sister."

He left the room, his tea untouched.

AT LEAST THE MEADOW was the same.

The old house had been his father's fathers', the woodsmen who hunted deer for the village before great quantities of fresh meat could be transported any distance, who cut down trees for lumber and firewood and who foraged for mushrooms, berries, honeysuckle, any sweet special thing the forest ever had to offer. Darragh's nanny had told him stories of them, and he'd loved to hear of them as a child—until his father returned from sea with fresh tales of waves that could crush the tallest, oldest, thickest trees, and fish larger than the ship he sailed on. The scale of maritime stories had been more exciting to Darragh than the quiet deliberateness of the forest.

The meadow was the result of his grandfathers' efforts; they cut the trees down in a vast swath of land behind the house they'd built, and dug up the roots and stumps as though clearing it to farm. But then, they'd let the land do as it willed. Wildflowers bloomed; and an occasional tree sprouted up, slim and unassuming; and the deer came. The woodsmen never shot the deer that came to eat the tender petals and grasses, and so the animals never learned to fear the meadow or even the house at its eastern edge.

They were out now, in the dusk, keeping close to the tree line but otherwise unbothered by Darragh, seated halfway between the house and the darkening forest. This was about where he had built his captain's cabin, but the scar in the meadow from when he'd burned it had healed. When his father had asked him why he'd done it, he'd told him that he no longer needed it, that he no longer wanted to pretend. Father had taken this as a sign and had moved the family into the city so that he could manage his little shipping empire and teach his children the business. Those three years had been the most exciting of Darragh's life. He had spent hours on the docks, spoken to hosts of people, learned so much about the world—he'd met others like him, had his first kiss, wandered the city looking for people who could teach him any small skill. He had worked little jobs for his father and others, and he had bought his suit of men's clothes. He had flicked his blood into the sea in the harbor, into the river north of the city, over the great waterfall that thundered into the bay, and his body had changed.

Had there been signs that the change would be unwelcome? Undoubtedly, though Darragh had not had the sense to notice. He'd assumed that their time in the city, among all those people so different from them, would open his father's mind as it had his, for all his father's brooding remarks at dinner. He had wished his mother could be there too, to reap all the benefits of the city; perhaps confinement to the country had made her run away. What else could explain it?

It had all made sense after his fifteenth birthday, when he'd learned that his father's prejudices applied to him too. That love was not always a force for good.

As often as Darragh had remembered the stranger who came to him the night his tender budding breasts had frightened him out of bed, he had never wondered where they came from or how the thorn they'd given him had done its work. Some magic, he assumed—though it was unlike any alchemy he'd heard of, and unlike the prayer-spells used out on the sea. There was no logic to it, for one thing—flick drops of blood into a fire or water, change your physical form? And yet, it did as promised. Thirteen years now he'd used the thorn, and his body was what he wanted it to be, and with less discomfort and experimentation than Sidra had experienced in her transition, with the physicians and their apothecaries. He had told her the story, of course, and they had tried to summon the stranger with foolhardy teenage confidence, once she realized that she was like Darragh; but he knew nothing about the stranger, and had nothing more to say into the air than "please." No one had come, and Sidra had gone to the doctors.

The doctors had already been to his father, Vesta had said, and been outmatched by his illness. He would die, possibly without ever waking from the sleep he'd fallen into, and Darragh would never learn why so personal a thing as gender had made him repulsive to his father.

Would learning help him in any way? Sidra would say no, but as Janne had pointed out, Sidra's family had not batted a single eyelash at her coming out. Whether they understood her feelings mattered little, if at all. She had never had to contend with being utterly cut off from her bloodline, her history. But would that history be any more welcoming of Darragh than his father had been? Would his grandfathers the woodsmen have understood?

"Please," he found himself whispering. "All I want is a chance. I'm no longer afraid . . . but I must know. I must know if I have anything of a father left in this world."

His only answer was a breeze. He closed his eyes and let his head fall back as if that would keep the tears in his eyes, but they only slid into his hair, their wet paths chilled by the brush of air.

The breeze turned into a gust, smelling of an incoming storm— and something else—

Roses?

But it was gone, and thunder was rolling over him. Darragh stood and went back inside, through the old house, whose door was surprisingly unlocked. It was less of a surprise when he found Vesta sitting in what had been called their parlor, on the right side of the first floor. The room was full of furniture all covered, save the chair and table at which she sat, with dingy sheets, which looked like sullen sails in the soft light cast by

Vesta's oil lamp. Darragh could not help himself, and a small mirthless laugh escaped him.

"So that's why you did not knock this place down," he said. "Storage."

"I thought you might want to see Mother's letters," she said, ignoring his comment. She raised a small bundle tied with a frayed ribbon.

Darragh took them from her. "So few."

"Two a year. On your birthday, and mine. But they're useless. She never says anything to hint at where she is," Vesta said.

He could see she was correct; the missives were mainly small notes, not even folded, addressed to him and Vesta respectively, saying little more than that she loved them and wished them well. "It's more than Father ever sent me."

"But she didn't send them to you, did she?" Vesta said. "She sent them to Belinda."

"I can see that," Darragh snapped. "She left before—"

"I remember." Vesta sighed. "I'm sorry. I cannot seem to hold my tongue. I have missed you so much. I want us to be close again, I just—I'm hurting too."

Vesta. His father's accomplice and successor, to the shipping business, at least. Would she continue his excommunication too, unless he made nice with her? That was his pain speaking; he found it difficult to imagine that she alone had been unscathed in all her years with their father. He looked her in the eyes and asked, "Because he is dying? Or . . . is it perhaps better for him to leave us than to stay?"

"It has been ten years, Darragh," she said. "He's changed."

Darragh stared down at the letters in his hand, letters that proved his mother had still thought of him after she left. Were they enough to prove that she still loved him? What proof could satisfy that question, from her . . . or from his father?

He found Vesta's gaze again. "Then loan me a horse. We shall see how much he's changed."

"I do not understand," Vesta said.

"I mean, keep him in this death-like sleep until I return, for I will find the means to revive him, and when I do, I shall have my interrogation," Darragh said.

She frowned. "And how do you intend to cure him, when all the doctors have not?"

The thorn felt warm against his chest. He said, "Only do as I ask, and you shall see."

THE STORY OF
THE SILVER LEAVES

nce upon a time, in a kingdom by the sea, there lived a beautiful princess who struggled to choose a spouse from among her many suitors. One day she called them all before her and said that she would marry the one who brought her the most special gift. Many of the suitors called out with questions, but the princess offered no more explanation; she felt she would know the right gift when she saw it, and that the one who found it would be the one who knew her best and would make the best spouse.

The suitors scattered across the kingdom and beyond in search of the thing that would win the princess's heart. Some purchased grand silks and other clothing; one tamed the most beautiful horse; another hunted dragons in order to bring the princess a magnificent trophy. Though the princess appreciated their efforts and thoughtfulness, none of these gifts was the most special.

One of the suitors was a baker's daughter. In her family, it was her duty to go to the farming villages to collect the wheat and have it milled into flour. She despaired of finding a special gift for the princess before the other suitors, some of whom were renowned heroes; but while she was out in the villages, the baker's daughter heard of a forest away in the North, at the center of which stood an enchanted mountain. The trees on this mountain grew straight from the rock, without soil, and had silver leaves that sparkled in the sunlight.

When the baker's daughter heard this, she knew at once that this was what would most please the princess, who loved growing things and kept a garden full of plants from all over the kingdom. She gave the wheat responsibilities to her sister, and set off for the forest in the North.

She could see the brightness of the leaves long before she reached the forest, and when she entered the trees, she attempted to keep as straight a course as possible in the direction of the mountain. But the forest was thick and green with summer, and she was soon hopelessly lost.

"I have been traveling hard for a long time; perhaps this is simply the forest reminding me to rest," she said. So she found a mossy patch in the crook of a tree's roots and slept there.

When she woke, she heard a pitiful crying, and went in search of the source. She found a fox kit stuck under a fallen tree branch. "Poor little kit!" she cried, and set immediately to digging it out. When it was free, it slipped out, but it was weak and could not stand on its own. The baker's daughter asked whether its home was nearby, and if she could help it get there. The kit dragged itself forward a little, then looked back at her, so she picked it up and walked in the direction it had tried to go.

While they walked, the baker's daughter heard a frantic bleating and the loud rustling of sticks. She stepped a little off the path to see what was happening and found a goat whose horns were caught in a bush.

"Don't worry, billy!" she said. "I'll get you out." She tucked the fox kit safely into her hip pouch and set to the bush, pulling the branches apart so that the goat could free itself. When it did, it pranced happily around her, and she laughed.

"You're welcome. I'd best be on; I need to get this kit home." She checked on the kit in her pouch. "Oh, it's fallen asleep. Billy, do you know where the foxes live?"

The goat tossed its head and bounded down the path. The baker's daughter followed it, and it led her through trees that grew ever larger and thicker, so that it was almost too difficult for her to pass through. But then, all of a sudden, the trees ended, and she stumbled out into a place with no trees but rose bushes as tall as her chest, covered with huge blooms. The baker's daughter stopped and stared at the roses, and then at the high stone walls beyond. Shielding her eyes, she looked up and saw the trees with the silver leaves atop the stone. She had made it to the enchanted mountain.

"What are you doing here?"

The baker's daughter looked down again, at a large gap in the stone. There stood a slim person with skin the dark umber brown of rich earth, and black hair molded into a great fall of locs adorned with flowers. The goat pranced over to em and butted against eir hand; so rather than be afraid, the baker's daughter carefully retrieved the fox kit from her pouch and held it out.

"I found this kit stuck under a fallen branch. I think it is quite hurt," she said.

"How did you get here?" the person asked.

"The billy goat led me here after I freed it from a bush. I wanted to bring the kit home."

The person came toward her, the roses parting to allow em passage, and collected the kit from her hands. "Thank you," e said. "It will be all right now."

The baker's daughter smiled, and the person headed away from her. She looked up again at the magical trees, summoned her courage, and said, "Is this the enchanted mountain?"

The person had knelt just past the gap in the stone, and the baker's daughter watched while e laid the kit down. The kit glowed, briefly, and then bounced up, perfectly healed. The person told the kit to be more careful, then smiled at the baker's daughter as if in answer to her question. Her heart swelled with happiness.

"If I may—I've come with the hope of retrieving a cutting from a silver-leafed tree," she said.

"Why?" asked the person.

"It's a gift for a beautiful princess whom I love very much."

The person stood and regarded the baker's daughter, head tilted as if considering her with new eyes. E looked at her for a long time, and what e thought, she couldn't have said. At length, e told the goat to climb the wall and get what she asked for. The goat did so, scaling the almost sheer face quickly and confidently. It came down in the same manner, with the cutting in its mouth, then trotted over and offered it to her.

"We grant you this cutting on two conditions," the person said. "First, you must never tell whence it came. Second, you must always remember that it was not your love for the princess that let you come near this place; it was your kindness to those in need."

The baker's daughter nodded solemnly and accepted the cutting. She thanked the person, the goat, and the fox, and bid them farewell. Her journey back to the kingdom by the sea was long, and toward the end of it, she began to fear that she was too late. Surely some other suitor had brought some other gift worthy of the princess. If that were the case, she vowed to herself that she would return to the enchanted mountain and give the cutting back. But when she reached the palace, she was told that the princess was still unattached, and so she went before her to offer her gift.

When the baker's daughter drew the cutting from her bag, the princess gasped at its beauty. When she held it in her hands and saw that it was no jewel but a live plant, she wept and kissed the baker's daughter, and thanked her for such a perfect gift. They planted the cutting in the princess's garden, where it grew into a magnificent black-trunked tree with sparkling leaves.

The princess and the baker's daughter married, and lived happily ever after.

5
CHOICES

Darragh left at dawn, changed horses at the inn, and made it back to Cathal in the early evening, the sun still yellow over the western hills. He was obliged to leave his frothing horse at the city gate, for the animal was too exhausted to mind his direction in the active streets.

If the stranger who had given him magic would not come to him, he would seek them out.

Vesta would have scoffed, but she could not deny that the stranger's power was true, not when Darragh stood before her. He must and did agree with her that the chance of the endeavor's success was vanishingly small; still, he was committed to the attempt, for then at least he could say he'd done whatever was in his power to heal his father. Whether gratitude and acceptance, or fury, or failure and death waited on the other side remained to be seen.

The Sorcerers' Guild was on the north side of the city. Its campus sprawled from an ancient tower like blood in water, coloring all it touched, growing, attracting to it the sort who were always searching for the next piece of flesh into which they might sink their teeth. It was not that the Guild was disliked, or feared;

though the campus itself was richly outfitted, the buildings all lovely, those who lived in the apartments surrounding it did so because they could not afford to live outside the Guild's shadow, away from the taint of magic. It was a place of confusion for most, who did not understand the grandiosity of those whose trade was so . . . intangible.

Darragh had been twice to the campus's easternmost building, the college of wind-singers, a tower taller than any other building in Cathal and the first landmark visible on the horizon to a ship bound for the city. Wind-singers were expensive to hire, and thus were contracted only for the most crucial of shipments in the worst times of year, unless the owner of the ship was flaunting their wealth. Most sailors disliked them, for it diminished the faith in their skill, if they be known to sail too often with one.

He went to the ancient tower, the original sorcerers' hall, positioned just inside the old city wall, and entered through a door that was small by modern standards but suited his stature just fine. There were no windows on the first floor, but it was lit by orbs the size of his fist, which blazed with the same yellow light of the sun outside; he could see clearly the murals that covered all the walls, depicting battles, mainly. Occasionally amid the shine of armor and glow of fire was a more tranquil scene of contemplation or discovery, often set in the woods or atop some rocky hill. The people most prominent in these scenes wore elaborate robes, mainly of emerald green, even in battles—in which their dress seemed not to matter, for they stood atop parapets or quarterdecks.

Darragh had time to see all the murals, making a turn of the room that encompassed the entire ground level. It was empty, save for a bare antique table with two benches in the middle of the room. On his second turn, he paused at the bottom of the stairs that curved along the wall and disappeared into a dark opening in the ceiling. He thought it odd that the front door should be unlocked when no one was there to mind it; perhaps he had been mistaken, and the tower was not the hub for the guild he'd imagined it was. It seemed likely, obvious even, in that moment, that the sorcerers had relocated their administrative offices to a grander and more modern building.

Feeling a little foolish, especially once he realized the light of the mock suns had gone orange, he turned to leave, and then he saw a person, older and beige-skinned with straight brown hair that came to their jaw, standing beside the table. They wore a normal-looking shirt and breeches with a vest; the emerald cowl that draped their shoulders was the only thing about them that hinted at the lineage painted on the walls.

"You would leave without saying a single word?" the person asked.

"Forgive me," Darragh replied. "I assumed I had the wrong place to make inquiries, and did not wish to disturb anyone."

The person smiled. "We are an insular group; sometimes one benefits from a little disturbance."

"How can one know whether one's intrusion is welcome, or beneficial? It is better, then, not to disturb."

"I can tell you now, I welcome your appearance," the person said.

"I meant beforehand," Darragh said.

"I know."

Darragh looked away from the person's oddly intimate smile and said, "In any case, I haven't disturbed you; you have now come to me."

The person laughed. "So I have. It is fortunate for me that I saw you enter, though not with these eyes, and heard your footsteps, though not with these ears. Otherwise, I should never have known, and we should never have met."

"Fortune remains to be seen," Darragh said. "I need to find someone who uses magic."

"Then your quest is complete," the sorcerer teased.

"A particular person," Darragh replied. He would need to be direct, he realized. "Though I admit, I have very little to go on. They helped me some years ago by giving me a magical item."

"What was the item?"

With only a moment's hesitation, Darragh pulled the thorn from beneath his shirt. "This."

The sorcerer approached him, serious at last, until they were close enough to take the thorn in their own hand and peer closely at it. They gestured, and one of the small suns floated over to them, brightening to a noontime white that made Darragh squint. He could feel the sorcerer's breath on his face, for they were taller than he, but not so tall that their face was beyond his sight, though he looked straight ahead, focusing on the fabric of the cowl where it stretched over their shoulder.

"This is old magic. Very old indeed," the sorcerer said finally. "You know nothing of the one who gave this to you?"

"Nothing," Darragh sighed. "They appeared to me one night when I was miserable, and gave me this as remedy."

"What does it do?"

"Mitigates that which caused me pain."

The sorcerer smiled again at that, but hungrily. "It is possible to gain the information you lack from this item, to discover the location of its originator. But I would need to make a thorough examination of it; you would need to leave it with me."

The light of the suns was red around them, save for the one giving light to the sorcerer's scrutiny. Darragh pulled the thorn gently from their grip and took several steps back. "I will consider it," he said, sounding more calm than he felt.

"Do," the sorcerer said. "And when you have decided, return here to me."

Darragh nodded, sharply, and went for the door. Before his hand met the knob, the sorcerer spoke again.

"My name is Gabin."

On this occasion, Darragh let his manners be as rough as his looks, and left without another word.

THE MAIDEN'S LANTERN WAS busy but not full, for it was only an hour after sunset and there was time yet before the upper-cliff bars emptied and their patrons began their trek farther and farther down the winding path, from one barrel rack to another until they could stomach no more, passed out too close to the road's edge, and were collected by the night-barrows whose job was to save these people from accidental death.

Darragh was two draughts into his evening and no closer to a resolution of his feelings. The thorn felt heavy around his neck as it never had before; the thousand forgotten pinpricks on his fingertips throbbed anew. He had never let the thorn leave him. Replacing the leather cord with the chain had been the first time he'd removed it from his neck since placing it there thirteen years before.

He chided himself for dramatics. It wasn't as if Gabin the sorcerer had asked to keep the thorn, only to borrow it—and that to find the stranger who had originally given it to him. That was what he wanted, wasn't it? Gabin would give the thorn back to him when they were finished with it. He would make them swear it; he would stay with them while they worked on it and got the information he needed. Still, the thought of parting from the thorn even for a moment—he did not know what would happen to him if the worst should happen, and he did not get it back in time. Would all its magic be undone? Was the life he had so fragile? Things he had never thought to ask when he was still a questioning child. He had not known then what the form he wanted would be, and it seemed to him the stranger had known that; that was why he had been given an impermanent form of magic. That must have been why.

Old magic. Somehow Darragh didn't think Gabin meant thirteen years. A thought struck him, and he pulled the book Perrin had gifted him from his bag.

Wailing, suddenly loud, pulled him from his thoughts. In the near corner, the tavern-keeper was shouting at someone while several children, crammed around a table, cried at varying volumes. Darragh stood and approached, the better to hear the commotion, and soon he discerned that the parent had brought their family in to eat without any apparent intention of paying.

"A mother does what she must," the parent said. "I will accept any punishment you think fit; or let me work for the food—"

"I've no need of more hands, and as for punishment—shall I call the magistrate, when you've stolen enough to make a hanging offense?" the tavern-keeper snarled. "I have my own family to feed, you selfish—"

"Will you trade, sir?" Darragh asked.

The tavern-keeper turned to him, anger gone save for the redness of his cheeks. Darragh knew the man but little, enough only to know it was not cruelty that made him berate the mother and her children; he kept his business to a tight leash, and if he had not the money from such a large meal, he would be in debt to one of his suppliers. He looked at Darragh in his rough sailor's clothes with skepticism and asked, "Have you anything that matches the value?"

"I have that which exceeds it, if I judge rightly," Darragh said. He unclasped the fine black chain, slid his thorn off it, and held it to the light so the tavern-keeper might see it.

The tavern-keeper cupped the chain to steady it for better examination, and after a moment, nodded. "Aye, it does that. I will change the rest for you," he said.

"No need. Let it be given to the family," Darragh replied.

They looked to the woman, whose face was a blend of shock and concern; but she nodded, and so did the tavern-keeper. He left to get the coin.

"You needn't have done that. I knew what would follow from my actions," said the woman.

Darragh bent his head in apology, but also to hide the dark smile he could not immediately suppress. He had interfered, and though it might have been beneficial, he had not known whether it would be welcome. By his earlier declaration, he should not have done it. It was difficult to feel wholly regretful, while the children—all under ten years of age, by his guess—were calming down; when he lifted his head he saw that their parent, too, had not so firm a grip on her anger as before.

"I am sorry," he said.

"And I am grateful," she replied.

He dipped his head to her again and returned to his table, but he had hardly exhaled the tension in him before a shadow fell across it. A tall person with yellow-brown skin deepened in tone by the sun stood before him, dressed in breeches without hose and a shirt with a waist sash providing cushion for a thick leather belt. Their coat had toggle closures but hung open, and its sleeves came only to the elbow in a loose bell shape, with a large armscye for mobility—a boater's coat, exactly like his, though in better condition. The person's shirt sleeves were pushed up to the elbow, revealing a faded but elaborate triangle tattoo on her right forearm, which further confirmed her as a sailor and identified her as a woman who paired with other women.

She sat, and he saw that she was considerably older than he, at least double his age; she was smiling in a knowing, friendly way, and holding up a leather cord.

"I saw you slip something off that chain. Thought you might need a replacement for it," she said.

Darragh chuckled. "I do. Thank you."

She watched him while he took the cord and threaded the thorn on it, then fastened it around his neck. He smiled when it settled into place, more comfortable than the chain ever could have been.

"Earrin," the sailor said by way of introduction. "That was kind of you."

"Darragh." He shook her hand. No title to signal the proper way to gender and address her; other sailors, like him, would read her tattoo. Darragh's own was on his neck, a stylized mermaid's purse tangled with a harpoon. "Kindly meant, perhaps. But I should have kept out of it."

"Why?"

Because it is better not to disturb? "It was none of my business. She knew what she was doing; she was prepared."

"And if one is prepared to suffer, we should let them?" Earrin asked rhetorically. "Who raised you?"

Darragh frowned, but Earrin was chuckling and shaking her head; she hadn't meant it seriously. He swallowed his thoughts about who had raised him—or rather, who had not. "We cannot expect others to fight our battles for us."

"Agreed, and some battles cannot be fought by anyone except ourselves," Earrin said. "But which battles those are can be hard to judge."

"Everything is hard to judge," Darragh groaned, suddenly exhausted. "I apologize. It isn't you that's brought this on me. My thoughts have been lately mired in some dark places."

"So you turn to folklore. For escape, or for advice?" Earrin asked, gesturing to the book.

He chuckled again. "I am not sure. I haven't opened it yet."

"Well, the advice is usually to be kind . . . and mind your own business." She grinned at him, and he couldn't help smiling back. "May I?"

He nodded and she picked up the book, flipping through it as if looking for something in particular. When she found it, she smiled and turned it round to show him a tale called "The Hundred Promises."

"This one is about my family," she said.

"Is it?"

"Oh, yes. That copy you've got is a valuable antique. The new collections, they've taken out all the kind stories and filled them with all terrible ones to show the Enchanter in a bad light."

Darragh scanned the story—a barren family went into the woods and traded rose seeds to a mysterious stranger for a tree; when the tree bloomed, the family conceived. *At first, the farmer thought the Enchanter had not marked him; but then e turned eir head, just so the light fell golden on the crest of eir brow* . . . Darragh's mind filled with the memory of his stranger, the way the light had caressed their face. He raised wide eyes to Earrin, who quirked her eyebrow.

"Why would they want to show the Enchanter poorly?" he asked.

She took the book from him again and flipped around, but this time she shook her head. "This one is from before it happened," she said.

"Before what happened?"

"Before the trees bled."

Darragh sighed and looked for the "Promises" story again. There was so little detail. "Where is your family from?"

"The north," Earrin said. She tilted her head and scrutinized him. "Why do you ask?"

"I need to find the Enchanter. I think … e helped me once, when I was a child, and now I need eir help again," he replied. "I simply don't know where to start. I went to the Sorcerers' Guild, but—"

"They wouldn't know," Earrin said. "The Enchanter worked in old magic, older even than that ugly old guild tower; they'd never understand it nor know how to come near it."

Darragh nodded, until one word registered. "Worked? Not works?"

"Aye, for no one has seen hide nor hair of the Enchanter for more than a hundred years." Earrin looked thoughtfully at him and said, "Except you, apparently."

"You believe me?"

"Should I not?"

He sat up straight and felt the thorn resting against his chest. Proof more solid than any he could have wished for. "I need to go north."

Earrin smiled. "I think our meeting must have been arranged by some favorable stars, Darragh, for as it happens, I am captain of a river barge. We set off again in the morning."

"It will only be favorable if you have need of extra hands, for I cannot pay my passage by any other means," Darragh replied.

"Oh yes. I will certainly put those hands to work," she said, laughing.

THIS TIME, SIDRA LEFT Janne's apartment with Darragh and they walked together until they found a quiet alley between two seaside buildings; they settled against the walls at its edge, the hill slanting sharply below them. The night was a muddle of blue broken only by the white light of the moon and stars winking in the water. The orange fire lights of the lower hillside and the alchemist lamps of the upper were hidden by the angles.

He told Sidra what he had found when he returned home, what Vesta had said, what he had learned, and what he intended to do. She listened without comment until he was finished, and then she said, "This is not merely about your father, Darragh."

"No. I suppose it isn't," he said. "I have wanted something for a long time now, and I've yet to find it at sea. Now I think I must search for it in the forest."

"What is it that you're looking for?"

"I am not sure . . . I feel its lack, as if I felt it once and forgot everything but the shape of where it once sat in my soul. Mayhap it is my father's love, or . . . I do not know. But I have been unsettled by this, and I know that I must resolve it somehow."

Sidra peered at him in the dark, and her eyes filled with tears. When one fell, he brushed it from her cheek, and she, to his surprise, laughed; then she reached for him with both hands and wiped away the tracks of tears he had not noticed trickling from his own eyes. Yet more came, for with their recognition came the full force of his hope and his sorrow. Sidra pulled him into her arms and held him while he sobbed and shed the stress of the days since Vesta's visit, and of the years of quietly arguing that he had everything he wanted.

"I suppose you want leave for this journey, then?" she asked when he quietened.

He laughed. "Yes ma'am. If it's convenient."

"You had damn well be ready to meet us at the nearest port when you've completed this quest."

He laughed again and kissed her cheek; they held each other tightly in the dark, to delay the first long separation they had ever faced.

THE STORY OF
THE STATUE

n a village at the edge of a forest lived a woodcarver's apprentice. The apprentice was well-liked by all who knew him, for his skill was great and his heart was kind.

In this village there lived also a young shepherd who was in love with the apprentice, and determined to marry him. So on the day he came of age, the shepherd asked the apprentice to become her spouse.

"Alas," said the apprentice, "you are a very good friend to me! But I will not marry you; I cannot love you as you love me, and I fear this would lead to discord between us. Come, let us stay as we are and be friends."

This vexed the shepherd very much, but nothing could move the apprentice to change his mind—he insisted he could not fall in love and would not marry. The shepherd sighed and sighed, until an idea came to her of a way to help the apprentice. She ventured into the forest and sought out the Enchanter who lived there, and found em seated on a boulder before a great waterfall.

"Enchanter! My friend is broken and cannot fall in love; please, give me a love charm for him," she said. "I will pay any price."

The Enchanter stood and looked fiercely down at the shepherd, who was in that moment afraid, for the Enchanter was powerful and that power radiated from em like an oppressive heat.

"You are very cruel to your friend, to say such a thing and to seek this charm, which is an evil kind of magic," the Enchanter said. "Begone and do not attempt to hurt another in this way."

The shepherd fled from the anger of the Enchanter and was for a little while deterred from seeking a love charm. But her ardor for the apprentice continued unabated, growing with every day, so good and handsome was he. So she set out again in search of magic that would make him hers. She found a sorcerer who told her he could give her what she wanted.

"Take thou the blood of thy beloved and thyself, and mix it, and this herb I give thee, into a bread dough. Bake the loaf, and serve it to thy beloved without their knowledge," the sorcerer said. "Then they will be enamored of thee."

The shepherd returned to the village in high spirits. She invited the apprentice to come and sit with her while she took her flock out, and to do his carving at her side. He agreed. While he carved, the shepherd made her plan; when he was very focused, she screamed and startled him so that his knife slipped and cut his hand. The apprentice hissed in pain but asked what was wrong, and the shepherd told him she thought she had seen a wolf, but it was only a dog. She used her handkerchief to bind up the apprentice's wound. When he stood up to leave her, the cut had stopped bleeding, and so the shepherd took the handkerchief back, though the apprentice wanted to wash it for her.

When she came back to the village, she set to the making of the bread dough. Into it she added the blood from the handkerchief, and from her own hand, and the sorcerer's herb, and baked it all together. When the loaf was ready, she carried it to the apprentice and offered it as an apology for his hurt hand.

The apprentice, suspecting nothing, thanked the shepherd and cut a slice straightaway for himself and for the shepherd. They ate of it together, and the shepherd watched the apprentice carefully for signs of love.

Unbeknownst to the shepherd, though, the Enchanter, who was a friend of the apprentice, had become suspicious of her target and given the apprentice a talisman against such magical coercion. When the apprentice ate of the bread, the talisman grew hot and bright with the release of its protective magic, and he dropped the bread in alarm.

"How could you betray me this way?" he demanded. "You have tried to force me into loving you—you are no friend of mine, and never shall be again. You are too cruel!"

"You are the cruel one, to be so cold with me!" the shepherd replied. "You have a heart of stone!"

The apprentice glared at her and said, "You had all of my heart that I could give you, and you spat on my affection. I shall never speak to you anymore."

He threw the remaining loaf into the fire, and the shepherd stormed away from him. She wept bitterly for several days, out on the fields, and then her hurt feelings condensed into rage. She returned to the sorcerer and this time asked for a potion with which to punish the apprentice for withholding his love. The sorcerer gave her such a potion, and when the shepherd returned to the village, she poured it into a jug of milk and went with an expression of penitence to the apprentice.

"My friend, I am so sorry," she said. "You are right, I have betrayed you and thought only of myself; it was very cruel of me. You have been my most dear friend, and I miss you sorely. Please, share a cup of milk with me, and let us reconcile."

Though the apprentice was still in great pain, he had faith in other people and believed his friend to be truly remorseful. So he agreed, and accepted a cup from the shepherd. Alas, his talisman was spent. When he drank of the milk, a great pain seized his body and he ran from the house—but he had not taken more than a few steps toward the forest before he was turned completely to stone. The shepherd was satisfied and went away quickly, before she could be connected to the magic.

Not long after this, the Enchanter came through the village on eir way home to the forest, and found eir friend the apprentice turned into a statue. E knew at once what had happened, and went to the shepherd. Though e appeared calm before her, e was filled with anger.

"Shepherd, I have been thinking of your request for a love charm," the Enchanter said, in a mild voice that caused the shepherd no alarm. "I may be willing to give it, but before I do, you must answer three questions for me."

The shepherd, not wanting to alert the Enchanter to what had already come to pass, said, "I will answer any question you ask, with full honesty."

"Very good," the Enchanter said. "The one you love—would you willingly cause them to bleed?"

"No, I should not wish any harm to come to them," the shepherd replied.

"Would you knowingly deceive them?" the Enchanter asked.

"No, I should only ever tell them the truth."

"And would you ever abandon them?"

"No, never! I would sooner turn to stone."

As these words left the shepherd's lips, the Enchanter smiled— they were all lies, because she had indeed done all of these things to the apprentice. The stone curse upon the apprentice was broken then, and his flesh turned soft again; the Enchanter left the shepherd behind and went to the apprentice, to help him and ensure his health.

The shepherd, meanwhile, was herself turned to stone as punishment. The statue of her still stands among the grazing fields.

6

ON THE RIVER

THE BOOKSELLER JUMPED, AND Darragh had the grace to look ashamed for having rapped hard on the glass the moment they'd come into view; but they opened the door to him, though their shop was not to open for another two hours, by the sign on the window.

"Have you the most recent *Callistan Folk Tales*?" Darragh asked.

"Recent!" the bookseller laughed. "Why, it's older than you are."

"May I see it?"

The bookseller waved him in and went to retrieve it. "Off on the barge this morning, are you?"

"How can you tell?" Darragh asked.

"Merely a guess, my young friend. You young people are always in such a rush, it is getting more difficult to say," the bookseller replied.

They found the book and handed it to Darragh, who looked at the list of stories contained in it. There was no "Hundred Promises," but there was one called "The Bleeding Trees."

"I'll have it," he said. "How much?"

The bookseller raised a hand and shook their head. "A gift. I do not get many sailors in here eager for reading material."

Darragh smiled and thanked them, not needing to ask how they had known him for a sailor. He put the book carefully in his sack, which was quite full of treasures now—two books and a fine jug—and hurried up the hill to the river.

The river port, Sergius, was the northwesterly point of Cathal, having been its own city before the modern age of shipbuilding had brought greater prosperity to the seaport and given it the power to absorb the river docks as well. The Erastus River was a calm and a wide waterway until it began its descent to the sea, just west of Sergius, in a series of short waterfalls and frothing rocky runs terminating in the Great Falls, taller than the wind-singers' tower. Just beside it was the aptly named Great Falls Elevator, which hoisted cargo straight up until it reached the ledge, where it was taken the rest of the way to Sergius by mule teams cutting a zigzagging path up the hillside. Those teams had once used the main road through the Cathal hillside, before the elevator had been built; though the Cathals feared the elevator, they were pleased enough to send the mules to the north of the city.

Earrin's business was shipping cargo, rather than passengers; that was clear the moment Darragh laid eyes on her barge, the *Celestino*. It had one deck with a small cabin at the stern, and a furled sail on a single mast with crates and barrels stacked fore and aft of it. He also saw at a glance why she had accepted his offer to work his passage without any questions regarding his water-worthiness: on either side of the barge were rows of oar benches. He almost laughed at himself, but of course it made sense. There might have been a sail, but under any but the strongest winds, they would need to row against the current to go north. It was likely that Earrin took on new rowers at every stop she made. Darragh rolled his shoulders and approached.

The captain spotted him crossing the plank and came to meet him. "Welcome, Darragh!"

"You might have said I'd be rowing. It would not have frightened me," he said, smiling at her.

She laughed. "No, I suppose not. Do you favor port or starboard?"

"I will sit whatever bench you require."

"Good man." She led him toward the bow and gave him his place. He was partnered with a pale but ruddy-faced person with a circle tattoo in the center of eir forehead. E introduced emself as Amon. Darragh judged em younger than he but near twice as wide; when e teasingly offered to sit where the pulling would be harder, Darragh readily agreed, which made Amon laugh.

"Nothing to prove, then?" e asked while Darragh sat and settled himself.

"Not anymore," Darragh replied. "I know my strength, and I will trust yours, and all will be well."

Amon's smile softened into a more thoughtful, appraising expression, and Darragh turned away lest he offend with the smirk he could not quite contain.

The *Celestino* set off before the sun had crested the eastern horizon, and Darragh, Amon, and their fellow oar-pulls poured all their focus into the task at hand. Earrin stood before the cabin by the drummer, while her first mate stood at the bow. It was smooth work for most of the day, and when the sun was high Earrin came down among the benches, tapping alternating pairs to rest and eat. Amon offered to rub Darragh's back, an offer he accepted gladly, and in return, he massaged Amon's hands while he watched the changing coast roll past them. The land had been flat around Sergius, but now the horizon was lumpy and yellow-green with new grass. He saw sheep and cattle along the hills, small shacks occasionally. They passed a ramshackle pier that looked as if it would split should they attempt to tie against the current on it.

"How far is the next river port?" Darragh asked.

"Two hours at this pace to Ovidia. We'll likely stop there overnight," Amon said. "This is your first time upriver?"

"Yes," Darragh said. "My family comes from east of Cathal. I've been to the northern seaports, but never up this way."

"And do you go north now by choice or necessity?"

"Both." Darragh laughed. "I am choosing to finally answer, if I can, a necessary question. And you?"

"I have been on the river three years, and I won't leave if I can help it," Amon said. "It's too beautiful, and I meet too many interesting people."

Darragh laughed, but did not answer, for it was time to row again. As the landscape changed, so did the shape of the river, and the first mate at the bow now called instructions for navigating the windings bends before them. Darragh struggled at first, for rowing out of the doldrums or out of a storm at sea required no such fine turning, but with Amon's guidance he soon found the feel of it and had no more trouble. When the barge docked at Ovidia, Darragh was exhausted but happy, especially when he and Amon were given permission to go ashore at nightfall, after business was done.

Amon took him to a tavern full of river travelers, where it was so loud they leaned in close to speak to one another and eventually gave even that up, communicating only by looks and smiles; once they reached that point, they were not long for the tavern floor, and went up to the room Amon had taken. It had only one bed, and Darragh laughed.

"Is it rude of me to be so transparent?" Amon asked.

Darragh came and stood close to em so that their clothing brushed, and said, "Not to me. Do I take this for permission to kiss you?"

"Please consider everything permissible until I say otherwise," Amon replied.

Afterward, Darragh lit the candle on the small nightstand and retrieved his book of folk tales, the older one, then returned to Amon on the bed. Amon clung to him and saw the title. E kissed each of the tattoos on Darragh's bare chest and asked, "Read one to me?"

Darragh lifted his hand from where it played with Amon's hair, flipped the pages to a random story, and began to read. It told of an apprentice who did not fall in love, and the cruel friend who would not accept such an answer, who tried to force love with magic. But the Enchanter refused, punished the friend, saved the apprentice. Darragh read the lines mentioning the Enchanter over and over again once he'd finished, but he could not describe the effect those lines had on him.

Amon seemed likewise entranced; e reached up and grazed the words on the page. "I have never heard this story before," e said dreamily. "I am that way—aromantic, like the apprentice."

"Oh?" said Darragh.

"Yes. How old is this story?"

Darragh checked the front of the book. "This collection is . . . damn. One hundred and twenty-seven years old." Earrin had not lied when she called the book an antique. Had he known, he might not have carried it with him on the river; he had to hope the oilskin he wrapped around it would protect it should they come through a storm or rough water.

Amon sighed. "Alas that so little should have changed in such a long time."

"This is why you will not leave the river?" Darragh asked.

"No, not in any large way. It is why I came to it, though."

"I understand. I ran to the water, too."

"You are aromantic?" Amon asked.

"That is not why I ran." Darragh shut the book and set it on the nightstand.

"Was it this?" Amon asked, tapping the three-faced tattoo on Darragh's left breast, the one that meant he was a different gender than the one given to him at birth.

"Yes."

He felt Amon nod against his shoulder. "Have you been in love, then?" e asked.

"No," Darragh said again, after a moment.

Amon said, "Perhaps you are aromantic and just don't know it yet."

Was he? He supposed he could be. The stories of his childhood were full of grand romance that struck and sparked and burned all before it, and when he was young, that had seemed both possible and desirable. As he aged, though, what he felt was less consuming than those stories had led him to believe it would be, and it became more difficult to imagine giving himself over entirely, and for years or more, to what he felt for another person; yet the harder it became to imagine, the more he wondered about it and, he now realized, wished for it. Did wishing for it mean he could feel it?

"I'm sorry, Darragh," Amon said into his silence. "I only meant to tease you."

Darragh rolled on top of em and kissed em deeply. "I don't mind it. You might be right. But then again," he said, pausing to kiss em again, "I might fall in love with you by morning."

Amon grinned, and they spoke no more.

DARRAGH WOKE BEFORE AMON; he rose from the bed carefully and looked down on eir lovely sleeping form. What did falling in love feel like? For his throat was tight and his eyes hot with emotion; he felt so lucky to have met this person, to have shared his body with em and been granted the pleasure of eirs. He thought em kind and charming and if he had to leave em that very moment, he would feel joy at the prospect of meeting em again. Was that love? Was that, as he had told the metalsmith what felt like so long ago, hands weaving a blanket together, or sailing a ship together, or any of the other things he'd so firmly said? More likely, he knew nothing—no more than the shepherd who had tried to force her friend to fall in love with her.

If he left Amon that moment, with no promise of seeing em again, would he feel sorrow to lose em? Was romance in that pain?

He did not have an answer and he did not like the question, so he caressed Amon's face until e woke.

After three days, Darragh could understand why Amon loved the river life so much. The rowing was hard but steady; the weather was mild, the scenery was beautiful, and going ashore every night if one wished was an indescribable luxury. Amon's friendship was a large part of why the journey felt special instead of tedious, Darragh knew. Though they spoke no more of romantic love, he thought about their conversation while he rowed, attempting with each pull to draw in some kind of answer, only to have the current drag it away from him again before he could grasp it.

On the third evening, Darragh was assigned to the night watch, and settled onto the sacks of grain at the bow with his lantern and the new book of tales.

"Have you read them all now?" asked Earrin.

He looked up, watched her walk toward him with her hands deep in the pockets of her culottes. "All the old, ma'am. I got myself a new copy as well."

"Ah, so now you are learning how cruel the Enchanter is." The captain laughed and sat on a crate beside Darragh.

He understood her sarcasm, because the Enchanter portrayed in the new tales seemed a different person entirely to the one in the old. The old one had helped families conceive, guided children lost in the forest, helped those who were in danger or in miserable circumstances—this was the Enchanter Darragh recognized from his own encounter. But the new version stole children and ate them, jealously punished youth and beauty, hoarded treasure, and worse.

"At least one of the old stories is true. What of the new ones?" he asked. "If people can change and become terrible, cannot enchanters too?"

"People do not change; they show their true colors," Earrin replied.

"I think that is sometimes true. Perhaps it is even true in the majority of cases," Darragh said. "But sometimes, adversity forces us to make choices that may seem cruel from the outside."

Earrin smiled slowly. "You are very philosophical for a sailor."

"Sailors have a lot of time to think, and isolation is a ripe venue for philosophizing."

"And you've been ten years a sailor; have you the meaning of life yet?"

"Not yet," he said, laughing. "But with enough time, I may suss it out."

She laughed with him and looked toward the river docks, alight with the inns and shops necessary to every river town. "Isolation can be a ripe venue indeed, but not a pure one," she said, her voice soft and thoughtful. "We bring all our poisons with us."

Darragh nodded, and they sat a moment together in the silence of the river, which is to say, surrounded by the constant splashes of water, the calls of toads and the rustling of marsh grasses on the steep, muddy banks, the human noise of laughter and shouting and music and stomping. Ripe and impure, and in its own way, comfortable—comforting. But perhaps that was only the presence of Earrin, whom he found himself admiring very much; her teasing intelligence made him feel at ease, because he felt compassion in it, too, and he was not afraid of her insight.

"Ma'am . . . may I be so bold as to ask you, what do you think love is?"

She raised her eyebrow. "Has Amon told you—"

"Yes, e has. That is not why I ask. Well—not in the way—e asked me if I had ever been in love, and I said no, and since then I have not stopped wondering whether I should even know if it happened to me," Darragh said.

Earrin hummed a little noise of understanding. "You are not the first to wonder, and won't be the last. For all we humans purport to exalt love, for all that our kingdom is built upon an institution that supposedly enshrines it, yet we struggle to define or differentiate it."

"You must have some idea."

"Oh, aye," she said. "For me, I think love is an instinct, a resonance that draws people together. It is not always a *good* instinct; sometimes it is wrong, as sometimes I feel afraid when there is nothing to fear."

"Then what is the difference between friendship and romance, or kinship?"

"There is none. Love is only a feeling, and one we have no true control over. Relationships, though—whether of friends, lovers, or family—they are made up of choices and actions. And before you ask me what actions constitute a relationship, let me say, that is something people must decide for themselves."

Darragh sighed, for he realized that his breath had been coming shorter while they spoke. "You've thought deeply about this," he said.

"I had reason to," she replied, her smile a little dark. "I was married to a man who performed all the proper actions—he courted me, he married me, he provided for me and my children— but our relationship was a site of pain and resentment, and so I decided to leave it."

"And your children?"

"My girls," Earrin sighed. "He did not love me, but he loved them; I could see it in the way he treated them and spoke of them. They were safer left with him, rather than on the run with me."

It was lucky that Darragh's life had taught him how to disconnect from painful situations that could not be escaped; Earrin's words conjured painful old questions in him. He felt his whole posture slacken while his mind retreated to the bow of a different ship, the sound of different water, a memory where the ocean air was chill and sharp upon his face. If Earrin noted the change in him, she gave no sign; she stood, clapped his shoulder, and reminded him to keep a keen watch before leaving the ship.

Even after she left, it took some time for Darragh to rouse himself from that comforting place where the world was open before him and the wind was strong enough to carry away his troubles. His watch relief arrived before he had fully recalled himself, and he nodded dimly before trudging to the stern. There was a small deck space behind the cabin, and Darragh stretched himself out on it, his book clutched to his chest and his eyes on the stars. He could go into the town; Amon had given direction for where they might meet. But though he imagined Amon would be kind to him in his present distress, he wanted to be alone. The conversation with Earrin had hurt him in the places of his heart devoted to his family; again, he felt guilt and confusion that he could not let them all go—Vesta, his parents—and be happy in his friendship with Sidra and their crew. Worse than that was the fear—that Vesta would not keep her word and hold their father in the death-like sleep; that despite the potion, his father would die before Darragh made it back; that he would wake and banish Darragh all over again; that it did not matter what happened, and Darragh would have this aching hollow inside him for the rest of his life.

7
INTO THE NORTH

THE BARGE REACHED ITS final port a week after setting out, a city called Varrun, the Gateway of the North. Darragh stood on the *Celestino*'s deck and studied the river, which stretched as far as he could see in the same manner it had the entire journey, but there were mountains on the horizon, from which the Erastus sprang.

"They seem so close," he said to Amon.

Amon laughed. "It's a day's ride yet to the nearest. Is that where you're headed?"

"Perhaps," Darragh said. "I'm not fully sure of my destination yet."

"I wish you all luck, and hope you find what it is you're looking for. If you can, wait for us when you make your return, so you can tell me everything," Amon said.

Darragh embraced em. "No matter what happens, I will have no regrets of this journey, for through it I met you."

"You are a sentimental one, aren't you?"

"Rather that than other masculinities I've seen," Darragh replied.

Amon laughed again, and kissed him. "I look forward to seeing you again, Darragh Thorn."

Smiling, Darragh took his leave, and would have quitted the barge immediately had he not been stopped by Earrin. She handed him a pouch heavy with coin.

"Wages," she said. "You're a fine oarsman, Darragh, and are welcome on my crew any time."

"But—I agreed to work my passage," he said.

"I don't take passengers. Now, listen: if you go due north from here, you'll find an inn at Iarom-by-the-Barrow. That's where most of your tales were recorded, told to that collector by the innkeeper." She slung a crossbow from her shoulder, offering it to him with a small quiver of bolts. "And you'll need this north of here. Not much in the way of markets for buying food."

He nodded. "Thank you."

She lingered, uncertainty in her posture, and then she said, "Darragh, may I put my arms around you?"

Surprised, he met her eyes and saw a kind of concern there that rattled him, but he nodded again, and she folded him into an embrace that felt easy and warm and familiar. Despair washed over him, and Earrin's hold tightened, as if she knew. "May your path be smooth," she whispered; then she clapped him on the shoulder and turned away to her business. Darragh sighed, marshaled himself, and disembarked into Varrun.

It was a rustic city in comparison to Cathal; Varrun had not yet torn down the wall around its fort, set upriver of the docks and very old-looking even at a distance, crenellations rising above the mix of thatch, wood, and slate roofs. Indeed, the slate shingles were the most modern thing Darragh could see, besides here or there a smooth glass pane in a shop window, without rippling and of the thinness only achievable by the alchemists in the south. Darragh avoided those shops; any place that would pay the truly absurd price to not only order such a pane, but have it shipped this far, would have nothing for the likes of him. He kept himself to the ones without any glass at all, and found good hose, thick socks, and a proper land coat like the ones he saw others on the street wearing. He'd not spent long on land in the north, but he knew that even if the days grew warm, the nights would still be chilled.

His next errand was to the fort, the only place he was confident of finding an accurate map to study. The fort was a rectangular affair that had lost many of its more fearsome components; being so inland and part of a united nation, it had been insulated from attack these last two hundred years at least. When he passed through the entrance, he saw only the wooden doors, and no portcullis. There had been some improvements made to it along those peaceful lines—Darragh could not believe the gold braziers were a military decoration—and it managed to pull together into a noble aesthetic, the balance of might, history, and refinement appropriate for government offices.

Darragh sought out the records office and was duly presented with the most recent official map of the north country.

"Just last year they made this," the young records officer said proudly. "They surveyed for more paving at the same time." They pointed at the dashed lines branching from the thick black path of the paved roads.

"That's exciting," Darragh said.

"I think so, yes. Not everyone does, which I suppose is understandable after what happened the last time the government tried to improve the roads—"

"Oh, don't start with that again, Ceara," said another officer. "Don't pay her any mind, good gentle. It's only a story."

"It's not," Ceara said. "If it was, would we be importing lumber when there's a massive forest less than a hundred miles away?"

The older officer huffed and returned to their desk, and Ceara smiled at Darragh in triumph; her look brightened when she saw that he was intrigued. "What happened last time?" he asked, quietly.

"The first time they tried to set the roads, people moved up north in a rush; everyone was mad for timber. This was one hundred years ago, after the War."

"The Great Build," Darragh said.

"Yes, exactly," Ceara replied. "And the road meant that people could get the logs from the forest down to Iarom, where the river was deep enough to send them south."

"Iarom. Iarom-by-the-Barrow?" Darragh asked.

Ceara pointed it out on the map. "It's the largest town that far north. At least, it was then. More people leave those places now than are born in or move to them."

"If it's on the river, why is this the northernmost river port?"

"The Erastus is too fast to go upriver, once it rounds that bend north of the city. That's when it starts to narrow into the mountains."

Darragh noted the course of the river, and Iarom's place on it, and nodded. "So what happened to the forest?"

"It wasn't just the forest. There was some huge storm, a quake, a cataclysm, they say," Ceara said. "There were floods and rockslides; the road broke into pieces, houses collapsed. Plenty of people died—that's when the Barrow was built. And the trees *petrified*. You can't cut them at all now."

"A natural disaster," said the older officer.

"A storm doesn't turn trees to stone," Ceara shot back.

"What does?" Darragh asked.

She looked back at him, eyes wide, and said, "Magic. But not like the alchemists. My gran, he said—"

"Your gran is so old he hardly remembers his name."

"Yes, so old he was alive when it happened!" Ceara replied. "He was too young to remember himself, but his parents told him all about it, and they always warned *my* parents to stay away from the forest, because something dark and powerful lived there. It got angry when people chopped down the forest, and it punished them."

The older officer huffed again, more forcefully this time. Darragh glanced at them, then leaned into Ceara and said softly, "I believe you."

She smiled and, suddenly shy, bobbed her head and left him to study the map.

THE STORY OF
THE BLEEDING TREES

nce in the far north, not so long ago, there was a village at the edge of a great forest. This village was home to many woodcutters and sawhands, who would fell trees for firewood and for lumber, to sell down south where the timber had been exhausted.

This great forest was presided over by a terrible enchanter, however, and e came to resent the villagers for diminishing eir lands and damaging eir trees. Soon the Enchanter came to the village. E came to the newly built town hall, the largest building in the village, and tapped eir staff upon the door three times. The people gathered, from within the hall and without, drawn perhaps by the Enchanter's power. All trembled to look upon the hunched, cloaked figure.

"Be not afraid," said the Enchanter. "I come as a friend with sage advice."

The mayor of the village said, "Then let us hear it."

The Enchanter's expression changed from a smile to a face as stony as the mountains beyond the forest. E pointed with eir staff at the town square and said, "Pile high all your axes and saws in the center of the village and burn them. Let the handles be kindling and the blades become horseshoes. If you do not, I shall cause the forest to be forever closed to you."

A great cry of dismay rose up from the people, for timber was the lifeblood of the place. The mayor called out, "Why do you give us this advice?"

"Have I not been generous? Have I not allowed the pillaging of what is mine for generations of your pitiful lives?" the Enchanter said. "Be grateful I do not take revenge, and cut down one of your kin for every tree of mine you have felled."

This time there was no cry, but rather a petrified silence, for all in town knew that e could do such a thing with one sweep of eir gnarled staff. In this silence, the Enchanter walked away, returning to the forest, and once e had gone, the townspeople wailed.

"What shall we do?" they moaned. "Oh, what shall we do?"

The mayor, green about the face, said, "We cannot burn the saws and the axes, or we should have no way to live. But let us have a bonfire in the square so that the smoke rises high over the town. The Enchanter will see it and think we have done as e asked; and let none go lumbering to the forest for a week. That will give us time to find a resolution."

So the bonfire was built and lit, and since the night was fair and the mood was fearful, much of the town slept around it, huddled together. The morning dawned gentle and clear; the sun burned off the mist, and the villagers breathed a sigh of relief.

Alas, the days passed quickly in meetings and councils, which all proved unfruitful. The Enchanter's forest nigh surrounded them, and so there was no other land from which to harvest lumber. The river had fish enough for children to catch, but not to sell beyond the town; and the south had sheep and wool of their own, so weaving could not sustain them. The oldest member of the oldest family said they might return to the days before the war and the great need for wood, and live to sustain themselves, and never mind the soft-handed people of the south; but as the mayor reminded them, it was a world of coinage now, and if the village lived by subsistence only, they would soon fall into decay and irrelevance.

Each day brought new ideas and new refutations; each sunset saw a stalemate. Several youths grew tired and frustrated of the discussion and the fear. Foolhardy, they took their hatchets and went into the forest. They chopped off green branches for no other reason than to show the Enchanter they could.

The next morning a great storm descended upon the town. It raged for several days, until the villagers began to believe that the Enchanter meant to drown them all, but at last it ceased, and with it ended all negotiation with the Enchanter's terms. There was no way around it. The village must fell trees and send them south. When the ground had dried again, the woodcutters went out to the forest to resume their work.

As they approached, the sun burned away the morning mist and revealed a horrible sight: the thousands of stumps left by the saws had burst into tall, thick trees once more. Yet they were unlike any trees the woodcutters had ever seen. They shone like armor from roots to leaves and flashed in the sunlight so that the people had to squint and shield their eyes. A brave few inched forward and saw that the trees' bark was indeed like metal, and the leaves were sharp as knives, with a reddish sheen as though already bloodied.

The woodcutters retreated in fear, for they rightly perceived that this was the work of the wrathful Enchanter.

Now, the eldest daughter of the oldest family, whose name was Fionn, went to the forest's edge and contemplated the sentinel trees. She did not think it likely that the Enchanter would turn every tree to armor, for what life was that for a tree? So she went carefully into the rows of sentinels until she reached trees still covered in bark. With her small ax, she chopped free a low branch as proof, and returned to the village with news that there was still timber to be had. The woodcutters returned, and just in time, for many families were running short of food and gold.

When the Enchanter felt their axes again, e grew furious and caused the earth to shake tremendously in the night. The villagers wailed and fled their homes. By morning, the tremors ceased. At first, the villagers did not understand, for there was little damage to be seen. They concluded that the Enchanter meant only to frighten them, and for a day or so, they kept away from the forest.

Soon enough, the woodcutters and sawhands went back to their work; but when the first blade hit the first tree, a terrible shriek rose up, as if the ax had bitten the flesh of a child. More horrible still, the breach where blade met wood ran with thick red blood. Again the woodcutters fled, and nothing could induce them to return, even when their children began to cry with hunger.

They sent word to the king, and the king sent eir son the prince to free the village from the Enchanter's tyranny. In his golden armor, the prince entered the forest, and the villagers cheered knowing they would soon have relief from their troubles.

But the prince soon became lost and could not find the river in the darkness of the forest. So, to show he was not afraid, he drew his sword and called out, "Enchanter! I summon thee. Come, and we shall speak of how to resolve thy conflict with the village."

So the Enchanter came to him, emerging from the fog and the shadows with a slow and silent step. E looked upon the shining prince and said, "I am resolved, O prince."

The prince saw that it was true, and knew he had no choice but to dispatch the Enchanter. He raised his sword and struck with all his might, but the Enchanter knew his mind and was unhurt. E turned the prince into a beast, a great golden bear-like thing with claws as black as slate and eyes as red as coals. The beast whined and ran away, and the Enchanter took the prince's sword with em as a prize.

When the prince did not return, the village despaired and

began to flee south. The king learned of eir son's disappearance and sent word throughout the land that whosoever could save the prince would be greatly rewarded according to their desires.

Fionn, woodcutter, eldest daughter of the oldest family, did not flee her village. She stood often in the back door of her family's cottage, smoking her pipe and contemplating the glinting forest. Her family knew the Enchanter of old, and so she formed a plan. She packed a bag, bade goodbye to her parents and her siblings, and set out for the Enchanter's waterfall.

She could not tell when night came, for the forest was shrouded in twilight that neither ended nor varied, so she walked until she was tired, and then settled down upon the moss to rest. She was close to sleep when she heard a violently shivering voice moaning gently somewhere nearby. She rose and called out, "Who is there? Why do you shiver so?"

A small, old person came into view around a tree trunk, hugging themselves tightly and shaking with cold. "I am a hermit who lives in these woods," they said. "I used to line my burrow with hanging moss to keep it warm, but now the forest is in this perpetual evening, and my eyes are so old, I cannot see to climb. I have been cold ever since; I can hardly find my way home."

Fionn looked up and saw the moss the hermit spoke of, cascading in gray-green chunks from the branches of the trees. She said, "Wait here, and I will gather moss for you, for I can see well enough."

Though her limbs were tired and her fingers cold, she climbed, and lifted bundles of moss from the branches and let them fall to the ground, where the hermit began to exclaim with delight. Soon they called up to her, "That is plenty, dear friend! Please come down!"

She came down, and the hermit offered her profuse thanks. They said, "Come with me to my burrow, and I will give you something good to eat."

Fionn was hungry, so she followed; the burrow was nearby, formed of trees that had been guided to weave together into a small round hut. A door was braced into it by an arch made of stone. Fionn had to crawl through it on hands and knees, but she found that inside it was tall enough for her to sit comfortably, while the little hermit could stand. The burrow was lit with fairy lights, small golden orbs fluttering against the living roof, and Fionn gasped, for it seemed the roof was alive with stars. The hermit turned a twinkling eye on her and smiled.

"Yes, so you see what I am," they said. "And your goodness shall be rewarded, for I will tell you how to save your village. There is a rose hedge in the middle of the forest, the most beautiful roses in the world; these are the source of the Enchanter's power."

Fionn frowned. "Then surely they must be well protected."

"They are, but I will help you, as you helped me," the hermit said. "Eat this mushroom when you set out tomorrow, and the Enchanter will not know of your approach."

They held up a little toadstool, which Fionn took and put carefully in her pocket. Then, the hermit held up a river rock, smooth but for one sharpened edge.

"Strike this stone, and the resulting spark will catch and burn the roses up," they said.

Fionn took the rock and promised to follow the hermit's instructions.

The next day, she set off into the perpetual twilight in the direction the hermit pointed her. Even with that help, though, she had never been so deep in the forest, nor under such conditions; and the huge trees and thick roots often forced her to veer this way and that. Soon, she was lost. More than that, she heard a creature following her. She stood still and did not reach for her ax, in case it was another helpful fairy, like the hermit.

"Come out; I will not harm you," she said.

Then emerged a huge golden beast, with fearsome red eyes, and Fionn gasped. But the beast whined, and then she saw upon its brow a dark line, like a crown, and she guessed this was the missing prince.

"Do you know where to find the rose hedge?" she asked.

The beast gave no answer but walked away, and Fionn followed. They came to a path, emerging gradually from the undergrowth of the forest. Along this path, the light returned, and the foliage around them became bright and yellow again, and she heard birds for the first time since passing the sentinel trees with their sharp-edged leaves. She laughed in delight, and the beast made a warm rumbling noise before disappearing into the forest.

The canopy above seemed to thin, and Fionn remembered the mushroom; she paused to eat it, and with its sweet, dusty flavor on her tongue, she approached the rose hedge.

It loomed before her like something from a giant's garden, each bush half again as tall as she, each perfect bloom as large as her head. The petals were a pure rich red on one side, and purple underneath, each as soft as the finest velvet. Fionn cried to look upon such beauty, and to smell the lovely odor of each flower. But she saw too the thorns, as large as her hand, on each stem, and knew what she must do. She took the rock given to her by the hermit, and one of her flint rocks; striking them together, she sent a spark into the rose hedge.

It needed no tinder, no blowing; it caught at once into a fire that raced through the hedge until it all burned with a pure white flame. Fionn stumbled back in awe, and then again when she heard a high, sharp scream behind her. She turned, and there the Enchanter stood, clawing at eir face. When e saw Fionn's face, e cried, "You!" And then e glowed white like the fire, and disappeared in a plume of smoke.

All at once, the flames went out, leaving no trace of the roses, but revealing the prince's sword, which the Enchanter had thrown into the hedge. The sun grew bright, lightening into the farthest reaches of the forest, so that Fionn could see nearly to the hermit's burrow through the golden filtered light. Fionn laughed and clapped her hands.

Suddenly the prince emerged from the forest. He smiled and grasped Fionn's hands and kissed them, saying, "You have saved me, and you will have my gratitude forever."

THEN HE PICKED UP his sword, and together they left the forest. The king joyously offered Fionn her heart's desire as reward for her courage, and her heart's desire was to marry the prince, and his to marry her. So they were wed in the capital in great state, and instead of flowers, they carried hanging moss woven with fairy lights.

8

IAROM-BY-THE-BARROW

THE WEATHER WAS BLISSFUL when he set out from Varrun, so Darragh removed his boots and hose and walked barefoot along the road. He had a half day's walk to Vicus, where the paving ended, and had rather save his boots and his feet in them for any rough terrain or dry grass; it was a lovely damp spring, though, with fine light rain intermittently coming down, not enough for mud but enough to keep the new flora green and soft. It was like the purest memories of his childhood meadow all around him, and he was alternately elated and destroyed by the feelings his surroundings inspired.

From Vicus, he abandoned the dirt roads and cut across country, keeping the river always in sight to the west. There was not much settlement; the roads went off to the northeast, for as Ceara had said, the river was fast and a little rough at certain sections, fit or safe for nothing but those ill-won logs. Occasionally, he passed large sharp stones that jutted inexplicably out of the ground.

The going was slower than his walk home had been, for the country was rolling, in such a way that the hills never looked that large and yet he might take half a day just to crest one. Then he would stop and gaze at the horizon all around him, at all the things that yet looked small at their distance—the river, the mountains, and eventually, the forest, creeping into view to the west. It was from such a vantage point that he finally realized that the thin sharp stones he passed in more and more frequent clusters were likely the remnants of the first paved road into the north. Whatever destroyed it, it had certainly been violent; the paving wasn't simply split or cracked, it had been broken with such force as to tilt the pieces almost vertical, perpendicular to the ground like knives through sailcloth. Darragh took to touching them when he passed, wondering at the anger, or anguish, that could have produced such magic.

At length he saw a town, and beyond it an isolated hill that was not a hill at all; he had reached Iarom-by-the-Barrow. The mountains were close enough to have deep shadows, and for him to discern the tree line. The forest likewise would have been near enough for detail, except that it was shrouded in mist, though it was midday and warm. The trees of its edge could not have been more than two hours' walking away. Whoever lived in Iarom-by-the-Barrow had no fear of the dark thing in the forest, it seemed.

Darragh descended into a shepherd's pasture. The sheep paid him no mind. He saw someone standing in the field and called out to them, but they did not respond, nor even move, not even when he came within a horse's length of them—but then he realized it was a statue. It depicted someone wearing a short dress and breeches, an old-fashioned style, with a scarf holding back their long hair. It had been painted to appear more lifelike, but up close he saw that the paint was old and quite chipped. The face was nearly worn away, but the pose, now he could observe it from all sides, was a frightened one.

He looked around at the placid sheep. Was this meant to be some kind of scarecrow? Unlikely, given the evidence of its use as a perch. Darragh shook his head and went on toward the town.

Walking through it was a dismal affair. Many of the buildings appeared empty and disused, for some time, with thin thatch and broken shutters, crumbling daub. There were no shops, or at least, no signs, except on the large building Darragh took to be the inn: its wooden sign, hanging from a bar, showed a crudely carved and painted hearth. The inn itself seemed in good repair, as did the houses immediately around it; the inn's first floor was made of stone, its second of wood, and there was thick glass in diamond-patterned iron frames on the first floor's two front windows. Darragh could not see the roof well, but he thought it might be wood shingles. There were chimneys at either end, a necessity in the north.

He knocked on the inn's door. It opened to reveal a person about Darragh's height, with reddish dark umber skin, warm brown eyes, and salt-and-pepper hair in small, tight braids running flat along their scalp to the nape, where the braids hung loose and long, to the small of the person's back. The person smiled at him and said, "Welcome to Iarom. I am Dom Berin, proprietor."

"Goodman Darragh," he replied.

Berin gave no sign that e noted the lesser title he gave himself; he was as entitled to *master* or *sir* as anyone, for it had long been used informally to signal respect and, since the end of the sumptuary laws, gender. But he always stumbled over such things. He had been called Able Seahand for six years, and after that, Midshiphand, and now, Second Mate. Those were the titles to which he was accustomed, but this far inland, few would recognize them; and in any case, they wouldn't have told Berin which pronouns he used. That information was always read in tattoos or volunteered soon enough aboard ship or in sailing circles; sailors had no need of gendered titles to facilitate.

"I invite him into my house," Berin said, rather formally, to show e had understood. The script of civility had been mostly dispensed with in the south, but Darragh still remembered the second part.

"I accept eir hospitality," he said.

E nodded, and stood back to let him enter. He was shown to a modest room, yet still one with a fireplace; it had a small bed with a straw mattress, two blankets, and a rag pillow; a washstand; a trunk at the foot of the bed; and a rack upon which to place one's clothing.

"Dinner will be served in an hour," Berin informed him.

"Thank you. Is there a bathhouse?"

"At the back. I'll show you."

Darragh removed his second set of clothes from his bag, and followed em. The bathhouse extended from the kitchen, for the ease of heating water, presumably. It had two large metal basins separated by a greased, hanging cloth. Beside each was a screen and a small lacquered table, upon which sat soap, a washcloth, and a sheet for drying.

"The pump is just outside; if you collect the water, Horace will heat it for you." Berin smirked, but with a friendliness that was forcefully familiar. "You're lucky we're roasting dinner on the spit, otherwise the cauldron would not have been free till after."

"I have always had excellent timing," Darragh replied, smiling.

Berin laughed and left him to it. Darragh took up the bucket he found near a set of cabinets, which proved to have extra linens, and went out to the pump. He faced the forest while he worked it, marveling at the mist, which was heavier even than that up the mountains beyond it. He could imagine all sorts of stories inspired by such a scene; it was certainly an unwelcoming prospect.

The forest cleaved to the mountains' base as far as he could perceive, south to north; to the north, both stone and trees swung widely to meet and cross the river in another cloud of mist, this likely produced by a waterfall. Iarom seemed to stand in a basin of sorts; nature curled around it on all sides but the southern. It could have been sheltering, or surrounding.

He filled the bucket and took it into the kitchen, where a tall, thick, ochre-skinned youth was chopping vegetables and arranging them in a roasting pan. They looked up and smiled. "You must be Darragh," they said. "I'm Horace—Mister Horace, that is. I think. Forgive me, we haven't had a guest in quite a while. Winter, you understand."

"Of course. I am pleased to meet you," Darragh replied. He lifted the bucket.

"Oh yes, here," Horace said. He swung out an iron pot already over a fire; when Darragh had poured the water in, he replaced the lid of the pot and returned it to the flames, then handed Darragh a second bucket. "If you can manage it. It'll only take two more buckets, and you may as well get them together."

"Obliged." Darragh smiled at him and set to the task.

He bathed quickly, so as not to miss dinner; he was tired and would have enjoyed a long soak, but he was also ravenous from being excessively careful with his rations. He would leave the water, he decided, and if it was still warm after he ate, then he would climb back in and relax.

The dining room of the inn was comfortably sized, with a table large enough to serve sixteen people, more if the seating were tight. The hearth faced the long side of the table and had a fire in it, which made the room a little close. Darragh welcomed it, though, having stepped out of the scalding bath into the rapidly cooling night air mere moments before. He was embarrassed by his wet hair, but neither Horace nor Berin made mention of it. The three of them gathered at the center of the table, rather than either end, so that they were near the fire. The meat that had been roasting—mutton, by the look of it—was set on a carving board. Next to it were the vegetables Darragh had watched Horace prepare earlier.

Berin served Darragh first, then Horace. When each plate was full of food, e smiled at them both and bade them eat.

"What brings you so far north, Goodman Darragh?" Berin asked.

"Please, just Darragh is fine," he replied. "I am here to seek someone I knew once."

E raised an eyebrow. "Someone from Iarom? Tell me who, then; I have lived here all my seventy years, and I know the name of every person who has set foot in this town since I was a child."

"I do not know eir proper name; I suppose I do not even know if e has one," Darragh said. "I think e is known in these parts as the Enchanter? I've been told e lives in the forest."

The instant Darragh uttered the name, Berin's face turned stony. "What foolishness; the Enchanter does not exist, except in old stories."

Darragh chewed his food, schooling his expression toward neutrality. He did not want to argue with his host, but he was curious about eir hostility toward the subject. "Do many come from the south, seeking em? Do those seekers make a nuisance of themselves?"

"Not many come," Berin said after a moment. "Sorcerers and treasure hunters, mainly. They go into the forest, and we never hear from them again."

"Surely that speaks to some magic or force in the woods," Darragh said.

"You are not a woodsman, are you?"

"No," he replied. "I am a sailor."

Berin nodded. "I know I am ignorant of many dangers presented by the sea. Likewise, until you have grappled with the forest, you cannot imagine the myriad ways an unwary traveler might meet their end in such a place."

"You go into the forest?" Darragh asked.

The innkeeper sighed. "Not I. It's a hundred years since a person could go there and have any hope of a healthy, safe return. But we keep the wisdom alive, from our parents and grandparents and great-grandparents."

The three of them ate in silence for a few moments. Darragh considered his next inquiry carefully. Not without some trepidation, he asked, "Who made the statue in the pasture?"

Horace dropped his knife. Berin gave him a stern look, then said to Darragh, "What statue?"

"It reminds me of a story I read once," Darragh said. "About a young apprentice put under a selfish curse. The Enchanter was in that story, I think; e turned the curse back on the shepherd who cast it, and she was turned to stone out in the field."

"It must have been made by some artist who was inspired by the story, then," Berin said.

Darragh laughed. "I suppose that is a more likely explanation than that the story was a factual account."

Horace laughed with him, a little nervously, and Berin, too, smiled, looking more like the wry and friendly host who had greeted Darragh at the door. Darragh drank of his wine while he contemplated how to proceed. He was not afraid to go into the woods with only the information he already possessed, but he would prefer to know more of the ancestral wisdom Berin mentioned. Did e truly believe the Enchanter to be naught but a fable, or was e deliberately obscuring eir existence? What could Darragh say, to convince em of his earnestness? He had proof only that some magically gifted person had given him a portion of their power; he could not say for sure that it was the same Enchanter rumored to live in the misty woods. He had not even proof of his claim of transition by magic, if Berin argued that.

"I am sorry your trip has been a waste of time," Horace said.

Darragh smiled at him. "Do not be sorry for me. To journey is my work, and there is always something to enjoy in it."

"Horace, will you clear the table, please?" Berin asked.

He nodded and performed his task. When he was gone, the innkeeper said, "Have you come to kill the Enchanter?"

"What?"

"I see it in your face; you do not believe me. There is not even a small glimmer of doubt." Berin chuckled sadly. "So you know I am lying, which means you know more than all the others combined. Are you a sorcerer? Have you come to break the curse, to steal eir power?"

"No, I—" Darragh thought of Gabin, then, the sorcerer he had encountered at the guild in Cathal, and the way their eyes had gleamed once they saw the thorn. His instincts had warned him away from that person, and now he thought he understood why. "Please," he said to Berin. "I know less than you think, and though my reason for coming is selfish, my goal is not the amplification of my own power. Not in a magical sense. I wish to ask you for full honesty, and in that spirit, I will bare all to you. When I was a child I observed my older sister with great fear, for in her I saw my future, and I was terrified. After the blood came to me, I was visited by a stranger, who gave me this thorn."

He drew it out and held it close to the candle flame. "The stranger told me to use this thorn to cast my blood into either fire or water, and that by doing so, I would gain the form I desired. The stranger spoke true; their power helped me become the man I am today. That was thirteen years ago."

Berin stared at the thorn, eir expression shifting from suspicion to wonder. "Then what is your selfish reason for coming here?"

"When my father learned the truth about me, he exiled me from his house," Darragh said, tucking the thorn away. "Now he is near death, and I do not want him to die without hearing, from my own lips, the devastation his rejection caused in me."

At that, Berin gave a dark laugh. "Selfish indeed. But no one could fault you for it."

"I believe the stranger was the Enchanter from the *Callistan Folk Tales*, and I believe that Enchanter lives in that forest," Darragh said. "I've been told this is the inn where those tales were first recorded for publication."

Berin nodded. "My great-grandmother was keeper of the inn then. When the Enchanter went out to visit the people, e started and ended eir journey here. My family heard all the tales, from the Enchanter emself and from others who followed em. E was . . . much beloved by this house, at that time."

"What is this curse you spoke of?" Darragh asked. "There's a story that tells of bleeding trees, but someone in Varrun told me that the trees petrified."

"The story tells of the Enchanter's death, too," Berin said. "What say you to that?"

Darragh huffed. "That I know to be false."

"How?"

"The book in which the tale is told was published before my birth. Before I met the Enchanter."

"This could as easily prove it was not the Enchanter you met."

"Indeed," Darragh said, smiling softly. "Every story in the set of bad tales conquers the Enchanter in some way. I understand that if e is seen as a villain, this must be so, for the health of the people—"

"*Seen* as a villain? Sir, that person threw a fit when e did not get eir way, cut off this town's means of income, and abandoned us to a long, slow death that is very nearly complete!" Berin stood roughly from eir seat and turned away from him, leaning against the mantel. "E swore to provide for and protect us, but when e was required to give an inch, e destroyed our lives in a fit of pique. Is there anything more villainous than that?"

Darragh had been leaning forward during the rapid exchange; now he sat up straight against the unforgiving high back of his chair and sighed. He could not argue for any virtue on the Enchanter's part, for whether the trees bled or petrified, the truth was as Berin said—a timber-rich town had lost its access to that resource and deteriorated because of it. The story of the bleeding trees had drawn the Enchanter in gross terms, but even so, reading it had only increased Darragh's empathy for em. This pique, as Berin put it, added a sense of humanity that had been lacking in the earlier tales; of those, only the story of the statue, which showed the Enchanter's anger, had hinted at any true soul within the powerful and benevolent figure. He didn't want to condone or ignore the harm the Enchanter had caused—but he thought of how sad the stranger who came to him had looked, and could not muster any feeling but tenderness when he thought of em.

He stood and walked toward the door.

"If you insist on finding the Enchanter," Berin said, "look for the roses."

Darragh looked back. The innkeeper was watching him with a guarded expression. "What?"

"Eir castle is protected by a great rose hedge . . . the most beautiful roses in the world. That is how you will know you have found em," Berin said. E touched the mantel lightly, and Darragh noticed that the carving on it was of roses.

"Thank you," Darragh said.

The innkeeper shook eir head. "Don't. You will die in that forest, like all the others. And I want no thanks for that."

DESPITE THE COMFORT OF his room, Darragh found himself plagued by the echoes of Berin's words. They crawled within him, sent chills across his skin; the sensation was not unlike biting into a biscuit that still had weevils hiding in its center, unmoved by the most vigorous knocking of the stale, hard crust against the beam. He could no more catch these doubts than he could the skittering insects, could not spit them out. He must simply swallow them.

But had he any acid in his heart, in his mind, to match that in his stomach? If words could be as weevils, then these bore out of his organs into his blood, his bones. For the first time, he cursed his unexamined affection for the Enchanter. It shrouded him like a thick fog, and he felt that he could hardly see his own hands, let alone the shore toward which he sailed.

He knew better than most that one incident of kindness could not predict a good heart generally—any more than one act of malice predicted a bad one. Groaning, he got out of bed and went to stoke the coals in his hearth, as if that would smooth the gooseflesh along his arms. Crosswinds of thought buffeted him. He couldn't know the Enchanter the way this town had, an ancestral memory that Berin had access to. Yet from what he had heard, no one living had met the Enchanter but Darragh; mustn't that count for something? And even if Berin's word was to be trusted— and he felt it must be—the events that had caused such strife had taken place a century ago. Was the Enchanter unchanging as well as long-lived? Could any living thing with sense go unchanged in their thoughts and behavior for more than a hundred years? Even the ocean changed in great, slow ways, its levels and currents and tides; even the shorelines. So even if Darragh would have hated the Enchanter of the Iarom cataclysm, could he not care for the Enchanter of his meadow?

Yet . . . were some things unforgivable? Should a good person who had done a great enough wrong be shunned forever? Had not Vesta tried to make this very same argument to him about their father?

Darragh stretched out before the hearth and lay on his back, staring at the ceiling. His heart thudded in his chest and his breath came short, the way it did during storms or in dangerous ports. He had no real justification for why he was disposed to accept the Enchanter's goodness, or at least eir improvement, and not his father's. Perhaps the fact that he had so much more knowledge of his father made the possibility less available.

Or, perhaps it was all down to the knot in his chest, a rope of longing he could not have unpicked if he'd tried, that only felt loosened when he remembered that lovely, kind, miserable person in the meadow.

9
FOREST

DARRAGH LEFT THE INN before dawn, in no mood to tempt further hostility from Berin or even from Horace. He understood their position, even if he would not adopt it, and no argument would sway him from his purpose. When he woke, he put his room to rights and slipped out of the dwelling with all the stealth of a ship's cat, on his bare feet. Upon his pillow he did leave, with his payment, a sketch, done upon an endpaper torn from the new book of tales, depicting a shark, its body curved with the movement of its powerful tail fin. He knew not whether the sailor's symbol of wandering would be recognized in such a place as Iarom, but he wished and hoped it would be understood that he'd left secretly, swiftly, not in cowardice or shame but because it was not in him to linger.

The grass sparkled with dew, so Darragh left his boots off and rolled his pant legs to his knees; even so, the wild grass of the field between the edge of Iarom and the forest brushed and caught the fabric, and it accumulated a little dampness from the tip of each wispy blade. The predawn mist never lifted, for he was at the forest's edge by the time the sun rose; he came upon it without realizing it. He had expected the quality of the mist to change, but it never did. It was the same small, gathering moisture he was used to, and in the increasing light it looked as gray and soft as any mist he'd seen before—but his bare foot found a cold, hard root, and he paused in his stride.

Darragh lowered himself to the ground, where there was a very little clear space, and examined the root. It was thin, far from its trunk, and pewter in color. Darragh lit a match to view it better, and the root caught the orange glow of the flame as well as any sconce. It had the pattern of bark but no texture; it was smooth to the touch, yet its surface rippled like laminated steel. And it was cold—cold as only metal can get.

"You really did turn them into sentinels," he said quietly, snuffing the match. The morning chill was in him, though his face and chest felt hot from his brisk pace. It must have been that meeting of hot and cold that left him unsteady in that moment. Lifting his hand carefully away from the metal root, he took several deep breaths. He did not move again until he felt his equilibrium return. Nothing changed around him.

He crawled along the ground, following the line of the root in search of its trunk. When he found it, he stood slowly, with one hand on the trunk to guide him, the other warily reaching into the mist for the bladed leaves. He reached his full height, arm extended above him, without being bitten, and laughed; it seemed that all the greedy woodcutters of Iarom's past had been taller than he. He proceeded, still cautious, into the trees.

It was dark. The sun had got above the forest in the east, he was sure of it, but its light could not burn off the mist, could not pierce the canopy, which was so thick he could not discern how high it was. If not for the trunks he touched to guide his way, he should hardly have known where one tree ended and another began. Eventually, his eyes adjusted as much as they were able; but it was a moonless twilight, and the stars were distant indeed. When Darragh's jaw began to ache, he realized he had been clenching it, hard. He rubbed at his stubble with one rough hand to loosen those muscles, and put one foot in front of the other.

Having no celestial bodies by which to track the time, Darragh walked until he felt hungry. The trees had become craggy with bark again, which was some comfort, but he dared not break them for firewood, lest they scream. He nestled himself against a large trunk and ate his rations — rye bread and hard cheese — in the dark. He had hard biscuits, jerky, even some dried fruit as well, but he would be spare if he could. When he'd outfitted himself for this final leg, down in Varrun, he had imagined being able to hunt — well, at least to make the attempt. His experience was more in fishing, though he'd been lucky enough when shooting sea birds; he had his line and hooks but had been glad of Earrin's gift of a crossbow. But he had neither seen nor heard any kind of creature. The forest was not silent — the trees groaned, the leaves rustled, dry twigs snapped under his still-bare feet — but it seemed to Darragh that any living thing with freedom of movement had long since fled this forest.

Even the air seemed . . . lonely. It was unexpectedly breezy in the forest, as if the wind were trapped and forever seeking a way out. Or perhaps it was more personal, like a ghost seeking another soul, for Darragh was buffeted by it from all sides, continuously, while he walked. It had stilled only when he sat; perhaps, while he was stationary, so too could the air be. Such a thought would have felt absurd anywhere else.

Look for the roses, Berin had said. Darragh did not think looking would do him much good, in such light. When he stood and prepared to set off again, he sniffed the air, but he was surrounded by earth, wood. A wanderer he might be, but he lacked a shark's sense of smell.

His compass would not settle, which perturbed but, so far, did not ruffle him. Still, he feared getting turned around, without the sky to guide him, so he set off for what he guessed was east, where the river was not too far off. Had he known the conditions within the forest, he would have simply followed the river from the beginning, but he had been a little overconfident, perhaps. If it had not been so dusky, so empty, he might have laughed at himself. He was not afraid, but he was beginning to understand that his confusion in this place was not merely a seahand's inexperience of land. The forest was more dismal and unbroken than the open ocean, not a cloud nor spout to orient oneself by. Each tree, which ought to have been a landmark, shrank from his gaze into the shadows until he could not tell how close it stood to him, whether it was beech or oak. His feet could feel no difference between dirt and leaf litter, between root and rock. The indistinctness of the shapes around him made him wonder at his eyes. He stopped and closed them, as if they needed rest, but when he opened them again all was as it had been before: dim, soft, and silent.

It was a comfort when at last he could hear the water, when he finally caught the scent of it, unmistakable for all its lack of salt. He was surprised by how it reminded him of the *Augustina*; the freshness of the water tainted by the decay it wrought upon everything it touched. He smelled mold and rot, wood soft to the touch and slimy vegetation. He walked toward it until he saw it, more like a cavern below him than a river, and felt the earth slope beneath its surface. He was still barefoot—he had never thought to put on his boots; in the dark he had been grateful for the grip of his callused feet—so he felt the cold pebbles of the riverbank, smoother than coins, and the chilly water when it lapped his toes. He walked in to his ankles and let his head fall back as the whole of his body relaxed, sinking into the mud.

Had he been born a creature of the water? Had his childhood dreams of the high seas come to him from some internal place, or had he molded himself in his father's image? Had he grown to love the ocean genuinely, or because he had no love elsewhere?

How long he stood in the river, Darragh took no note of. He opened his eyes only when he felt it necessary to do so, because something was looking at him.

Upriver from him, on the same bank, he saw a beast, standing on all fours but its shoulders taller than Darragh by a head, if he could judge correctly in the half light. The shadows under the canopy went from brown to black, dim to dark, and it was difficult to tell where the creature ended and the shadows began. Its coat looked thick, like the hair raised on a dog's back; the color shifted in the awful light: stone gray, shadow black, sometimes almost tawny gold when the beast's body rocked, as if it were a snake readying itself to strike. Its eyes were the only clear and constant thing in its form, red and luminous as the setting sun heralding a calm night at sea.

There was an odd calm upon him—as if the forest were a liminal realm in which time held no sway, and so, he was at his leisure for contemplating the beast before him. Was it a bear? He had never seen one. He had seen a wolf, once, down south, but this animal seemed larger than it had been. He did not think bears had red eyes. And it was the only animate thing he had seen since entering the forest. Why had it not fled with all the other creatures?

Why hadn't it fled?

Then time caught up to the forest all at once, and Darragh remembered where he was: the dead forest fortress of a powerful Enchanter.

When one spots a shark in the water, one swims to safety as slowly and gently as one can manage. Where was safety, in a forest too frightening even for animals? He was a good climber with fewer handholds than the trees offered—but then he would be trapped, with no promise that he could climb higher than the beast was tall with enough speed to save him, or that the beast could not simply climb up after him, or use its bulk to fell the tree or knock him out of it.

The beast curled its lip, revealing large, thick teeth that seemed smoother and blunter than a shark's but were equally capable of sending Darragh's stomach into his throat. He took a step backward, achingly slow, as he tried to keep the water around his feet silent, to find a firm foothold in the unseen silt, knowing that to fall would be the end of him. He put his arms far out to either side for balance and took another too-careful step away from the beast.

It stepped forward. Its great paw came out of the river, and Darragh thought he saw the metallic ripple of water coming off claws in the instant before the paw descended again, with a surprisingly gentle sound, below the surface. The beast's one step was worth two of Darragh's. When he retreated again, his foot in its haste did not come entirely free of the water, and the whole step made a splash that echoed off the surrounding trees, clear as a bell.

The beast roared, and Darragh turned and ran.

He left the river and fled without sense of direction—the only direction that mattered was *away*—but the beast's roar, a deep bellow overlaid with a high whining tone, like a gull's, followed close on his heels. He ran but was not accustomed to such terrain, and before he had run as far as the trees around him were tall, he tripped over a root and tumbled to the sticky forest floor. He had but rolled onto his back before the beast leapt on top of him. The nearness of it, its great heaving chest a foot above his face, was accompanied by an awful cold such as Darragh had never felt before; he knew not whether it came from the beast or from his own certainty of death. His blood was ice, and his body came to utter stillness as the beast looked down at him with its bright red eyes.

His right hand had fallen on his crossbow, which was lashed to his hip; his left rested on his stomach, just above the sheath of his seax. But whether it was the chill upon him or some other sense he could not make sense of, Darragh thought of both and answered himself, *no*. He met the beast's gaze, exhaled all his breath, and closed his eyes.

When warmth returned to him, he thought he must be dead, though he had felt no pain, and he felt a little gratitude toward the beast, that it had killed him so quickly he had not had time to feel the slightest prick of tooth or claw. But then he felt the sharp insistence of a rock underneath him, pressed against his spine; he shifted away from it, opened his eyes, and saw the forest exactly as it had been before he spotted the beast, if only a little darker. He had lost the river, and his boots. Though he could not be sure the darkness meant that night had fallen, he decided to treat it as night and try to rest. He found a soft hollow between two large roots and wrapped his blanket around himself. His only comfort was in the hope that having been once spared, he was in no more danger from the beast.

10

CANOPY

MORNING CAME WHEN DARRAGH woke, for it was all as dim and dark as it had been before; but it was not unlike the hold of a ship, and he was not very discouraged. He ate with great difficulty—that is, it was difficult not to eat too much, since he had had no dinner the night before and was obliged to regret it. Shortly he set off in search of the river, not without trepidation; perhaps the river was the beast's hunting ground, and going there again meant asking for another encounter. But following the waterway was his best chance of getting into the interior of the forest, and so he went in the direction he thought was east.

After hours of walking, for a farther distance than he thought he could have fled, he had found no signs of the river. Either it had vanished, or, more likely, he was very turned around indeed. So he ate the last of his soft bread and determined to climb a tree, to see if he could spot the river from the canopy. He left his pack at the base without fear of it being disturbed, and put his fingers and toes into the craggy bark of his selected helper. It was a tolerable easy climb, and soon he was among the sturdy branches. There, he paused to see what he could see, which was very little. The branches of his tree and those near it were thick with growth, but also with the tangled skeletons of branches that had broken but never made it to the ground, and great sheets of hanging mosses. Darragh looked above him and thought he could see a lighter blue-green where the leaves met the day, but it was high and the path thick and obscured. He was sure he could do it, but how long would it take? He began to despair now of the scheme's success at all. Could his seahand's eye spot a river below the trees? It had not been so very wide, and with the branches of each tree so twined with its neighbors', and each so very tall . . . but as much as he doubted his ability to gauge the forested landscape, he knew that at least that if he could find the sun, he should know his cardinal directions, and that would help. So he climbed.

It was hard going, for the web of vines and branches, and later for the growing thinness and unsteadiness of his footholds and even the trunk, which soon was indistinguishable from the other limbs of the tree. But up and up he went, trusting the strength of his hands and his feet to keep their holds, and that of his arms and legs to hold him, and he kept himself pressed close to the branches at the center. Eventually he made it, and when at last he put his head above the leaves, the cold wind that met him felt divine on his hot, sweaty face. He allowed himself a few moments with his eyes closed, breathing deeply of air more fresh than he'd dared hope, before he turned to his purpose.

He thought it must be afternoon, but he could not find the sun, so he guessed that it was behind a mountain. There were mountains on two sides of him, though, nearly a half circle around him; which was west? Carefully, he shifted around to see if he could find the river south of the forest, for he doubted he had gone in so very far as to be out of sight of the forest's edge. Here the mist thwarted him, for it stretched like snow to the horizon wherever there were not mountains.

Fear gripped him then. He had listened to the warnings, from the people in Varrun and from Berin, but had felt that for him, it would be different. He had felt that—that perhaps he would be *expected* in the cursed forest. Indeed, he accepted that it was cursed but had partly believed that its effects would not apply to him. His foolishness astounded him, for he had always considered himself practical, perhaps too practical—but perhaps that was why he had not fully allowed himself to believe in a curse, for what was more impractical than that?

With effort, he brought his attention back to his body and climbed down with barely contained trembling. The worst was the last section of trunk, below the last branches, and he did find himself asking if it was not too high to simply jump down; it was, and at last he dug into the bark and went down belly to the trunk like a lizard. He sat then on a root and looked out before him— toward the forest's edge, he hoped, for he had been obliged to move around and around the trunk to find the best way down. Exhaustion ran over his limbs, sometimes as the pounding of a drum and sometimes as light fingers plucking harp strings all down the length of him.

His fear faded. The feelings that rose at the thought of dying in the forest, as Berin had said he would, were not fears but regrets. He had come on this journey seeking the removal of one regret, a resolution of his relationship with his father, even if that resolution came in the utter destruction of that relationship. Yet he would carry that into oblivion, and now with it the regret at never seeing Sidra again, or his other crewmates, or Amon and Earrin and the other friends he had made on the journey. Strong, too, was the disappointment of never seeing the Enchanter, if for no other reason than that he would never be able to show em what he had become, and thank em for saving his life.

Down under the trees again, the forest seemed darker than ever, and his eyes would not adjust, but was it night? Night fell when Darragh slept.

11
THE LABYRINTH

DARRAGH HAD NOT NOTED the scent of the beast when it had been on the verge of killing him, his sense of smell preoccupied with his own fearful sweat, or perhaps shut down entirely. But he had grown accustomed enough to the wet, warm stench of the forest that when the new odor reached his nostrils, it was noticeable. Half sleeping, half waking, he inhaled it, and it smelled like the breeze over a dead wheat field—dry, cold. Dusty, almost. A little malty. He inhaled again and thought it smelled of the rigging on the topmast, earthen rope fibers stripped of aromatic depth by the sun and the wind and the salt. He should not have known it was the beast's smell if he had not opened his eyes and seen it sitting before him.

It was full as large as it had been before, but though it was taller by virtue of its sit than it had been when its head hung in a prowl, it was not threatening. The posture, haunches on the ground, back legs almost disappeared into the shaggy fur, lacked the delicacy of a cat's but was more graceful than a dog's. Darragh had never seen a bear and wondered if the beast was more like such an animal than it was like a wolf; in bulk, this was certainly true, but he was certain of nothing else.

The beast saw that he had woken and leaned toward him, head dipping below its massive withers as it stretched. Darragh scrambled to stand, then bowed.

A bow should have made no difference to a normal animal, but there was nothing to suggest the beast was a normal animal, so Darragh hoped to make up for his rudeness and prejudgment the day before with courtesy now. In response to his bow, though, the beast sniffed at him, its breath puffing up Darragh's clothes and hair. Then it stood and slipped away between the trees.

Darragh held still a moment, and then he followed it.

The beast took an inscrutable path that was at least no more difficult to traverse than the ones Darragh had picked out himself. It got quite far ahead of him, though it did not appear to be moving swiftly, but just when he thought he might lose sight of it, it paused and looked back at him, and waited awhile before moving on again. After many hours of this unceasing hike, Darragh's every limb protested the unusual contortions required to get around the trees and over the irregular ground, and his stomach flexed with displeasure at its emptiness—he had not eaten since the previous midday. But he strove to marshal his discomfort to keep pace as best he could with the beast, for he was sure now that it was his only hope. Of what, he was not sure. Finding the river, and the way out? The Enchanter? A quick death? He pushed on.

When he came to a clear path, he stumbled. The sudden absence of roots and vines, rocks to step over, in favor of plain dirt, meant that all at once his legs were lifting too high and coming down too far, and it took several flailing steps for him to regain his balance. Darragh stopped and looked about him, but it was truly a path, a trail such as one might see through any meadow or wilderness where humans often trod. It was not flat; rather it was a kind of miniature cavern, with sloping sides down which the forest crept in an attempt to reclaim the corridor. The path seemed wide to Darragh for all its precarious appearance, and he realized why when he saw the ragged trimming of the bushes on each side. The path was the width of the beast; the beast was its keeper.

Darragh looked down the path at last and saw the beast watching him. When he met its eyes, it began to walk once more.

Darragh's stomach growled, and he considered stopping to eat, now that he had the path. But, as a secondary benefit of the path, walking became easy enough that he could draw rations from his pack without stopping, so that was what he did. His hard biscuits were a chore to eat, but he consumed them almost too fast to think of their unpleasantness; the hard cheese he sliced, and ate half the slice, then sucked on the other half a bit to make the act of eating last longer. Again with difficulty, he restrained himself from eating his fill, lest he be too soon reduced to gambling with the forest's mushrooms.

It seemed to Darragh as he followed the beast down the path that it got lighter rather than darker, though the day must have been wearing on. Despite the path, there was no gap in the trees above him; rather the canopy to either side had tangled together across the wound, reaching and grasping like lovers across a wall.

He was gazing up at this intercourse when he accidentally kicked something softish, which rolled from the force of his foot. He looked down and saw an apple.

The fruit took a moment to place; though he had passed a fair few apple trees on his way north, still dusted with flowers, he had seen nothing so bright or appetizing since entering the forest. He bent and picked it up; it was sticky, having split upon its fall, and torn from being kicked, but it was fragrant and an inviting lovely red. Darragh brushed the dirt away and took a bite. His mouth filled with glorious sweet juice; the apple's tender flesh melted in the heat of his mouth and his tongue tingled with the precious, fresh flavor. He looked for the apple tree, and when he saw it, he said, "Thank you so much. Your fruit is perfect."

When he turned his attention once more to the path, he could not see the beast. It had abandoned him at last, but the path was before him, and the farther he walked along it the more fruit he found, fruit that had no business being so far north, no business being ripe at that time of year, in the middle of a rotting forest. His mouth watered; but though he took from every tree and bush he saw, he took no more than one, even from the berry vines, and he thanked each plant for the gift of its fruit. Part of him remembered just how many of Perrin's folktales had begun with children lured into danger by delicious food, but he was, after all, looking for the Enchanter, so he was not afraid. Besides, he'd seen no other creature, man or animal, who might bear the burden of eating the fruit and spreading the seeds, though it seemed these plants had no need of natural help to thrive.

Yet just as he had that thought, a songbird swept in front of him; it fluttered down and perched upon his hand, which just then held a pear. The bird dipped its beak into the white flesh of the fruit again and again, while Darragh marveled at its size and delicacy, a far cry from the great white gulls that would near wrestle a sailor for their hardtack, and often win. He held still and let it eat, and soon it was joined by another. When he took a cautious step, the birds fluttered away and then returned, and so he walked on again while they feasted.

There were butterflies in the air soon enough, and more birds could be heard if not seen. A fawn danced into his path, and then a fox, who trotted beside its natural prey as placidly as any farm dog herding lambs to safety. Squirrels and mice and chipmunks darted across the gap between brush with fat acorns stretching their jaws, and they gave no more respect to Darragh's dirty feet than they did the soil beneath them, running over his skin and catching it with their tiny claws. He winced and shook them off and laughed when they looked back at him, sometimes curiously, sometimes indignantly, but never with fear. The light did increase as he walked, but rather than making his way brighter, it saturated the forest so that he was surrounded by a hundred shades of green and yellow. All the shadows were blue and all the bark tinted maroon.

If this was how the forest had been before the cataclysm, Darragh could sympathize with the loss that Iarom must have felt.

Suddenly, the forest opened.

Darragh squinted in the daylight, soft with late afternoon but more intense than he'd become accustomed to. The path disappeared into undisturbed green grass, which led to . . . a rose hedge. He could smell them now, such a sweet and subtle scent that was distinctive even to him, one that seemed to come from within rather than without, that bloomed inside an inhalation rather than being drawn in. The hedge was taller than he and so thick he could not see through it. He approached and looked closely at the huge red blossoms. Some of them were robust, and as Berin had said, the most beautiful that Darragh had ever seen; but more were limp or balding or blackened with rot. These he looked on with sadness, for he could guess it was no matter of life cycle causing the roses to die.

The hedge was as much thorn as it was bush, thorns he recognized instantly as of the same kind as the one about his neck. He could not push through, and he could see that to cut through would be not only tedious but disastrous to the hedge and his knife. Squatting, he saw that there was a slim gap between the bottom of the hedge and the ground; less than a foot, but enough that he could crawl under without too much injury.

He removed his pack and crossbow and seax, and set them on the grass; they would not fit under the roses with him. He removed only his blanket, which he thought to hold over himself for some small protection from the thorns. After a moment's consideration, he removed his shirt. He could better lose the blanket to damage than an item of clothing, and he hoped the Enchanter, if e was on the other side of this hedge, would forgive him for his informal appearance. As for his trousers, he could only keep his hips to the ground and hope.

The earth under the roses was cool to his bare skin, a little damp to the touch. It was difficult to hold the blanket in place while keeping his hands clear of the hedge's underside; he found himself clutching the blanket near his ears and bracing with his elbows while he pushed forward with his legs, his toes digging into the dirt for leverage, his heels brushing the lowest branches. Occasionally the trunk of a bush impeded him, and he sometimes had to slither in tight curves but without the benefit of a snake's powerful muscles; his, though strong enough to serve him in most other things, were simply not designed for his present task, and so he proceeded through these obstacles with alarming slowness. He could not know how far into the hedge he had gotten, nor how far he had left to go. The dark did not frighten him, but the closeness sometimes caused flashes of panic; his aching body screamed to stretch, to run, to force its way out. In those moments he was obliged to stop and breathe, lifting his head slightly so as not to inhale the dirt, until he felt calm enough. In other moments, he let his tears fall, so long as he could still crawl forward.

Even when he reached the end, he held his pace slow until his feet were completely free; and then he flung himself out on the grass and took great gasping breaths, tears flowing freely down his dirty face. He shivered with exhaustion and the chill of being exposed again, and wrapped himself in his blanket as he curled up, imagining that the trembling shook off the strain of the experience, so that he soon felt steady again, and sat up. He had meant to stand, but found his hands and feet still felt too light and fragile, so he must stay as he was until they were solid again.

Then a hand, golden-brown and large, came into his field of vision. Darragh clasped it; it pulled him up and steadied him.

The hand belonged to a person, tall and columnar, a uniform width in body from the tunic-covered chest down, with shoulders broader by half than Darragh's. They had a mane of ruddy brown hair with thick eyebrows to match; their face was wide and smooth and handsome, most of all in their eyes, pleasant dark brown peering out from below eyelids with no crease, framed by a slight black fringe of lashes.

Their free hand, the one not still holding Darragh's trembling one, chafed Darragh's chill bare arm. "There, there. You've made it," they said. "You are welcome." The hand that called warmth back to Darragh's skin drifted to his chest, hovering just over the long thorn resting there; the person's brow furrowed in thoughtful surprise, in suspicious wonder. "You are welcome," they said again, softer.

"Are you the Enchanter?" Darragh asked, though he did not think so. This person was less melancholy than his memory of the one from the meadow; but then, if he didn't think people could become happy again, or happier—then his thoughts were too dark.

The person smiled. "Only a man. My name is Frederick."

"Darragh. Goodman Darragh."

Frederick squeezed Darragh's hand and said, again, "Welcome. Come to my hearth."

It was then that Darragh noticed the great stone structure before him, a wall that rose to the height of three tall people and stretched to the edges of his vision on either side. Though it was difficult to see, looking straight up in such proximity, it looked as though trees grew on top of the wall as well, though how that should be possible, Darragh knew not. The stone was gray, and flecked with something that caught the light that shone so brightly on this patch of the forest. The mist and darkness through which Darragh had come seemed miles away, or seemed to exist only in some nightmare he had had. He thought of it as a wall, this edifice, but only because of its uniformity, for it was all one, no bricks or individual stones to be seen; it seemed to have sprouted from the ground like any tree.

Frederick led him by the hand through an opening, opposite where he'd exited the rose hedge, and Darragh saw as they passed through that the wall was thick, thick enough that one could probably walk along the top comfortably, even pass another person or creature without fear of falling. He saw too that the stone structure was not simply a wall; there were walls inside too, as if he had entered a building, a castle. No—a labyrinth, for Frederick guided him along curving, wandering halls not unlike those in the wind-singers' tower in Cathal. If not for the moss under his feet, which had replaced the grass, or the open sky above him, Darragh might have been inside any ancient bailey along the coast.

They walked through a kind of twilight, the stone around them rendering the sun distant; Darragh's much-abused eyes adjusted begrudgingly, tired from the darkness of the forest to the sunshine of the rose hedge and now to the half-light of the labyrinth. He suddenly felt as though he could sleep for a hundred years.

At last they went into a large round room, the hearth Frederick had mentioned occupying the center. It was bounded by stone that, like the walls of the labyrinth, seemed wholly unformed by human hands. Frederick released Darragh's hand at last to tend the coals. Above the hearth was a kind of canopy, also of this natural stone, which seemed to capture the heat and keep it to the ground level, so that the room was comfortably warm, and the temperature was steady as Darragh circled it. A bed stood nearby, looking woven out of hundreds or thousands of small branches; where a mattress should have been was a thick growth of moss, covered by several soft wool blankets. There was a table and chairs, which seemed to have been made by the same method as the bed—from small branches twisted and braided and somehow, Darragh discovered as he let his fingers make contact with a chair, made solid and unyielding. It would have taken anyone a lifetime, he guessed, unless magic were involved. He watched Frederick, suspicious of his assertion that he was "just" a man; but Darragh felt no fear.

There were shelves in the walls, alcoves in the stone, as if someone had said, "I need a space to put this," and the stone obliged. Inside these miniature caves were two sets of bowl, plate, cup, and spoon; several jugs and clay urns of varying sizes; a pot, a pan, and what looked like a kettle; and, much to his surprise, a small collection of books and scrolls. A larger chest of wood, banded in iron, stood between the bed and the wall; to this Frederick went when he finished stirring the coals, and revealed it to contain linens and clothes. He drew from it a tunic like his, long sleeved and knee-length, split from the hem to the hip to allow for riding and freedom of movement, and a fur-lined surcoat. These he extended to Darragh, who at that moment realized that he had forgot his blanket at the rose hedge, and that he was cold.

"Thank you," he said, accepting them. He set the surcoat on the bed to get the tunic on, and when it touched his skin he was surprised at how soft it was, for it was thick and warm, and he instantly felt some of the tension in him uncoil. He laced the neck loosely, out of habit, before noticing that the tunic fit him, which, if it were Frederick's, should not have been possible. He looked up at his host in amazement.

Frederick was grinning at him. "Do you like it?" he asked.

"How can it fit me?" Darragh replied.

"I think that perhaps you are fitted to it."

Darragh frowned thoughtfully, but proceeded in donning the surcoat. With that accomplished, he was at last warm and comfortable. "I do like it, and I am grateful, to you and to whatever former guest of yours left it behind."

"I am honored by your gratitude, and by your assumption that I have had guests before you," Frederick said.

He gestured at the table, and Darragh sat in one of the stony wooden chairs that was, inexplicably, plush. Frederick looked into a cauldron that hung from the hearth canopy, over the lower coals, and asked if Darragh was hungry. Having received an affirmative answer, Frederick ladled stew into both of his bowls and set them on the table with their spoons. After retrieving the cups and filling them with water, he sat, and looked at Darragh; and he laughed at the expression Darragh wore, which must have conveyed the consternation he felt at Frederick's remark.

"Come, Goodman Darragh, you must know that this is a magical place; is it then more likely that I have had a guest of your exact shape, or that the clothing in the chest adapts itself to the present need?" he said.

"Put in those terms, I concede the point," Darragh said, smiling a little.

"You are too sly," said Frederick, though his tone seemed to say he did not mind. "You know now also that you are the first to make it through the forest; do you think that is significant?"

"I am the first to make it through the forest during your

tenure," Darragh replied. Frederick laughed and nodded at his correction. "But you flatter me in any case, for I did not make it through the forest on my own. I followed a beast, who led me to the safe path."

"Followed a beast, did you?" Frederick said, his eyes dancing. "And what did you think of it?"

Darragh set down his spoon, which he had been about to dip into the steaming bowl, and thought for a moment of how he could describe what he had seen; but he was distracted by the teasing tone of Frederick's voice, the merriment in his eyes, and the memory of his host's large, warm hand.

"It was you," he said, looking up at Frederick.

The man grinned again.

"Why did you decide not to kill me?" Darragh asked.

"You had your crossbow, your knife, and never drew them," Frederick replied.

"Some would call that cowardice."

"You know the limits of your power, Darragh; that is what I learned about you. You knew you could not save yourself with your weapons, you could only cause us both to die; and so, rather than take me down with you, you surrendered yourself to me. I have never seen such a thing in humanity, not when I was human myself and not since I have guarded this place from the ones who came before you." He smiled. "That is why you did not deserve to die."

12

THE BEAST

FREDERICK WOULD NOT ANSWER any more of Darragh's questions, insisting that his guest eat instead, and under the twin impositions of his hunger and Frederick's evasion, Darragh relented, forming new inquiries as he ate. Yet when he finished his stew, exhaustion overcame him entirely, such that when he woke in a moss bed with a pearl-blue sky above him, pale with morning, he did not even remember having fallen asleep.

The bed was the same as the one he had seen the day before, but as he discovered when he sat up, in a different room. It was smaller, with a fireplace and chimney projecting from the wall into the room rather than an old-fashioned hearth like Frederick's. The surcoat had been removed, though he still wore his tunic and trousers; he remained barefoot, but his feet were not cold. He'd not remembered to look at Frederick's feet the day before. He did have hose in his pack, which he had abandoned beyond the hedge but woke to find set neatly upon a large wooden chest. For the time being he set them aside. The jug he carefully removed and unwrapped, relieved beyond words to see it was intact. He'd feared that he'd landed on it in his flight from the beast. Finally, he removed the letters from his mother, which he had slipped into the lining of his pack through a small tear. These he smoothed as best he could, checking them for damage, before returning them to the pack; it seemed the most secure place for them.

The beast—Frederick. What did it mean? Was Frederick a fairy of some kind, a forest guardian? Or, was he a man, as he'd said; but not *just* a man?

Something tickled his hand. He lifted it slowly and saw a spider there on his knuckle, a fat garden weaver, and he looked around. "Do you find many flies here, little friend?" he asked. "Or have you gotten yourself stuck?"

There was a root along the wall, growing down from above; he lifted his knuckle to the bark and nudged the spider onto it. Then he went back to his unpacking.

The two books of folk tales were undamaged, and Darragh thanked whatever stars had seen fit to bless him, because he knew his clothing shouldn't have been enough to keep his treasures safe. He put the books in a shelf, caressing their velvety spines, then went out into the labyrinth.

Roots and vines shrouded the hall on either side of him like tapestries, woven with flowers and embroidered with spiderwebs. It was like nothing he'd seen the day before, and again he wondered how large the labyrinth could be. Were the walls there as thick as the ones he'd passed through? He searched out the wall for a bare spot he could climb, sparing a moment to miss his stiff-soled boots, lost near the river. That hard leather would have made it easier for his feet to find purchase; but though the wall was uniform it was not smooth, and he found friendly holds enough for him to climb even in the dewy dampness. It was no more difficult than climbing a mast, though he missed the pegs here and there for resting.

His fingers found the top's edge, covered in moss, and looked for something to grip so that he could clamber over the lip; a root obliged him, and he lifted one leg and then the other to stability atop the wall. Panting, warm from the effort, he twisted and sat with his legs dangling over the wall he had just scaled, and gazed with wonder upon a second forest, sprawling before him like something out of a dream: inky black bark on willowy trees growing upon the thick stone walls, silver-leafed branches that twined together to form an open but shielding canopy over the labyrinth; soft gray-green moss that blended into the stone; flowering vines that decorated the tree roots and cascaded over the edge to form curtains in the maze below. The air shimmered with the movement of flies and butterflies, the sun flashing off iridescent wings. Squirrels, chipmunks, rabbits scurried all over the flora, giving it a rippling effect that almost seemed like breathing. Songbirds vocalized with abandon, protected from raptors as long as they stayed below the interconnected branches.

Darragh had never seen anything so beautiful. And it was large—the trees were not so thick that he could not see some distance, and it stretched considerably far in the direction he faced. He stood and turned to look behind him; less far, so at least he knew there was some constraint to the size of the labyrinth.

He walked through this upper forest, keeping the nearer edge to his right, until the wall began to curl in toward the center, away from the edge. Then he backtracked and found what he thought was the narrowest point between it and the next wall, toward the outside of the labyrinth. Could he jump it? He wanted to find his way out, back to the start, so that he could begin anew and see if he remembered the way to Frederick's room; but he was afraid if he went down the wall, he would commit himself to a path he could not control.

Assuming, he thought, *I am not already on such a path.*

If Frederick was the beast, then Frederick had led him to the labyrinth. He said he was not the Enchanter, but surely he must know em, if it was true that the Enchanter had once lived in this forest. Could he trust Frederick? Frederick had fed and clothed him, which normally afforded protection under the rules of hospitality, but with fae folk Darragh was less sure of norms and customs. The folk tales in his books told him to trust good magic implicitly and to distrust bad entirely, but was often conflicting on how to tell the difference. Kindness and beauty were no guarantee; cruelty could wear a mask.

"There you are," said Frederick, approaching. "How did you like your room?"

"Very well," Darragh replied, feeling a little ashamed of his suspicion. Frederick was not just beautiful, he exuded warmth and goodwill; it felt absurd, under the glow of his smile, to think it was feigned or that some malevolent purpose lurked behind it. "Though I don't recall getting to it."

Frederick sat, and Darragh joined him on the moss. "This place is not for the faint of heart. You needed rest."

"Is that why you were so secretive last night?" Darragh asked.

"Secretive! I prefer enigmatic." Frederick laughed, and Darragh chuckled with him; but then he looked thoughtfully at Darragh and said, "You don't seem very fool-hardy."

"No one has ever described me that way."

"Yet still you came, against all warnings."

"How do you know I was warned?"

Frederick gave him a sad look, and did not answer. Instead, he asked, "Where did you get your thorn?"

Darragh sighed. "If you led me here to tease me, I must tell you that I have teasing in spades at home."

"And where is home?" Frederick asked.

Where indeed? The *Augustina*? The place where he'd been born, where his people had lived for three generations? Darragh looked wearily at his host, and said, "Why do you think I have come?"

Frederick appraised him for a long moment, during which a breeze lifted the scent of the rose hedge up to greet them. "Have you ever trimmed a rose bush, Goodman Darragh?" Frederick asked.

THE ONLY ROSES DARRAGH knew with intimacy were those carved on the figurehead of the *Augustina*, woven into the hair of the nymph that blessed their progress. He had always been careful around them with his scraper and rag, freeing the ornament from mold and moss, from bird shit and all the detritus of the sea. But for all his gentleness, those roses were made of wood, hard wood lacquered against the moisture and extremity of life at sea. These roses in the living hedge seemed fragile by comparison.

Frederick stood beside him, describing how to observe the entire plant before beginning, what to look for—the dry, shriveled, black branches, the musty-smelling blooms. With his knife, he cut one such branch until the inside showed white, which Darragh could not help but think of as bone. Frederick showed him the angle at which to cut, told him that the cut must be smooth and clean, while Darragh nodded along.

"Remove any branches thinner than your smallest finger," Frederick said.

"You have been doing this a long time?" Darragh asked.

Frederick glanced sideways at him, then said, mildly, "Longer than you have been alive."

This was fresh teasing, for Frederick appeared no older than Darragh. He handed Darragh the knife and the leather gloves he wore, thick working gloves a world apart from the velvet-lined ones of Vesta's world. What was Vesta doing at that moment? Was she planning a funeral—or attending one? Darragh frowned and said, "I have not come to seek a gardener's apprenticeship."

Frederick's face grew somber, and he replied, "I know. But I must ask for your help, because I cannot tend the roses, and they are dying because of it."

"Why cannot you tend them?" Darragh asked.

Frederick turned away from him, walked back to the wall of the labyrinth. Darragh dropped the tools and followed him, catching his arm. "Is it to do with your curse?" Darragh continued.

Frederick huffed. "What do you know of my curse?"

"Nothing!" Darragh said. "Are you a prince, bested by the Enchanter? That is what the tales say when they speak of huge golden beasts. Are you some fairy yourself? You are tricky enough to be thought so. You say you are just a man. I know that cannot be true; but I *am* only a man, I can see only what is before me, and I have not the time for mysteries and games. Tell me the truth, or let me leave."

This time, when Frederick huffed, it was almost a laugh, and his gaze was soft upon Darragh's face. "You wrong yourself, Darragh. I think you see much that is obscured." He sighed, and said, "I am a prisoner here, but not by the Enchanter's hand. There was a sorcerer once who wanted to marry me, but I refused her. She turned me into a beast because she said I had no heart, no soul. The Enchanter brought me here to keep me safe and mitigated the spell as best e could, so that I could be human inside the labyrinth, but the sorcerer's magic is strong and dark, and e—" He broke off, sighed again, tears in his eyes. "E could not break the curse."

Darragh's hand, still on Frederick's arm, slid to his hand and gave it a sympathetic squeeze while he reflected on this information. Then, a realization dawning, he said, "The statue—you are the woodcarver's apprentice, the aromantic one whose friend could not take no for an answer."

Frederick laughed sadly. "It seems I feature in many tales; I am quite famous. Yes, that is the truth. I was a woodcarver's apprentice, and the sorcerer was my friend. So I thought."

"I am so sorry," Darragh said.

"It was more than a hundred years ago, and my fate could have been worse," Frederick replied. "I have grown happy here, though I do wonder whether . . . the world has changed."

Darragh thought of Amon. "A little—a very little."

They stood in silence for a moment, and then Darragh let go Frederick's hand and retrieved the pruning tools.

"A gardener's apprentice after all, then?" said Frederick, a little of his lilt returned.

"I understand now," Darragh murmured, seeing how the roses near the wall were well trimmed, but those farther out were choked and dying. Frederick could only work within the reach of his human arms, and the hedge sprawled far beyond that reach. So Darragh put on his gloves and took the knife. He found a gap where his slight frame could pass, where he could get to the bushes beyond the inner row; and he began to work.

Where was the Enchanter? he wondered. The mention of em had made Frederick sorrowful, and he spoke of em as if e was gone. Dead? Gone from the forest? If e was not here, then Darragh knew not where to look, and despair touched cold upon the back of his neck. Perhaps Frederick knew, but could not go to em because of his curse. If so, Darragh could venture out to find em and bring em back, or at least bring news back to Frederick. He doubted that the Enchanter was dead. Surely, his host would not tease him so much as to hide that from him, knowing that he had come in search of that person.

The thorns of the branches around him did not scratch him, and it was more than just his caution that did this; in curiosity he put his finger to the point of one, deliberately, but could not make it draw blood. He smiled and whispered thanks, and it seemed to him the flowers shook themselves with pleasure in response. It occurred to him that they might be thankful for his attentions; the small, weak buds at his elbows, blocked from the light by their dead fellows, brushed his skin with what felt like insistence. He amassed piles of branches, and then returned to gather fallen petals off the ground; and then he said goodbye to the hedge for the day and went back to the clear space between the hedge and the labyrinth wall to sort his gleanings.

Frederick watched with interest while he sat, cross-legged on the ground, and turned one large pile into many: the intact petals, the leaves and branches, the thorns, and then the last, that of material too black and decayed to be saved.

"I thought you had no experience with gardening," Frederick said.

"Not the pruning," Darragh said. "But this . . . my mother taught my sister to do it, and my sister taught me. They used the petals for tonics and cosmetics; they're also good for placing over small cuts."

"The branches?"

"Good for kindling." He frowned, and added wryly, "Or for a switch."

Frederick nodded, his expression careful. "And the thorns?"

After a moment, Darragh laughed. "The ones at home were not straight like these; they were sort of hooked, like a claw, and very small. We would file them down until they would not hurt us, and then we threaded them onto necklaces and pretended they were shark's teeth we had collected, like the kind my father's captains wore on their belts."

"And so you used every part."

"Yes. Father hated it," Darragh said, the mirthful memory fading. "He bought us pearls; and soon enough, Vesta favored those. But I wore the thorn necklaces for a long time. I will wear one for the whole of my life."

Suddenly Darragh looked to the sky and asked, "What day is it?" He had lost time in the forest. His next quarter was coming soon.

But Frederick took his hand and said, smiling while Darragh looked on him amazed, "Do not fear; you have three days yet."

13
THE WATERFALL

THE LABYRINTH WAS A place of peace and bounty such as Darragh had never known, for all the wealth of his childhood. As the days passed, the walls seemed to open to him until the disorientation fell away and he knew it as well as his ship. He discovered the modest crop fields, which were just then birthing tender spring greens, and met the goats and deer who picked a delicate path through the rows, looking for weeds to eat while leaving the cultivars alone. Wherever he went, small hares attended him, hopping into the depressed grass left by his feet. Birds landed on his head and rubbed their faces against the stubble of his hair, which was growing and which, for the first time in years, he did not feel compelled to cut.

Frederick's home was lovely and self-sustaining. Though much had come, he said, from gifts to the Enchanter originally, they propagated and provided food in the long-term—like wheat from sprouted grains, and cuttings of herbs. Each had their preferred place, and Darragh found food gardens spread throughout the labyrinth, in shade or sun, in gravel or clay, near rock to climb or stood alone in a meadow.

It was endless, and perfect, and teeming with life. Not only goats and deer and gentle animals, but wolves and foxes came too, to rest in the sun or curl up in a den deep inside the stone walls. Badgers had their burrows, snakes had their holes, spiders and bats sought out the high dark places. It was not a place without death; and often, Darragh and Frederick, at work on the rose hedge, would pause to listen to the scream of a hare or a frantic flap of wings. But it did not trouble them any more than it troubled those creatures who lived in the shelter of the labyrinth.

"Is this what the whole forest was like? Before?" Darragh asked one day while he looked for more branches to trim.

Frederick, obscured by rose bushes, said, "Yes. The Enchanter was its keeper, along with some lesser sprites, and under eir stewardship all was kept in balance."

"The people from Iarom too?"

"Yes. Until their greed outweighed their sense."

Darragh gathered his trimmings and returned to the wall, where Frederick sat on the ground with his back to the stone wall, frowning. Darragh did not like to see such an expression on the face of one so kind, but his host had been in the labyrinth some hundred and fifty years, he'd gathered; it was a long time to be in a place so . . . stable.

"Everything has a lifespan, does it not?" he asked. "Even a forest?"

Frederick looked up, his mouth almost hinting at a smile. "True. And everything can be murdered—even a forest."

Darragh sat on the grass in front of him. "The tale says the Enchanter grew angry over the diminishing of eir dominion."

"In a way, that is true," Frederick replied. "But not as a question of size, or landholding power the way humans define it."

He said no more. Darragh brushed the soft grass under his fingers, and into the silence said, "When I arrived you told me you were just a man, but . . . do you no longer consider yourself human?"

Frederick sighed. "I admit that it is sometimes difficult to feel kinship with those who treated me with such . . . incredulity and disrespect."

"Change comes," Darragh said.

"Change. *Change* has no substance; the word has no true meaning. My people always knew the forest would change; the Enchanter always knew the forest would change. But that knowledge told us nothing of what that change would be," Frederick said.

That made Darragh smile mirthlessly, for he was right. And Darragh was right too; many things in his life had changed, in ways he could never have predicted, in ways he never wanted. For every good thing, there was just as likely to be something bad. Something always changed.

"Still," he said. "Change does come, and it does not come from nowhere. It comes from choices."

"Did you choose to leave your father?" Frederick asked.

"Yes," Darragh replied. "That is, when he told me to leave, I chose not to go back. I chose not to beg his forgiveness; I chose to stay true to myself. And he chose the same, it seemed."

Frederick's face lightened then, and he smiled at Darragh with something that looked like fondness. "I did not expect you to give such a wise answer," he said.

Darragh returned his look. "It took me a long time to feel that way. But it is the truth, and it helped me to contend with what happened to me. That should be the end of it, but now, with his illness . . ."

"Such things have a way of birthing regret where we have never felt it before," Frederick said, nodding.

Darragh's chest grew tight, the things he felt grasping at each other like survivors of a shipwreck, adrift, clinging to anything that might lift them above the rolling surface of the water even if by pushing themselves up, they pushed another person under. No matter which emotion rose to gasp for air, Darragh still felt choked. He stood and said, "Might I explore the forest? Will I be safe on my own?"

"Of course," Frederick said. "The wolves know you. And if you feel in danger, only call for me, and I will help you."

He smiled and thought he managed to keep it from looking too sad, and turned to go; but then he turned back and asked, "How do I get through the roses?"

Frederick chuckled and replied, "The roses know you now too."

The roses, as if to prove his words, bent toward Darragh slightly when he faced them again, and he found himself smiling genuinely. He lifted a hand to them, and stepped forward into one of the spaces he had found for trimming. When he did so, he found another space beyond it, which he stepped into; and there was another space before him, then another. Thus the roses made way for him, and soon he found himself on the other side of the hedge.

"Keep to the east," said Frederick's voice.

Darragh glanced back at the labyrinth, which rose beautiful and calm, its upper forest shining in the sunlight. Then, he stepped into the murky green of the lower forest.

The farther from the labyrinth he went, the more the forest matched his mood, and it was the gloom he had sought. Even so, the dark dampness was not so unnerving as it had been on his way in, and he wondered if he was simply getting used to the closeness of the forest. Or perhaps it simply felt less restrictive, knowing that the labyrinth was there and he could return to find open space, fresh air, sunlight, like belowdecks was tolerable because the sun and sea and wind were all there for the taking if he had a mind. He kept walking. Would he reach a strip of forest so overgrown that it was dark as a moonless night? Or would he reach the mountains first?

Near to the rose hedge he met with some deer, who nuzzled his hands and huffed when they did not contain any treat. A little farther on he saw the wolves, resting on some rocks, their muzzles red with a fresh kill. One pup came alongside him and trotted in his steps for a few paces before an older wolf called it back with a grunt.

After that, he saw a salamander here or there, a crow, but

no other life. He was not so attuned to its hidden presence as Frederick, who could seemingly look at a rock and find no less than three kinds of creatures on it; so though he saw no other living thing around him, he trod as carefully and respectfully as he could, and in focusing on that his melancholy mood soon began to loosen.

At the river, he wondered if he should search for his boots. Before he could decide, though, he spotted a flash of orange in the blue and purple shadows around him. On the other bank, a fox emerged from the bushes, sat down, and stared at him.

Darragh stepped forward, his toes just at the edge of the water, in a place where it pooled into a little world of its own, temporarily protected from the current by large smooth rocks. The fox didn't move. So he tugged his breeches over the knee and stepped into the river.

The fox waited until he neared the other bank, then trotted some distance, where it was still visible to him but would not be splashed by his exit from the water. He followed it, and soon it trotted two or three horse-lengths before him, stopping in particularly thick or winding sections to wait for him to find it again. Darragh felt a tingle of familiarity, for it was not unlike the way Frederick had led him from the river to the labyrinth. Where would this fox take him? It seemed to him they headed north, but as before, he quickly lost his sense of cardinal direction below the thick canopy. The terrain grew rocky, and the path turned uphill, and so he felt sure he was headed toward the mountains—but north, or west? Frederick had said to keep to the east . . . but why?

Soon, he felt the chill of water in the air, though the river was far behind him; then he heard the churning, splashing noise that told him the fox had brought him to the waterfall he'd guessed lay near the mountain's base. When he broke through the trees and saw it at last, he smiled.

It was not so large as he'd thought; it rose so high that even at a distance Darragh had to crane his neck to see the top, but it was minuscule compared to Cathal's Great Falls. A pool was at its base, deep and green, which fed into a gentle creek, undoubtedly joining the Erastus River at some point in the forest, or perhaps being joined by smaller creeks to become the river, for it was wide enough, though shallowing quickly from the pool. A huge rock, high enough that if he climbed it he should be staring straight into the center of the falls, stood opposite the white cascade, which tripped over a slanting rock face until just above that middle height. From there the water fell, unobstructed, in a sheet. Beyond it was only darkness. To one side, Darragh saw a kind of rough staircase, slippery with moss; he could climb to the top of the falls if he wished, and keep going up into the mountains.

The fox stood at this staircase.

Darragh made his way carefully to it, for the spray of the falls dampened all around it, and began to climb, his hand on the stone wall to his left to guide his way, his right arm out for balance. The fox found its way easily, and halfway up, hopped from those stairs onto a slim ledge. Darragh saw that the ledge widened and led to a cave behind the waterfall. He looked at the fox.

The fox stared back, then walked behind the falls. It stopped and looked into the cave, then back at him; and then it went to the other side of the falls and disappeared.

Sighing, his orders clear, Darragh cautiously mounted the ledge and edged to the mouth of the cave. What was the fox trying to show him? He could not see, and there was nothing nearby dry enough to light; he could hardly hear over the noise of the falls, or his own heartbeat pounding in his ears. His back grew damp from the spray, and perhaps from nervous sweat, for as he looked into the yawning darkness of the cave he felt—change. As if the rudder beneath him shifted of its own accord and a new course lay before him; he knew not whether it was better than the one he'd charted.

"Hello? Is anyone here?" he asked.

Something moved, and Darragh looked toward it. As his eyes adjusted to the shadows, he thought he could make out a human form, leaned against the wall and draped in dark fabric. While he stared, the shadows deepened, and the walls began to shake. The bats roosting in the walls woke and flew about in distress, shrieking. Darragh held his arms up to protect himself and continued to stare at the form against the wall, but the more he looked, the harder it was to see, until it was all blackness and thunder around him.

"Please, I only wanted—" His words were lost in a rush of wind. Lightning cracked and illuminated the cave; he caught a glimpse of the form, hunched over, before the light faded. Then the form opened its eyes, which glowed bright white in the darkness.

"Leave."

The wind pushed Darragh toward the waterfall, needlessly; he fled through it of his own accord and leapt into the pool below.

Interlude
THE LARGEST HOUSE

ALL WAS SOFT IN the deep blue of night. The leaves caressed each other, a soothing hiss pervading the air of the forest; in answer, the animals hushed themselves. Steps were taken with care by all beasts and not a stick snapped to shatter the quiet flowing between the trees. Only on such a night could Merrigan freely fill eir lungs. The world grew ever more oppressive. Was this age? How many lives had e lived already? E breathed in the velvet atmosphere, sucked it into eir core.

E pointed eir feet toward the town with reluctance, with resolution. Business must be conducted, however distasteful, and as e left the forest e was indeed beset by the awful taste of smoke, of decay and the filth of civilization. If e could have offered a reprieve, to emself and to the poor soul e went to attend . . . but a bargain had been struck, and e was as bound to it as he who had sought it.

In every window, through the threshold of every door, firelight flickered orange and red. In every hearth, a fire smoldered. Left over from cooking, perhaps, or a comfort against the darkness of night—there was no chill in the air. As Merrigan walked, e let eir eyes unfocus, experiencing the changing light at the edges of eir vision and the shadows in eir path. E let emself go away from eir destination, until the last possible moment. Nights such as that one, business like that which e ventured to conclude hardened eir bones until e felt petrified inside, dull and senseless as the cobblestones beneath eir feet, trapped by eir obligation. The dark side of the power e wielded.

The house e sought was the largest, for it belonged to the wealthiest family; that was to say, the family that could maintain the house was the wealthiest in the town, for the house and its land were both the source of and the drain on the family's income. If badly managed, the family would wither. E had seen this come to pass with four families in eir lifetime. Some lasted quite a while; the tenure of others was very brief. The character required for the astute management of land, as well as the compassionate support of a household, and in this case, much of the town . . . was not hereditary.

It was two stories and had been rebuilt in stone perhaps fifty years earlier. It had been ten years since Merrigan's last visit; in that time, the kitchen had been removed to the side yard, a separate building connected to the main house by a covered path. E stared at the little outbuilding, and remembered when the fires were in the center of the houses, when the cooking was an opportunity to bond and the smell of roasting meat and the sound of sizzling fish were all one needed to be reminded of home. The children of this house did not sit by their parents while they cooked, picking pinbones from fleshy white fillets, and crunching on the vertebrae of bony fish. The kitchen looked lonely.

A porch had been built in front of the house, more wood cut down and laid across the earth, for no reason Merrigan could discern. E had resigned emself to the wooden houses long ago, but the porch seemed excessive. E sighed; then e tapped the base of eir staff upon the ground three times.

A wail went up from the house.

The door remained shut.

Thrice more e tapped eir staff, though e did not have much

hope of their cooperation. In truth, e had never had hope. The price which the desperate were eager to pay always seemed too dear when it came time to settle the debt.

The wailing continued, but the door did not open. E lifted eir hand and directed the knob to turn, the hinges to swing. They obeyed, for turning and swinging were what they did best, and the unsteady light of the front room's fireplace crept over the threshold. Merrigan stepped up onto the porch, the wood cold and firm beneath the soles of eir bare feet. At the opening of the door, all sound from within the house ceased, and eir heart was made heavy by the sorrow of she who cried, for it was not she who had struck the deal with em. When had she learned the terms? Had she known all those ten years? If so, she was complicit, for she did nothing to meet them. But perhaps she had tried. Perhaps she had been unaware until that very night, when her husband had made his ineffectual precautions against eir coming. In that case, Merrigan was very sorry for her indeed.

A bar of iron had been laid across the door, just inside. Sprigs of rosemary nailed to the frame, and likely to the frames of all the windows. But Merrigan was only half fairy. The iron did not hurt em, and the herbs were pleasant to smell. E passed the frame and entered the room.

The family was gathered in the front room, which had once been one of only two rooms. Now, its hearth cast light upon a comfortable sitting area, with cushioned, upholstered benches and chairs, small tables with books and cards and dice upon them. This was a pleasure room, a leisure room only. Well. There was no pleasure in the space now. The old man sat in a chair that had been backed up to the corner farthest from the room's entrance; with all the lamps snuffed, he was deep in shadow. Before him, his wife sat upon a bench with their youngest child, nine years of age, perhaps. The child appeared uncertain but aware of their mother's distress, and looked upon Merrigan with fear. Two more children, youths just beginning to taste the prospect of maturity, stood when e entered the room, and quickly sat again upon taking in eir appearance. Not mature enough yet, it seemed. Merrigan's weariness grew as e looked upon them, and when e could not bear it, e turned eir attention to their parent.

The old man acknowledged em with a heavy sigh; the smell of alcohol upon his breath reached em across the room and overwhelmed the poor rosemary upon the door.

"Merrigan. I might have lived happily had I never seen your face again," the man said.

"Yet you have lived well these ten years knowing I must come," e replied.

"Well. Lived well." The man grunted. "Have I lived well?"

"By every metric you requested, you have."

Ten years ago, the man had called upon Merrigan to save the failing estate he had inherited. He had no food, he cried at eir feet then. He had no livestock, no money. His children were dull and listless, his wife fatigued and weak. He wished the Enchanter to grant them the means of their survival, the materials to thrive, and e did so—with conditions, for magic must never be freely given.

"Where is the school?" e asked.

"There is no school," the man growled.

"Why do the houses around yours crumble? Why does the wind whistle through them?" e asked.

"They are not mine to care for."

"Why does the smell of sickness rise from the houses?" e asked.

"Because these villagers will not hire a doctor." The man rose from his chair, anger singeing his despair enough to reanimate him. He stalked toward Merrigan, the skin of his face pulled tight across his skull. The heat of his unspoken words radiated from his mouth, but they stayed behind his teeth; there was no argument he could lay before em.

"Has your table ever been empty?" e asked.

The man leaned upon the mantel and looked into the fire. His wife answered for him. "No," said the woman.

"Have your assets grown?"

"Yes."

"And has your family grown strong in both body and mind?"

She glanced at her husband, then said, "Yes."

"Meanwhile the town has decayed around you. Our bargain was that as you thrived, so should those who depend upon you in this wilderness. Your wish was granted not to you for your merits, but upon you because of the number of lives connected to your success," Merrigan said. "You have not fulfilled your portion of the bargain."

"We'll do it now!" the woman said. "From now on, we will help our neighbors. Won't we, my love? We can bring a doctor to town, and a teacher. We can repair the houses."

She must not have known what would be required of them. Merrigan wondered whether, perhaps, the old man had told no one, the better to renege on his promises and keep all the good fortune to himself. "Those were not the terms," e said gently, though e knew no sweet tone of eirs could prevent further tragedy for this woman.

"What were the terms?" the woman asked. She looked to her husband, brooding silently over the flames. "Husband, what are the consequences?"

The chimney was not quite good enough to prevent a haze of smoke in the room, and it irritated Merrigan's nostrils to breathe it. Though e opened eir mouth only to speak, and spoke quickly, the bitterness attached itself to eir tongue and eir saliva could not relieve em of it. Not yet, not until e returned to the clean air of the forest. Eir intentions were to be tender with this family, but eir patience was nearing its end. The man did not answer his wife, as if not speaking the thing would prevent its happening. He knew better; Merrigan was ashamed of him.

"All that you have gained, you shall now lose," e said.

The woman turned wide eyes on em, and she clutched the child beside her. Merrigan pitied her in her marriage. Perhaps he had been a worthy husband once. Alas that selfishness had a greater part than love in some souls; alas that selfishness could grow, like a disease, as it must have in this man whose pleas for his family's health had been so sincere ten years ago.

"I won't allow it," the old man said.

Merrigan ignored him, and kept eir eyes on the woman. She wept and shook her head. "Please, don't."

E had no choice. E was as bound to the magic as the man. Once, e would have experienced guilt, but such things had passed. Guilt was a deterrent; it was meant to prevent one from doing harm in the future, to spur one to make amends. E offered help and always made eir terms clear. E took nothing which was not promised, e took it only under the agreed-upon conditions. It was pointless to feel guilt for such transactions.

The floorboards rumbled. The parents looked down in alarm, and the youngest child began to cry.

"Something for the children—please, they had no control over this, over their father," the wife said, standing and gathering all her children to her. "Can you do something for the children?"

"Do not bargain with this devil!" The man barreled forward, attempting to get between his wife and Merrigan.

Merrigan blocked him with eir staff, and considered the woman. Her jaw was set, her eyes wide and filled with anger. She had not looked at her husband since eir pronouncement. E observed her soul and saw that she believed in the old stories, in magic; she had grown up with a wary respect for it.

"If I do this—" The words died in Merrigan's throat, unexpectedly. E could do nothing to mitigate the punishment of the man, but e felt that the magic of the bargain was gentler with his family, unknowingly and without consent included. This was not because magic had any inherent fairness or morality; the simple fact that these humans had not verbally agreed to the bargain left it weaker with regard to them.

"I will agree to anything," the woman said, holding eir gaze with her fiery one.

"You are banished; you must leave your husband and this town, this region," e said. "Make your home elsewhere. These are the conditions."

"And if we abide by them?" she asked.

"You will never be rich. That much of your husband's bargain, I cannot ease for you. But I can promise that you will never go hungry or come to harm, so long as you make kindness your guiding principle."

She gave a relieved sigh and nodded. "Yes." After glancing at her children, getting nods of understanding from them, she nodded to em again. "We accept."

Merrigan looked away. "Go collect your provisions, quickly. Leave as soon as you are able."

The four them were quick on their feet indeed, and instantly gone from the room. Merrigan was left alone with the husband, whose anger seemed drained by his wife's shunning of him; he had returned to his chair in the corner. Eir work was over and eir mouth was thick with smoke; e left the house, though not quickly enough to avoid hearing the man curse eir name one more time.

When eir feet touched dirt again e stopped, and filled eir lungs with the marginally cleaner outdoor air, and tried to disperse the tension in eir back. Movement caught eir eye: the woman and her children, cloaked, exiting the kitchen building. They returned not to the house, but set off down the road away from the town. E raised eir hand and sent eir small blessing after them. Something chill brushed eir face, and when e lifted eir fingers to eir cheek e was surprised to find it wet.

Behind em, the house groaned. The ground shook. And then life burst from the dirt.

Saplings appeared, vines; they wedged themselves between every stone of the house. The plants were stronger than their mundane counterparts. They broke the mortar, and those stones that were not caught up in the rapidly growing web of branch and bark tumbled to the ground and lay like abandoned skulls on the dark earth. The cold wood of the porch warmed and warped and sank into the dirt until it looked like any other snarl of roots. The fire inside was snuffed; the chimney collapsed and became a stone spire, a trellis around which the tallest tree grew.

When all went still again, the grand house was reduced to its original two rooms, enclosed, with a door, but walled and roofed by living things. In the silence, Merrigan heard the man inside screaming.

E could not control the consequences of magic, and e was glad of it, for e did not think e could bear such a burden as that. But as e looked upon the manner in which the magic had taken back what it had given, e approved.

It had woken the other townspeople, though, and they had begun to congregate around the house. The night filled with their sounds of alarm and dismay, their pity and their contempt alike. Merrigan stepped onto the road and walked against the tide of humans, back toward eir forest. A few of them noted the Enchanter and pointed em out. E did not stop to hear more of what they said.

People in that town and those near it had told a story once of an enchanter who had saved a good family on the brink of starvation. Merrigan wondered what story might be told now.

PART II

14

THE KING

THE KING OF VARRUN was a proud man. He was overlord to a dozen dukes and counts, who all paid tribute to him and served him in his sworn duty to protect their lands and his. But his nobles were wealthy themselves, and when he traveled with his household to their fiefs to see to orders of business, he saw how their halls were filled with tapestries, and their robes were made of velvet, and their hair was bedecked with gold. He disliked that they were as richly dressed as he, and that they gave gifts of gold to their own subjects, even to the serfs.

So, long before Merrigan was born, he decreed that velvet and silk were to be worn only by the nobility, and that colors requiring rare pigments were to be reserved for himself. Ermine and the soft furs he likewise reserved for the royal family. The amount of gold that could be worn was delineated by rank, so that the king could wear twelve pieces; the queen, ten; the nobles, eight; and so on. The serfs were allowed one gold earring, to wear only on feast days.

He likewise ruled that men must wear caps and women must wear veils, men breeches and women skirts that showed not their ankles, and that this was suited to the station of each. Namely, that men required breeches for their freedom of movement, that they might accomplish their labor; but women moved only within the home and needed no such freedom.

Thus were the sumptuary laws enacted. Punishment was to match the degree of the offense.

15

CHANGELING

THE CHILD DOZED NEAR the hearth; eir parents thought e did not hear them, but the coals burned low and the night was calm, so there was nothing to block the sound of their voices in the little cottage.

"Merrigan is nearly ten years old," said eir stepmother. "It is time! We have indulged this behavior long enough."

"Peace, wife," said eir father.

"It is bad enough, the comments of the other mothers," the stepmother said. "They are afraid for their own children, and I do not blame them. It is too strange. If it continues, we will be driven from the village, I'm sure of it. Oh! Why you ever brought that changeling into our house—"

"Enough," said the father. "Merrigan is *my* child. Say no more about it."

Silence fell, neither peaceable nor dutiful. Merrigan opened eir eyes, and it almost seemed to em that e could see the wedge driven between eir parents, and it was shaped like em.

MERRIGAN LEFT THE COTTAGE and fled into the forest before first light, knowing none would follow em, for the villagers believed the forest to be full of fairies and other magical creatures, some of which meant harm to country folk. Yet e had never felt that fear, and often walked along the forest's edge; the villagers said it was because e was a changeling that e could stand to be so close.

When the youth had exhausted emself with running, e collapsed and leaned against a powerful dark tree to rest. E fell asleep, and did not wake until dusk, when e felt something cold and wet at eir hand. Eir eyes fluttered open and focused on what had touched em: a little orange fox, difficult to see in the dim evening light, watching the youth carefully. The fox made no movement, so the youth ignored it and looked around. It was dangerous to be in the forest after dark, even more so than during the day, to hear the old villagers tell it. But the youth was unafraid, and only sighed against the tree.

"What brings you here in such a state?" the fox asked.

"And in what state must I be in order to come to my home?" Merrigan replied.

"Is not the village your home?"

"No more," e said. "Perhaps it never was."

The fox tilted its head to one side. "Why should you say that?"

"You are very curious," Merrigan said. When the fox gave no reaction, e sighed. "The villagers say I must act like a man, or if I cannot act like a man, then I must act like a woman. I do not—I am somewhere between the two, perhaps, or outside of them entirely, I—I don't know. But I know this, that I am neither man nor woman and I cannot pretend to be." E sighed again, and eir jaw tightened. "I cannot go back."

"Why do they say you must act one way or another?" the fox asked.

"They say that unless I choose to be a man or a woman, I will have no trade, and I will never find a spouse, and I will be spurned wherever I go," the youth said.

The fox shuddered, and for a moment the youth's heart dropped into eir stomach, thinking the fox agreed with the villagers' prediction; but then the fox's ears twitched, and Merrigan realized it was laughing.

"Why do you laugh?" the youth asked.

"Humans have grown so strange!" the fox replied. "To think such things. Well. There is hope for you yet, and you must show them how they are wrong."

"Why? I want none of this. I simply wish to live my life!"

"You shall! But will you live here, in the forest? Or do you wish to live beyond these green borders?"

The youth huffed but gave consideration to the fox's words. Truly, e did not want to hide in the forest forever. E wanted to see the ocean, to climb the mountains in the north; e wanted to fall in love, and know all there was to know. So e sat up straight, and stretched, and smiled down at the fox. "What must I do?"

"Do what your heart desires," the fox said.

With that, the fox disappeared into the dark forest. Merrigan settled into the silence, leaning back upon the tree again. E slept, the question of eir heart's desire swirling through eir mind; and when the sun came gently through the leaves above em, e stirred, and went back to eir parents' cottage.

Eir father wept and held em close. "I was so worried! I thought your mother stole you back from me."

"No, Father. I only went to the forest to think," Merrigan replied.

"And what did you think about?" eir stepmother asked.

"About what I want to wear after my birthday."

Eir parents shared a look, and then eir father asked hesitantly, "And did you decide? What do you want to wear?"

"Yes," Merrigan said, smiling. "I want to wear breeches, like you."

Eir stepmother grimaced and said, "But dear, you . . . have not the figure for breeches."

"It's all right, Mother," the child replied. "I want to wear skirts too. Just not all the time."

"Dear one," said Father. "I am sorry to say that you do not have the right to decide."

MERRIGAN WOULD NOT OBEY. Eir stepmother tried many tricks and cruelties to force em into the clothing required of em, even to the point of burning all the clothes e had. But then e would reach into the fire, unbothered by the flames, and pull from it what e wanted: breeches, skirts, tunics and hose, new garments that blended elements of the old, forged anew by the coals and Merrigan's touch. For Merrigan *was* a fairy child; eir father had been beloved of a fairy in the forest and lain with her, then been given the child to bring up.

Eir proclivities were attributed to this, and much of the village grew wary, even as they came to Merrigan and asked em to repair some small thing, irreparable by normal means. E mended holes in leather so that it seemed it had never grown thin at all; e regrew wooden beams that had been eaten away by pests and saved houses. E found lost sheep and lost children, lost tools and lost seeds; e saved spoiled milk and restored rotted grain. So there was a strange kind of love in the village for em, but the villagers knew that if word should ever get out of how e flouted the sumptuary laws, the whole village might pay. For if even the lowliest village child could disobey the king, why could not his highest lords?

Merrigan sometimes wondered if the villagers were right, and if eir gender was a fairy thing. But as e grew, e thought not, for e talked sometimes of it with eir father, and the other children when their parents were not nearby. So e knew that e was not the only one who felt the limits of *man* and *woman*, both in the flesh and in the law. One friend, a boy called Otto, had nimble fingers and could make stitches so fine they disappeared into a seam; and another, Sybill, though she was a girl, could chop wood for an hour and still split logs with a single blow of her ax. Sybill had a maternal glow about her, too, and cooed at any infant she saw, while Otto used his nimble fingers for much more than sewing, and always had liaisons to confess when the monks came round. Otto, Sybill, Merrigan, and even their parents all fit and broke in turn the wisdom they received from their betters; but while Otto and Sybill would gnash their teeth in frustration, so too would they, in the end, shrug, where Merrigan could not.

One day when Merrigan was nearly sixteen, as e was passing through the square, the shepherd's boy likewise crossing through caught eir eye, and shook his head as if to warn em not to continue on; his eyes were wide and flicking to a group of adults clustered before the wall of the meetinghouse. Among them was Merrigan's father, stony-faced while the village elder gestured vigorously at a parchment nailed to the wall. Merrigan could see the seal of Varrun on it. Merrigan receded, unnoticed.

That night eir father said, "It is the society that is so firm, I think."

Eir stepmother was asleep; the two of them sat alone near the low-burning hearth.

"What do you mean, Father?" asked Merrigan.

"Well, think of your mother. Your stepmother, I mean," said Father. "Is she all goodness and patience, meek, under my command? That is what women are meant to be, but she is not. She is good, and patient, yes, but she is knowledgeable and capable. I could not manage things without her; if I did not have her, if it were entirely on me to decide and command, I think I would die of the stress."

Merrigan nodded. "I have observed this throughout the village."

Father stared into the fire, his expression thoughtful and sad. "We all live by these expectations, which we call laws of nature . . . yet is not nature that which plays out around us every day? Should we not draw laws from what we observe, rather than perpetuate some false thing that crumbles weakly before the truth of our lives?"

Merrigan's eyes burned then with tears, and e went to eir Father. He put his arms around em and held em close, and Merrigan felt his tears fall on eir brow.

"I wish I could protect you from this, my sweet child." He wept.

The next day, the duke came.

Merrigan's father shook em awake when the day was yet pale, and the first thing e saw when e woke was the whites of eir father's eyes.

"Come quickly," he whispered.

Merrigan dressed with all the speed e could muster while eir father watched both the door and his bed, where eir stepmother slept on. Eir father would not speak, though, until he had taken up a sack and Merrigan's hand, and led em out of their cottage to the forest's edge.

"The duke comes fast this morning to our village," Father said finally, in the silence of the misty meadow. "Your mother sent a warning; he comes to flay you for your disobedience in dress and behavior. To make you an example. You must flee into the forest and never return."

"Father! No, I shall hide until he leaves and then come home," Merrigan said.

But eir father shook his head, tears in his eyes. "He will not stop. Too long you have asserted yourself, and now the king knows of it; he will not stop until he sees you punished. You must go."

Merrigan wished to protest; e wished to fight—the duke, even the king if e must, to wield eir magic in eir own defense and win the right to live eir life in peace. But e could see the pain such a war would bring down upon eir father, eir friends. For the time being, at least, eir father was right. It was better to go into the forest. It was better to hone eir skills, until e could be sure of success. So e threw eir arms around eir father and said goodbye, then went into the forest.

Eir father hurried back to the village, meaning to return to his bed before the duke came to his door. But he was too late; the duke bore down on him from atop a great white horse, with his knights behind him, their armor wet and glinting as the sun rose and the mist condensed on steel. They spoke not to the man when they saw him, for they knew who he was, and since he was coming from the forest, they knew what he had done. So they rode past him, into the forest, in chase of Merrigan.

E soon heard the hoofbeats pounding, the screams of the horses as they twisted this way and that to avoid branches and roots, as they jumped fallen logs, as they splashed through streams. E heard the flutter of wings as they disturbed birds, and the groaning of the trees as they stirred themselves to the invasion. Merrigan ran as fast as e could, but the horses were faster; they gained on em, and e began to weep, sure that e was going to die and angry that eir life would be extinguished for the pride of one jealous man.

Then e stumbled into a clearing, and all fell silent.

The grass smelled sweet under em. The sun was warm on eir back. The birds sang their morning greetings, unbothered by hungry men. Merrigan lifted eir head and heard only the gentle forest silence, the birds and the rustling of leaves, no martial sounds of hooves and metal scraping. E seemed to have reached some oasis, some refuge; e looked behind em and the narrow path e had followed was empty, though e could have sworn the duke was at eir heels. In wonder, e looked forward and saw a creature standing in the center of the clearing. They smiled at em, and all at once e felt enveloped in a love tinged with regret, and e knew this was eir mother, and e knew this was the fox who had told em to do as eir heart desired.

E dropped the sack eir father had packed for em, with clothes and food and the small carved toys of eir childhood, and walked to meet eir mother. She stood draped in orange robes the color of fox fur, her black hair spilling over her shoulders. She opened her white arms to em and embraced em. Together they sank to their knees, and she held em and rocked em while e sobbed.

As e wept, stones burst from the ground around em, great rings of stone that grew and grew and grew.

16
THE THREE PRINCES

THE KING WHOSE LAWS had banished Merrigan grew old, as humans do, and he considered his sons. The eldest had been thoroughly schooled, to the highest standards of the region, could read and speak all the official languages, and even write in one; yet he had seen the attention and time paid to his education as a punishment, especially as his younger brothers grew with what he saw to be more freedom. So he was well-trained but resentful and rebellious. He longed for the throne only so that he could finally do as he wished. The king, who, though cruel and selfish, was canny, knew his eldest son would make a poor king, and a poor steward for all that his father had accomplished in uniting the fiefs.

His second son had been reared for public service of a different kind, and unlike his brother he had taken to the education that centered mindfulness and assistance, compassion, if only to those deemed deserving. So he too would be a poor king, in his father's mind, for he would not be strong or skillful enough to keep the powerful dukes and counts in vassalage to the throne.

The youngest son, as is often the case, had learned from the examples of his elder brothers and taken upon himself their best qualities while avoiding their defects, and his father the king loved him above the others. Yet he knew that if he named this son as his heir, his elder brothers would find some way to do him mischief, so the king devised a plan to ensure the safe succession of his favorite.

The king gathered his sons around him and said, "My worthy sons, I love you all so well, and you are all such fine young men, that I know not which of you to name successor. So, we shall give it up to the will of heaven and set a test for you. Whosoever succeeds will be king when I am dead. In the great forest of the north, there is a cave where sleeps a dragon guarding a mighty sword. This sword, in a righteous hand, will ensure victory to whoever wields it, and prove who should be king of this realm."

The brothers rode out together from the fortress of Varrun into the north amiably enough, but when they reached the forest's edge, the eldest brother said, "I will go into the forest, but you two must wait. Since I am the eldest, I deserve a day's head start. Besides, I have heard that this sword burns horribly the unrighteous hand that grips it, and as I have been trained for the kingship already, it will be safest for me. Better I take it up, so that you do not hurt yourselves with it."

The younger brothers exchanged a look, but they agreed, and so they made camp while the eldest brother went into the forest.

The next morning, the second brother said, "I will go into the forest, but you must wait. Only I among us have been schooled in righteousness, and so the sword must be mine, but our elder brother needs to feel the sword's heat before he will accept this. I would not wish for you to hurt yourself, though, so give me a day's head start to find the sword."

The youngest brother agreed to this and kept his camp while his second brother went into the forest. The next morning, he broke his camp and entered the trees alone, leaving his horse to graze in the meadow.

Merrigan had lived in the forest now for some years, learning magic from eir mother and learning the forest through hours of exploration. E knew the trees and was known to them, and had learned to hear them when they spoke; e helped them when they were sick, cleared them of twigs and leaves when they shed their growth each autumn, and listened to the stories from their long, long memories. E knew the animals, from the great lumbering bears to the tiny flying insects to the fungi that connected everything together both above and below the surface of the soil. E had grown older too, though with eir fairy blood, e would long outlive the king.

E knew the moment each brother entered the forest, and so e stood in their paths and waited for them each in turn. When the eldest brother came upon em, still mounted on his warhorse, he scoffed down at the tall, slim youth with earth-brown skin and a spray of locked hair.

"Spirit of the forest," he said. "I seek the dragon's cave. Lead me to it, and you will be rewarded."

"I know the cave, and the dragon," Merrigan said. "I will take you to it if, when you are made king, you repeal the sumptuary laws."

The eldest brother laughed. "Why should I do that? My father had good reason to enact them. Take me to the cave immediately."

Merrigan refused, and with sudden anger the eldest brother drew his sword and charged at em; but Merrigan nimbly disappeared into the forest, and the eldest brother could only vent his rage upon a tree, hacking it to pieces. When that rage was spent, the eldest brother rode on, grumbling, to find the cave himself. Merrigan emerged, laid eir hands upon the wounded tree, and helped it repair itself.

The second brother soon came down the path, sitting atop his mule, and saw Merrigan waiting. He smiled at em and said, "Good youth, I seek the dragon's cave. Lead me to it, and the heavens shall reward you."

"I know the cave, and the dragon," Merrigan said. "I will take you to it if, when you are made king, you repeal the sumptuary laws."

The second brother sighed. "To this, I cannot agree. I think the laws are a good reminder to the people to be humble, and to know their place. But if you will still lead me to the cave, I believe you will find that reward shall come, even if its form is unexpected."

Merrigan refused; the second brother sighed again and rode away.

For a day and a half Merrigan waited for the third brother, until at last he came down the path on foot, his rucksack heavy with the things he had taken from his saddlebags. When he saw Merrigan in the path, he smiled and set down his sack. "Hello there, forester," he said. "Will you share a meal with me?"

Merrigan tilted eir head in a small flash of surprise, but smiled and said, "Yes."

The youngest prince sat and opened his sack, pulling out dark traveler's bread, salted mutton, a jug of wine, and a waterskin.

"This salting keeps the meat very well, I find, and is more delicious than smoking," he said. "But it does leave one very thirsty. I am sorry, but I have no cups."

"I do not mind sharing," Merrigan said, a little shyly, for it had been years since e had had a meal with anyone other than the fairies and the creatures and the trees.

The prince smiled, and handed em the jug of wine, from which e took a small sip. Then they ate the bread and meat in companionable silence, while the prince looked all around him. It was spring in the forest, and so all was yellow in the sunlight far above them, and the scent of earth mingled with the sweet odor of the pollen released by the flowering trees.

"I have never been here before," he said, wonderingly. "I am glad my father's quest has given me an opportunity to visit. I will come again, I know that much."

"What is the quest?" Merrigan asked mildly.

"I must seek the cave of a dragon who guards a magical sword," the prince said. "This sword burns the unworthy but grants victory to a deserving wielder. My brothers are already ahead of me in seeking it; have you seen them?"

Merrigan shook eir head, and the prince merely nodded and said no more. At last, Merrigan said, "I know the cave, and the dragon."

The prince smiled at em. "Is it a wise dragon, or a ruthless one?"

"Wise," said Merrigan. "She will let you touch the sword, for it is true that it burns those who should not bear it, and if it does not burn you, she will let you take it."

"That is a great relief to hear," he said. "I did not relish the idea of doing battle with a dragon." He frowned and added, "I only hope my eldest brother does not kill her."

Merrigan nodded, but did not say that e had sent word to the dragon, who planned to leave her cave when the eldest brother approached. In fact, she had done so already by this point, and watched the eldest brother scald his hand on the hilt of the sword. In his shame, the eldest brother had tried to steal some other treasures from the dragon's hoard, and so she swooped down and ate him whole, and his horse too. Merrigan learned of this later.

The youngest prince finished his meal and prepared to set off, all while Merrigan watched, waiting for the request his brothers had made. When it did not seem the prince would make it, Merrigan stood with him and said, "I will take you to the cave if, when you are made king, you will repeal the sumptuary laws."

The prince looked at em a little closer, and asked, "Why do you want the laws repealed?"

"So that I can visit my father safely," Merrigan replied.

Slowly, as if weighing this information, the prince nodded. Then he smiled and said, "Very well. You are very kind to offer your help, and in return, I will do all within my power to repeal the sumptuary laws."

Merrigan grinned but said nothing, suddenly shy, and then e gestured to the path and led the prince on. They walked through the trees and into the mountains, up a switchback path where the air grew thin and cold. The prince offered Merrigan his cloak, but e declined, for e felt not the cold as he did. Soon they came to the dragon's cave. By now, the second prince had come, and he was still there, for the pain he felt when he touched the sword had been so great that it rendered him unconscious. The dragon had settled him to sleep against his mule, kneeling on the ground.

When the youngest prince saw his brother, he cried out and went to him, but saw that he was alive and breathing, though his hand was burned. Sighing, he turned to the dragon.

The dragon was dappled gray like the rocks of her cave, so fitted to her surroundings that were it not for her golden horns, the prince should not have been able to see her. She looked at him with eyes as white as new snow and said, "Why come you to my cave, young prince?"

"I seek the sword of the righteous, by the order of my father the king, in order to show whether I am worthy or not to rule when he is gone," the prince said.

Merrigan went to the fallen second brother and took his hand, and sealed the burn so that it would heal without infection. E felt his head, and was confident that he would wake with no adverse effects.

The dragon lifted her wing to reveal the sword in its scabbard, laid out upon a threadbare velvet cloth. The prince went to it and gripped its wooden scabbard. Then, cautiously, he put his hand on the hilt. The wooden hilt remained cool to his touch, even as several heartbeats passed, and he smiled first at the dragon, then at Merrigan.

"You may take the sword with you and show your father its result," the dragon said.

The prince bowed to the dragon, then returned to his brother, and saw the change in his brother's wound. He looked long on Merrigan, who did not notice, for e had gone to greet the dragon.

The second brother was strapped to his mule, and Merrigan and the youngest prince led the mule carefully down the path back into the forest. The sword was strapped to the prince's back, under his rucksack, and Merrigan could see it catch the light of the unobscured sun; it winked and flashed and left bright spots in eir vision. E wondered if the prince would keep his word. He seemed like he would be a better king than his father.

Merrigan walked with them to the edge of the forest. E could see the prince's horse beyond the tree line, perking up and waiting as it spotted its rider returning. The second brother had woken in the forest and was now watching Merrigan and the youngest prince. Under his eyes, the youngest prince only smiled and clasped Merrigan's hand while he said, "I thank you, worthy forester, for your company and your help. Again I promise you, I will do my best to fulfill your request."

Merrigan only nodded, and watched them while the prince re-tacked his horse and rode south with the sword on his back.

THE YOUNGEST PRINCE BECAME king in due course, for none challenged the results of his father's test. When he was crowned, he called the barons together and asked them to repeal the sumptuary laws. Were they all so insecure in their power, he asked them, that they must impose such petty rules upon the land, that they must take such malicious interest in how the people dressed? Had the laws not been in fact a way for the king to put them down, and put limits on them?

But times were changing, and there were tradesmen and artisans and others who began to gather their own wealth, and the poorer lords were, like the king, afraid of these new middle classes usurping the glory to which the nobility, even the poor nobility, were entitled. And the second brother reminded them all that the laws were not merely to protect noble hierarchy, but also the hierarchy of each home in the realm, which was itself a reflection of the hierarchy that kept them all safe in the world and in the heavens.

So, though the prince had become king, he could not persuade the barons to repeal the laws regarding dress; and as times had changed, so had the kingship, such that he required their approval to do so. He lamented that he could not fulfill his promise to the kind forester. In an effort to do some small thing, he inquired around the villages of the north and found Merrigan's village, searching for eir father, that he might at least tell him that his child was alive and well.

But Merrigan's father had died, some two years previous to the quest. This, Merrigan did not learn until much later.

Merrigan waited for the prince to return as he'd said he would, with news that the laws had been repealed as he had promised. He never did. The walls of the labyrinth grew.

17

THE ENCHANTED MOUNTAIN

MERRIGAN'S MOTHER WAS A wanderer at heart, and after Merrigan had sufficiently grown up—some seventy-five years since eir banishment—she said goodbye and took a new form, one of a barn owl, and flew away to seek new adventures. Merrigan had grown up indeed, and so e smiled at eir mother's diminishing form and wished her well.

The labyrinth had by now become as it would be when Darragh came to it, its walls tall and thick and as far-reaching as Merrigan's sorrow, but crowned too with the beautiful upper forest, which had begun to grow as e settled into the routines of the forest and eir new life. It was a magical forest in the purest sense, for the flora was rooted in stone and there was no soil to be had—the ground was gray-green moss to provide a cushion. This elevated ecosystem was home to birds and insects, sprites and rodents, beyond the reach of other animals; the only exception was the occasionally ambitious goat, from the colony that had left the mountains and formed a new home on the labyrinth's north side.

The only way up to the forest was to fly, or to climb. Merrigan set eir hands to the stone, finding handholds a little above eir head;

e set eir toes into a foothold, and with a small push against the dirt, e was headed upward. The urge to be aloft seized em often. Luckily, there were crannies and ledges suitable for eir extremities at all points in the labyrinth, and the enchanted forest was only a short climb away. E loved the climb. To carry emself to such heights with just the power of eir body invigorated em—perhaps it was the climb e craved more than the forest above, which was very like the one below, after all.

E kept close to the stone as e climbed, eir muscles warm with the task of lifting eir body. Eir fingers secured themselves on large grips and slim cracks alike; e knew them all, had used them all on one climb or another in the past seventy years. E found the top of the wall, moss and roots spilling over the edge, and lifted emself, twisting as e did, to sit with eir legs dangling over the wall e had just scaled. None of the beings living there marked eir presence; they were one and the same, e and them, thriving in their own sanctuary.

But for how long? Merrigan had learned that change was inevitable; whether small or substantial, life could not help but shift over time. All but eir life. Seventy-five years since e had fled into the forest. E shivered and emptied eir mind of those thoughts, those knives, waiting just out of sight for the perfect moment to slide a gentle death into eir flesh. If e thought too long on them, they would come.

If e thought too long on them, e might welcome them.

THE SILVER LEAVES OF the upper forest rose above the trees surrounding Merrigan's labyrinth, and could be seen from the highest hills in the south as a glittering spot in a sea of green. It confounded the philosophers, who climbed these hills to ponder the mysteries of the universe, and later, to examine it all with new tools that allowed them to see far and wide. The forest had long had a reputation as being a place of magic, and it was thus treated with caution; but it was a curious age come upon the kingdom, thanks to a period of relative peace under the new kings. They found hills closer to the forest from which to spy on the odd light, and when they found no more hills close enough, they built the towers of Varrun as high as they could and looked from there. It seemed to them some kind of mountain in the middle of the forest. They speculated over what it could be, and what might produce such a shine, like polished metal. They concluded that it was an enchanted place, a mountain with some kind of forest made of precious metals growing straight from the rock. In this they were more or less correct, though they could not prove it, for no explorer of the forest ever came close enough to tell.

It being a time of peace, when the eldest daughter of the two kings grew up and began to think of marriage, her fathers thought that they need not arrange one for her, for they had other children and no immediate need of new treaties or alliances. So they told her she could decide for herself how to sort through the many suitors who were coming to court her.

The princess, who was a thoughtful, loving sort of person, thought long about a way to discern which suitor would suit her best, what test or question could show her both what kind of person they were and what kind of person they thought *she* was. She spent long hours in her garden, tending to the plants that were her pride and joy, searching among them for inspiration, remembering how she had chosen them or how they had been gifted to her. And there she found her answer.

She called the suitors in town to her, and told them she would marry the suitor who brought her a gift that would stir her heart, a most special gift that would reveal in the gifter a kindred spirit. Many of the suitors had questions and asked for more specific instructions, but the princess gave none, and indeed had none to give. She was seeking something different from what she had felt before, and therefore could not tell the suitors how to find it.

The suitors, these sons and daughters of her fathers' noble vassals, scattered far and wide across her kingdom, into foreign realms, and even into uncharted territory seeking the most special thing that would win the princess's heart. Despite the glorious things they produced upon their return, the princess's heart remained unstirred. She admired their efforts and the beauty of the gifts, but felt that none of them proved the suitor a match for her. She wanted neither silks nor gowns nor clothing, nor beasts tamed or slaughtered. Her fathers sighed with her as each suitor proved a disappointment, but still she waited for one who might succeed.

Merrigan noted the entry of the baker's daughter into the forest, and relegated eir notice of her to the back of eir mind with all the other temporary visitors to the forest. A settlement had cropped up not far from the forest's edge, and its inhabitants were often taking short trips into Merrigan's domain for firewood and hunting. Their impact was small; e folded them into eir balancing of things in the forest easily. So when the baker's daughter came, it raised no alarm or interest in Merrigan.

The baker's daughter did not keep to the edge of the forest, though; nor did she keep to the river, as the hunters and foragers did. Merrigan spent more attention on her the deeper into the forest she came, and when the baker's daughter stopped to rest, Merrigan called a sprite to em.

"When she wakes, take some innocent form, helpless, in some predicament," Merrigan told em. "Discover her purpose and her character."

The sprite did so, appearing to the baker's daughter as an injured fox; Merrigan watched her free the little fox and divert from whatever her goal was to return the creature to its den. Merrigan summoned eir favorite billy goat and said, "Put yourself in peril in her path; let us see if her kindness persists."

The goat did as e asked it and tangled its horns up in a bramble. The baker's daughter freed it, and its pleasure, and the sprite's, radiated through Merrigan's own chest. Merrigan silently instructed the goat to lead the baker's daughter to the labyrinth and flew home to meet her there. When the goat, and the sprite, and the baker's daughter arrived at the labyrinth, Merrigan stood before its entrance, wearing green robes modeled after the ones eir mother had worn. The baker's daughter looked at em with awe, but without fear, and held the sprite out for Merrigan to see.

"I found this kit stuck under a fallen branch. I think it is quite hurt," she said.

Merrigan studied her. She was young but not a child, and fit, unbothered by all her trekking through the woods. Her arms were fat and strong, as was the rest of her so far as Merrigan could tell, for she wore the many skirted layers required of women under the long-dead king's sumptuary laws: a smock, a wool kirtle, and over-tunic. The baker's daughter had taken two points of the kirtle's hem and tucked them into her leather belt to provide at least some increased mobility, revealing her hose, snug on her thick calves. Merrigan noted that these garments, though familiar to em, had undergone subtle changes since eir flight into the forest; they were better shaped to match the curves of flesh. But had anything else changed? Could this brave adventurer have worn breeches if she'd so chosen, and spared herself the washing of mud from her hem? She wore good leather shoes, at least, high and with laces wrapped many times around her ankles.

"How did you get here?" Merrigan asked her.

"The billy goat led me here after I freed it from a bush. I wanted to bring the kit home," she said. She smiled, stretching the gray linen of her veil.

Merrigan approached and took the kit from her hands. "Thank you," e said. "It will be all right now." The woman's skin glowed dark gold in the light of the setting sun, which would soon be gone to them. After a moment of considering, e said, "Come with me."

The baker's daughter followed em into the dark labyrinth, which blazed to life, lit by thousands of fireflies gathered in the stone halls, hovering above the heads of Merrigan and the baker's daughter. She gazed up in wonder as Merrigan led her through the labyrinth, for they lit the path, moving in tandem with Merrigan. The baker's daughter gasped with delight when Merrigan lifted the fox kit above eir head, and it transformed into its natural form, not unlike a firefly itself but larger and iridescent.

Merrigan smiled to hear the young woman's pleasure, glad she did not feel tricked.

They came to Merrigan's room, in roughly the center of the labyrinth. E waved eir hand over the hearth dug into the center, and the embers there flared up into a healthy flame. The fireflies dispersed to their own affairs, and Merrigan bade the baker's daughter sit. She paused in an examination of the chairs and table, running her hand over the braided, twisted wood.

"This is beautiful," she said.

Merrigan smiled, ladling a cup of goat's milk out of eir clay urn. "Thank you."

"How did you make them?"

"I gathered fallen branches and persuaded them to join together; and when that was not enough, I asked the trees to give me larger, sturdier boughs." E set the cup of milk before the baker's daughter and sat opposite her. "It took a long time, but I enjoyed it, and so did the trees, I think. Tell me, what is your name?"

"Aurelia," said the baker's daughter. "Is this the enchanted mountain?"

"You are not in the mountains yet."

"Yet this must be it, for they say the silver forest grows straight from the rock," Aurelia said.

"Ah, I understand. They see it from a distance; I suppose then it must look like a lonely mountain," Merrigan replied. "You must have come a long way, Aurelia."

"I am used to traveling; I must go to all the farmers, and collect their wheat and take it to the miller, and then take the flour home to my father."

"All that walking must hastily wear out your hems," said Merrigan, watching her carefully.

Aurelia shook her head. "I have a cart. But I do wish I could wear breeches, because it is a business getting up and down from the seat."

Merrigan nodded, eir heart sighing; the laws were still in place, then, if such a practical and active woman as Aurelia could not wear breeches. E had long suspected that the youngest prince had not kept his word, but it was still a fresh disappointment to have the confirmation. Aurelia finished the goat milk in Merrigan's silence and set the cup down, taking note of her host's distant expression; but then Merrigan roused emself and smiled at her.

"Why have you come so deep in the forest? Did you seek the enchanted mountain, as you call it?" e asked.

Aurelia turned nervous and clasped her hands in her lap. "If I may—I've come with the hope of retrieving a cutting from a silver-leafed tree."

"Why?" Merrigan asked.

Aurelia's face flushed, and she said, "It's a gift for a beautiful princess whom I love very much."

Merrigan sat back, as if to see the whole of Aurelia, and tilted eir head. The baker's daughter flushed more red and covered her cheeks.

"You must wonder how I can say such a thing, when I am the daughter of a baker and I have never spoken a word to her," Aurelia said. "I cannot deny it; I only know that when I see her, I feel such a lightness in my chest—but an ache also—knowing she is there brings me joy, and being apart from her brings me pain. When she smiles, all my dark thoughts are cast out before it, as shadows flee before the sun. I think of her so many times throughout the day, hoping that she is happy, that her life is what she wants it to be. I do not know what else to call this but love."

"Indeed, this seems as good a description as any I have heard," Merrigan replied.

"The princess wishes to get married, and her fathers have given her control of the process, so she called for suitors to bring her gifts, to see who will fit her best," Aurelia said. "This is my only chance; it will be enough to meet her, and give her some token, though I know she cannot choose a baker's daughter."

Merrigan narrowed eir eyes thoughtfully at Aurelia, then stood and said, "Rest here for the night; sleep in that bed, in safety. I will consider your request, and we shall return to it in the morning."

Before Aurelia could say aught else, Merrigan left the tower. E wandered through the dark paths, needing no fireflies to light eir steps; then e put eir hands to the stone and climbed up to the forest with the black trunks and silver leaves. Those same leaves glowed in the light of the moon, unobstructed by any other canopy. Merrigan lifted eir hand to them; then e nestled emself in the roots of the trees, on a thick cushion of silvery moss, and stared up at the branches all through the night.

When morning came, e climbed down and returned to eir tower room, where Aurelia had woken and set a clay pot to warming in the dull embers. When Merrigan appeared, she jumped a little in surprise, then smiled.

"Forgive me; I thought I might prepare a breakfast, as thanks for your kindness in letting me spend the night," she said.

"Thank you," Merrigan said.

Aurelia nodded and continued the preparation of the pottage, seeming at ease and not inquiring about the cutting, though surely she must have been eager to know the result of her quest. She found the materials required for her task without trouble—there were not many items in Merrigan's room—and, when the pot was warm enough, she added some grain to it from her pack, covered the pot with its lid, and gently shook it, holding the handle and lid through her apron, to toast the grains against the warm clay. Merrigan watched this with interest; e had not eaten grain since e came to the forest. Indeed, eir fairy blood meant that e required very little food at all, and e subsisted mainly on wild greens, honey, goat milk, and occasionally meat. E had nearly forgotten grain.

When the grains were toasted to her desire, Aurelia put the pot back in the embers, added water to it, and left it to cook. She dusted her hands on her apron, out of habit, it seemed to Merrigan, and smiled as she took her seat at the table.

"That will take awhile now," she said. "I was so rude yesterday, I did not ask your name."

"It is Merrigan," e said after a small hesitation.

"Have you always lived in the forest?" Aurelia asked.

Merrigan sighed thoughtfully. In all eir contemplation the night before, e had not wondered about this—what to reveal. Aurelia was only the second person e had spoken to at any length since fleeing into the forest, and e had not told the prince eir name or anything about emself, except eir reason for wishing the sumptuary laws repealed. But that had been a long time ago. E had now lived in the forest for more than four times longer than e had lived outside it; two human lifetimes, almost, had Merrigan dwelled more among trees than among people, though the trees were quick to remind em how young e was. Eir father must be dead now, e knew that; and whether he had had more children, whether Merrigan had any human family left in the village at the forest's edge, e did not know.

"Yes, I have always lived in the forest," Merrigan said.

"Are you . . . ? Can you . . . ?"

Aurelia seemed to struggle with her question, but Merrigan perceived what she wished to ask and pondered how to show it to her while she sought the words. E noticed the fraying sleeves of her kirtle; so, silently, e reached out and touched the wool with one finger. Aurelia watched the motion, and then, with widening eyes, saw the wool reconstitute itself, at her wrists and, when she looked, at her hem as well. And so her question was answered; yes, Merrigan could do magic. The woman smiled.

She was curious, but not prying, and they spoke of other things while they waited for the grains to plump up and become tender. Aurelia rose occasionally to add more water from a second pot, warming in the embers, while she told Merrigan of all the villages she visited collecting barley and wheat and rye for the miller. She told Merrigan how her younger siblings spent their days separating the bran from the rest of the wheat, so that they could make fine white bread delivered specially to the wealthy houses, how they had their own special mill to make that flour because they were the only ones who would bake such bread; it took too long and involved too much effort for the other bakers and millers. Merrigan was surprised how much e enjoyed hearing all of this, how things had changed. E did not tell Aurelia that there had been no bakers or millers when e was a child, but a shared mill if the village was lucky, where they pooled their grain and took turns at the millstone, and allotted the flour to each house, which made its own bread.

When the pottage was done, Aurelia mixed goat milk into it and drizzled it with honey, over which she cooed with pleasure, and they ate the fine breakfast in contented silence.

Finally, Merrigan called for the billy goat, which trotted in carrying a cutting of the silver-leafed tree in its mouth. This it delivered to Merrigan, who held it up before an awestruck Aurelia.

"We grant you this cutting on two conditions," Merrigan said. "First, remember that it was not your love for the princess that let you come near this place; it was your kindness to those in need."

Aurelia nodded vigorously. "I understand. Love itself is not a virtue; it is not the same as goodness."

"Yes," Merrigan agreed. "Second, if the princess likes your gift and chooses you for her spouse, you must promise that during your reign the old sumptuary laws will be repealed, and that each subject of your realm will be allowed to dress in the manner that befits them."

At this, Aurelia narrowed her eyes, perhaps in surprise that such a thing would matter to an enchanter deep in the forest, but she nodded again and said, "I promise."

But Merrigan was not so trusting as e had been with the prince. E said, "If you fail to keep your promise, the tree that grows from this cutting will die, and with it all the bounty of your land. Do you understand?"

Finally, Aurelia felt a tinge of the fear she had seen in the others who spoke of the enchanted mountain, the wariness of magic that other people seemed to have, and she realized that Merrigan's magic could do more than mend fabric. But she saw no reason why it was not reasonable to fulfill the Enchanter's request. So she nodded a third time, and said, "I do."

She took the cutting, bid farewell to Merrigan, and the billy goat led her out of the forest.

THE PALACE GUARDS TRIED to prevent Aurelia from presenting her gift, but the princess heard of it and ordered that she be allowed through. When she saw the baker's daughter, she felt her heart quicken unexpectedly, and when she was given the cutting, she knew it was the most perfect gift, from someone who, though they had never met before, saw her for who she truly was. The princess kissed Aurelia, and they were shortly married. During their ceremony, they planted the cutting in the princess's garden together.

That night, while they lay in bed together, Aurelia told the princess the story of how she came to possess the cutting, and of the promise she had made to the Enchanter. The princess agreed that it was a reasonable promise, and that when they were queens, they would keep it.

At length, first one king and then the other died, and Aurelia and the princess were crowned and anointed rulers of the realm. They did not forget their promise, and so they spoke to their barons about the sumptuary laws. These barons, the sons of the sons of the prince's barons, had grown accustomed to showing their wealth in other ways than through clothing, ways that were inaccessible at that time to even the wealthiest merchants, so they were persuaded to agree with their queens, and the laws were repealed.

Aurelia had the writ copied and sent to the forest, along with two sacks of grain. The villagers at the forest's edge knew not where to deliver it, even if they were willing to go deep into the woods, so they left it in the meadow. Merrigan collected it emself, and bore it back to the labyrinth. E had never learned to read, but with a little magic, the scroll was legible to em; and when e read it, e wept with joy.

18

THE SORCERER

MERRIGAN CHOSE EIR CLOTHING carefully. What e had bore little resemblance to that with which e had fled into the forest, for e had grown, and it was more than one hundred years old, longer than even such sturdy clothing could naturally hope to last. E had kept it fit by supernatural means, with eir magic and with the help of eir fairy cousins. Through such means had e changed the items to suit eir desires; skirts split and turned into trousers, tunics slimmed and shaped, embroidery added and removed. E loved each piece of clothing, those modified from eir human garb and those of fairy make, the robes that smelled of all the forest all at once.

But what to wear to the village?

E had waited several years since Aurelia's writ, knowing that it was unlikely for people to change their behavior all at once. Now, though, e hoped to meet with others who had been freed by the repeal of the sumptuary laws; but how could e show them that e was one of them? E settled on a knee-length tunic, over which e wore a long surcoat and breeches with hose and tall leather shoes. It being summer, e needed no cloak, but e covered eir hair partially with a length of fairy fabric, shimmering pure white in the sunshine.

Thus garbed, Merrigan set off for Iarom.

IF NOT FOR THE river, e would not have recognized the village of eir youth. It had tripled in size, which was more than e had expected, though e of course knew it had grown a little. Yet everything about the village seemed larger. The people were taller, even the children; the buildings had walls that were as tall as Merrigan, unlike the low stone and high peaked thatch of eir youth. Oh, the roofs were still thatch and the walls still partially stone, but by looking at them, a grown person could walk from one wall to another without having to duck their head. This was made possible by the wood the people cut from eir forest: they removed the roof, built the wall higher with a wooden frame on which they daubed a kind of earth, dung, and straw plaster. Merrigan had grown quite used to high walls, but still e had not envisioned this, and e almost laughed at emself.

But e had not long to admire the village, for e was soon spotted, and a cry went out. Soon adults and children alike were standing outside their homes, gathering loosely in a central space too fluid to be called a town square. They watched Merrigan walk into the town, from the direction of the forest; that, and eir strange bright cloth and unusual garb, gave them to know who e was: the Enchanter.

Merrigan heard this name whispered around em and wondered at it, but said nothing. If tales of eir home as the enchanted mountain in the enchanted forest were entrenched enough that a baker's daughter might quest to find them, e doubted that any word of eirs could correct the misapprehension. Instead, e smiled at the people, to show them e meant no harm, while eir eyes danced over them and their clothing. The children were all garbed in long, baggy tunics, but that was the same as when Merrigan had been young; they would wear that tunic until it no longer fit, over breeches or a kirtle once they were old enough. Beyond that,

Merrigan saw no one whose dress might be called ambiguous; their garb was as Aurelia's had been ten years ago, each part recognizable to Merrigan even if the skill and style of its construction was improved, and each part of a distinct set worn by distinct genders.

E comforted emself that perhaps there were some who did not want to mix and match as e did, and wholly took on a new mode of dress; or perhaps there were simply none here who felt as e did. It was still a small village.

Merrigan stopped eir progress in what seemed like the center of the crowd, and looked around for anyone with eir father's features, but saw none clear enough to be sure. While e looked, a village elder came forward, on the assistance of both a cane and the arm of a young person, who, when they reached Merrigan, set down a stool upon which the elder sat. Merrigan looked at the ground beneath em and asked it to rise a little, forming a small mound where e could sit level with the elder; the villagers gasped while e settled emself upon it.

"Good Enchanter of the forest," said the elder, who wore a coat and hood despite the warmth of the sun. "What service can we be to you?"

Merrigan was surprised to be so greeted, but e smiled, and said, "There was a man here, some two or three generations ago; Abboid was his name. If any remember him, I wish to know if he has any family yet living, in Iarom or elsewhere."

The elder nodded. "I have heard of this man. He died some twenty years before I was born, but his wife remarried, and their descendants live yet in the house closest to the forest." He raised a gnarled hand, and two beige-skinned youths approached, both wearing the kirtles, surcoats, and veils of womanhood. One of them was pristine in her appearance, clothing so clean Merrigan wondered if magic had been used; the other had a leather apron over her clothes, and carried ashy leather gloves in her hand. Her face was ruddy and streaked with sweat, but she smiled.

"I am Branwen," she said. "And this is my sister Gabin. What interest have you in our family?"

Merrigan stood and offered them each eir hand. Branwen took it immediately, Gabin with greater caution but with interest bright in her eyes.

"Abboid, your ancestor, was my father; he got me on a fairy of the forest, and I was raised among the people of Iarom at the beginning of my life," Merrigan said. "Maud, your ancestor, was his wife, my stepmother. Therefore, though we do not share blood, I will make free to consider you my kin, and help you in any way I can, should you ever have need."

"Then let us make you welcome, cousin Enchanter!" Branwen said.

E smiled. "My name is Merrigan."

IN GRATITUDE TO THE village, Merrigan asked them if there were any small favors e might do for them, as e had used to do. E made repairs to walls, daub and stone alike, and encouraged thatch to be waterproof, and be rid of pests. E located several lost items and importuned the old millstone—the same one from eir youth—to remain whole, and continue to serve the needs of the village. The village elder asked for nothing, but Merrigan asked him if he was in pain from his age; and because he was an honest man, he said yes. So Merrigan, with his blessing, touched his fine wooden cane so that when he laid his hand on it, it would lessen the aches in his joints. The cane was happy to do this for him, because he had carved it himself when he was young, and spent most evenings polishing it.

This led a woman, who had been quiet during all the other requesting, to ask Merrigan for a more than small favor. She led em to her house, and as soon as e entered, e knew what it was she sought, for it smelled of bile and sweat. Alone in the large bed was a small child, brown skin ashy with sickness.

Merrigan had healed animals in the forest before, though more often from injury or from eating the wrong thing than from a sickness like the one e saw in the child. Still, e thought that the way to go about it would be much the same. So e laid eir hand on the child's brow, and closed eir eyes, and looked inside them. E looked for the place of disturbance, the place where things were not as they should be, and found it in the child's gut. Some infinitesimally small creature had got inside, multiplied and made its new home not in the food that had borne it in but in the dark wet warmth of the human body.

Exerting eir power, Merrigan exhorted the tiny creatures to leave, to gather together and to pass entirely out of the child, to seek some other place to thrive. It took time, far longer than it felt to em, while the family and Branwen and Gabin and some other villagers looked on, crowded into the cottage. But while they watched, the child's face smoothed, and the perspiration on their brow did not return when it was dabbed away, for though it would take time for the creatures to leave, Merrigan had done what e could to ease the symptoms of their presence.

At last, e stood, and the mother fell upon her child, who slept peacefully; she wept and blessed Merrigan unceasingly.

Merrigan felt an odd tightness in eir chest, and an uncomfortable flush of heat in eir neck. E left the cottage and walked away from the people, who in fact were giving em an awed berth. Only Gabin followed.

"Cousin Merrigan," she said. "How is it that you can do these things? Your fairy blood? But surely you cannot be as strong as a pureblood fairy."

"Cousin Gabin," e said, giving her a small smile, weariness finally settling on em. "To be honest, I do not know how strong I am. I have never tested the limits of my power. I am sure it does come from my mother's blood, though."

"But how is it you use it?" Gabin asked.

Merrigan sighed. "I have not really considered the how. I . . . simply look at some thing or some creature as deeply as I can, as deeply as I need to. Repairing objects, finding things, this does not require much depth. Healing, or asking for a favor, for these I must go deeper. I must see, and hear, the . . . inner layers of its life."

"Well," Gabin said, smiling, "there is no doubt that however you wield it, you have true power. Do you think—do you think humans can ever do what you do?"

Merrigan looked up, thoughtfully. "I do not know. I suppose anyone could learn to look as I do; but I do not know."

"It seems so effortless to you," Gabin said.

"It is," Merrigan agreed. Gabin made a small sound of surprise, and Merrigan chuckled. "Perhaps you did not expect me to say so. But as I said, I have not tested my limits. I am sure that someday, there will be something that costs me greatly to do, or that I cannot do at all."

"Let us hope it is worth the effort, or that, if you cannot do it, no harm comes of its being undone," Gabin said.

"Hear, hear," Merrigan replied. E reached for Gabin's hand, and this time, she was quick to take it. "I am weary, perhaps from my journey, perhaps from all this magic. Good cousin, tell them I will return soon, to see after the child."

Gabin nodded. "I will deliver your message."

Two weeks later, when Merrigan did return, e found the child wholly recovered, awake, laughing, their skin full of colors that spoke of health and life. The family could not contain their joy, and they tried to shower Merrigan with such gifts as those of their station could provide; e refused most of these, accepting only a loaf of bread. But there were gifts to be had from more than just that family; for the villagers of Iarom had told tales, in the market to the south, of Merrigan and eir favors, and there were people come to Iarom in search of em. Some of them brought with them that which they asked Merrigan to repair, or bless, or heal; others requested help for things that could not be moved, and they begged Merrigan to come to their villages to provide magic.

Merrigan had never gone south; so e agreed. E traveled to the next village, and then the next. And every time e went home again, and then traveled out to visit those e had helped, and check on the progress of those e had healed, or reexamine some thing e had repaired, there were more people from farther south, more requests. And so Merrigan kept traveling, and helping. E became known enough that strangers knew that e was neither man nor woman, and that e used a different set of words to describe emself. And soon, as the years went on, Merrigan met others like em, who asked for clothing that fitted neither man nor woman; or who had made their own such clothing, and asked for some way, some aura, to make others immediately aware of their gender.

And Merrigan met too those people for whom a change of clothing was not enough, who wished their body to be altered in some way. These people, Merrigan stayed with for weeks at a time, puzzling out the process of making such changes. This was the first test of Merrigan's limits, for e had never had to look so deep before, or make so great a shift. It was an easy thing to convince a tree to grow in a slightly different direction, or to pause growing while some other problem was resolved. But the human body was complex, and eir magic needed time to learn it as thoroughly as e had learned the trees. Merrigan did what e could for these people, another kind of kin to em, and always came to see them when e traveled, every time improving their situation, and becoming friends.

In these years, Gabin moved away from Iarom, to the city of Varrun. Merrigan visited her there whenever e passed through, and she told em of others she had met who wished to know the mechanics of magic, as she did. She and Merrigan talked long about these philosophies, until she moved farther south still, to a place Merrigan had not yet gone.

Branwen stayed in Iarom, where she was the sole black-smith; before long, the cottage whose foundations had been laid by Merrigan's father was home not only to her, but to her lovers, Callum the farmer and Tavish the herdsman. Together they built a fine and prosperous life, for themselves and for Iarom; but the years of their marriage wore on, and still Branwen did not conceive a child, something all three of them dearly wanted. The three of them held each other and wept, and began to fear that they would never have the family they wished for.

When Merrigan returned to Iarom from the south, e stayed

with eir cousin and her family, and listened to their troubles. "Can you help us, cousin?" Branwen asked.

Merrigan took her hands, and then Callum's, and then Tavish's, looking inside them; and e was astonished to see *Gabin* inside each of them, an inexplicable shadow over their generative resources. E opened eir eyes from this deeper exploration and looked to Branwen.

"I will do everything I can for you," e said.

E went south the next day, and not by cart, as e had been accustomed. E flew, past Vicus, past Varrun, farther south than e had ever gone before, until e reached a fortress by the sea and the tower where e felt Gabin would be found. Merrigan strode into the tower and found Gabin there at a long table with others, all of them wearing emerald-green robes that shimmered, but in a poor mimicry of eir own fairy garments. Gabin stood, eyes wide for a moment before she schooled her expression.

"Cousin, welcome," she said.

"We must speak alone," Merrigan replied.

She sighed, but nodded, and her colleagues emptied the room. When they had gone, she said, "You found it, then."

"How did you do it?"

"By studying that which you intuit," Gabin said. "I cannot converse with the materials of the world, as you do, but there is a kind of power in mirroring them; what was only a theory in my time at Varrun has now been proven. By creating a charm out of things that are symbolic of my target, I can put spells on it. In this case, a sheep's womb, dried over a fire where I burned raven feathers, dove feathers, and a branch grown in exact symmetry."

"You use your observations of my magic, the discussions we have had, and this is what you produce?" Merrigan scowled. "You have learned nothing from me."

Gabin glared back at em. "You *learned* nothing! I do not begrudge you that with which you were born, but you have no right to scold me for experimenting to increase my knowledge of and skill with something that has been as natural to you as breathing. I have worked for every scrap of magic I have."

Merrigan sighed then, seeing her point; but still, eir heart ached. "But why your own sister?"

"Blood strengthens all magic," Gabin said, after a long pause. "Using it on someone with whom I share blood increased the likelihood of its success."

"Well, it has been successful. Now you must undo it," Merrigan said. "Your sister and your brothers-in-law suffer."

Something tightened in Gabin's jaw, and she said, "I cannot."

"You must."

Gabin slapped the table. "I *cannot*. I have tried; as soon as I was sure it had succeeded, I tried. But nothing has worked. I destroyed the original charm. I made a new one, one to bolster their fertility. But still these tear-stained letters come to me—and now you, so I know there is truly nothing to be done, if you could not remove it."

"I have not yet attempted it," Merrigan said.

"What?" Gabin blinked. "Why did you come all the way down here, then?"

"Because it is easier to remove magic than to counter it with new," Merrigan said. "At least, in the way I know of these things. And the one for whom it is easiest to remove magic is the one who cast it."

Gabin nodded. "Yes, that makes sense. But . . . I tried, Merri. I swear on my life, I tried."

Silence rang in the hall between them, until at last, Merrigan said, "Then let this episode be a lesson to you."

"Be hesitant to destroy something, because destruction is not always reversible," Gabin whispered.

"Just so," Merrigan said. "I will endeavor to rectify your disaster, and I will not tell Branwen what you have done. You should do that. But know that if I ever learn of you producing such magic as this again, all ties of kinship between us will be broken."

With a mirthless smile, Gabin answered, "Just so."

19

SEEDS FOR A SEED

THE LABYRINTH HAD CREEKS, and small pools, but what it did not have was a waterfall. For that, Merrigan traveled to the northernmost end of the forest. There the woods converged with the long death of a mountain range, and the major river of the land broke the edge of the wilderness on its southern journey.

The waterfall was not grand; the river was still tentative, a shadow of what it would become. Merrigan considered them similar in that way, emself and the fall. An odd thing to say when one had lived three human lifetimes; but e had spent much of that time first marveling at, then contemplating eir new position in the world. Only in the recent decades had e ventured once more beyond the edge of the forest.

E put eir hand in the fall, closed eir eyes, and sent eir magic downriver. In this way, e could see all the river saw, all the villages and fields, all the creatures come to eir banks to suck life from em, like infants, like vampires. But e was grown wide and deep and swift, strong enough to kill, unstoppable until e joined the green sea.

With a shudder, e withdrew eir hand and took eir usual place on a tall boulder, facing the fall, overlooking the pool that collected before the water went on its way. The rocks before em were wet and black, dotted with green moss. The water looked white where it caught the sun and flashed, but it turned brown at its base, thick with silt. Cranes patrolled the edges of the pool; a snake sunned itself on a smaller rock beside eirs. Predators, all, but if the fall were a little stronger, it would be dangerous to them; the same could be said of so many things. E hugged eir knees into eir chest and tried to light on a new direction for eir thoughts.

How to help Branwen?

This was no small repair; like eir efforts with eir gender kin, this required deep understanding of the human flesh, and of the magic Gabin had so foolishly used. Merrigan's knowledge of the body had greatly increased over the years, such that e was now beginning to manipulate its shape and processes—but that was not the issue for Branwen. Branwen's misery was of a natural process artificially interrupted by violence. Merrigan struggled not to be continuously angry with Gabin—e had done eir share of interrupting the process of generation, but eir method involved singing the person's reproductive cells to sleep, convincing them not to emerge and seek to grow. Altogether less painful, and easily undone. Gabin could not do that, perhaps would never be able to. E could not be angry at her for this.

Yet e could be angry at her, because she had not been trying to help a person who desired to put off having children. She had, in her own words, experimented, using her sister's womb as a target because, with blood and this concept of mirroring, it had the highest chance of proving her theory. This was cruel, and this deserved anger. Merrigan hoped only that Gabin had indeed learned the lesson in it.

Merrigan went back to Branwen's home, and took her hands, and Callum's, and Tavish's again. There the shadow still lay within each of them, darkest within Branwen; but beneath it, all seemed well, if dormant. So Merrigan had an idea, and told

Callum to come to the waterfall in four days, and e would have a solution for them.

E returned to the fall and began to craft this solution: a seed, for a new kind of tree. Merrigan brought all eir knowledge of trees and humans to bear, and coiled a purpose into the seed. The tree that grew from it would send its roots to the nearest house, and it would resonate with those who lived in it; its branches would sing when the wind blew through them, songs of health and happiness that would invigorate the flesh. This would waken Branwen's womb, if it had survived Gabin's spell, but to deal with the internal shadow, fed by their dashed hopes, something else was needed.

Callum arrived, tall and pale, and found Merrigan seated on eir rock by the falls. His footfalls frightened the snake off its rock and into the shadows of the underbrush. "Cousin, I have come as you asked," he said. "Please tell me you have good news for me to take home."

Merrigan rose, descended the rock, and stood before him, smiling. E held out eir hand; in eir palm rested a large seed. "Plant this near your home. Every day for one hundred days, you and your family must visit the tree that grows and offer a promise to your future child. If you do this, and if every promise is sincerely and lovingly offered, your family will conceive."

Callum took the seed, holding it like a precious thing, and tucked it carefully into the pouch hanging from his belt. Then he threw his arms around Merrigan and embraced em. "Thank you so, so much, my dear cousin," he said; Merrigan could hear the tears in his voice.

Slowly, carefully, Merrigan put eir hand on his back, applying a slight pressure, and in this way returned his embrace. "You are welcome."

He left, eager to get back to Branwen and Tavish, and Merrigan resumed eir place upon the boulder. E listened to Callum leave, the crackling and snapping of his footsteps audible for quite a distance before the unquiet silence of the forest reasserted itself. E did not know how long it was before the snake returned to its place as well; but eventually it did, curling on the warm rock. E smiled down at it, then stared into the waterfall.

MERRIGAN MADE MANY VISITS to Branwen's house over the hundred days, and indeed, e arrived there on the hundredth day, and as e approached the door e saw that the tree had sprouted its flowers. Branwen appeared then, opening the door before e had even got close enough to knock. Her face glowed, and though she wore no veil she ran toward em and said, "Merri, I felt it! I felt it quicken in me!"

She reached for Merrigan's hand, and e gave it; and then she placed it on her abdomen, not noticing Merrigan's rueful smile. It would have been too soon yet for anyone but Branwen to feel the life inside her—anyone except Merrigan, who looked with eir magic, and saw indeed that a seed of a different sort was growing in eir cousin. E told her so, and she wept and kissed eir cheeks, and brought em inside to celebrate.

It became clear that Gabin had never confessed what she'd done, and doubtless never would. Merrigan wondered whether it was now eir responsibility to disclose it, but e could not muster emself to disturb the joy in that house. Someday, perhaps; but not now, not when the shadow had at last been lifted. Eir seed had worked. The tree had woken the bodies of Branwen, Callum, and Tavish, after the trauma of Gabin's spell, and the act of promising to care for the future child, of imagining the life they wished to give them, had helped to lift the shadow. Merrigan was well pleased with this work.

As the sun set, while Branwen dozed and Callum stoked the fire, Tavish went to get something from a cupboard and approached Merrigan shyly. "Good cousin, as a thank you, we would like to give you a gift: seeds for a seed," he said. "My mother's roses, which are the most beautiful in the world."

Merrigan accepted the seeds, and left the three of them to rest and bask together in their shared joy.

While e walked the long dark path back to the labyrinth, e wondered about the so-called guild of sorcerers that Gabin had joined away to the south. It seemed natural to em that humans make use of whatever magic they possessed, just as e did, just as the fairies did, just as all creatures did. But while e knew that there was kindness in humans, e knew that there was fear and viciousness too. E had often been asked both to inflict pain and to alleviate that which had been inflicted; and sometimes, e had dispensed a kind of justice, when that of the dukes failed or when the one in need of justice feared to make use of the formal systems in place. Merrigan knew that such systems were fraught with their own troubles—the sumptuary laws that had plagued em long ago had not been the only unjust statutes in the realm. E used eir judgment, not only of what was right or wrong, but what was good or bad to get involved in, what would end with eir involvement and what would cascade into a series of unreliable consequences.

Would the humans be so circumspect? Gabin certainly had not been, but she was still young, even by human reckoning, having not yet seen three decades of life. Part of Merrigan thought that e should return to the tower, to offer guidance, but eir guidance had not prevented the affair with the sheep's womb; how could e be sure these sorcerers would not take eir words, eir knowledge, in directions e could not foresee? E wished that e could go and observe them for a long, long time, as e had done with the forest. This was not possible, though. Even if e could hide emself among them, could e watch what they did without acting to stop them, if they did wrong? Perhaps before, e could have. But Merrigan had been now some fifteen years among the humans, and grown fond of them, and did not think e could hear of someone willfully hurting them and do nothing.

E sighed, and tried to put the sorcerers from eir mind. E would simply listen for news of them, try to keep an eye on them from afar.

It was a small comfort that eir reputation was so well-established in the northern towns that no one there thought of a sorcerer, for the most part. They knew Merrigan would come to them, and if it was urgent, knew where e could be found, for eir travels began to coincide with the seasons and followed the same route every year.

It was full dark when Merrigan returned to the labyrinth, but the moon and stars were bright above em and the light reflecting from the silver leaves of the upper forest cast the whole clearing in a white glow. E stood at the edge of the path, staring across the clearing at the great walls of stone; and then e cast the rose seeds before em, into that space.

A year and a day from the moment e scattered them in the earth, the seeds erupted into fully grown bushes, sporting deep red blooms as large as eir head. E sat in the path between them, shaded by the height of them; e could not say how many hours passed thus, while e worried a fallen petal to wilt between eir fingers.

20
TIME

TIME PASSED, AS TIME will.

21
FREDERICK

FREDERICK WAS A CHILD when he crossed Merrigan's path the first time, stumbling out of the bushes at the side of the forest trail in pursuit of a little fox kit. He tripped over his shoes, hand-me-downs from an older child in the family or the village. They were still too large for Frederick's feet, and their sliding caused the child to fall right in front of Merrigan.

The fox kit escaped. Frederick stared after it in silence, the afternoon air turning almost muggy with his disappointment.

It had been some two hundred years, at this time, since Merrigan's exile, and e had spent more than half of that in eir role as enchanter to the northern towns. E had observed generations of children in Frederick's village, healing them, occasionally amusing them; e had never in that century seen a child take a fall so well. E knelt beside him and ducked eir head to get a look at his face under his curtain of dark gold curls. Eir movement roused his attention, and he lifted his gaze to meet eirs.

"Well met," Merrigan said.

"Well met," he replied, voice small, as though he was still

dazed. He blinked several times, and then his brown eyes filled with light. E had been recognized. "You're the Enchanter!"

"My name is Merrigan," e said.

"I'm Frederick."

"Why were you chasing the fox?" e asked.

"He bit my sister and wouldn't apologize," he replied.

E laughed. "I think he's too little to have learned manners yet."

Frederick frowned at em. "*I* am not too little, and he is the same as me."

E tilted eir head, but made no answer while e considered the declaration. Children were fanciful, e knew this. Frederick's earnestness was endearing; he couldn't have been older than five years, and undoubtedly he believed infant foxes were the same as infant humans. While e considered him, Frederick rocked onto his bottom, stretching his legs out in front of him. His knees were bloodied, with pieces of grass stuck to them. Myriad scratches covered his shins, from the attempt to follow the kit's trail. Frederick observed his injuries, frowning deeper, then looked to Merrigan.

"Will you heal them? The cuts?" he asked.

"What will you give in return?"

"I don't have anything to give," the child said.

"Ponder a moment. I'm sure you have something."

Ponder he did. He gave Merrigan a stern nod, then set to thinking. He seemed still oblivious to eir scrutiny, for though e stared baldly, he never met eir gaze, not even as his head fell back, searching the sky for something to offer in return for eir magic. Birdsong filled the air; e tried to remember what season it was. Spring, or summer? Eir ministrations to the village helped to ground eir sense of time, but when alone e often found emself slipping. On such an afternoon, mild and sunny, while the forest sounds muddled into a pleasant hum—it was easy to lose oneself, and e had no greater joy. Not anymore.

Frederick sat up—he had lain flat out while Merrigan dozed—and exclaimed, "I'll give you my favorite book!"

"A book?"

The child nodded, grinning, obviously proud he had come up with something. Merrigan extended eir hand; Frederick shook it, and the deal was made. E turned eir attention to his wounds. They were superficial but must surely have stung and throbbed. In the early days of eir magic, Merrigan would have happily healed such scrapes at no obligation—but e had learned that favors had a tenuous and easily corrupted definition, which humans were particularly adept at manipulating. Or perhaps they were no better at it than any other being, but e had been caught off-guard by their expectation. Fairies, for example, were well-known exploiters of favors, and so one was always prepared to be suspicious of exchanges with them. Humans were harder to learn; their numbers overwhelmed all other beings with whom e had had contact, and though they were of one culture, the mood and practices varied so from settlement to settlement, even year to year. But e did eventually learn to ask for something in return for any magic, for any person. For most works, e offered no suggestion of payment, for e needed little, and e was fascinated by what was offered by different people, for equivalent and for disparate magic.

E held eir hands above Frederick's legs and coaxed the debris out, encouraged the skin to close up. It was the work of moments, and soon the child was dashing ahead down the path, imploring em to follow him down to the village for payment. He kept to the greenway this time, with no diversions into the dense scrub. Given that he ran forward and was constantly obliged to wait until Merrigan reached him at eir own steady pace, e attributed this responsibility to an eagerness to fulfill their bargain, rather than any circumspection on the choices leading to the exchange.

Before long they had left the trees and had only to cross the wide meadow between the tree line and the village. The meadow reminded Merrigan at last that it was spring, for the grasses were bright and new, the flowers sparse and just spreading their petals. Out in the open, a chill breeze ruled the air; it ruffled eir robes.

Frederick barreled down the gentle slope to the village; the ring of small cabins that had once been Merrigan's home, which e had watched grow for decades. The old millstone, finally broken, had been replaced by one which Merrigan had asked to roll down from the mountains, and shaped as it made its slow and careful way down through the trees. The largest houses had replaced their thatch with wooden shingles, and now had second floors, and fireplaces in the walls instead of central hearths.

The cabin where Frederick's family lived was empty when they reached it, save for a young hen rooting through the grass that had escaped the bounds of the mattress at the back of the room. It ignored Frederick while he reached into a small basket and extracted an item. Thus equipped, Frederick gestured Merrigan outside once again. They sat against the cabin wall, in the sunshine, and he presented em with the book.

It was fragile, pages made from leaves that had been apparently pasted into sheets with sap. These pages had been carefully sewn together with a bit of twine. As for the content of the book, there were no words; the narrative was conveyed with faint, shaky drawings in a purplish ink, clumpy in places. The child had crushed berries for it, undoubtedly.

Merrigan had learned to read without the aid of magic, during eir travels and eir visits to scriptoriums in the remote places of the north. That had been the only place to read anything at all, other than royal edicts, for a very long time, though in some of the larger cities there were now libraries that anyone with coin could access. With this in mind, Merrigan had wondered what sort of book the child could possibly offer em; e had been pondering the ways he might have been exposed to books or come to have one in his family's possession. As to the latter, he had obviously made the book himself, a rather marvelous surprise. E imagined him sitting in the forest, painstakingly collected materials strewn about him. He must have worked at it for hours, days even. Merrigan's heart swelled with admiration; e found emself unable to look at him, silent and patient beside em, for fear e would burst into inexplicable tears.

The drawings answered eir first question, for they were clearly the story of the first time Frederick saw a book. E recognized an adult figure wearing plain robes, with a ring of hair just above their ears. Monks had visited the village, bearing one of their illustrated histories. Frederick must have gotten a decent look at it and been inspired. Gently, Merrigan shut the little book and held it lightly in eir hands. It was a more wonderful price than e should have wanted him to pay for such small magic as e had done for him; e wanted to say e couldn't accept such a precious thing. E turned to Frederick with these words on eir lips—but e saw his pride in his flushed cheeks and bright eyes, and e swallowed eir rejection.

"Thank you, Frederick. I vow to treasure it forever," e told him.

"Good!" He stood up. "I must help my sister now."

Merrigan got to eir feet, careful of the little book in eir hand. When e lifted eir head, e saw that Frederick had not left.

"You will come for the planting?" he asked.

Merrigan smiled. "Yes, I will come."

MERRIGAN'S GREEN ROBES WERE quite out of place in the landscape of reds and golds as e made eir way home again at the end of harvest-time. To occupy emself as e walked the long, dusty path, e contemplated little spells e could cast on the fabric. E could make it change color as the leaves did; e laughed to emself and wondered whether the fabric should not shrivel up and die come winter, and leave em bared as the tree branches were. Such might be the cost of trivial magic. But e was not very invested in the contemplations from the start, for e did not mind the juxtaposition of symbolism. E was recognized in green, in the fairy robes e wore, and it was the color of spring. With winter approaching, the people of the land were always happy for a reminder of spring. They smiled at the green, and both it and Merrigan were always welcomed.

The last village before the forest came into view upon the horizon, and with it Merrigan saw a youth, seated at the side of the road not far before em. A long staff stretched into the path, such that e felt lucky to have seen it, otherwise e should have tripped over it. As e neared, e saw that the youth was Frederick, who had grown much in the ten years since they'd met. He almost looked like an adult: gold hair cropped short for the harvest, arms and legs muscled with the labor, tawny skin further darkened with the sun. He was bent over the top of the offending staff with what smelled like an oiled rag.

Merrigan paused near him, but so focused on his work was he that he took no notice of em until e said, "Well met, carver."

He looked up and smiled. "Hello, Merrigan! I thought you might be back today."

"And you predicted right," e replied. "It is lucky for you that I'm not too weary from my travels to watch my path."

He frowned a moment, then looked down the staff and laughed sheepishly. Using the staff, he stood; then he gave the shining brown wood a final buff with his rag, and held it out. "I made this for you."

Merrigan smiled and felt eir heart lift. E *was* weary, with walking and with work, but Frederick's kindness reinvigorated em. Slinging eir bag over eir shoulder, e took the staff into eir own hands. It was very well crafted indeed, straight and tall, smooth to the touch with sanding and conditioning. The base was capped with a little round of iron, which weighted and protected it. But the top, which had so consumed Frederick's attention to the last moment—the top took eir breath away, for it was carved, exquisitely, in the shape of a proud fox's head.

He saw em staring at it, and said, "For the first time we met. I was chasing a fox, remember?"

A fox—eir mother? Her foxes had never left Merrigan; they were eir most constant companions in the labyrinth, though she herself had been long absent. Though Frederick could not realize the true significance of the symbol he'd carved for em, e was nonetheless grateful, and moved, and widened eir smile as e set down the base of the staff and leaned upon it. Eir weight settled into this new arrangement immediately, so well-fitted was the staff to eir hand and eir body.

"Thank you, Frederick. It is magnificent," e said. "What shall I give you in return?"

"Your continued friendship," he said, grinning.

Merrigan laughed. "Freely and gladly. I do have a gift for you, though. For your birthday." E opened eir bag and pulled from it a large block of a dark brown hardwood, its grain streaked with black, which e handed to a gaping Frederick. "It comes from far to the south; I received it in trade from a merchant in Varrun."

"Then I cannot take it, it is your fee!" Frederick said.

"I asked for it for you. What should I do with it?" Merrigan said, laughing again. "Make something for me from it, if you like, but it is yours."

"It is beautiful," he murmured, distracted from his protests by the fine, oily smoothness of the wood. At last he looked up and said, "Thank you."

Merrigan smiled. "Shall we on to home now?"

"Yes, of course," he said. They took two steps on the road, and then he stopped and said, "You must say the staff was a gift from someone else."

Merrigan paused with him and cradled the staff against eir shoulder—already such a natural motion—as e considered the sudden dark cast to his expression. "Of course, if you need me to."

Frederick looked down the road to the village, his brow furrowed; he sighed. "They tease me . . . about you. Since I was little. They say that I am sweet on you."

Merrigan sighed too. It was true that e and Frederick had developed a deeper bond than the one e had with any of the other villagers. Their mutual interests in nature and stories and artistry had given them much to talk about, or rather, much for em to relate to him from what e saw on eir travels. E had considered asking his parents if he might travel with em next year. But in all of this, e felt e had been remiss, and not taken notice of the consequences of eir singling him out, however unintentional.

"These jests give you discomfort," e said.

"Great discomfort," Frederick agreed quietly. "You are my

friend and mentor, and of course I love you. But why must they liken it to romance? Why is everyone permitted friendship but me?"

He paced, and his voice rose, strained with agitation; he punctuated the end of his sentence with a sound kick to a rock in the path, which sent it flying into the meadow. Merrigan stepped out of the dirt and into the dry grass, sitting down a little way from the road. Frederick followed, and Merrigan patted the grass beside em and said, "We may tarry awhile, I think."

His relief was obvious; he descended to the ground and not only sat but sprawled out on his back. His brow furrowed again, but he did not speak further, so Merrigan laid eir beautiful new staff across eir lap, closed eir eyes, and tilted eir face toward the sky. A breeze tickled eir skin and dropped a dry leaf into eir face. E brushed it aside, swallowing eir laugh, for there was no chuckle from Frederick. He had not taken note, which told em just how deep in his thoughts he was. E could imagine the struggles he had to tell em, but e cleared eir mind and waited, rather than indulging in speculation.

The sun was still warm, though on its downward journey. E shed eir outer robe, exposing eir arms and back that eir skin might soak up the light. These travels, for the planting and the harvest, were the only times during which e really experienced direct sunlight. Eir dark skin hungered for it, though, and while e sat there basking, e felt emself grow luminous with it.

"Merrigan . . . are there people in the world who cannot fall in love?" Frederick asked.

"Why yes, of course there are," e replied, opening eir eyes.

The youth bolted upright, staring at em, eyes wide with a certain kind of hunger. "But why? What's wrong with them?"

"Nothing at all."

"But are they all unhappy forever?"

E raised eir eyebrow at him, and Frederick sat back with another sigh. "I am sixteen now, and my parents say I should be thinking about starting my own family," he said. "The adults have always teased me about you, but now other youths in the village begin to. And not only about you; they jest about pairing me off with each other. They chase me and sing songs about marrying me. It is all they talk about this last year at least. But I do not want to marry anyone, not if marriage is what they describe."

"What is their description?" Merrigan asked.

Frederick scowled. "Love, and babies. It—it is so confusing, Merrigan, because they speak of partnerships based on loyalty and honesty and respect, of caring about another's happiness, of mutual support. These are all things I want, and things I hope I give to my friends. But they say that love is different, that it is *more*, yet they cannot tell me what this *more* is. It seems to me that love is all those things, with the desire to live together, and perhaps to raise children together, to be together almost constantly. Is that . . . am I understanding correctly?"

Merrigan's heart went out to this youth; he was in a difficult and confusing position indeed. "That is very commonly the form romantic love takes, yes."

Frederick ran his hands rapidly over his shorn hair, face twisting and eyes glistening with unshed tears. "I do not want that. I support my friends; I would do anything to help them! But if that is what romantic love is, then I do not feel that, not for any of them."

Tears began to fall, and he dashed them from his eyes. Soon there were too many to deny, and he hung his head and sobbed freely. He reached for Merrigan, who took his hand, matching the pressure of his grip. They sat in this manner until the sun lost its warmth and the air turned chill. When the sky was lavender with oncoming night, Frederick lifted his head and dried his face on his sleeve.

"No one believes me," he said. "They say that because I kissed Minerva, I must be in love with her. I am not—I am *not*. But my parents and I have argued about it, and they said that if I cannot fall in love with someone, I will be unhappy and broken forever, and always alone."

Merrigan covered their joined hands with eir free one, and

looked into his eyes. "They are wrong. There are others like you, and many of them live just as they wish, without romantic partners but with strong friendships, and they are very happy. There have always been those like you, and they are just as happy as any other kind of person."

His expression remained flat, the look of one who was weary from the effort of existing. Merrigan realized then that Frederick's pain over this was not as recent as he would have em believe. Undoubtedly the teasing, the planning, the pressure had worsened since his birthday and his passage from childhood into what short-lived humans considered adulthood. But e recognized his look and sympathized with the experience of spending much of one's life knowing that one is just outside a space that all others seem to inhabit. To grow up that way was to stand above a rose bush as it grew, becoming more and more trapped by its branches, pricked over and over again by the developing thorns, while one's fellows stood by admiring the blooms.

An orange glow flickered on the horizon. The night fires had been lit. Frederick looked toward them, and Merrigan's heart sank that all trace of his earlier joy had gone. Even as e felt gratitude to have been there and able to listen, dissatisfaction settled inside em like a bitter seed stuck in eir throat. The further e got from a standard human lifespan, from the scope of human existence, the less eir patience with them. Why must their first reaction always be to pull away from difference? Why did not their curiosity and ingenuity encompass their own lives, the feelings and experiences of themselves and their fellow humans, rather than just the tools they could produce or the feats they could accomplish? Was imagining the total satisfaction of friendship more difficult than imagining a castle made of stone? Was accepting an unfamiliar identity a greater challenge than improving one's farming methods for greater crop yields?

Two hundred years alive, and still e did not understand the human love of exclusion.

"Thank you for listening, Merrigan," Frederick said at last. "I confess that is part of why I waited here for you. I knew you would understand."

Merrigan tore three strips of eir outer robe and braided them. "I shall offer my ear whenever you have need of it, my friend." E held up the braid. "Wear this as a bracelet. When you need me, lay your hand upon it and call for me in your heart. I will hear, and I will come to you. Will you take it?"

"Yes! Oh, thank you." He extended his wrist. Merrigan circled it with the braid and touched the ends together. They glowed briefly, and when the light faded, the fabric was joined in one unbroken length. Frederick smiled at it, the first happy look in him for hours, and Merrigan smiled in return.

He stood and said, "Now we had better return to the village." He offered his hand to Merrigan, who grinned and shook eir head; e used eir new staff to push emself to stand. Frederick chuckled, weak and hesitant at first but strengthening before it fell off, and some worry sloughed itself from Merrigan's shoulders. They turned toward the firelight.

"Why have I never heard of other people who don't fall in love?" Frederick asked as they walked.

Merrigan shook eir head. "Even in my experience, it is not widely admitted. Many of them *have* married, because of pressure like that which you are under, or because they have found partners who are like them or accepting of them, and they want to build such a relationship. But most likely, it is because when *most* people are one way, they tend not to acknowledge those who are not also that way—and so the stories of those who are different do not spread easily."

Frederick nodded grimly, and Merrigan thought that might be the end of it; but at the edge of the village, he stopped suddenly and seized eir arm. "Merrigan, what shall I do? How can I resist these expectations when everyone around me tells me I must marry or there is something wrong with me?" he asked.

Though the light was dim, e saw tears welling in Frederick's eyes again. E opened eir arms, and he stepped into them, pressing his face against eir shoulder while e embraced him tightly. E held him and wished e could enchant the whole village, the whole world, so that this would not happen to Frederick or any other person. There was no magic for this. None without a devastating price.

"Do what your heart desires," e whispered to him.

22
GABIN'S APPRENTICE

WHILE FREDERICK UNBURDENED HIMSELF to Merrigan in the fields outside the village of Iarom, Gabin was in Varrun, interviewing apprentices, one of whom was a beautiful shepherd.

She reminded Gabin of herself in many ways, chiefly the glint of hunger in her eyes. She, too, wanted more than the quiet life in that little village, and magic seemed the best way of getting it. Luckily for her, she also had some aptitude for it. Gabin and her colleagues still could not come close to Merrigan's intuitive and deeply integral magic, but they had expanded their theories of mirroring and representative magic. They were so skilled that Gabin had even been able to tie her life-force to that of a long-lived tree, which was kept in a secure garden in the campus of the Sorcerer's Guild. This was now common practice among sorcerers; some chose trees, as she had, and others chose perennial plants, so that they might hibernate a brief period of every year and emerge in the prime of their life, for many many years. Gabin thought that method foolish. Why seek near immortality only to waste much of it sleeping?

The Iarom shepherd agreed; and so Gabin took her on.

THE SHEPHERD, BREDA, WAS already in love with Frederick by the time she met Gabin, but he was safe for two more years, while she tried to court him in more traditional ways. These he endured, without reciprocating, hoping that eventually, she would transfer her affections to someone who wanted them.

That did not happen.

At last, she asked him to marry her. He declined, and confessed to her that he was aromantic and did not feel romantic love the way she did. Though he swore he would always be her friend, she went away with angry tears on her cheeks, and Frederick grew wary. He went to the meadow at the forest's edge and used his bracelet, Merrigan's gift, to call for em. E came, and walked out of the forest without eir robes, in the breeches and skirted tunic e wore under them, an expression of worry on eir face.

"Frederick, what is it?" e asked.

"I . . . I am sorry, it may be nothing. But she has been a sorcerer's apprentice these two years, and she was so angry."

He explained what had happened, and Merrigan nodded grimly. E had been watching Gabin and her apprentice, and was also wary of the ruthlessness that seethed beneath their skins, waiting for its opportunity—and this was indeed an opportunity for a young, rejected love to wreak havoc.

"You are right to take precautions," Merrigan said. E stepped back inside the trees and chose a length of vine with a single leaf on it; this, in eir hands, became a braided cord with a wooden charm in the shape of that leaf. E put the cord around Frederick's neck. "This will protect your heart from any enchantment, and it will notify me if such is attempted, and I will come to aid you."

Frederick sighed with relief and embraced Merrigan tightly, and Merrigan returned the embrace fully, something e had learned to be comfortable with, if only with Frederick. But Frederick did not pull away after the usual time; instead, his body began to shake with sobs. His face was pressed against Merrigan's shoulder uncomfortably, for he was now taller than em and so his shoulders were like a vulture's in this posture. Yet he did not seem able to lift his head. So Merrigan guided him to sit, and they leaned together against an old tree at the forest's edge, the one that always welcomed Merrigan home from eir journeys to the south.

What could Merrigan say to comfort eir friend? Nothing had improved; e knew this. No, if anything, the pressure on him to feel as others felt had only increased, especially now that he was old enough for marriage, and, as a skilled tradesman, a desirable husband. That he was so good-hearted and handsome to look upon likewise only made him more sought-after in the way that caused him so much pain. Would that e could switch places with him; but Merrigan had long ago resigned emself to loneliness. Frederick's friendship was all the relief from that e needed—but what friendship could e offer in return? E could protect him from charms, but not from the constant erosion of the spirit caused by the village's expectations.

"I have to leave Iarom," Frederick said, calm at last.

"Frederick . . ."

"I know. I am sorry," he said. "I don't mean to say that this is the same as what happened to you."

"It is," Merrigan replied. "Is your exile less painful because they are not chasing you with swords? Blades come in many forms. I do not sigh because you are exaggerating your circumstances. I sigh because I know them well, and I am sorry for you, because I think you are right."

"I thought to ask you if I could go south with you next spring," Frederick said. "But now I am not sure I can wait."

"You should go now," Merrigan said. "Before the winter weather comes, while the roads are still dry."

E felt him nod against eir chest, then he sat up and looked at em, his young face drawn with sorrow. "I love you," he said. "You are the only person I can say that to, outside my family, without being misunderstood."

Merrigan touched his cheek, and smiled. "Go home now, and begin to pack. I will come to you tomorrow evening to help you plan."

But while they spoke, Gabin and her apprentice were likewise making plans, and that night, while Frederick slept, the sorcerer's apprentice used magic to sneak into his room and prick his finger. She gathered the blood into a vial.

FREDERICK WAS PACKING HIS bag when the sorcerer's apprentice came to his room carrying a loaf of bread wrapped in good linen.

"I wanted to apologize," she said, offering it to him. "I have been so selfish, but I hope—are you leaving?"

She had noticed the pack, his clothes, his bundle of carving tools and one or two little figurines he was yet finishing. Frederick, his heart racing, tried to smile at her and think of some way to explain that would not anger her. "I am," he said, "but only for a few weeks. Merrigan has found a commission for me; a lord of Varrun is building a fine new house, and many carvers are required. My master is too busy with her work here, but she thinks it is a good opportunity for me."

The sorcerer's apprentice nodded. She smiled at him. "Are you off immediately, or can we breakfast first?"

"There is time for breakfast," Frederick said, relieved. "I do not leave until tomorrow."

"Wonderful. Come, sit with me while I warm the bread."

So he joined her by the hearth, the new fireplace built into the wall with the chimney that channeled the smoke away into the sky. Frederick's grandfather, a stonemason, had built it. While the sorcerer's apprentice arranged the fire and set a tray above the embers, Frederick sat at the long trestle table continuing work on one of his figurines. He intended it to be a bear, but had absentmindedly trimmed too much from the middle, so he thought he might make it a lion instead.

The sorcerer's apprentice warmed the loaf on the tray, then

sliced it and drizzled it with dark gold honey from a vial in her pocket. She presented this to Frederick. "All is forgiven, isn't it?" she asked.

Frederick, more relaxed from his carving, smiled and said, "Yes, of course. Thank you for the bread, and the honey."

He took a bite.

Then he yelped and spat it out, stumbling over the bench as he leapt from the table, clutching his chest, where the talisman Merrigan had given him burned hot and bright. Frederick held the wooden leaf away from his body by its cord and looked in horror at the sorcerer's apprentice, who likewise stared, wide-eyed, at the charm he held.

"That . . . that *witch* gave you some spell! You asked for protection, didn't you? How could you suspect me?" she shrieked.

"You never gave me any reason to believe you could accept me," Frederick said miserably. "Now you have utterly broken my heart."

"You have no heart!" the sorcerer's apprentice growled. She seized the figurine he had been carving and brandished it at him. "You are no better than a beast, no heart, no soul, no humanity inside you at all! Be a beast then, until true love sets you free!"

She brought the figurine down on the vial of honey, which contained Frederick's blood mixed with hers; and though she had no spell in mind, her anger was powerful enough to join with the blood and the wooden creature born of Frederick's hands, and work its own terrible magic. Merrigan's talisman was spent, and this curse was not on Frederick's heart. He was unprotected. Frederick's body groaned, and he roared with pain as his bones expanded; his skin grew tight around his swelling muscles until it split and revealed a newly-grown hide with tawny fur. His handsome face grew horrible to look upon as the bones of his skull rearranged into a snout full of long sharp teeth, thick and white.

He was a beast; his transformation was complete when the

house shook and Merrigan appeared in the doorway, summoned by eir talisman's activation. E saw the situation at once; but Frederick bellowed with ongoing pain and shock, for he was still himself inside the beast, aware of what had been done to him. Fear rippled through his powerful body, and Merrigan knew that it would be worse for him if that fear escaped while he was still in the village. So e took the staff—the very fox-head one Frederick had carved for em—and moved it in a slow and steady circle to focus him and lull him to sleep.

While e did this, the sorcerer's apprentice escaped and fled south, as if she thought to run the entire way to Varrun, where Gabin waited. Perhaps she only meant to get far enough away to call for her master's aid. Merrigan did not give her this chance. While she ran and Frederick slept, Merrigan found her, reaching out with eir mind; e tapped the slate floor of Frederick's cottage with eir staff, and the sorcerer's apprentice turned to stone.

The sleep e laid on Frederick was not strong enough to still the erratic tension in his body, still reacting to its transformation. E laid eir hands on his flank and spoke to him, of calm and quiet and of his human self, while e tried to understand the spell that had been cast. It roiled under Frederick's skin like a snake thrown into a fire; it hissed and curled away from Merrigan whenever e reached for it.

The little house filled with people—Frederick's parents, other villagers who had seen the house shake, heard Frederick's roaring, seen the shepherd flee, and watched her turn to stone. These people cried out in horror when they saw the beast, and Merrigan beside it.

"Where is Frederick? What have you done to him?" cried Frederick's father.

Merrigan ignored him, and the others and their muttering. Eir only wish was to ensure Frederick's safety, but the human's magic was still unsettled. E needed time with it, time to listen and look. E rose from Frederick and turned; the gathered humans recoiled, but e took no notice. E saw what e wanted—the sticky figurine, the honey now visibly bloody. Merrigan took it and put it in a pocket of eir robes, then returned to the hulking body that was Frederick.

"I must take him to the forest with me," Merrigan said. "Healing him will be difficult."

"What happened, Enchanter?" Frederick's mother asked.

"The shepherd cursed him; she has been studying with my cousin Gabin, and used that magic when Frederick rejected her," Merrigan replied.

"So you turned her to stone?" said someone else, incredulously; this person was the shepherd's father. "Isn't that too harsh a punishment? How long will you leave her like that?"

Merrigan looked over eir shoulder at him. "I have no intention of freeing her. Let her master restore her, if she sees fit."

A dreadful silence fell upon the people in the house, which Merrigan ignored, turning eir attention to the problem of getting Frederick out of the house without further damaging it. E considered the roof, with its wooden beams and shingles; and then e raised eir hand and eir staff and reached out to the wood. It was more difficult, because the wood was disconnected from roots and leaves, but it was not yet completely dead. It roused itself to Merrigan's request, and the shingles pulled away in two great sheets, and the beams bent themselves with a great groaning, until a hole large enough for Frederick opened up in the roof of the house. If the people gathered were screaming, Merrigan did not hear it. E held the roof with the staff, and used eir other hand to lift Frederick, coaxing the breeze under him to raise him up and out, to set him down gently in the grass outside. When that was done, e called the roof back into place, and darkness and silence fell inside the house again.

E left the house, put eir hand on Frederick's mane-covered shoulders, and raised him with the wind again; then they flew together to the labyrinth.

THE VILLAGERS CAME AT sunset.

The modern villagers were not so afraid of the forest that they would not come near it at all; but they came only so far as was required to get their timber, their firewood, their herbs. Merrigan had often wondered why they should be so nervous, why they should fear the forest, when they knew e was there to manage all and to protect them. There were predatory creatures among the trees, of course, but they would not approach with menace while Merrigan was present; surely the villagers knew that.

The villagers came, with torches against the darkness already thick beneath the canopy, and it occurred to Merrigan that e had been hasty. In eir worry for Frederick, e had not explained eir full intent to the villagers, to his parents; so when e sensed their entry to the forest, e went to meet them, determining that e ought to allay their concerns. E raised light with em, slowly, so that they could clearly see em while they spoke and not be startled. This was unsuccessful; the humans still jerked back with surprise when they noticed em.

"Where is Frederick?" asked a person e recognized as the blacksmith; not a descendant of Branwen's.

"Frederick is safe," Merrigan said. "He has suffered a trauma. I have brought him to my home so that I can heal him in a calm, quiet place."

The woodcarver, Frederick's master, stepped forward, her angry expression made even more striking by the shadows from her torch. "Wanted to make sure he couldn't run off before you took him, eh?"

Merrigan did not smile. "Be easy. Once Frederick is well again, I am sure he will return to you."

"This is all your fault!" cried the shepherd's parent. "You corrupted that boy—he should have just married her!"

"You bewitched him, for sure. He's loved no one but you since he was a child," said the woodcarver.

"Don't speak such nonsense," Merrigan hissed.

The villagers stumbled back from eir voice as though it had been a whip. Tension rippled uncomfortably up and down eir spine; e was incredulous that they could speak so about Frederick, but after all, hadn't he told em that this was what they thought of him? E had no patience left for this.

"Begone, and leave Frederick in peace until such time as he chooses to seek you out again," e said.

The voices of the villagers rose in argument—Merrigan did not discern their words, e had no interest in giving further consequence to their little absurdities. E slammed the base of eir staff upon the ground; the soft light e carried flashed like lightning. The villagers screamed and ran from em. E listened to their pounding feet break sticks and crush leaves, heard them trip and fall in their haste, until they had left the forest behind.

E walked back to Frederick. The tightness in eir body continued, causing em to jerk and shiver as e moved; e paused, and laid eir hand upon a tree, letting the texture of the bark mesmerize em and calm em until e was still and relaxed again. Though the humans were all gone, their screams clung to em, echoing in eir hearing.

Merrigan understood then that the creature they feared in the forest . . . was em.

23
PUNISHMENT

MERRIGAN PLACED FREDERICK UNDER a deeper sleep; then e flew across the black sky to Varrun. E told emself that Frederick's sleep was for his safety, but in the darkness e admitted to emself that e did not want eir friend to see this side of em. Eir turbulent emotions almost hindered eir flight, which would have looked erratic to any chance observer. All eir life, e had eschewed vengeance, seeking justice instead. Part of em loathed to give in to it now . . . but justice and vengeance were sometimes difficult to distinguish—and she had been warned.

Varrun was almost a city by this point, the clusters of buildings outside the fortress made of timber, and even some of stone instead of turf, but the fortress stood just as it had two hundred years ago, when the king had sent his duke forth from it with orders to flay a teenager alive for being neither a man nor a woman. The thick stone of the baileys was dark with age now, but it still hid Merrigan's enemy. E slipped through an arrow slit, and made eir way to the room where e knew e would find her.

There was a charm on the door, but it was easy to break—too

easy. Still, Merrigan lifted eir hand and broke it, caused the door to open, and stepped inside.

Gabin had no fire lit. E saw her in the shadows, sitting up on her bed.

Waiting.

"I knew this would do it," she whispered. "I knew it would be this that brought you back to me."

"And you gave her what she requested despite that," Merrigan said.

Gabin laughed, an oddly rasping sound that made Merrigan's gut clench. She sounded ill. Merrigan gestured toward the brazier and ignited it, so e could look upon eir cousin. E should have been long dead, like Branwen, but she was using a tree to keep herself alive. She had been among the first to use such spells; perhaps something was going wrong and the spell was failing. But she did not look ill after all. She looked drunk.

"What is wrong, cousin?" Merrigan asked. "Why have you done this, knowing it would anger me?"

Gabin laughed again. "I want you to understand."

"Understand what?"

"You judge me," Gabin said, the laughter suddenly gone. Merrigan said nothing, and the sorcerer sighed. "You may have been human once, *Enchanter*, but you've grown too distant from us now. You can't see that we *are* selfish and cruel. You will not give love charms because they are unethical, because they force one person to bend to another's will. But that is all humans want to do—all we want is to subjugate others for our own purposes, be they of pleasure or power. You are fighting a losing battle."

Merrigan adjusted eir grip on eir staff, the beautiful staff Frederick had made. "You betray your own humanity by thinking that I am fighting at all," e said.

"What are you doing, then?" Gabin demanded, standing. "Why ingratiate yourself with us? Why come to punish me, if we are not on opposite sides?"

Why had e come? Out of anger, spurred by eir desire to hurt

the one who had hurt eir friend. Perhaps later, e would reflect on this and be amused that even as the sorcerer anticipated eir revenge, she sought to accuse em of being too alien to understand such human propensities. In that moment, though, Merrigan found the calm e had lacked on eir flight, and knew what needed to be done. Though Gabin may not have believed em, e had long ago given up any hope of changing human hearts or human minds. The villagers of that evening, in the forest accusing em of corrupting Frederick, were no different from the villagers of two hundred years ago, worried that young Merrigan would corrupt their children and make them question the strict rules of dress and behavior under which they lived. That was why Merrigan had had such pitiful advice to give Frederick. E was an enchanter, not a teacher, not someone who dispensed lessons. E had magic, not influence—but magic was all e needed.

E made no answer to Gabin, but tapped eir staff twice upon the ground. She stiffened, and her hands glowed, though not through any power of hers, and her eyes widened with fear. Merrigan raised eir staff, and the light in Gabin's hands lifted from her skin, dissipating in the air like steam.

"What are you doing?" she asked, through clenched teeth.

"I am removing the spark that allows you to create magic," Merrigan replied.

"No!" Gabin cried. "You cannot do this! My livelihood—"

"You shall still be able to make medicines, which is all you should have ever done."

When all the light was gone, Merrigan released her, and she staggered back onto the bed. Merrigan turned and left without another word; e took to the sky and flew faster than e ever had before.

What was e doing? A hundred years helping humanity—but their memories were short, and they feared em as much as eir stepmother had when she threw around that word, *changeling*. What had e gained with eir service, other than a way to pass the time?

The wind scraped eir face, tore eir robes, rattled eir bones, but all was silent and soft in eir mind. E felt . . . empty. Cold. But unafraid. The warm rush of anger and fear in response to the assault on Frederick had been unexpected, and not unwelcome. Yet this place within em, cold and dark and alone, was eir heart's true home, and where e would always be safe.

24
FREDERICK IN THE FOREST

MERRIGAN RETURNED TO FREDERICK. E worked for three days while he was under the enchanted sleep; then e woke him. He gasped and shuddered and fell into Merrigan's arms, and trembled there for long minutes while he came to realize he was not in danger. When at last he was relaxed, Merrigan pointed to the water and bread e had placed next to him.

The light rose around them, golden and warm, filtered through the autumn colors of the canopy. Frederick, with his tawny skin and honey-colored hair, blended marvelously with the hues of the season. The beauty of how completely he belonged in such a tableau lifted some of the darkness from Merrigan's mind, and when he next caught eir eye, e smiled more fully at him. He returned the expression, then sighed and looked seriously at em.

"I don't want to go back," he said.

Merrigan shook eir head. "You cannot. Not yet. I have mitigated your curse, so that within the boundaries of the forest you are human. But if you leave the trees, you will become the beast again. I promise you, though: I will break the curse and free you."

Frederick took this news with grace and nodded; still,

Merrigan felt a twinge of guilt. The curse was a difficult one, for the shepherd's accusation—that he had no heart, that he was a beast without humanity, all because he could not love her—had tangled itself up in Frederick's own insecurity and guilt, his secret fear that something *was* wrong with him. Frederick seemed to understand that Merrigan, in working to free him from the curse, had learned all this, but the love of friendship between them was strong, and so he trusted em. Merrigan felt both grateful and unworthy.

"You may dwell freely in the forest while I work," e said.

"Thank you," Frederick said. Somewhere nearby, the leaf litter rustled, and Frederick looked toward the sound. His expression was merely thoughtful, though, so Merrigan concluded he was not frightened, but simply needed a moment to collect his thoughts. He continued, "I . . . I cannot imagine returning to that village. To Varrun. Ever."

Merrigan said nothing, only waited.

Frederick went on, "I tried to do as you advised, to let my own desires guide me and stand my ground. It was successful with some people in the village, but there were others that I could never sway, who begrudged me any mention of my stance on love or marriage. Even before this . . . incident . . . it was frequent enough and painful enough—their words, their looks—like sandpaper on my skin. And now that Breda—" He shook his head, swallowing the words.

"I am so sorry, Frederick," Merrigan said.

"I trusted her. I believed she was my friend." He covered his eyes and growled in frustration, then dropped his hands. "I shall never feel safe there again."

A tight knot formed in Merrigan's gut at the look of defeat on his face. E could not look at him, and stared into the glowing leaves instead. "I regret that my advice to you was not better."

"No! Your advice gave me courage. Knowing you had been in something like my position before, and got through it and found such strength—I am still grateful for your advice," Frederick said.

"You told me how *you* had overcome this struggle, and it did help, and I will still strive to learn from those words."

Merrigan stood then and turned eir back on him, for e did not want him to see the tears come to eir eyes. When e advised Frederick to do as his heart desired, e had not intended to give him the impression that e had done any of the things he just said — e had not. E got through nothing, e overcame nothing. E had experienced a few years of contentment doing as e desired without giving consequence to those who questioned the crucial parts of emself. It was not enough to protect em, and in the end, e had run. The only thing e had learned was that one could not truly ever be safe from the machinations of others.

But that was too harsh a lesson for one so young as Frederick.

"Merrigan?"

E clenched eir jaw; e hated to stand in that way, knowing eir posture must seem harsh. Could e tell him? Could e explain that e was not so strong as Frederick believed?

If they two were different than they were, perhaps e would have waited. Perhaps e could have saved the disillusionment for later. Eir young friend had already declared that he might never feel safe again in the place he had lived all his life, though; and for eir part, e had only ever found strength in honesty. E turned round again with a heavy sigh and knelt before Frederick.

"Someday, Frederick, I will tell you the full story of my youth," e said. "For now, let me say that I was given the same advice I offered you. I followed it, and it was the same for me as it was for you — for all that it helped, it could not completely erase the harm done, nor prevent new harms from occurring. And in the end, it did not protect me from losing everything I held dear. I offered — I offered it because despite my very long life, I have not yet found any better way. So you see, we are both still learning."

Frederick reached up and caressed eir cheek. "We can learn together."

Merrigan nodded, then led him into the forest. At length,

they came to the labyrinth. Merrigan stopped a distance from it, so that Frederick might have a moment to observe without being overwhelmed. He approached it slowly, the roses parting for him, and asked, "What is this?"

"Your home," Merrigan replied. "For now."

He placed his hands upon the stone, gazing up, squinting at the sunlight flashing off the silver leaves of the upper forest. Merrigan waited while he explored, entering and going some hesitant distance before returning. "It's a maze," he said.

E smiled. "It is much more than that. It is a sanctuary, home to thousands of creatures."

Frederick had not lifted his hand from the stone since he first touched it. The emotions that beset Merrigan as e observed his consideration of eir words were difficult to parse, twined together, inextricable, but the experience of them was familiar enough that e needed to expend no great energy in contemplating them.

"What do you think of it?" e asked.

He leaned toward the stone, as if it had spoken quietly in his ear, and he wished to better hear what it had said. "I think it has been waiting for me."

MERRIGAN HELD NEITHER HOPE nor expectation of how Frederick would settle into the labyrinth. It was quite a different life than the one he'd had in the village, or would have had in the wider world; and e worried that he would struggle, being wholly displaced from all he knew. But if e had formed ideas of what should happen, or when, then Frederick would have made em a fool by them.

He learned the labyrinth quickly, no small feat considering its size and complexity. Soon he was beloved by all the small creatures, so much so that the butterflies would follow him while he roamed and settle onto his shoulders when they were tired. The goat kids of the north wall challenged him to climb faster than they, and he obliged, though he never surpassed them, which was just as they preferred it. The greatest hinderance to his total acceptance was the wolves of the south wall, who sent Merrigan many a baleful look in the first weeks of Frederick's residence. With effort, though, he won them over, mainly by giving them their space and occasionally being of use to them, and of course, seeking their advice on forest matters, which was what wolves loved best.

Frederick spent his days, while the weather was good, roaming in the labyrinth and beyond, guided by the foxes who had taken a liking to him; and every night, he slept in a different nook in the labyrinth, until he found a tower not unlike Merrigan's, though it had a roof of vines and stayed quite dark, even during the day. He showed it to em, proud and unbothered by the darkness, because he loved to explore and considered his tower more of a den than a home, a place he would come to sleep and use for storage but not much else.

"Where shall you relax, and eat?" Merrigan asked.

"With you, of course," Frederick replied. Merrigan laughed and said he would always be welcome.

While he roamed, Merrigan went to the waterfall, meditating on his curse and how to undo it. *Be a beast then, until true love sets you free.* That was what the shepherd had said. If her emotions had been weaker, it would have been broken already, because her words were not careful enough to serve her purpose: love took many forms, all of which could be true. The love of Frederick's parents could have sufficed, or even the friendship he and Merrigan shared. But the bitter shepherd had had strong, malicious intent, and her curse built itself around the passionate, possessive, selfish version of romantic love she had in her heart. After weeks of study, Merrigan was no closer to determining the mechanism of true love's liberation, though. Did someone have to love Frederick truly, romantically? If so, that was easily done, for he was easy to fall in love with—not a good curse. More likely, the curse required *Frederick* to fall in love to the degree the shepherd had felt, which made it a very good curse indeed.

Still, a curse was built like a wall, and like a wall it could always be demolished. Merrigan just needed to find the right tool.

When the cold weather came, and all the denizens of the labyrinth came home, Frederick came with them and made his way to Merrigan's chamber in the center of the maze.

E was reading when he came, eir usual practice in the afternoon. He appeared in the threshold and smiled at Merrigan, who closed eir book and set it down. "How are you?" e asked.

His smile widened. "This place is amazing. But I haven't seen much of you. Have you been here in the tower all this time?"

"No. I've roamed a little myself."

"Where?"

Merrigan thought of showing him the waterfall—e had thought several times of doing so, but decided against it each time. "Here and there," e replied.

Frederick laughed softly. "Perhaps in place of that secret, you will tell me another."

"Ask, by all means."

"Have you ever been in love?"

He leaned, deceptively casual, against the frame of the entrance. His face held a light, curious expression, holding on to the lingering shape of his laughter. Despite his efforts, Merrigan could tell—from the tension in his arms, his hands where he twined them before his chest—from the stillness of his mouth—that the question had been on his lips for quite a while. Perhaps for years.

"Yes," Merrigan said. "A very long time ago."

Frederick nodded, his features relaxing, and joined em at the table.

"Why do you ask, Frederick?"

"I hardly know," he replied. "A last attempt to understand what romantic love is, and whether I am capable of it. Whether I should even want to be."

Merrigan sighed, and they were quiet together for some minutes. Then e said, "Romantic love . . . is any other relationship you may have had, but taken to extremity. It removes you from yourself, makes you confuse the emotions of another being for your own. For some, it settles down into comfort and contentment;

for others, it never does, and is a constant swing from the highest highs to the lowest lows. It can bring happiness, but that happiness is no different from any other kind. That joy is no different from, no greater than the joy I felt when I climbed the labyrinth wall for the first time and beheld the upper forest in all its beauty. Likewise the sorrow this love brought me was as deep and hurtful as sorrow from any other cause. No more. No less. There are those who would like to pretend that to be consumed by love, to desperately attach oneself to another, is noble in some way—that it is necessary and right. But in my experience, they are only justifying their own obsessions, preemptively defending their decision to forget their friends, to abdicate their responsibilities and even their mundane pleasures, and to, at least temporarily, devote themselves entirely to adoration."

"And it perpetuates itself. It is passed on from one person to another; it is enshrined in our definitions of family, of humanity," Frederick said. "That is what they feel, and therefore everyone must feel it."

"Yes. Because they cannot imagine differently, and because if everyone feels love this way, then their actions in service of it are beyond reproach," Merrigan said.

He shook his head. "I don't believe anyone would reproach them at all."

"Ideally, no. But imagine if most of the world were like you, if romantic love were a strange and perhaps a perverse thing to feel. You see how their impulse is to scold you. So they imagine they would be scolded in turn, without the protection of this assumed universality," Merrigan said.

"Why not just accept difference, when it does no harm?"

Merrigan frowned. "Because humans are creatures of fear. You do them harm, Frederick; at least, they think so, because you force them to question their received ideas. You shake the foundations of their truths."

Frederick sighed and looked about, ready for another subject. "May I look at your books?"

Merrigan nodded, and he went to them. Most of them were very old, hand-lettered on large vellum pages, the spines bound with stitches and uncovered. E kept them wrapped in soft cloths. The shelves the books occupied were the most extensive in eir tower. In another few decades, e would need to expand, probably up, which would mean fashioning a ladder or handholds. It would be worth it. The books brought em joy.

Frederick flexed his hands. "Where did you get them all?"

Merrigan joined him before the shelf. "They are my preferred form of payment. Some I purchased the conventional way."

He reached for a thick, leather-bound volume but hesitated, then lifted a small velvet bag instead and raised his eyebrow in question. Merrigan only smiled and watched while he lifted the flap and extracted the volume within: a little book made of dry leaves pasted together, sewn with a bit of twine, containing a pictographic story drawn in crushed berries.

"You kept it," he said, laughing.

"I promised I would treasure it."

He put the book back, carefully, and dashed unshed tears from his eyes while he scanned the spines of the other books. "May I read one?"

"You may read any and all of them."

MERRIGAN EXPECTED TO HAVE Frederick's curse broken by midwinter, before e set out to check in with the villages under eir care. But then Cathal, the great city by the sea, invaded the north. This was the start of a conflict that would later be called the Unification War, which ended when the king of Varrun submitted to Cathal and the nation of Callister was born.

The Enchanter was much invoked, for all e made the humans nervous. They desired eir protection of their fields, their homes, their children fighting on land and on sea. Varrun had a handful of sorcerers, children of the north who were loyal to their homeland, but many more sorcerers fought on Cathal's side, since that was where the guild was based. The dukes of Varrun begged Merrigan to do as the sorcerers did, and stand with the generals on hills or quarterdecks, flinging magic upon the teeming infantry.

E refused. E protected the fields and the homes, so that they could not be razed and the people would not starve. E healed soldiers who were wounded, and e charmed and organized the camps to prevent the spread of disease. This saved many lives, but it did not win the war, and the North grew bitter toward the Enchanter, who seemed to them a hypocrite. How could one who could punish so cruelly decline to hurt unjust invaders?

The magic cost Merrigan greatly as the war dragged on for nearly twenty years; and what was worse, it consumed so much of eir energy and power that there was none left for breaking Frederick's curse. Every time e returned to the forest, more ragged and gasping than before, e said to him, "Ask me to stay, and I will. Ask me to leave them all to fend for themselves, and I will, gladly."

But every time, Frederick smiled and said, "They need your help more than I do, Merrigan. Go."

So e went.

25
THE INEVITABLE

THE WAR ENDED, AND the trouble began.

Or—Merrigan finally realized the inevitable consequence of eir return to the human world.

26

THE GREAT BUILD

THE WAR HAD DEVASTATED the land south of the region under Merrigan's protection, south of Varrun; stripped it of its forests, for war in those days was always hungry for timber. Arrows and spears, shields for the lowly, conscripted infantry, great siege machines and long spines of anti-cavalry pikes, charcoal for the blacksmiths' furnaces and kindling for the cooking fires. Temporary fortresses with whole trunks buried close and lashed together, and the constant need to rebuild villages that would only be burned again the following spring. Even the game parks of the nobility had been pillaged to feed the beast.

Merrigan could not get the screaming of the southern forests out of eir ears. So much death hung in the air of the new Callister. E watched the humans move through it, oblivious, optimistic, even. They didn't know how it clung to their skin and their clothes, how they breathed it in and shoved it into their mouths along with the butter on their bread. They mourned and moved on, for the most part.

They thought they could put right what they had destroyed.

They thought that all they needed was waiting for them in the forest at the base of the mountains, so vast it was a kingdom unto itself, so unendingly green it seemed immortal.

27
THE SURVEYORS

WHEN THE NEW CROP of would-be lumberers came to the village of Iarom, Merrigan waited and watched, but it seemed things would be all right. E had rested for a year following the end of the war, and with the help of the forest spirits was strong enough to guide all the sawhands to the trees ripe for felling, and temper their harvesting. They could only take so much at a time, for the trunks needed to be hauled from the forest back to Iarom one at a time. These were small, family operations at this time, the richest of which had two mules and could therefore haul a trunk faster. But it was a slow process, felling the trees, preparing them. Merrigan preferred it to be slow. The dilapidated south did not. Nor did the merchants who came to investigate the industry, with their sharp eyes and their taste for efficiency. It was only a matter of time before more workers, more mules, larger carts, and better saws were brought north.

The meadow between Iarom and the forest was eaten up by camps, and then cottages, and eventually sawmills. But these changes were a cascading force, inspiring new ones. Sending whole logs down the river to be processed was no longer necessary or ideal; yet the new timber-lords did need a more efficient way to send their product to the south, where it was worth more than gold, in those years following the war. They tried to dredge the Erastus River at Iarom, to make it so the river barges could come all the way to them; Merrigan did not need to intervene in this, for the river fought them on its own. So instead, they appealed to the king. He was already planning improvements to the roads. It was easy for him to extend those plans north.

AT THE END OF the harvest, Merrigan began the long trek home. Eir cart made slow progress, rolling along beside em under its enchantment. The weather was fine, and e matched eir pace to the cart's, strolling along the road. The charm e'd laid on the clouds would break soon, and then there would be balancing needed. E would hurry along later, when the storm began.

It was not much of a road. The path e followed was a narrow swath of dirt where grass knew not to grow, lest it be flattened by the passage of feet; parts of it had forgotten that lesson, and roots had taken hold in patches. Merrigan lifted emself and eir cart over those ill-advised settlements, but the enterprising blades of grass only waved em on and paid no mind to eir withering look.

Talk of roads had been all over the region e serviced. The king wished for the land to become a wealthy one, but it could not very well trade with other countries if its villages could not even trade with each other, so the court said. Merrigan looked down at eir cart, diligently rolling over the uneven ground, bumping and shuddering at rocks in the soil. The villagers spoke gleefully of the project: paved roads, freed from mud, easy on the feet and on cart wheels. Why shouldn't they be pleased?

The storm came. Merrigan had picked up eir cart by its handles and moved along faster once the sky had darkened, and when the rain began, e was within sight of the little inn of Iarom, the swinging wooden emblem of the hearth with its brightly painted flames a beacon in the sudden grayness of the world. Merrigan deposited eir cart in the stables and gave each horse there an apple;

after e had draped eir cloak over a beam to dry, e entered the main room. It was as unchanging as eir own tower. The old building had been covered with wooden slats on the outside, but the inner walls still showed the earth between the beams, and the floor was well-packed dirt. One long table dominated the room, and functioned both as a preparatory and a dining surface for the meals served twice a day. Two benches accompanied the table; the only free-standing chair was next to the fireplace, and it was occupied by a person Merrigan had seen grow from a red-faced child into a solid woman as warm as the fire which constantly burned in her grate. She was Branwen's descendent—but it had been long since Merrigan called anyone cousin.

"Well met, Valencia," e said to the woman at the hearth.

She looked up and smiled. "Well come, Merrigan! I've been expecting you—but I should have remembered, you're never here till the rain comes."

"Am I truly so predictable?"

"You're a creature of habit, I think," Valencia said. She bade em come sit, so e joined her there, and she gave em a warm roll with butter. Soup bubbled in a pot over the flames.

"Are there many with you tonight?" e asked.

Valencia nodded, stirring the soup. "I'm full of surveyors—that's what they call themselves. On the king's business as regards the road."

Merrigan focused on the pleasant softness of the bread and said nothing. But Valencia knew em and smiled a little nervously. "I gather you're not in favor of the project? I suppose you don't travel by land," she said.

"I often do. As to the road . . . it will bring change," Merrigan said.

Valencia looked around the room, considered it, and e saw the first flickers of sadness in her countenance that e had ever seen, in all the years e had known her. Was it easier, or more difficult, to take change in stride when life was finite? E no longer remembered what consequential changes felt like within one human lifespan.

E finished eir roll and dusted flour from eir hands as e stood. "Have you any wishes this evening?"

Valencia shook off her reverie and smiled, this time purely with affection. "None that can't wait until morning. Please, sit. I'll serve your supper. The surveyors will be in any moment, I'm sure."

Merrigan resumed eir place upon the bench, and gratefully accepted the bowl of steaming soup she set before em. It was too hot to eat yet, so e left the spoon where Valencia set it; at that moment, a group entered from the side door. The surveyors, undoubtedly, four persons with skin in varying brown tones, dressed in what appeared to be uniform under-tunics. Merrigan imagined their coats were drying on the beam next to eirs, given the dripping from their hair. Valencia tutted and handed them each rags to sop up the rainwater, and they smiled at her and thanked her.

While the surveyors sat themselves and remarked on the suddenness of the storm, Valencia set four bowls upon the edge of the table, then turned to the cauldron. One of the surveyors, the youngest and the darkest to Merrigan's eye, leapt from the bench and was at her elbow in a moment with the first bowl. She laughed and said, "Thank you, dear."

The apprentice blushed and held the next bowl out for her to ladle soup into.

"Very efficient," Merrigan said, smiling.

Valencia laughed again. The youth, by contrast, started when their eyes met Merrigan's. They seemed riveted, though not distracted enough to neglect their assumed responsibility over the soup bowls; when one was weighted down with its contents, the next was offered with a smooth motion. Undoubtedly this youth's only duty was to hand things off to the more senior surveyors, and they had mastered this well enough to give space for daydreaming.

"What is your name, prentice?" Merrigan asked.

The youth frowned and said, hesitantly, "Fionn."

"Where are you from?"

"Cathal."

And probably of a well-off family, then, who had purchased

the apprenticeship—but was the prentice an eldest child of a modest family? Or the younger in a noble one, expected to take a profession to support themselves once their elder siblings had inherited all their parents' wealth?

"What is your age, and how shall I address you?" Merrigan asked.

The youth laughed. "That's not how you ask," they said. "You're doing it all wrong."

Merrigan blinked at them, thrown for the moment. In the time since Aurelia had succeeded in squashing the sumptuary laws related to gendered clothing, there had of course been consternation and confusion among the people as to how they were to determine a person's gender, if not by clothing and occupation in life. In the north, in the best cases, it was either volunteered along with one's name or asked for directly; but even decades after the repeal of the laws, few enough people took advantage of the freedom that often, the subject was simply ignored, and people made their own assumptions or gleaned the information from other clues. A person in skirts who called themselves the wife of so-and-so, it was reasoned, could safely be called a woman. Merrigan knew several of eir gender-kin who struggled greatly with this attitude.

"I pray you will forgive my ignorance and help me avoid giving offense in the future," Merrigan said. "What is the correct way?"

"You're supposed to ask who I am, and then I say Fionn she Torcall of Cathal," the youth said. "My given name, my pronoun, my eldest parent's name, and my birthplace."

Merrigan smiled, and said again, "Very efficient."

Fionn's blush returned. "I am seventeen. That's not included." She paused a moment, then said, "Why should you care to know who I am and where I'm from?"

Merrigan dipped eir head apologetically. "Forgive my curiosity. You are good to help Valencia with the serving, that is all; I admire it."

Fionn shrugged. "Serving is one of my duties on the road."

With that pronouncement, she turned and carried two bowls to the other three surveyors, who sat at the far end of the table away from the fire. An odd choice, but not inexplicable. Merrigan was known to the populations of all the villages around the forest, and due to eir predictability—eir habit, as Valencia called it—it was possible the surveyors had been told of eir presence and furnished with a description of em. Their reluctance to join em was not wholly unexpected; e was surprised, though, that they forewent the fire merely to avoid being in conversation with em.

E was warmed. E had no more need of the fire, and the smoke began to be bothersome. E rose, intending to take eir dinner in eir room.

"Where are you going?" Fionn asked.

She had sat herself across from em, rather than with her superiors. What an intriguing child. First she seemed startled by em, then she pushed back against eir questions, and now she wanted to sup with em? E sat back down and scrutinized the youth. Brown skin that was warm and yellow in the firelight; reddish brown hair, and dark eyes that reminded em of Frederick's. A wide, well-formed nose and firm jaw. Her under-tunic was sleeveless, and Merrigan observed her muscles; undoubtedly carrying gear was part of her duties as well, and given the name of the profession she studied, e imagined she carried gear great distances.

"Will you not introduce yourself?" she asked.

"My name is . . . Merrigan e Abboid of Iarom," e said.

She smiled. "It gives me joy to meet you."

E raised an eyebrow. "Why?"

Valencia burst out laughing, loud enough that the other three surveyors briefly paused their conversation.

"You'll have to pardon Merrigan, child. E doesn't leave eir stronghold above thrice a year, and—so far as I know—only sees us village folk," she said. "E hasn't learned the latest niceties."

"And never shall, if truth be told." Merrigan shook eir head, amused and a little embarrassed.

"Stronghold? Are you a duke?" Fionn whispered, as though elevated rank must also make eir ears sensitive.

"No."

"Then it is a metaphor."

Merrigan thought of the labyrinth, secure and impenetrable. "No."

Fionn narrowed her eyes at em, but the answer she sought was not written on eir face. She huffed and looked to Valencia for assistance, but the innkeeper shrugged.

"Where is your stronghold?" Fionn asked em.

"Nearby."

"Your age?"

"Greater than yours."

"Your profession?"

"Different from yours."

The youth frowned. "I answered *you* honestly and directly."

Merrigan bowed eir head again. "And I thank you for that."

"Will you not do me the same honor?" Fionn asked.

Merrigan regarded her and contemplated the unusual animation e felt. Typically at the end of a harvest, e was exhausted, and indeed e had been when e arrived. Perhaps it was just the fire, or simply a matter of seeing eir old friend. It was certainly not the soup, which e had yet to taste—Fionn, too, had forgotten hers. But perhaps it was this youth, by turns reverent and impertinent, but always curious, who revived em.

"I will give you three truthful answers," Merrigan said. "On the condition that your questions will be different from those you have already asked, and that you will keep my answers secret; they will belong to you and you alone."

Fionn licked her lips and opened her mouth; Merrigan held up a finger. "Take care, and ensure that you ask what you truly wish to know. You may take your time to think."

"I have a condition," she said.

"What is it?"

"That you answer clearly and directly as well as truthfully. I don't think you were lying before, but I learned nothing; I don't want more of those vagaries," Fionn said.

Merrigan laughed. "A good condition. Of course. I will answer in plain, honest words."

"Good," Fionn said. "Now I'll think."

Merrigan smiled, and at last focused on eir soup. It was a little tepid, but a subtle tap upon the bowl remedied that. Fionn also ate during her contemplation, though she seemed focused wholly inward. Her spoon traveled between her bowl and her mouth over and over without variation, and Merrigan found emself wondering what she was always thinking about, if she had no cause to think of the repetitive tasks at hand.

The surveyors at the end of the table spoke in hushed voices, but with a little effort, e could hear them. They spoke of the forest, bemoaned that the main source of lumber for the Great Build should be at such an annoying distance from the villages that were destined to be towns, and the towns that were destined to be cities. It pleased Merrigan to hear such talk, though e knew that the irksome logistics would not long protect eir home from the greed of development.

"Plenty of willing laborers, though," said one of the surveyors, a wry lilt in their voice.

Another surveyor laughed. "They'll be disappointed. Hard work and no treasure."

"You don't believe in it?" the first asked.

"Undiscovered treasure hidden in the forest, guarded by a sorcerer?" The second huffed. "Of course not. I give no credence to these northern fairy tales. They only cause mischief."

Had Merrigan been alone, e might have laughed out loud. E agreed with the second surveyor emself, since when a fairy's duty to its home was discharged, its entire energy was devoted to such little games and tricks as it could conceive of for amusement. Further, e knew beyond a doubt that the type of treasure in which an ambitious human laborer might be interested was not to be found in the forest, guarded or unguarded. If lumberers signed on to such a project in order to prospect for gold or jewels, they would be disappointed indeed.

"I have my questions," Fionn declared.

Merrigan smiled at her. "Then ask."

"Where do you live?"

E frowned—but the question was different from what she had previously asked. She kept her face neutral while she waited for em to answer, a clear sign that she knew how clever she was being and wished to appear innocent. Despite emself, Merrigan smiled again. "I live in a labyrinth."

E could see the next question—But *where?*—form in her mind, but wisely, she dismissed it.

"What sort of work do you do?" she asked.

A complex question, and one to which Merrigan could give an incomplete answer and still be within the terms of their bargain. E felt that Valencia was watching em as well as Fionn. The good woman knew the usual course of eir work, that of the blessings and the wishes and the small useful enchantments. E could answer in accordance with that aspect and remain as welcome as ever, in that inn at least. Yet, within Merrigan grew a desire to be honest with Fionn in a more full sense of the word. E did grant wishes and give blessings, and was appreciated for those things, but in the end, such magic was minuscule in the scope of eir life. They were distractions which kept em occupied, provided reasons to interact with the human population, and insulated—though not as well as they had once done—em from the loathing which was necessarily born of the ill-fated bargains e struck with others.

"Merrigan?" Fionn's voice was soft, and when e looked at her, her brow was furrowed with concern. E smiled to reassure her that she had not offended em, though e could not be sure of the expression's effectiveness. A dark cloud settled, like a weight, upon eir shoulders, and it was with effort that eir posture did not slump under it.

"I am a steward of this land and its inhabitants," e replied.

The concern wrinkling her brow shifted into wrinkles of perturbed confusion, and again Merrigan saw the supplementary questions. As a citizen of Cathal, an apprentice to royal surveyors,

Fionn would know the official hierarchies, the names and ranks of the nobles who were, nominally, stewards of the region. She glanced quickly at Valencia, but the woman ducked to avoid the scrutiny and made a show of stoking the fire. Perhaps Fionn would question the innkeeper later, and perhaps Valencia would offer further explanation; let her. Merrigan had given eir truthful, plain answer, and eir end-of-harvest exhaustion began to fill em again, and make eir limbs heavy.

"Ask your third question," e said.

Fionn hesitated, then asked, "Are you happy?"

Despite emself, an incredulous chuckle escaped Merrigan. E had the impression that the question was not her original idea, but was inspired instead by the change in eir mood which she seemed to perceive. "What is happiness?" e countered.

The girl frowned. "It—it's itself!" She gave a forceful, frustrated sigh. "Satisfaction, joy, comfort—"

"If happiness is the combination of other pleasurable factors, then yes, I am happy," Merrigan replied.

"But it is not so simple. It is—it has its own energy, its own activity, that elevates it above mere contentment," Fionn said.

"There is nothing mere about contentment," Merrigan said.

Fionn was unmoved by this comment. "Do you understand me?"

Merrigan stared into her earnest, impassioned face, and said, "I do. This conception of happiness is particular to you, and you must learn to allow that for others, happiness may not be so active. Or, the activity of it will be different than yours, or what you imagine."

"What is happiness for you, then?"

Merrigan sighed, drained at last of eir emotions as well as eir physical energy. E devoted little time to contemplations of happiness or unhappiness in regard to emself, though the pursuit and experience of such was often the subject of the books e and Frederick read and therefore their discussions of those texts. Like most of life, e considered it to be separate from emself, considered it unreasonable to assume that e could sustain happiness—either contentment, or the energetic feeling Fionn envisioned—over eir centuries-long existence. E was satisfied; e was comfortable; e felt joy. E had given Fionn the truthful and plain answer she required. Beyond that, even if e had been able to explain, e could not have expected a seventeen-year-old to understand.

"Our bargain is fulfilled," e said. "I wish you happiness, Fionn."

E held out eir hand as e rose from the bench. Though she pressed her lips together in tight disappointment, she took eir extended hand. E squeezed her sturdy brown fingers. Fionn gave a sharp intake of breath. When their hands parted, there was the slight mark of a leaf at the outer base of her thumb. She ran a fingertip over it hesitantly, then offered em a relaxed smile, her frustration gone. E returned the smile, pressed Valencia's hand, and went to eir room.

Laid out in eir bed, e lifted the hand that had touched Fionn's; eir skin was still warm with the magic that had flowed between them. E hadn't called it up, nor had e directed it to etch the little shape of the leaf. Eir own hand was unchanged.

28

HERO

MERRIGAN WENT HOME AND did not see the surveyors again, though the sprites and birds brought em news of their work, all their traipsing about, casting their appraising gaze over the landscape, measuring this and that and constantly scribbling notes. They consulted frequently with the timber-lords in their camp, which edged ever closer to Iarom. Soon, if things progressed, the places would merge into one great lumber town.

The wolves left that side of the forest, and Merrigan did not blame them. The humans attempted to kill them on sight, afraid that they would attack the livestock or chase away the game in the forest—as if the hundreds of sawhands blundering into the trees every day had no effect on the deer, the boars, the turkeys. It was a quirk of humanity, or perhaps a deliberate obfuscation, that they rarely considered themselves part of an ecosystem, and so did not consider how their coming would change things; then they looked about and asked themselves, where did the deer go? Where are the fowl? Even the original villagers of Iarom yearned for the days when any child could go snare a rabbit in an afternoon with no trouble, without acknowledging why the burrows were now so far away.

Merrigan did not leave eir tower, but Frederick often went to observe the sawhands at their work, and this was how he discovered a terrible truth.

The spring after the surveyors came, Frederick invited em to walk with him and observe the first openings of the flowers. He had developed a particular talent for this, and knew exactly which flower would open first, and when. Even Merrigan could not discern whatever signs he saw, and e was duly impressed every year. Frederick took great pleasure in this ability of his, and in eir admiration of it. As they walked, e attempted to usurp his prediction, pointing to this bud or that and insisting it was the one that would open first. He laughed and shook his head in amusement, every time.

After they had gone a decent way from the labyrinth, he asked, "Are you all right?"

"Of course," Merrigan replied. "All is well."

Frederick sighed, and it felt to Merrigan as if that sigh emptied eir lungs too, for it was one of disappointment. When Frederick left eir side and continued moving in the direction of their trek, away from the labyrinth, e knew what was coming.

There, in the middle of the forest, Frederick crossed some unlabeled threshold, and became a beast.

He stood there, staring at Merrigan with large red eyes that were sad instead of vicious, and Merrigan began to weep. E stumbled backward into the trunk of an old, solid tree, whose branches seemed to sag as if it wished it could embrace em. Frederick stayed where he was, which was best, because Merrigan did not think e could bear to be touched. Eir power was waning. After the war, after eir year of rest, e thought it would return steadily to normal, but it had not. E could see and sense all that e had before, but it was more difficult than ever to effect change. But this would have been bearable had not e felt eir mitigation of Frederick's curse begin to fray. Such was the shame e felt that e had not even been able to warn Frederick of it, and he had had to discover eir weakness for himself.

Frederick at last took a step toward em, but stopped, abruptly and at attention. Merrigan silenced emself, and they waited, motionless—even the wind. Soon enough, a person stalked into sight, coming from the direction upon which Frederick's attention was fixed. This person was tall and well-muscled, wearing forest clothes that helped them blend in to their surroundings. They carried a bow and arrow ready. A short sword was fastened to their hip.

Frederick stood tense but not alarmed. When the person was close enough to speak and be easily heard, they stopped and put back their hood, revealing skin of a whiteness Merrigan had rarely observed, and hair as fine and yellow as autumn grass. They released their ready hold on the bow, holding it harmless and aloft as they stared at Frederick, an expression of wonder on their face.

"I found you," they said.

Frederick narrowed his eyes and stepped forward, over that arbitrary threshold between man and beast. The person gaped while he transformed; and when he again possessed the human organs of speech, Frederick said, "Go in peace."

"Why should I go in the same instant I've come?" the stranger asked. "If I must, let me go to the Enchanter, and put an end at last to your torment."

Frederick did not glance in Merrigan's direction. The stranger had not noticed em, all green and brown, against the tree and partially shaded by its boughs.

"My . . . torment?" Frederick asked.

The stranger's face flushed. "Everyone knows the story of the poor boy taken by the Enchanter and turned into a beast, kept prisoner deep in the forest. I have come to free you."

Merrigan might have laughed if e had not felt a cold prick of fear on the back of eir neck. Had Frederick's true curse made it into this tale? How did this stranger propose to break it? Did they think that they had only to kill Merrigan? E had heard such stories before, in taverns where the teller either did not realize who e was, or told them especially for eir amusement, winking at every strange and false turn in the telling of real events. Merrigan remembered how the village had reacted when e'd spirited Frederick into the forest. E doubted the tale remembered em kindly.

"You have been misinformed," Frederick said. "I have no need of you. Go now, while you may still pass in peace."

"I—I have wandered these woods for the last year in search of you and the Enchanter's stronghold," the stranger said.

"Then be glad of the time you have spent in the forest, and return home aglow with those memories," Frederick replied.

The stranger refused to believe this was true; they put away their bow and arrow and drew the short sword, with the apparent intention of getting past Frederick's guard to come murder Merrigan whether the "beast" wished it or not. Merrigan lifted eir staff from its resting position against eir shoulder.

Frederick said, "Stay back," with a glance over his shoulder. Merrigan could not guess whether his words were meant for em, or for the stranger.

"You . . . you're not the prisoner at all. *You* are the Enchanter!" The stranger hefted their sword and charged Frederick, who ran to meet them, launching into his beast form.

Merrigan slammed eir staff against the ground, causing a flash of light and a boom of sound to disorient the stranger. E seized them by the arm and launched into the trees, carrying them to the forest's edge. E left them there insensible, either to rouse themselves or be found by others. Then e staggered as far into the dark depths of the forest as e could, though still within sight of where e had left the would-be hero. There, Frederick shortly found em, his great sides heaving with more than just exertion. Merrigan got emself onto Frederick's back, and they headed toward the labyrinth.

When they crossed the boundary of Frederick's curse, he gathered Merrigan up into his human, but still strong, arms, and continued walking. Eventually they passed a magnolia tree, dotted with flowers and the tips of yet more tentative petals, waiting for the morrow to make their debut. Frederick gently set Merrigan down long enough to point at one flower, soft and white in the shade.

"This one was the first," he said.

THE ROAD WAS BUILT. Laborers came and went more easily from the sawmills, and with them went the stories of the beast in the woods. Sometimes he was Merrigan's victim, sometimes an accomplice; sometimes they became the same person. They were always guarding something, some treasure. Usually it was great piles of gold or other conventional wealth, but sometimes it was some magical item, or a captive royal who served as a key to wealth. The stories became more romantic with the passage of time. Merrigan heard them from Valencia, mainly, but often from Fionn, who had returned to Iarom perhaps a year or two after her first visit. She married Valencia's son.

Eventually, Merrigan learned of the book. Fionn showed it to em, bringing it down from Valencia's room: a small volume of folk tales, bound in green-dyed leather. It bore no author's name, but the introduction, an invitation for readers to immerse themselves, was written in the first person, addressed to *Cousin*. It required little effort to discern Gabin's presence in the work. Merrigan pretended to Fionn to be flattered, given eir saintly depiction on the page, but e spent long days at the waterfall afterward, brooding over the meaning of the book.

Fionn seemed eager to learn about the forest, so Merrigan would meet her at the edge and lead her around, occasionally joined by some of the younger sawhands. E showed them how to find the trees that would be best to fell, not only for their ease and yield of useable wood, but for the health of the forest. As receptive as eir students seemed, though, it made no appreciable difference in the assault on the forest. Merrigan could not help but remember Gabin's assessment of humanity from so long ago—that humans *were* selfish and cruel and only wanted to subjugate all before them. E began to hate that e could meet people who seemed kind and good, because every Frederick, every Fionn, gave em cause to hope things could be better. But they never were. E remembered, too, telling Gabin that e was not fighting humanity's nature at all. It had been easier to believe that when e thought humanity's nature tended toward kindness and cooperation. Now, though e did not want to fight, e was, as Gabin had said, losing.

More heroes came. Frederick, with his usual talent for discernment, became very adept at recognizing a so-called hero in the forest, and would immediately respond to their presence with aggression.

Merrigan and Frederick took other precautions, as much as they could when Merrigan became so easily tired. E encouraged the forest to grow tightly around them, to obscure all paths to the labyrinth that a human could distinguish. Though the tide was stymied, it was never staunched entirely, for the heroes had no qualms about taking to the trees and bushes with their blades. Indeed, they seemed to view the obstacles as a sign of the worthiness of their endeavor, almost as an omen of their success. Though Merrigan sought as much as possible to handle the heroes emself, Frederick was more and more often required to use the weapons he possessed: his claws and his strength were called upon for their protection.

During this time, Merrigan tried to continue eir rounds, but was met with more and more suspicion. Soon, Iarom was the only place where e would go, but even there, the mood toward em began to change with the influx of people from the south. Merrigan went among them with cautious pleasure at first. It pleased em to hear their adulation of nature. Many of them came from Varrun, from Cathal, some from even farther cities, and they reveled to be free at last of the city stench, the clinging odor of shit and sweat and smoke. The fields and the forest had all those things, of course, but there were breezes too, and sweet grass, and the perfect scent of fertile earth. These were marvels to the newcomers, born and raised in the dark narrow streets bursting with bodies.

But those newcomers needed homes.

Merrigan felt the axes fall, and watched the edges of eir home bleed into boards and beams, built to wall the newcomers away from the very landscape they adored. It was the future, and e had seen enough futures to know that e could not fight it. Instead, e collected seedlings and led the village children to the forest's edge, helped them plant the forest's future, to replace what it gave to their parents. They sat together on the stumps while e taught the city youth about rural necessities.

Eir efforts were not universally looked on with kindness. The newcomers were wary, perhaps because of the stories, perhaps simply because at every point, at every change, Merrigan was there to pronounce dire predictions. Always caution, always fear—eir perspective was in total opposition to the mood of the age, pleased with itself for surviving a war it had started, eager to continue the activities that had inspired the conflict. Always expansion. Always consumption.

Perhaps, if Merrigan had remained gentle, things would have been different. But e had grown tired, and e had no gentleness left for humanity.

E went to Iarom, walked, as e had countless times before, along the side of the hateful stone road until e reached the building that was now the largest in the village. A town hall, they were calling it. A building used only for meetings, for governing. E stood before it and tapped eir staff upon the ground three times.

In another time, eir knock would have been answered immediately. E had no expectation that it would now, so even as e struck a third time, eir other hand lifted and called on the double doors of the hall to open. The doors revealed a long table with people crowded around it. These people stood and looked at the doors in confusion; when two of them came up to shut the doors again, they saw Merrigan and frowned.

"It's the Enchanter," one of them said. Merrigan recognized em as Amity, a sawhand. "Mayor Thaddeus?"

"Merrigan," said the other. Fionn. She did not smile; she looked worried.

Thaddeus approached, a slim older man Merrigan knew well. Yet the look on his face when he lifted his eyes to eirs was one e had never seen there before: regret. Merrigan could not bring emself to offer him any look of comfort or understanding at all. E looked at Fionn and Amity.

"You must halt the lumbering for a while," e said. "The forest is suffering."

The other people from the table moved toward the door; e was now addressing a small crowd.

"What are you talking about? It's fine," Amity said. "There are plenty of trees."

"The field of stumps is larger than this village several times over," Merrigan snapped. "Some of those trees were older than human civilization."

"And yet it is only a fraction of the forest's whole," Amity replied. "The forest will adapt and survive."

Merrigan narrowed eir eyes. "It's true, the forest will outlive all of you. But just as a village is made up of individuals, so is the forest. Would you say the same, that Iarom would adapt and survive, if I were to kill a fraction of the villagers?"

"Trees are not individuals," said someone in the group. "They're just trees."

Amity and Fionn, who had both heard Merrigan's lectures in the woods, turned red; but Amity did not lose eir scowl, and Fionn only looked more miserable.

"Trees breathe. They grow. They bleed. They communicate and they form bonds. It is not their fault you cannot hear them," Merrigan said. "And the more of them you kill, the more the forest compresses."

E lifted eir hand and called a shimmering, floating model of the forest into the air, hanging lovely and green at the level of eir waist. White light flowed through and among the trees, representing the various beings, the flow of life in the forest. The group leaned forward, their scowls momentarily replaced by wonder.

"Watch," Merrigan said quietly.

The trees at the forest's edge faded. The white animals retreated from the edge until the flow of the full forest was replaced with a writhing, tangled mass. "Prey cannot escape predator, and too many get eaten," said Merrigan, almost whispering. "When there is less prey, the predators begin to starve. Those creatures that eat of plants have fewer to pull from, and the plants are stripped of all they have and cannot reproduce, and so the creatures who feed on them starve too."

The white tangle grew brighter and brighter as the forest got smaller, until at last it winked out entirely in a flash that made the humans flinch. When they looked back at the illumination, it was small woods, empty except for a handful of tiny, faint white specks.

"The forest will adapt. But first, everything in it will die," Merrigan said. "And you . . . you will see only its death in your lifetime."

Merrigan shook eir hand, and the illumination disappeared. Silence surrounded them, pregnant with animosity and fear.

After a moment, Mayor Thaddeus spoke, his voice still rumbling despite his age and slight appearance. "Merrigan, we can do nothing but what we do now. We must build; people continue to come here."

"Let them turn back." E pointed down the road with eir staff, away from the forest. "Let them stay where they are. If you stop building, they will stop coming because there will be no room."

"The town profits by their coming," Thaddeus replied.

Merrigan inhaled, slowly, and eir throat burned with all the odors of civilization. Tar and smoke and metal. Acrid. Hot. An infection that had taken the village, so that they were now beyond eir power to heal. The town profited, Thaddeus said. How did the town define profit in this age, e wanted to ask. E wanted to ask whether every person of the town profited, whether everyone felt some benefit. E had only to look around to know that had not been true; that had not been true for many years.

When e exhaled, e breathed out the last of eir patience. E was surprised to find that e also lost eir anger. For the time being, e had nothing inside em but sorrow.

E conjured a flower, one that had grown in the meadows at the forest's edge and was nearly gone, being trampled by the lumberers' feet, with no shade to protect it at the edge, not strong enough to compete in the interior. Its delicate pink petals bloomed first white in eir hand before blushing to their proper color. E handed it to Fionn, who gave em a small smile.

She touched the petals; they darkened to the color of blood and melted over her hand. She shrieked. She cursed em. But Merrigan was already walking away.

29
THE FIELD OF STUMPS

MERRIGAN WALKED THROUGH THE tree stumps.

30

SENTINEL

THE SURFACES OF THE outermost stumps were mottled now, the rings turning dark and craggy with exposure. Merrigan tried not to look at them. E had already mourned them. E walked through them, eir head held high. Eir feet knew the paths, eir shoulders remembered the shade and closeness that once protected em, and eir whole body shuddered. E fell to eir knees and wept.

Eir tears were silent at first, coming without effort—e had no energy left, none to give eir sorrow and none to stop it either. But the longer e huddled there, next to a large stump that had once been a guidepost for em, a tree older than emself that had helped em learn eir way into and out of the forest—the longer e cried, the more eir tears refreshed em. Like a cleansing rain, washing away the dust and sweat of a drought. E lifted eir chin, turned eir face to the sky.

E let out a scream, which e had been holding in eir chest for years.

The clouds came, and with them came the rain. The sky split and drenched em, pounded the dirt around em into mud. E dug eir hands into the earth. E tore it as if it were flesh—as if it were the flesh of the heartless, of the monsters who saw beauty and thought only of what *profit* could be got out of it. Water flooded the hole e made and e slapped it, over and over; with each blow, it obliged em by reforming, undamaged, until e exhausted emself.

Panting, Merrigan gripped the root of the tree. E squeezed it and e willed it to *grow*. E reached into the mud with eir power and e willed them all to grow, all the murdered sentinels. Grow, e said, with bark like armor. Grow impervious.

And they did. The stumps creaked and wheezed and then shot into the sky. Their bark turned silver and hard under eir hands; the leaves that burst from their branches were sharp as knives, and they glinted red in the sunlight. All around the forest, eir magic woke the lives that had been sawed away; where the lumbering had not taken place, e touched the trees that still stood, and they too joined the shining ranks of the forest's guard.

E sighed and staggered to eir feet, bracing emself against the cool metal surface of the old tree. Resting eir forehead against it, e closed eir eyes. The effort had exhausted em, but e was satisfied. No tree of this forest would ever fall under a human's ax again.

31
EARTHQUAKE

THERE WERE NO MORE books.

Eir days among the villagers were over. Frederick's chance at returning to a normal, human life—gone. E tried, in the days after the curse, to walk with him around the forest, to pretend the forest, the villagers, emself and Frederick all had not been grievously hurt. That e had not caused such pain. But the trees screamed, as e had known they would, because e had known the humans would not give up; and even after they stopped cutting down the trees, those screams echoed in eir ears.

It was Fionn who brought the humans back into the forest, she who looked at the hard, bright sentinels and guessed that Merrigan would not have cursed the whole of the forest to such a cold half-life. She led the sawhands with their packs and baskets of equipment—their carts could not pass through—on a careful march through the knife-edged trees until they found the ones who were rough with living bark. And they cut them down.

When Merrigan knelt again to the earth and screamed with all eir power, it was not the forest e called upon. It had given all it could already. Instead, e begged the mountains for their help, and they gave it. They stirred themselves and shook the earth, trembling along their great roots until the village of Iarom, the lumber mills, all of it was no more than a leaf in a thunderstorm. The road shattered and sank into the ground. The timber camp splintered such that there was hardly a trace of it left afterward. And Merrigan used the tremendous energy to cast one final curse on the forest.

Many of the people in Iarom died. Previously, the villagers had burned their dead inside stone pyres lit with fragrant kindling, but there were too many bodies after the earthquake. The southerners lent their new home their old tradition, and the survivors built a huge barrow where the dead could lie together and comfort each other in the afterlife, as well as those who had remained. The survivors had not enough time and too much misery to properly prepare for life without those who had been lost. They built the barrow to keep the dead close, and to remind themselves of the great evil lurking behind it in the forest.

The terrible irony was this: much of the town had been destroyed, and it needed to be rebuilt.

AGAIN, FIONN LED THE villagers into the forest. She loved Merrigan too well, despite everything, to imagine the darkness the others spoke of. Hers was the first ax to fall in a forest that seemed darker and more overgrown than before.

When her blade struck the tree, the tree screamed; and when she pulled it free, the wound wept not sap, but dark red blood.

MERRIGAN CRAWLED TO THE waterfall, into the cavern behind it, and did not leave. E slept, and woke, only to sit listless upon the bare stone until sleep took em again. The nightmares of eir youth returned. E could not remember them come morning, but they left em with a cavern inside to match the one in which e sheltered, a familiar dark place to which e was, in truth, happy to retreat. It was a kind of death, which e experienced for long enough that the air grew cold, and the leaves fell to the ground. When spring came again, e heard the birdsong—e saw the flowers Frederick brought to show em—and e thought e might move again. E thought e might try.

But e was as stony as the labyrinth itself. E slept, and e woke, and even as Frederick stayed by eir side, e was alone with eir nightmares.

32
NIGHTMARES

THE NIGHTMARES WERE NONSENSICAL, but no less terrifying for it. Merrigan dreamt that the forest was a refuge no more, but a carnivorous thing—e ran and the trees snapped at em, their bark parting to reveal red mouths, flowing with blood, that would dismember em if e stayed too long near them. E dreamt that e was a statue carved from a block of black granite, except that when e was free and fully formed, the sculptor continued to chip at em with their chisel and e turned to gravel on their studio floor. E dreamt that the forest *was* as it has always been, beautiful and stately, but that the hair on the back of eir neck warned of something that snatched em up the moment e so much as breathed.

33

TORCHES

Merrigan remembered another nightmare.

E was eighteen again, convinced e was the only one without gender, frightened by the declaration of eir parents that e would never have the things they valued, that e had been taught to value. E went into the world to prove them wrong and was met with torches and rage and fear wherever e went.

And the torches followed em to the forest, and instead of lush it was dry and overgrown and dying, and the sparks brushed leaves and found kindling and sent everything up in a blaze that was visible for miles.

And e was there hiding in the forest, and eir skin burned too, and e screamed and screamed and screamed and did not die.

34

MERRIGAN AND THE CHILD

Once, there was a dream.

Merrigan became aware that e was in a meadow at the top of a small hill. E looked around slowly; behind em was a little house, more of a cottage, perched at the round apex. In front of em, at the bottom of the long shallow slope, was a little woods, with trees tall and mature but still relatively young, their trunks thin compared to the ancients Merrigan had grown used to. Those trunks and the meadow bore the signs of deer, which Merrigan wondered at given the closeness of the house. But it was pitch black, the deepest part of night.

To Merrigan's left was a pile of sticks that, with effort, e discerned was a kind of shack that was that very moment shielding a human child. The child's weeping was alternately the harsh, desperate gasps of immediate danger, and the mewling whimpers of dread. At length, all weeping ceased, and Merrigan could hear only the slow deep breaths of sleep.

The night shifted and Merrigan turned to face the house, and the direction from which the sun would rise. The air swirled mild around em, and e felt curiously displaced by unfamiliarity. E had no wish to disturb the dream. For the first time in an unmeasurable stretch, e felt what e would have once called peace.

The child stirred inside their precariously arranged dwelling, and Merrigan began to wonder if this was a dream at all. Why should e dream of a child? E had nothing to offer children any longer. Yet if there was one thing familiar about the dream, it was the way the child had cried. E found emself asking, "Why do you weep, child?"

E had spoken more to emself than the child, but to eir surprise, an answer came from the sticks.

"I do not want to grow breasts, and there is nothing I can do to stop it."

Merrigan's throat tightened with unexpected emotion. "Do you fear to grow up?"

"No," said the child. "That is, I—must all girls have such things upon their chest?"

E almost could have laughed. So many friends, so many gender-kin had asked similar questions or had similar thoughts. *I could be a girl, if not for this. Must I be a man if I look like this? What if I want both? Neither? I don't understand. Why does it matter? Why won't they listen?* Merrigan had abandoned more than just Frederick to curses it had been within eir power to resolve. E marveled how quickly laughter could turn to tears.

Merrigan turned eir awareness to the child, reached out with those senses Gabin so envied, and studied the point from which their body began.

"No," e said to the child. "But they will grow on yours if they are not stopped."

The tremor of tears returned to the child's voice. "I know. I feel them coming, and there's nothing I can do."

"Why do you fear them?" Merrigan asked.

"I do not fear them," the child replied. "But I do not want them on *me*."

Merrigan realized e was nodding, though the child could not see em. That was how e had always felt too. And as e listened to the child sniffle, come almost to crying again, and then master themselves, e realized that e was not dreaming at all. Had the child somehow summoned em? Or had e been reaching out, unconsciously, searching for some mirror of eir own feelings? E put eir hands to the grass with more wonder, feeling how real it was, damp and cold and tickling against eir skin. The sky had shifted again, begun to lighten in accordance with the passage of time.

"Will you join me? The sun is rising," Merrigan said.

After a moment, one of the branches moved, and a pubescent child crawled carefully out from the hole. They were short and lean, their nightshirt dirty from sleeping on the ground; there were scrapes on their fingers and cheeks. Everything about them, their voice, their carriage, the expression on their face, spoke of that malleable time between childhood and adulthood when everything could still change. Merrigan smiled at them, already hoping e could find some way to make sure the changes they faced would make them happy. They smiled back, an adult smile, as though they already knew it was a futile hope.

Merrigan patted the ground beside em, and the child settled there. They both looked toward the peak of the thatch roof, waiting for the sun to make the straw into gold.

"You do not have to be what they say you are," Merrigan said quietly.

"Father says that we are what we are, and it is abominable to change that."

"He is right. But then who decides what we are?"

The child thought for a moment. "Our parents?"

Merrigan smirked and looked down at them. "Do they know your every thought and feeling? Will you tell them what you have told me?" When the child frowned, e laughed. "Then how can they know what you are?"

The child shivered and hugged themself. "If I told them . . ." They shook their head. "Father would never allow me to see the physicians. He dismissed our cook when she took her daughter to them."

Merrigan looked at the child more appraisingly. "You have considered this already."

"When the blood came," they said, with a resigned sigh beyond their age. "I thought perhaps that was all that would come."

They were silent for awhile. Merrigan watched the place where the sun would appear steadily, though e felt the child's gaze on them. The air grew so warm so quickly that e knew this was farther south than e had ever ventured on eir rounds. Even if disaster had not befallen the north, e would never have met this child, never have been able to help them anyway. E did not know how e had come to be in that meadow, after e had thought eir power exhausted, but e would make the most of it and do one small good thing. E turned to the child with a smile, happy with the warmth of the sun on eir face after decades without it. E reached into the sleeve of eir cloak, and withdrew a thorn from the labyrinth's rose hedge.

"Prick yourself with this thorn and draw three drops of blood; flick each into either a fire or water," e instructed. "Do this every day for three months, then every three weeks for three years, then every three months for the rest of your life, and you shall have the form you desire."

The child took the thorn and held it up to the morning light— but Merrigan did not get to see what they did with it, or even their reaction. The next instant, e was back in the dark cavern behind the waterfall, stiff as if e had never left, groggy as if e had just been startled from sleep.

The memory, whenever Merrigan returned to it, was wreathed in golden sunlight, keen where it caught in the straw thatch and in the child's dark honey hair. When e felt sleep forcing itself upon eir mind, e wished to dream of the southern meadow where the deer were not afraid to come, and of the little cottage at the top of the hill. But e never saw it again.

Interlude
BE HESITANT

IF GABIN WAS SURPRISED to receive an invitation from her hometown, she was more surprised to arrive to death, destruction, and suspicion. It took time to piece together what had happened, because there was so much anger and fear. It resulted in severe exaggeration. It wasn't until Gabin had a quiet dinner with her cousin Valencia and Valencia's daughter-in-law, Fionn, that the truth became clear, at least to Gabin.

It had been one hundred and eight years since she had seen Merrigan, that night when the Enchanter stole her spark of magic. Her existing charms were unchanged, which was why she still lived—her bond to the tree in the Immortal Gardens of the Sorcerers' Guild was still strong, the more so because it was against guild law for sorcerers to meddle with the plants in that garden. She trusted in that law, had to, because she hardly went to the guild anymore. She couldn't bear the snickers or the pity, or worst: the indifference. Though she had tried to be a doctor, she had been easily frustrated with the poor medicines available in the absence of magic, and so had given that up for a reclusive academic life that served her bitterness. She collected folk tales, hiring people to travel the length and breadth of Callister, recording tales of magical creatures, or great odds, or inexplicable heroes. Her first book had been a poor attempt to woo Merrigan back, full of the stories that showed eir goodness, a goodness that had made Gabin weep with jealousy and love as she edited the stories together. She could never forget eir words about the danger of destroying something; she had thrown their kinship into the fire and destroyed it, and she would never be worthy of it again. She alternated between despairing of that fact, and reveling in it, rejecting any desire for Merrigan's love.

The tales had changed in the twenty or so years since that first collection. Listening to Fionn relate the events of Iarom's earthquake, Gabin knew the second one would be wholly different.

Fionn, pregnant and newly showing—her husband had died in the cataclysm—led Gabin to the forest's edge, restored and closer to the village than it had been even in Gabin's youth. The sentinel trees were hard and cold even before Gabin touched them. The knives that made no attempt to disguise themselves as leaves swayed menacingly in a light breeze. It looked as though they were reaching for flesh to cut.

"And beyond these?"

"Worse," Fionn said darkly. "The trees bleed and scream, like stuck pigs."

Gabin grimaced and sighed. "If the elders invited me back in the hopes that I could do something about this magic, I am sorry to disappoint them. It is far too strong for me."

Fionn nodded, as if she had guessed this, and Gabin was glad to be spared explaining that she had no power at all. Silence stretched on between them. The young woman stared at the trees with tears in her eyes.

"How could e do this to us?" she asked, finally. "I thought e was my friend."

"Undoubtedly, e thought you were eir friend too," Gabin replied. She looked away from the forest, unable to bear it any longer; it summoned in her the same oscillating extremes of feeling as the folk tales, where it was impossible to sort out whether Merrigan was a hero or a villain. Fionn met her gaze, young and imploring, as if asking Gabin for some explanation of how everything could go so wrong.

Gabin put her hand, smooth and ink-stained, on Fionn's shoulder and said, "The most true thing Merrigan ever taught me was this: be hesitant to destroy something, for destruction is permanent."

PART III

35

HISTORIES

DARRAGH STAGGERED DOWNRIVER, SOAKED through and chilled to the bone. The voice from the cavern rippled over his skin, and if he shivered, he could not say whether it was due to cold or fear or the sound of that single word, *Leave*, striking him again and again. He saw a gap in the riverbank growth and hauled himself out of the water, started to run, and fell hard to his knees immediately, his legs too accustomed to running through water. He stayed there, on his hands and knees, panting and suddenly immersed in the totality of his exhaustion. He wanted to weep and did not know why.

When he looked up, the path was before him. The fox was there. It waited for him to stand, and when he started to walk, it disappeared into the trees.

Darragh made his way back to the labyrinth, through light that never changed, but when he passed through the rose hedge it was twilight. He stumbled to his room and the beautiful half-living bed, and slept deeply.

Frederick was not to be found when morning came. Darragh

tried to go about his chores as usual, but he was beset by twinges all over his skin, and could hardly focus on his tasks. The roses pricked him so many times that blood ran down his wrists in thin bright rivulets, until at last the stems pulled away from him entirely in protest of his absentminded handling. Sighing, wishing Frederick were about for him to talk to, he cast for some other occupation. Something tickled his shoulder and he twitched toward it, and found himself thinking of the waterfall.

And the dark shape in the cavern behind it.

He returned to his room and found the lovely little jug the potter had given him on the road, months ago. This he filled with fresh goat milk, stoppering it carefully. He noticed a plethora of fallen magnolia petals and gathered up the nicest ones, which he bound to a thin stick with a bit of twine so that it looked like a long-stemmed flower.

Then, he made his careful way into the forest, heading west. It was hard going, for he did not really know the way. Though he thought he saw foxes in his peripheral vision, none of them ever came onto the path. But he endeavored to empty his mind and think only of how much he would like to visit the waterfall and its resident, to give them these small neighborly tokens. He got properly lost, and kept going, the jug snug in the crook of his elbow, the crafted flower bobbing gently in his hand. At last, the air temperature shifted, and the smell and sound of water reached him, and he followed it to the waterfall.

He went carefully up the steps, to avoid both crushing his tokens and disturbing the resident of the waterfall too much. He went as close to the cavern as he dared, and placed the jug and flower lightly on the ground between the sheet of water and the shadows of the cave. Then he descended, with measured slowness. He climbed the boulder and settled there, imagining that if he let the resident of the cave see him from a respectful distance, they might come out.

Darragh did his best to avoid thinking of the resident of the cave as the Enchanter. Indeed, he let his focus move away from the resident entirely, now that he had given his gifts. Instead he breathed deeply of the cool damp air, almost weeping at the longing for the sea that stirred within him. He marveled at the soft moss beneath him, and smiled when a little snake found a boulder close enough to the water to be in the sun but far enough from the falls to escape the spray. He let his gaze take in the full height of the falls, then devoted attention to each part. The top, where it might have looked like a crenelated wall except that the water spilled over it and spoke of the land beyond that edge. The upper portion, where that water clung to the rock that no longer served to support a riverbed, the rock that began to curl away from the water like lovers drifting apart, like a parent setting their children free, like friends pursuing different dreams. The place where water met water and churned the pool's depths, leaving the mud unsettled, forever shifting and rising and falling in a cloud of unjoined particles.

But the most fascinating was the water in front of the cavern. Without anything else to support it, the water clung to itself to form ephemeral, lace-like patterns in the air. It danced, each molecule changing partners a staggering number of times in the seconds it spent falling from rock to pool; long lines of swinging, complicated quadrilles, droplet waltzes, too many glorious movements to follow, winking in the sunlight. Darragh sat and watched the water fall for hours, until the sun moved away and the darkness of the cavern overpowered everything.

He had perceived no movement. But before he slid down the boulder, he bowed his head to the dark.

MERRIGAN FELT HIM RETURN to the waterfall. A jolt ran through em, as though e had been struck by lightning; eir heart momentarily stopped, e exhaled eir last breath, and in the utter silence that surrounded em, e heard the wonder he felt as he beheld the falls. Heard it as clearly as if it had been music—and when eir heart started again, it beat in time with the drum of that song.

He was a creature of heat and light, like the fire that burned in all eir nightmares. If he came too near, e was sure e would crumble into ash.

Oh, but he was beautiful.

FREDERICK WAS WAITING WHEN Darragh came home. The starlight rendered the labyrinth pale and undefined, but Darragh had no trouble finding his way to Frederick's tower, where the orange glow of his fire seemed suddenly equal to the sun in brightness. Frederick was perched on his bed, arms crossed; he looked up when Darragh glanced in, and smiled, but said nothing. Darragh likewise remained silent. He had missed Frederick and wanted to talk to him, but now that he was there, any questions or stories he had seemed unintelligible even to himself.

At last he said, "Will not you ask me where I've been?"

"I know where you've been," Frederick replied.

Darragh joined him on the bed, slowly, waiting to see if Frederick would stop him or tell him to sit somewhere else. No such interdiction came; so he settled with his legs drawn up, leaning against the smooth stone. "Are you disappointed in me? You said I should keep to the east."

Frederick grinned and shook his head. "No, I am amazed by you. Have you no fear at all?"

Darragh gave an incredulous laugh. "Whether or not a person goes into danger is no indication of how much fear they feel," he said.

"True enough. I will be more direct," Frederick replied. "I understand that the Enchanter was kind to you when you were a child, but you have more information and experience now. Are you not afraid of em?"

"I am no more afraid of em than I was of the golden beast in the forest," Darragh said. "Which is to say, very; but once my life is in the hands of such a being, more powerful than I could ever be, the fear is no longer useful. My fate will be what it is."

"Yet I stalked you; I hunted you. *You* chose to put your life in eir hands, by going back to the waterfall," Frederick said.

"My life has been in eir hands since I was thirteen," Darragh replied. "And I have been content to leave it there."

"Why?"

"I felt . . . I felt that e understood me in a way no one else ever had, or ever could," Darragh said. "Eir gift to me was something I needed desperately and could not have even articulated to myself. I idolized em. You are right to say I have more information and experience now, but all that has added to my idolatry is a depth that has shifted it into a profound admiration, wreathed in sympathy for the change in eir circumstances."

Frederick stared at him, and it was difficult to meet his gaze, because it seemed to be too many contradictory things at once. Miserable, relieved, disgusted, loving. Darragh did not regret any of his words, but could not tell what effect they had had on Frederick, and knew not how to proceed. The silence became uncomfortable, until Frederick took Darragh's hand in his and held it tightly. His expression, now stable, was loss mingled with hope.

"We have been so alone here for so long," Frederick whispered, half to himself. "We have hardly even had each other these hundred years."

Darragh swallowed the lump forming in his throat. "Because of the Bleeding Trees?"

Frederick nodded. "Merrigan's power is not so great as you think. Not anymore. E used so much of it in eir final efforts to protect the forest. Then e crawled to that cave and has never come out since."

He began to sob. Darragh hurried to embrace him, and they fumbled until they came to a comfortable position, for Frederick was much larger than Darragh. They ended with Frederick's head and shoulders half in Darragh's arms, half in his lap, turned in toward Darragh's chest, where his surcoat soaked up Frederick's tears.

Darragh held him, staring out without looking at anything in particular, until the sky began to lighten and the fire was embers. Whatever he had expected to find, it had not been this: two people as trapped by their histories as he was.

36

MERRIGAN

THERE WAS NO SIGN of the jug or the flower when Darragh returned the next day to the labyrinth, not even their remains dashed on the rocks below the fall. He took this as a good sign and climbed the boulder again. He sat for a while, watching the water, as entrancing as ever.

Merrigan. Frederick had so named the Enchanter. The thought of it quickened Darragh's heartbeat; it felt like an intimacy he had never thought of achieving. Part of him wanted to stand proudly upon the boulder and call out to em by eir name, like some prince in one of the folk tales. But though he had spent so much time thinking of em, he could not know whether e would even remember him, or connect him to the wiry child who had once been caught weeping in a meadow. So he thought he might speak to em, introduce himself. The boulder was too far from the cave. He would have to shout to be heard.

He slid down onto the smaller rocks beside it, which he carefully traversed to the damp steps up to the cavern's ledge. He sat himself at the top of the steps, his legs hanging over the ledge, his bare feet catching mist from the water. There he sat in silence awhile longer, wondering what to say. Ought he to demand the magic he'd come for, healing for his father? Even had he known nothing of the Enchanter's strained power, he would never have been so bold.

He could wait. He trusted in the sleep-like death, the alchemist's gift.

"The rose hedge seems to have improved," he heard himself say. He started, then laughed under his breath. "I—my name is Darragh. I have lived several weeks in the forest, in the labyrinth. I help Frederick with its maintenance. The rose hedge, mainly. He—"

He remembered that Frederick could not trim the hedge because of the Enchanter's weakness, and stopped himself. Instead he said, "He is much larger than I am, and so I can get into the places where he cannot, to trim the bushes."

Birds sang, the pool churned, and fish splashed as they broke the surface of the water in their lunging for surface insects. Leaves rustled in breezes and tree rodents scratched their way into the branches. But the cavern was silent.

"They like the attention, I think. I suppose roses have that reputation, for vanity among flowers, but I'm a poor judge. I have spent so much of my life at sea, where there are no flowers. Though it's true I have seen some marvelous blooms in the places I have visited. But I'm not often ashore. I am second mate and I must stay with the ship, and our docking is usually only long enough for unloading, reloading, resupplying. Docks are not places for flowers. There are roses carved on our figurehead, though."

Darragh drew his knees into his chest. "I gather the petals that have fallen, but there are so many I'm often pressed to conjure a use for them. My mother used to make them into cosmetics, of which I have no need." He laughed. "Perhaps some hydrating cream would not go amiss on my poor windburned skin; I may try it after all, with the goat's milk, perhaps. But I would make a syrup if only I could get sugar. That would be a fine treat. Some of the petals I have set to drying, for I think I could make a serviceable tea of them; there is little in the way of a hot drink, unless it be broth, in the forest. Frederick tells me the coffee ran out long ago. The thing of a hot drink is that it is not merely for one's physical thirst, it becomes something of a spiritual comfort as well. It was always something to look forward to, on the *Augustina,* and the ships before it. It was a pleasant way to mark out the passage of time, rather than reckoning it by scrubbing decks or scraping barnacles or coiling rope or . . ."

Self-consciousness took his voice for the moment. Surely, the Enchanter had no interest in his seahand's philosophies. He crossed his arms on his knees and rested his forehead against his forearms, his breathing inexplicably labored. The desire to weep was upon him again, but why? This time, he did not fight it. He let his tears fall and imagined them mingling with the infant river below him, and wondered at them and the crush of indeterminate emotion in his chest.

Sailors often wept, down in the dark, cocooned in their hammocks; Darragh had, in his first year, shed many tears unassigned to any particular misfortune or brutality. Such a practice ceased once he found his footing, which he had long considered to signal emotional maturity. Perhaps it was only another kind of callus, one for his heart to match the ones on his hands and feet.

"It is not that I don't love the sea, or sailing," he said, uncertain for a moment whether he was speaking aloud again. "I do. As much as I am able. But in all my life I think only one love has ever touched my heart, for Sidra, who is my sister though we do not share blood."

A few more heartbeats, and he said, "I hate the word *love.* It conveys nothing; its meaning is only supplied by the hearer, and it is *their* meaning, and the odds of it matching yours are poor indeed. Passion? I have passion for nothing, not even survival, though that has been my whole occupation for the better part of two decades. How can I have spent so much of my life with this coldness inside me?"

This time, when Darragh fled from the waterfall, it was *his* words that frightened him.

"I WANT TO APOLOGIZE for yesterday," he said the next day.

The sky was gray through the break in the trees above the waterfall and the pool and the boulder. The light was enough to brighten the highest edges of the lacy water curtain, but it did not sparkle as it had before. Darragh felt likewise: awake, alive, if a little duller than usual. He had invited one of the nanny goats and her kid to walk with him a bit, and to his surprise, they had both followed him to the waterfall. The nanny goat had settled next to him on the cavern's ledge, while the kid tried its hooves on the chips and crevices in the rock face, called by some old mountain instinct. He scratched the ewe between her horns.

"I forgot that I was not speaking to myself, and my thoughts wandered to a place that . . . well, I should not have shared such things with you, until we know each other better. It was not my intention to overburden or overwhelm you, and I am sorry," he said.

"It is almost midsummer," he said. "I have taken to tracking the days by scratching the wall of my room. Not out of any sense of imprisonment; I have my own need to know the date. But it is hard, in this place, to feel time. Perhaps when autumn comes, and winter, it will be easy. Perhaps there are two seasons only, this far north. The garden helps."

"I WISH MY FATHER had let us learn more skills. I am determined to make bread; I know a sketch of the methods, but every time I consider the actuation of my desire, I encounter more questions. How fine should the flour be ground? How much is required? I must build an oven, but I do not know how large it should be, or how hot, or how many vents it needs. At least I know that I need not separate the bran from the germ. I had white bread recently, for the first time in years, and it felt oddly sticky in my mouth. There was nothing to chew, and it only coated my tongue and teeth, and I could not get it swallowed.

"I did more traveling on the path that led me here than I did in all my years at sea, it seemed. A ship is largely static. There is high turnover of able seahands, to be sure, but one never really gets to know them, and so their coming and going has less impact. But when I came here—well, first I went to my father's house, and back to the city, and then north, and I met so many new people. Oddly enough, I felt that I learned more about them, grew closer to them, over the course of a week or a day or even an hour, than I have to the vast majority of the people I have sailed with in my life. It is so easy to feel stuck, at sea. Sometimes there is such a powerful sense of movement, yes, a high wind or strong seas . . . but once one is used to the moderate winds and the steady sea, they begin to weaken, to feel endless and unchanging. It is a comfort sometimes. Sometimes it feels like a kind of hell. That is why the wind-singers are so coveted and well paid. A captain with a wind-singer need never fear the emptiness.

"At least this place is never empty.

"I cannot stay long today. Frederick is concerned, with summer upon us, about the overgrowth and the deadfall. He says it is a fire's dream. But I will come again tomorrow."

"BREAD REMAINS BEYOND ME, but I have made a rose wine, and brought you some. Well, a rose liquor, for we have no casks to age it in. I am well familiar with casks, so I'm sure I could make one, but we have no iron for the bands. Probably some kind of clay pot would serve; I should set some aside as an experiment. But distilling, that is something every sailor must learn, for we are happier to drink liquor than to feel weevils in our teeth. At least, I am. The distilling kills the weevils when nothing else will. I will say it is much easier to do on dry land than on a ship."

"WE'LL NEVER CLEAR ENOUGH," Darragh said.

Summer was nearly over, and as he watched the orange sun touch the canopy, all he could think of was fire.

He had cleared the rose hedge of its overgrowth, but any

improvement in it had stalled. He and Frederick had gathered deadfall out in the forest, disturbing great mats of dried leaves and sticks, moist and fungal underneath but a thick brittle layer above; pulling unending coils of downed vines that scratched Darragh's arms like old rope; hauling huge broken branches and trunks either to the labyrinth, for their hearths, or to some other place where it could serve safely as shelter or a brace. Weeks of work, crudely managed with Darragh's small human hands and Frederick's huge beastly paws, at which Frederick would look back not with satisfaction but with a shake of his head.

There had been no fire in the forest since the cataclysm, he admitted. But Merrigan had always said that fire was normal for a forest, that it was needed from time to time, that the longer it went between clearings, the trickier the next would be.

"Of course it is impossible to imagine two people clearing the whole forest," Darragh said to the silent cavern. "So we have been working in lines, at random, creating places that hopefully will calm or break a fire from sheer lack of fuel. I had not thought once of forest fire until he began all this, but now he has put the fear in me. But fire is a great terror at sea, too. I suppose I only imagined that on land, there was space to flee. Here there is too much space, almost. We have not come close to the edge of the forest, or to the mountains, which is where a fire must truly break. We will never clear enough, not this summer."

He laughed suddenly, and said, "Summer! I have been here so much longer than I thought to be. I do not even know for certain whether my father is still alive."

He sat silently for a few more moments, watching the sun's indistinct edge sink out of sight. His walk home would be dark, but that was nothing new; he often walked home in the dark these days, for he came so late to the waterfall that he could not spend any great time there if his intention was to gain the labyrinth by sunset. But Darragh no longer feared the forest in the dark, nor did it impede his homeward trek in any way. His stomach growled. He had come to the waterfall directly from their most recent zone of work, and had only eaten some fruit when he and Frederick took a break. Though he did not want to leave, he pulled himself away from the rock upon which he leaned, and prepared to stand.

"Your father lives yet," said the voice from the cavern.

37

COME INTO THE LIGHT

THE FIRST NIGHT AFTER Darragh came to the waterfall, Merrigan dreamt of a tree. A single tree, young, stood on its own in an unremarkable yard—the whole dream, e stood before the tree and watched the breeze flutter its blue-green leaves.

The second night, Merrigan expected to sleep, for e had never felt more tired in all eir long life. But e slept not; e was trapped in eir body, trapped with the beating of eir heart and the goose-bumps rippling up and down the length of em. For so long, this flesh had felt foreign to em, cold and disconnected, a thing e was supposed to inhabit and could not fit emself to, could not command. So much the better, e had said to emself for years, so much the better that eir flesh should be dead, for e had nothing inside em like the image of a living thing.

E wept in the dark, and e felt each tear that fell from eir eyes, even when they came in a torrent. E could not have given a reason for eir weeping, if pressed. E cried as an infant cries when it is pulled from the warm dark safety of its parent's body and subjected to the sting of the air and the burning of the light. E cried to fill eir lungs again; e cried at the softness of fabric on eir skin.

MERRIGAN DRANK THE GOAT milk, the first liquid to pass eir lips in countless years. It was so much sweeter than e remembered. When e had finished it, e spent a long time holding the jug in eir hands, admiring its smoothness. Its fine quality became beauty to Merrigan's eye, because it had come from Darragh.

E saw him when he sat on the boulder, in the sun, which made the hair falling to his jaw look like pure gold, and gave such depth of color to the skin of his bare shoulders that it seemed not just a reflection of light but a tangible warmth Merrigan could feel even at a distance. E saw, even from the shadows of eir cavern, the focus and understanding in his brown eyes. E longed for it and feared it.

E could have still watched him, when he moved to the ledge and out of sight of eir physical eyes, but e was content to listen only to his voice. His words were kind and charming and sincere, but the melody of his speech was entrancing. His voice was as clear as posture in conveying his moods, and Merrigan almost felt e could imagine the way he sat, the way his face arranged itself as he spoke.

Many times, e dragged emself to the edge of the shadows, so, so tempted to join Darragh, to speak to him. But eir voice was somewhere else; eir language was unintelligible. E relearned how to speak, listening to the sailor who, for all his scars and calluses, seemed the most gentle creature Merrigan had ever encountered. As often as e was drawn back to life by these tastes of some good feeling, though, e was slapped back to the dark by eir guilt, unknowingly resurrected by this or that comment, particularly when the talk of fire risk began.

Merrigan knew, from eir first sense of Darragh, why he had come. E saw the shadow of his father hanging over him. Yet he never made any request, hardly ever spoke of the man, and quickly changed the subject if he was mentioned. Why this should be the case, Merrigan did not investigate or speculate on. E allowed emself to exist with another being without expectations between them, until the guilt e felt at abandoning Frederick reasserted itself. E was preparing to slink back into the full depths of the shadows when Darragh laughed mirthlessly.

"Summer! I have been here so much longer than I thought to be. I do not even know for certain whether my father is still alive," he said.

Sometimes his comments were like this, more to himself it seemed than to Merrigan, but Merrigan always listened. This was some question, a concern Darragh could not talk himself out of, and so, Merrigan was moved to speak.

"Your father lives yet," e said.

Darragh stilled, like a hare when it hears the step of the fox; but he relaxed just as quickly, and turned so that he could gaze upon the darkness of the cave. The evening light was fading. Perhaps that was why his voice was so earnest, so eager, when he said, "Come into the light."

Merrigan tried to remember what e looked like. E moved eir fingers, tensed eir limbs, in a clumsy attempt to form some image of eir shape. E stood, stretching out as slowly as a sapling, hesitant and a little frightened, for e had forgotten how tall e was. The blanket that had shrouded em rotted away as e straightened eir long-hunched back. E stepped forward, and flinched when the light touched the fabric of eir fairy robes, as fine and shimmering as ever. There on the threshold between light and dark, Merrigan trembled, uncertain whether the sun would hurt em after so long.

Darragh held out his hand.

His palm was up. He was not seizing, but inviting. Offering help, and hope. His own hope, which had waited so patiently inside him, so quiet he might not have even realized it was there. Merrigan could taste his hope and it threatened to make em sick, for hope and fear went so completely together; Merrigan had never known a hope that was rewarded instead of punished, no pleasure that was without a bitter edge. Nor had Darragh, e thought. Yet still he extended that small, coarse hand.

Merrigan took his hand, and it was an anchor as e stepped out of the cavern, like the roots of the labyrinth's upper forest, which Merrigan had once used to climb up to that bright path. E had waited too long, and it was a murky twilight into which e came, and so it was not very dramatic when e came entirely out of the shadows and lifted eir eyes from eir hesitant feet to Darragh's face. E recalled that e was tall, a head and a half above Darragh. The world around them turned from the oranges and lavenders of sunset to a uniform muddy green, then blue laced with purples. It seemed to Merrigan the only brightness left was the sap-gold color of Darragh's hair.

Darragh smiled at em, a small, tender smile so fleeting that if the look of it had not stayed in Darragh's eyes, Merrigan might have questioned whether e had really seen it or only dreamt of it. E wanted to smile back, but e had forgotten how. E could only stare in wonder.

DARRAGH DID NOT LEAVE the waterfall that night. In silence, he and the Enchanter sat down on the ledge, leaning against the rock face, just outside the cavern. They did not let go their hands, even for a moment; neither did the grip relax. It remained a constant tension, the source of which Darragh could not discern, while he and perhaps the Enchanter drifted in and out of sleep.

The Enchanter was beautiful. In many ways, e was as Darragh remembered: skin as brown as new decking and as full of color as taffeta, eyes dark and deep like the sea at night. But the sadness he had only perceived in retrospect was powerfully tangible, more so than he had expected. Perhaps the Enchanter's magic made it stronger, or perhaps Darragh's imagination was not quite able to fathom the nature and magnitude of the Enchanter's hurts, as was often the case among people. Even if it was the latter case, it made no real difference. Darragh's grip on the Enchanter's hand stayed tight because it felt like the only way he had to communicate his sympathy.

They did not speak, and when Darragh woke completely,

with the sun beginning to peer over the canopy of the clearing, he felt dizzy with hunger, and more than hunger. There was no rest to be had in his body. He knew not whether the Enchanter was awake also, and dared not look over. He felt eir hand in his, still tense but perhaps, perhaps just slightly less than at first; he felt eir arm, bare, against the length of his. He felt the coldness of the rock on which he rested. He wanted to chafe his cold, dull feet, which had not worn shoes these months in the forest, with his free hand, but did not. Though he shivered with energy, he could not bring himself to move.

Then he felt it—warmth. Warmth like the sun coming out from behind a cloud, like slipping into a hot bath, like fresh hot stones between bedsheets in winter, and like putting weary feet in front of a fire. Warmth like arousal, coming in unpredictable blooms all over him, warmth that grew and spread like honey until it filled every part of him down to his bones with such languid and complete heat as he had not felt since the farthest trip south the *Augustina* ever took, when he forgot what cold even was.

"Your heart is not cold," the Enchanter whispered. Eir voice was deep and smooth, and sounded so much like e had never stopped using it that it seemed to surprise em as much as Darragh. E was quiet for long moments, while Darragh basked in the warmth like a snake and listened to his heart thump hard, waiting for em to speak again.

"It never has been," e said at last. "Do not judge the stirring of your feelings by someone else's measure."

Darragh expected to be struck silent with awe, but he found his voice still available to him; perhaps because if he had woken the next instant to find himself in his bunk on the ship, he would not have been surprised. He said, "Never has been?"

When the Enchanter replied, there was a thinness to the words that made it sound as though they were being spoken through a small smile or smirk. "Even as a child, you had great under-standing," e said.

"You remember me?"

The Enchanter laughed once, then again, as if in surprise. "How could I forget you?"

Darragh's heart beat so fast, he lost track of its tempo. "I am a great deal changed since then. I am unrecognizable."

The Enchanter pulled away slightly then, and Darragh did the same, and they looked at each other in the light of a new day. Eir gaze bore into him, narrowed, eir expression pinched with something that could have been suspicion or consternation but felt like sincerity. He said nothing, only drank in every sensation he could, for if it was a dream, he longed to remember it.

The Enchanter said, "Not to me."

Darragh exhaled; it took him a moment to remember to inhale.

"You know my name," e said. "I want you to use it."

"Merrigan," Darragh said. The syllables felt like seduction in his mouth.

E smiled. "Darragh."

He closed his eyes and sighed and leaned back against the rock. His head spun.

"You should go. You must eat," said Merrigan.

Darragh knew e was right. He had gone long without food before, and if he spent another day at the waterfall, it would be a terrible time getting back to the labyrinth the next day. He shook off the sleepiness of the warmth, shivered his nervous energy back into motion, redirected the tension in his grip into the rest of his limbs, and stood. But Merrigan did not stand with him, though he still held eir hand.

"I cannot go back," e said, so softly Darragh thought perhaps he read the words in eir face, rather than heard em speak them. "Not yet."

Darragh nodded. He did not know how to take his leave, to say goodbye, so he said, as he had every day since he brought the jug and flower, "I will come again tomorrow."

FREDERICK WAS WAITING FOR him, this time out in the forest, out of sight of the waterfall but close enough that Darragh met him quickly. He sprawled in the path, head resting on his front paws, seemingly at ease but for his gaze, fixed on the direction from whence Darragh would come. When Darragh appeared, Frederick lifted his head, then heaved himself up to a vulture-like posture, quivering on the knife's edge between fear and joy. Then Darragh smiled, and Frederick shook himself and held his head high. He knelt so that Darragh could climb onto his back, and bore him home to the labyrinth.

38

OUTSIDE LIFE

WHEN DARRAGH CAME THE next morning, he had a sack of
fruit with him: crisp apples and pears, and velvety plums, peaches.
Merrigan watched him climb the steps to the cavern's ledge with
ease and remembered the careful, cautious way he'd first scaled it.
The fruit was all from the labyrinth, he said. He did not say that
there was no fruit in the rest of the forest, but e heard it in his voice
regardless. He arranged the sack into a kind of bowl, rolling the
top down until it stood open mostly on its own, with its contents
exposed. Then he settled himself into a cross-legged position
opposite Merrigan.

He was even more beautiful in daylight, with the shadows from
the waterfall playing over his face and mirroring the patterns of
light and dark scars across his brow, his nose, his cheeks. His beard
was redder than his hair, except when the sunlight caught it and
gave it blond edges. He wore a sleeveless tunic over his breeches,
which exposed his wiry arms, but even without that, his whole
bearing told of strength and grace. This was a man whose every
movement was measured and controlled. Merrigan wondered
what it must feel like to inhabit a body so fully and completely.

"Can you eat?" Darragh asked.

Merrigan had not felt hunger for a hundred years. But for Darragh's sake, e willed eir arm, slack in eir lap, to turn over. For a long moment, nothing happened; then eir fingers twitched. In slow, halting movements, e turned eir palm up. Into it, Darragh placed a soft ripe fruit.

He looked away from em, watching the lace patterns of the falls, letting em sit with the fruit in eir hand for a long while before e was able to bring it to eir lips. He did not watch em while e held it there, not biting and chewing but shredding it with eir unwilling teeth and sucking down the sweet flesh, which e turned to pulp with eir saliva and eir tongue. And when at last he did look back— then, he smiled at em, and handed em a handkerchief for the juice coating eir chin and hand.

He was so gentle with Merrigan that day, and the next, and the next, until e began to be gentler with emself—until eir stomach remembered how to feel sated, until eir limbs desired to move from one attitude to another—until eir voice was once again the instrument of eir thoughts.

That was not to say that Merrigan came altogether back to life, or all at once. There were nights when e closed eir eyes with light in eir heart and optimism for the day to come, only to wake and tremble with rage e could neither explain nor suppress, and e bloodied eir fists upon the walls of eir cavern. There were days when walking the length of the ledge exhausted em. But there were also days when e sat unmoving not because e was captive to eir stony flesh, but because the birdsong echoed down to em and e could hear it better when e was still, or because the foxes had come to sleep among the folds of eir robe and e could not bear to disturb them.

Darragh bandaged eir hands; Darragh helped em back to eir makeshift bed; Darragh sat and listened with em.

One evening Merrigan wept in his presence and begged him to leave em, because e could not bear his kindness.

He said, "I'll go, for now. But I will come again tomorrow."

"Don't. Go home. Leave the forest," Merrigan said.

He was silent. Merrigan stared at the ground—e had fallen to eir hands and knees—and listened for him to leave. He did not; he knelt beside em and placed a careful, tanned hand next to eirs. Slowly, waiting, e thought, for a word of resistance, he lifted eir hand and placed it on his wrist, that e might feel the ridges of skin, of scars, there.

"I begged someone to leave me, too, once; and in the end I was glad they had not strayed far," he said, softly. "I will leave you alone a little while, because you ask me to. But I will not go far, and I will see you again in the morning."

He slid his wrist out from under Merrigan's hand. E longed to catch his fingers with eirs, to clasp them and try to convey eir gratitude to him, but e could not marshal eir body in time. He slipped away from em, and out into the forest. When he was gone, e rolled onto eir back and looked up at the stars and asked, why? Why did e want to dwell in this dark place, why did e think it was safe? It was the most grievous deception e had ever perpetrated. E could not even take comfort that it was only practiced on emself, for Frederick and now Darragh had been dragged into it, and despite eir efforts e could not convince them to leave.

E asked again, why?

Why should they stay? They were not empty, as Merrigan was.

E curled the fingers that had touched Darragh's scars, dug those nails into eir palm until it hurt. E had been full once. E had been bursting with dreams, and with love, and e had lost it. All of it.

E wanted it back.

DARRAGH WANTED TO CLIMB to the top of the falls. When he suggested this to Merrigan, e looked back at him with an expression that was already regretful, wistful as if e were remembering some distant and now unattainable pleasure. He wondered briefly whether it was too soon—he had been waiting, perhaps he had misjudged—but he saw how Merrigan's fingers spread and curled in eir lap, preparing for a climb. So he took those hands in his, and lifted em to stand, and led em slowly to the steps cut crudely into the rockface.

Merrigan's expression, as he led em, focused on him instead of eir feet, with a kind of apprehensive hunger in eir eyes that made Darragh's palms sweat. He released one of eir hands, put his hand on the small of eir slim back, and turned em to face the wall; e looked over eir shoulder at him until eir body was completely turned, and Darragh exhaled slowly. As he'd turned Merrigan, his other hand had trailed along the outside of eir arm. It hovered there now, unsure where to land, while the hand on eir back tensed but did not grip em.

"You've done this before," Darragh said softly. His breath brushed eir shoulder blades, exposed beneath an unlaced surcoat by the removal of an over-robe, and he could see Merrigan's shiver. "I will be below. I will catch you if you slip."

Merrigan laughed. "Surely I will take you down with me."

"That is no sure thing at all," he replied, grinning. "I've caught many a slippery-footed sailor heavier than you. But even if we fall, I will still catch you. I will pull you into my arms and cover you with my body and protect you from the worst of the impact."

"And have you done that before?" e asked. "For slippery-footed sailors?"

Darragh longed to move the hand on Merrigan's back to eir side, eir hip, eir belly. He held it in place. "One day you should look inside me and count the cracks on my ribs," he said, laughing.

Merrigan turned around, and Darragh's hand landed on eir hip anyway. E looked down at him thoughtfully. "You boast sarcastically, but I see more than the cracks in your bones," e said. Then the corner of eir mouth twitched in what could have been a coy smile, and e turned, stepped away from him, and set eir hands to the rock.

E climbed, occasionally stopping to tug the hem of eir long shirt up over eir knees, while Darragh watched and let the emotions wash over him. He was so happy to see Merrigan recovering, to glimpse the person Frederick missed so powerfully. He had expected intelligence and empathy; he had even expected the rage, and certainly the melancholy; and he rejoiced to see the legend become a personality.

He had not expected . . . His memory of Merrigan as a living person had been overwhelmed by the childlike wonder he'd first felt and the idolatrous gratitude that had sustained him into adulthood. Faced with Merrigan in the flesh, with eir eyes so full of feeling, eir voice like sunlight, eir skin and hands and nose all perfect? He had known neither sex nor sensuality when first he met em, but things were different now. He was not surprised, to realize his multifaceted infatuation; he was infatuated frequently, with all sorts of people. But now he felt it was inappropriate. He recognized that he had been too flirtatious when leading Merrigan to the wall and resolved to comport himself better.

"Will you join me?"

Darragh was jolted from his thoughts by a voice out of memory—its echo said, *The sun is rising*—but the sun was risen and Merrigan stood fully bathed in its light at the top of the waterfall, smiling down at him more brightly than ever before. Darragh chuckled and scaled the wall, slower than em, for he had never climbed this section. Soon enough he reached the top and took Merrigan's extended hand to pull himself over the lip of rock. Then he stood next to em and looked out, to the south. The waterfall was not so tall that they could see the stretch of the forest, but Darragh thought he could see the silver leaves of the labyrinth flashing off to his left. The color of the forest was still green, but shifting to yellow and orange. Darragh saw fire. He shook the vision off.

"Do you see what you wanted to see?" Merrigan asked.

"Yes," Darragh replied.

"What is it?"

"You, out of that cave."

He smirked at em, and e laughed, then sat on a large flat rock half in the water. When e let eir feet dangle, eir toes dipped into the river. Darragh sat beside em, with his legs pulled up and crossed beneath him; his would have fallen short of the water.

"The fire breaks are what the sawhands should have been making," Merrigan said.

It took Darragh a moment to place the words, which belonged to another conversation — his ramblings, before Merrigan came out, about his work with Frederick on the preparation for a forest fire that might never come. Or, when it came, it would be unstoppable and their work would be immaterial anyway. Frederick seemed to have thrown all of his nervousness at Merrigan's emergence into the discussion of fire and fire management. He was rarely in the labyrinth anymore.

"They wouldn't listen to me," Merrigan went on. "It was easier for them to peel away the trees at the forest's edge."

Darragh had thought, when he imagined this moment, that he would have so many questions about how everything had changed, what had gone wrong; he didn't. He understood. At least, Merrigan seemed to think so, for e gave him the same rueful smile he felt on his own face, and he nodded and e nodded and they sighed, together, at the difference between easy and good. They said no more for a while.

"What is it like? To live so long?" Darragh asked.

Merrigan gave a small shrug. "I hardly feel I have an age any longer. I am outside time, and being outside time, I am outside life."

Darragh looked around him and asked, "Is a tree outside life?"

When Merrigan looked at him, it almost seemed to him that e had rolled eir eyes. He made his face innocent, and e laughed. "That is different," e said, almost pleadingly. "Trees live on a different scale of time."

"So do you," Darragh replied.

Merrigan widened eir eyes at him, understanding that he was not teasing em. E huffed a little, then sat in silence, staring at the swift water. Darragh waited and counted the animals he saw or heard in the forest. It seemed to him there were more than he was used to; or perhaps he was only better at recognizing their presence.

"I have been measuring myself against human lifetimes,"

Merrigan said at last. "Fairies of my mother's kind are very solitary, you see. I have simply been more immersed in human culture than anything else. Even though I know, and knew, that the course of my life would be different, I still thought of myself as a human removed from time." E slumped. "It was a relief . . . to actually remove myself from the unrelenting progress of time."

They were quiet together for more long moments before Merrigan said, "My mother spent many decades with me after I fled to the forest, until she felt I had grown up. I was more than eighty years old." E laughed, first wryly and then giddily. "You ask me what it is like to live so long. My mother always seemed wise to me, so wise and capable, because she had seen and experienced so much. By my third century I felt only disillusioned, and I thought perhaps she was never so jaded because she had not seen such horrible times as I had. But I more than anyone should have known better."

"Disillusionment is the unifying quality of me and my peers," Darragh said. "We are now old enough to have been disabused, at least temporarily, of both the dreams we had in childhood and the hopes of our early adulthood."

Merrigan smiled at him, eir eyes a little teary, eir cheeks flush with embarrassment. "It seems that in my own way, then, I am no older than you, and no wiser."

"Oh, you are wiser," Darragh said. "We may be peers on the path of life, but you have explored so much more along yours than I have had time to. If you are still young, so be it, but do not discount the things you have seen and felt and learned."

Merrigan grew serious again, and put eir hand on Darragh's cheek.

"Take your own advice in this," e said. "Do not you discount your wisdom either, Goodman Darragh."

39
PURITY

AFTER THAT, MERRIGAN AND Darragh often climbed to the top of the waterfall, to enjoy the sun that could reach them there. Summer fought to maintain its primacy against the encroaching cool winds from the mountains, and there came a week that was unseasonably hot. They sprawled over the river rocks, more baking than basking, until Darragh sat up and plucked at his shirt.

"Do you mind?" he asked.

Merrigan shook eir head, and watched him lift it over his head, baring himself from the waist up. The hardness of him had softened a bit, for the rations were better in the forest than aboard ship, but he was thick with muscle that Merrigan could see moving under his skin. It almost made his tattoos come to life, especially the great whale on his upper left arm. Merrigan had thought it an isolated decoration, it and the tattoo on Darragh's neck, but e now saw that there were many inked images in varying degrees of freshness, concentrated on his torso where they had all been hidden by his shirt.

"Are all sailors so ornate?" Merrigan asked.

Darragh smiled. "Most. The images are part of how we communicate."

"How so?"

He looked down at himself, as if choosing a place to start, and then pointed to a length of rope along his side, with four knots in it and numerals to either side of each knot. All were well faded, but the topmost was almost illegible at a distance. "This shows that I've been on four ships; the loose end here is where another will be added if I change again," he said. He pointed to what looked like a glacier at the base of his sternum. "This marks how far north I've been." Some great leafy green plant, just below his navel. "And this, how far south."

"The whale?" Merrigan asked.

Darragh turned around, and e saw that the whales continued across his upper back, in varying sizes, so that they appeared to be—

"A family group," Merrigan said.

Darragh looked over his shoulder and nodded. "Sidra and I got these together. We only finished them last year, and we started when we joined the *Augustina*," he said.

Merrigan stood and resettled emself on the same flat rock as Darragh so that e could look closer. The largest whale, the one on his arm, was the oldest by the fading, followed by the second largest. The youngest whales, three of them, were fresh but lacking the detail of the larger two; they were hardly more than silhouettes of dark blue with scatterings of black dots for shadows. All of them, like the rest of his back, were spotted with scars, some splotchy and some whip-thin. Merrigan brushed the longest scar, a purple line that started thick near the bottom of Darragh's shoulder blade and thinned as it dragged up near his spine, the nape of his neck. E felt Darragh tense under eir touch, and drew eir fingers back just as he arched away from them.

"Is sailing very dangerous?" e asked.

"Yes," Darragh said. "Which is why there is always sailing work to be had."

He twisted to face em, and they were now quite close to each other. Merrigan held still, waiting, to see if Darragh would move again, distance himself from em, but this time he did not. Rather, he seemed to hold himself with the same stillness Merrigan had, and bit by bit, breath by breath, they relaxed together into this proximity. Merrigan could have remained there, gazing into Darragh's eyes, studying his face, until the light faded, easily; but e did not want to lose that ease, and thought that it might be preserved by drawing attention away from it. So e looked at Darragh's neck, the tattoo there that by now had grown familiar to em.

"Does this one communicate something to your fellow sailors?" e asked.

Darragh grinned. "Yes, a very important thing, in fact," he said. "This is the one that tells them to address me as a man."

"Oh! How clever," Merrigan said. "In the years after the sumptuary laws were struck down, as more people made use of that freedom, many still struggled with how to declare themselves. I was never sure how to help them except with some glamour that nudged the assumptions of others in the ideal direction. Have things improved?"

"There are titles with connotations, and little scripts of intro-duction," Darragh said.

"The last one I remember was . . . to say your name, your pronoun, your elder parent's name, and your place of birth," Merrigan said.

Darragh laughed again, and said, "We have dropped the place of birth, and we use family surnames, but the name-pronoun-name form still exists. It is all too formal for we sailors, though. We just look for tattoos."

"So this one," Merrigan said, eir finger hovering over the image. "Means manhood?"

"There are several versions to choose from, many more phallic and literal than this one," Darragh said. He traced the length of the harpoon, from the barb under his ear down along the muscle stretching to meet the inner point of his collarbone. "The harpoon is obvious. But the mermaid's purse is really a womb."

Merrigan leaned forward to look at it, wondering at the odd little sack. "Is it?"

"It's a shark's egg," Darragh said. "It gestates separate from its parents, a place of birth all on its own, flexible but tough, able to withstand all the dangers of the ocean with such delicate cargo inside. For some men, it's simply the shape of it that matters, and they like it for being representational, because it feels more polite in nonsailing circles. That was one reason I chose it. But mainly I enjoyed the symbolism. It felt especially fitting for my circumstances."

Merrigan nodded. Eir gaze wandered from the tattoo to the leather cord that skirted it, and to the familiar thorn that rested against the glacier in the middle of his torso.

"It is your day, is it not?" e said quietly.

Darragh nodded, and lifted the thorn on its cord over his head. Merrigan did not watch him, though e could see in eir periphery the three flicking motions he made. When he replaced the cord, when it had settled again onto the ring around the back of his neck that showed its long residence there, Merrigan said, "I am sorry I could not make this permanent for you."

Darragh said nothing for several moments, and Merrigan watched his bare, tanned chest rise and fall with steady breaths, focusing on the triple-faced image below his right collarbone. There were fine blond hairs along his sternum, down the middle of him, lengthening and thickening and curling under his navel so that the plant inked there seemed to be covered in dew catching the first light of day. Was this what Darragh had envisioned every time he pricked his finger, every time he offered his blood to the elements? Merrigan had never consciously changed eir body, though e gathered that as e grew, e had instinctually nudged it with eir childhood magic. If e had been obliged to choose, how should e have come to look? E was struck with sudden fear and shame—what if there had been things Darragh wanted for his body that the magic had been unable to provide?

But then he took Merrigan's hand, lifted it, held it against a chest that was warm with the sunlight that surrounded them. Merrigan looked into his smiling face, and the fear and shame burned away.

"What you gave me was perfect," he said. "You gave me the time and means to choose for myself. Any happiness I have had, I owe to that moment. I will always be grateful to you for that."

Emotion rose up swift and strong in Merrigan, and e managed to say, "I am so glad." But e pulled eir hand out of Darragh's and went to the water, putting eir feet below the surface to the cold bottom, as if the chilly mud there could siphon off some of eir heat. E let eir shirt fall, so that the hem was submerged and the cloth grew heavy, clammy with moisture.

"Merrigan?"

"I only wish magic were always so . . . pure," e said.

And if it were? What would have happened when the timber lords rose, if Merrigan had had nothing but goodwill and compassion to counter them? Would e have fled with the wolves to yet more remote land, gone to live in the mountain caves with the dragons? Or would e have forgiven the humans and stayed among them as a simple village healer, forsaking all duties except to humanity? No. Merrigan would not have changed history, if e could. Looking back, it all seemed inevitable. But that did not lessen the sorrow.

"Nothing is pure," Darragh said. "Why should magic be any different?"

"You believe that? That nothing is pure?"

He splashed into the river behind em. "I believe . . . that purity exists in flashes, in moments. Sometimes several together. But it is fragile and easily transformed into something else. Someone once told me we bring all our poisons with us; we bring our hopes and needs, too, every moment of our lives. Our experiences come to us through a fog of fears and desires. So we may see purity, but only for an instant, unless we are very careful with it."

Who is this creature? Merrigan wondered. *I see purity every time I look at you,* e wanted to say. But Darragh was right, and e must be very, very careful with it. E could not taint such perception and kindness with eir own unworthy sadness, no matter how hungry e was for the calm and assurance this man seemed to swim in, the confidence he had in his ability to make sense of the world. How was it that he could say something so seemingly pessimistic, that nothing was pure, in a manner that conveyed his equal trust in others to meet challenges with care and deliberation? Merrigan had once been able to do that. Merrigan had once believed in that ability, in emself and in others.

"It is refreshing, isn't it? The contrast of the cold water with the hot sun," e said.

"Yes," Darragh said, and e could hear the smile in his voice.

He splashed a little farther from Merrigan, who turned to watch him as he bent at the waist and dipped his hair into the water, saturating it before whipping back so that water sprayed in Merrigan's direction. E laughed at the gesture, at the shock of cold water falling on eir skin, and then laughed again at the spell of eir anxiety being momentarily broken. Darragh offered em a hand, grinning, water running down his face, and Merrigan took it. Together they settled back onto their rock benches. Merrigan tried to guess at the meanings of his other tattoos, or made up ridiculous ones for the images that seemed obvious, while Darragh laughed and shook his head, his hair clinging in artistic curls to his cheeks, his neck, his shoulders. He pulled it all over one shoulder and tried to comb it with his fingers, while Merrigan turned away from the arc of his neck and the warmth it inspired in eir gut.

"Will you go back to sailing?" Merrigan asked.

"Go back?"

"When you leave here," e said.

Darragh sighed, and frowned, and said, "I . . . suppose I must. I have very little money and no other trade. And Sidra—she loves sailing."

He said it as if it were simply a fact, that if he wanted to be with

Sidra, he must be a sailor. "Do you love her so much?" Merrigan asked.

"She is a truer sister to me than Vesta has ever been," he replied. "I miss her. I wish I could—there is so much I wish I could talk about with her."

Merrigan nodded, and they were silent for a few moments. Then Darragh said, "I do love the ocean."

"Describe it to me?"

"You've never seen it?"

E smiled wryly. "I was near it once, but I was concerned with other matters. I scarcely glanced at it. Sometimes . . . sometimes I have followed the river, in my senses, some ways south. But no, I have never seen the sea."

"Hmm," Darragh said, closing his eyes. "The sea is . . . everything. Anything. It can create and destroy. It can make you weep at its unfathomable beauty and its incomprehensible terror. It is every color you can imagine, not only blue. There are times when it is nothing but light, not a shadow to be found, and there are times when you may as well be in the bottom of a deep pit, for all you can see your surroundings. Its motion can lull you or make you sick. Its breezes will energize you or skin you. It is a partner and it is disloyal, aloof, and loving, in unpredictable turns. And you will never forget it, no matter how long you are away—nor will it ever forget you."

Merrigan put a hand to eir chest, where eir heart was thumping. "It sounds like magic."

"Does it?" Darragh smirked. "I see. That makes a certain kind of sense."

"Do you *want* to keep sailing?" Merrigan asked.

The mirth slipped away from Darragh's face, and he sighed again. "I do not know what I want. I have scarcely made any plans for my life since the day I bought a gentleman's suit. Almost as if . . . I knew that someday the past would rip me out of any life I had built."

Merrigan nodded and looked to the west, where the sun was beginning to brush the tops of the trees on its way into the night.

"What do you want, Merrigan?" Darragh asked.

The question surprised em; it was a surprise, too, when Darragh's hand covered eirs on the rock still warm from the afternoon. But how could it be, when their hands fitted together so well?

E did not know what e wanted, now that e had come back to life. E felt the seeds of that which e craved, the joy and contentment, but e feared all emotions save the sadness e knew so thoroughly. Eir time with Darragh seemed to be approaching a threshold, over which e must crash back into the flow of life, and e dreaded it. E knew that e could not cross it without his support, but that his presence drew it ever closer.

"I have not wanted anything for a lifetime," e said. "I am not sure I know how to, now."

Darragh squeezed Merrigan's hand then with an intensity e did not understand; but he said nothing, and they watched the sun set together. Then he took his leave.

40
HOME

ONE DAY MERRIGAN WAS waiting for him, perched on the
boulder in front of the waterfall. Darragh climbed up and touched
eir shoulder in greeting before sitting beside em, following eir
gaze to the pool below. It was swimming with fallen leaves in
various states of disintegration; the driest of them absorbing the
water and becoming mushy film on the surface, while others,
protected by their waxy texture, skimmed along like little boats
with well-proofed hulls. The churn of the falls created swirls of
repetitive movement, doldrums where leaves were deposited and
gathered into what was almost a raft, and every now and then, a
current that let a few slip downriver. When one escaped, Darragh
and Merrigan watched its progress until they could no longer see
it, and then they returned their attention to the crowd of brown
and gold and red jostling in the water below.

"Do you miss your mother?" Darragh asked.

"Sometimes," Merrigan said. "But I was older when she left
me than you were when your mother left you. And my mother had
different reasons."

"Do you know her reasons?" Darragh asked.

"Whose?"

Darragh laughed. "You must. To say something like that."

Merrigan shook eir head. "My mother left because I was grown. She told me as much. You were not grown, and yet your mother left; therefore her reasons must have been different. There is much that I can see, but I do not know everything, nor can I—for which I give thanks."

"I wanted to look for her."

He couldn't bring himself to say more, but Merrigan took his hand, and in the press of eir palm Darragh felt the rest of the conversation; that he didn't know where to start and was soon consumed with his own survival, and that his mother must never have thought of her children ever looking for her, so carefully did she obscure herself and scrub her letters of any clues as to her situation. He thought of those letters, in his room back in the labyrinth, so spare and yet so regular. There were undoubtedly some deductions he could make himself, if he had the mind to do so, now that the disillusion of his age had given him space apart from the hurt of the abandonment.

"I miss my father," Merrigan said. "He was a kind man, and he loved me. After I was driven away, I waited and waited for someone to change the law, to make it safe for me to return. I never once thought of using my magic to sneak back to Iarom. I never thought to send a message and welcome him to the forest. I loved him and he loved me, and yet I believed sincerely that our worlds were separated by an impassable wall. Not seeing him again, not even trying, is the greatest regret of my life."

There were more leaves in the water than were now on the trees. Autumn lay thick on the ground, and the trees bared themselves to the sky, waiting for winter's cool, fresh kiss. If Darragh had any thoughts of returning to his father's bedside, he must act on them soon. It had been weeks since Merrigan's reassurance that he still lived. Since then neither one of them had made any reference to the man, though he seemed to buzz around Darragh's head like a horsefly.

He tried to remember the anger that had filled him months ago, in his childhood home, watching Vesta cling to the concept of their father. It had been a kind of jealousy, though he could hardly discern the nature of it—that Vesta had a father she loved, and who loved her? That she had chosen a cruel parent over her brother? He had begun this search to fill a need, and he was no longer certain that confronting his father, as a man, over the injustices of his childhood would give him the peace he craved. But when his father was dead, would that provide the opportunity to reconcile with his sister, or would he lose her forever? Would that reconciliation ease the melancholy deep within him?

He settled into these thoughts as though climbing into a bed, and as the melancholy covered him as if it were the blanket, he realized that it had been weeks since he last felt it. Merrigan squeezed his hand.

FREDERICK WOULD NOT REST until the snow came. Darragh tried to tell him how things fared with Merrigan, how well e was doing; he tried to invite Frederick to the waterfall to see for himself. But just as Merrigan declined to go back to the labyrinth, Frederick declined to go to the waterfall. Darragh let it go, leaving it to them to decide the terms of their reunion. One hundred years was a long time to be apart.

The forest was as dry as Darragh had ever seen it. It had not rained for weeks. The air turned bitter, and every morning, Frederick could be found at dawn in the upper forest, squinting at the sky as if he could see snowflakes up in the clouds. Then he would frown, and out into the lower forest he would go, expending his anxiety in breaking and dragging dead wood to the pits and mounds where he and Darragh burned it. The labyrinth was heaped with charcoal.

Though his strength made short work of fallen trunks and large branches, Frederick was hopeless when it came to the leaves and twigs now matting together on the forest floor, so for several days together, Darragh felt obliged to help him gather this most dangerous of fuel. They burned terrific amounts of deadfall. But none of it satisfied Frederick. It was almost as if he'd had some premonition. He had focused them primarily on the space between the labyrinth and the river—an escape route.

One, Darragh noticed, that did not extend to the waterfall. But perhaps Frederick thought the river would be enough protection in that part of the forest.

While Darragh worked, he looked up at the bare trees against the gray sky and thought of how beautiful it would look once snow fell. The whole forest would be like the one that grew from the labyrinth's walls, black trees adorned with light. He wondered whether the river would freeze, like the ocean in the far north, or the creek in the woods behind his childhood home. He found that he couldn't wait to see the icicles that would form at the waterfall. Only once he had that thought did he realize: he had decided to stay for the winter.

Darragh told Frederick that night, as they sat near Frederick's hearth waiting for the pottage to cook in its bed of fresh charcoal. Frederick smiled in what looked like relief, for the first time in weeks. "You should go and tell em first thing," he said. "Then maybe the snow will finally come, and we'll be safe for a while."

Darragh frowned. "Do you ... do you think Merrigan has been holding the weather at bay? For my sake?"

Frederick's smile flickered, then he sighed. "I do not know. I suppose I did, but I do not know if e has that power anymore. Perhaps it is just a dry year." It didn't look as though the idea brought him any comfort.

"Perhaps. But it is coming to a close, and whatever comes of it, we shall be together," Darragh said.

He smiled at Frederick, whose own smile returned wearily; they clasped hands briefly before returning to their silent contemplation of the clay pot.

The next morning Darragh set off for the waterfall, wondering at himself and his lack of urgency toward his father's illness and imminent death. He remembered what Frederick had said when he first arrived, that such things birthed regret where there had been none; at the time, Darragh had fled from that idea, right into the waterfall. Now, though, he saw that Frederick was right, and what was more, that the regret he felt was less for the lost opportunity of reconciliation, and more that he did not want to reconcile at all. He had given up his father so completely, so long ago, that to give him up now was easy.

MERRIGAN WAITED ON THE path, leaning on eir fox-head staff, resting eir head against it. E had thought to go all the way to the labyrinth, urged by the very important thing e had to share with Darragh; but e had only made it so far. It had been several days since Darragh's last visit, but Merrigan was sure he would be coming that day, so e stopped when e had to, and waited. It was the first time e had been out of sight of the river in a very, very long time. It was disorienting. Trees and paths that had once been known to Merrigan as well as eir own body were now foreign. E looked around, but all eir landmarks had been grown over, buried in the unrelenting life Merrigan had fought so hard to protect, only to cut emself off from it. E reached out to a tree next to em, looking for recognition. When eir fingers touched the bark, that was what e felt, along with a heady mix of sadness and joy, welcoming and forgiveness. Merrigan snapped eir hand back as if stung, and held emself narrowly in the middle of the path, afraid of further contact.

At last Darragh came into view, dressed in long sleeves and his pleated sailor's trousers but still barefoot, as he had been all summer. Merrigan curled eir own toes against the dirt and tried to savor the smile that burned across Darragh's face when he saw em standing there. He jogged the rest of the way to meet em, grinning. His cheeks seemed flush, not with exertion, but with news he was bursting to share.

"Merrigan! How lovely of you to come meet me," he said. "Would you like to walk a bit more, or shall I escort you back to the falls?"

He offered em a crooked elbow, which almost made Merrigan

cry to look upon. E didn't move, and Darragh extended his hand instead, his face serious. It was still pink from the scrubbing he must have given it in the cold river, and dotted with scratches from his work on the clearing. How many times had he offered em that hand? Oh, how Merrigan wished e could return all that generous stability. E met Darragh's hand with eirs, but instead of placing eir hand in his, e came up underneath and gripped his fingertips gently.

"Your father has woken," e said. "He will die soon. You must go home."

Darragh's hand, his arm, went a little slack; Merrigan caught the weight and held it. Together they stood, holding each other up through that small contact. His cheeks drained of color; his jaw and eyes grew hard and distant.

"You are certain?" he said. Merrigan nodded, and after a moment, so did Darragh. "Then I . . ."

He hesitated, and his gaze came near to Merrigan again as his eyes filled with tears; he looked at em with the words he wished to say caught up in his throat. What they were, Merrigan could hardly guess. E dared not speculate. It was enough to see the indecision, the conflict, the shock in his expression.

"Go home," Merrigan said softly. It was different from the dark night e had tried to push him away, and both of them felt it. E let go of his hand, and when e lifted eir own hand again, it held a perfect red rose summoned from the labyrinth's hedge. One of the last to resist the hedge's long, slow death. "Take this to him, as a gift."

Darragh gave a little huff that, with more force, would have been a scoff, and made no move to take the rose. Merrigan stepped closer, rested eir staff against eir shoulder, and gathered Darragh's hair. It had been quite short when he first came, but it had grown shockingly long during his time in the forest, falling past his shoulder blades in golden-brown waves. These Merrigan twisted together, and through them, e wove the rose so that the stem held them into a glorious tangle at his neck.

Eir hands lingered there, at his neck, his collarbones; when they drooped lower, Darragh's hands caught them and held them against his chest, rounded only with muscle. E could feel his chest rise and fall with short, high breaths.

"Merrigan," he began.

"Go," e said.

Again, Darragh hesitated. Then he released Merrigan's hands and walked away.

When he was gone, Merrigan regretted eir cowardice. E was relieved by it. E longed to know what he would have said and tried desperately to shake the fantasies of it from eir mind. Feeling built within em until e could no longer make sense of the thoughts and sensations swirling through em. E began to weep, for fear and a kind of wonder, and sank to the earth. Eir staff clattered to the ground beside em and rolled until it stopped at the feet of a fox. Merrigan blinked at it, until e realized the truth of all that had happened.

"You brought him here," e said.

The fox became eir mother, who ran a finger along the staff. "It is good to see you out of that cave, Merri," said eir mother.

"I do not understand," Merrigan said. "Why? Why did you— what did you do?"

Eir mother tapped her chin thoughtfully. "I only led him to the waterfall. He made it to the forest, to the labyrinth, of his own accord. He won over Frederick by himself. After all that, I thought it was only right that he have the opportunity he sought, to reunite with you."

Seized with sudden bitterness, Merrigan spat, "So he could beg me for magic? That's the only reason anyone has ever sought me out."

Eir mother tilted her head. "Did he?"

Merrigan didn't answer; though he had come with a request in mind, he had never voiced it, and eir mother must know that as well as e did. More angry comments sprang forth in eir mind, but e tried to beat them back. E tried not to think of that prince, from so so long ago, the one who won the dragon's righteous sword when his brothers failed; the one who had been so kind, and who had not asked for Merrigan's help but accepted it happily when it was offered, and who had failed to deliver on his promises. He had never come back, and Merrigan had vowed never to let emself feel such sorrow again.

E wept harder, and felt very young indeed.

"I am in love with him," Merrigan said. "How could you do this to me? Why did you bring him to me?"

Eir mother curled around em, her orange robes covering em. "Because I thought he could remind you that there is beauty and goodness in the world as well as pain. I am not sorry to have been right."

"You forgot the most important lesson, Mother," Merrigan said. "With humans, nothing ever comes without selfishness and sorrow."

"My sweet child," eir mother said, gentle but immovable. "Sometimes it is up to us to put our hurts in the past, where they belong."

We bring our poisons with us, Darragh had said; Merrigan remembered and felt ashamed of eir own petulance, then felt ashamed for minimizing eir feelings. Eir experiences had been dark indeed, eir hurts were great. Perhaps e should not have sequestered emself as e did, but eir reasons for doing so must be understandable to any small empathy. Yet eir mother was right. Perhaps e was still strong enough to hope.

"Thank you," e whispered against eir mother's chest.

She held em tighter. "My heart, it is my privilege to care for you."

41
PASSAGE SOUTH

DARRAGH MADE IT BACK to the labyrinth, though he was not sure how; presumably it was by the memory in his legs, which had walked that path so many times. He felt only the looseness of the rose in his hair, its huge heavy bloom bobbing as he walked, brushing his ear. Though it felt unsecured, it did not come undone, and when Darragh at last looked up, he saw the labyrinth, and the rose's dead kin before him.

Frederick was in Darragh's room, but when Darragh entered, he seemed surprised. "What's the matter?" he asked.

"I have to go," Darragh said.

"I do not understand," Frederick replied. "I thought—"

"Yes. I want—but my father . . ."

Frederick noticed the rose, and he sighed, as if he understood more completely than Darragh did what had happened on the waterfall path. He retrieved the sack Darragh had carried when he first arrived, set it on the bed, and began to gather items to pack. Darragh watched him for a moment before coming round to himself. It was as if he had just fallen back into his body; he gasped and felt tears burn his eyes.

The next moment, Frederick was there, embracing him, huge and strong and warm. "You can come back," he said.

Darragh dug his fingers into Frederick, clinging, to steady his shaking hands. He said, "I will. When I have concluded this awful business, I will come back."

They released each other and set to packing. Frederick reached for the folktale collections, but Darragh stopped him. Nodding, Frederick left them on the shelf. There the two volumes stood, at the edge of Darragh's awareness. In the folktales, there were two kinds of leaving home. The first was as a victim, to be abducted or banished. The second was as a seeker, either to rescue someone or something, or to improve one's own lot by questing, for treasure or love or fame.

When Darragh left the *Augustina*, he had been seeking; he thought he had known his goal. Now, he could not help feeling banished.

BERIN OPENED THE DOOR of Iarom's inn to him, and screamed.

The last thing Darragh wanted was to talk of Merrigan, but the whole of Iarom—some forty people—gathered at the inn that night. There was not room enough for all of them. They crammed into the dining room until the only free space lay between Darragh and the hearth, behind where he sat at the long, solid table. The heat of the crowd matched that of the flames, but Darragh felt neither; he was cold to his core.

Berin sat opposite him with two others about eir age, whom Darragh took to be the village leaders. He might have called them elders had not most of the town been as aged as the three who stared at him with amazement and no small amount of suspicion. He had expected an onslaught of questions, but for many minutes together—he could not be sure how many—all the people stuffed into the room had simply watched him. There was silence even from those outside, some of whom were pressed against the windows, some, he understood, merely waiting by the front door for news to be passed along to them.

"That is assuredly one of the Enchanter's roses," said the elder on Darragh's left. "The most beautiful roses in the world. I remember them."

"No, you don't," said someone behind them. "You may be old, but you aren't that old."

"I was alive when the Barrow was built!"

"You were three years old."

"It doesn't matter if he remembers them or not," the other elder said. "That is undoubtedly the most beautiful rose I have ever seen. But more to the point, this young man went into the forest and came out alive."

"Did he?" Berin said. "He left my inn in the wee hours, when there were none to see him go. Maybe he went south."

Darragh let this speculation flow around him. Even if he had felt obliged to prove his residency in the forest, how could he? None of these people had been there; what could possibly convince them of what had happened to him? Now that he had left the shadow of the trees, he began to disbelieve it himself.

"His hair," said someone Darragh couldn't see.

The crowd strained to part until Horace, tall, smiling Horace, squeezed into the room, little more than a floating head. If Darragh had not known for himself how tall the apprentice innkeeper was, he might have thought he stood on a barrel.

"What do you mean, Horace?" Berin asked.

"You remember how short his hair was when he was here before," Horace said. "He had sailor's hair, cropped close to his head. Now look at it. Hair doesn't grow that much in only six months, not naturally. He's been somewhere magical."

Berin looked back at Darragh with wide eyes, and then laughed. The mirth did not linger long, because going into the forest in truth was a far more serious thing than pretending to have gone into the forest. *It's true* made a murmuring circuit through the room and then out of it, to inform the other townsfolk. But no one spoke. Hardly anyone moved. As keen as they were, it seemed to Darragh that none of them actually wished to know how things stood in the forest. Their own mythology was tied up in Merrigan's; their victimhood did not exist without an unsympathetic adversary. They had lived a generation under a fairy tale history without nuance—but nuance brought no comfort. Nuance asked them to recognize the wrongs done by their ancestors, and asked them to be kinder and cleverer than those same antecedents, if they hoped to avoid the same clashes. It made sense that they should be afraid of whatever news Darragh might bear back from the forest. To them, his survival signaled a change, and they were afraid of it.

He would have answered their questions, had he any sense of what they were; was it too simple to say that Merrigan was alive? If he told them e had left the cavern, would that mean anything? If he told them of Frederick's fear of fire, would they sympathize, or stare blankly at him?

Undoubtedly they were silent because *they* had no sense of their questions, either. Darragh had left his own largely unformed during his quest, into the north, into the forest. Once his only known question had been answered—once he knew that Merrigan was the Enchanter, was the person who had helped him, was alive—he was left with only an unintelligible jumble of impulse and hesitance that had less to do with Merrigan and more to do with his father. Devastating hope, and bitter cynicism.

He stood. "Please excuse me. I am very tired."

"Is e coming back?" Berin asked.

Darragh almost laughed, that that was eir first question. Fear or hope? "I do not know."

A moment later, Berin asked, "Are you?"

Darragh remembered Berin's resignation, the night before he left for the forest, when e told him to look for the roses. Eir certainty that he would die. Now, eir mature face seemed young, bewildered; a cornerstone of eir world had shifted and the whole foundation was in danger of crumbling. E had seen, in Darragh before the forest, that he did not believe the bad tales of the Enchanter any more than he believed e was dead. What did Berin see in him now? What made em look at him that way?

"Yes," he said.

"But did you get what you wanted?" Berin asked. "Did the Enchanter heal your father so you could tell him what you need to tell him?"

Darragh sighed. "That remains to be seen. But I will tell you of it when I return."

The crowd dispersed, some with agitation, most with relief. Darragh slept in the same room he'd had before, and woke early to leave. Berin sent him off without any words, only a pack of provisions. When Darragh stopped for lunch and opened the pack, a folded piece of paper sat atop the wrapped food: the shark drawing Darragh had left on his pillow months before. The symbol of a wanderer, more commonly inked into skin than drawn onto paper. Sidra had once encouraged Darragh to get it done, to go with the others he had—various animals, stars and navigational symbols, dates and place names—but he had declined. As much as he identified with the shark, perhaps he had always believed, deep down, that his wandering would someday come to an end.

THE *CELESTINO* WAS NOT in Varrun when Darragh arrived. He stalled for several days, picking up work loading and unloading barges at the docks so that he could pay for room and board. The other workers had not asked his name, but had begun calling him Beauty, for the rose in his long hair. This was a common practice among the itinerant laborers along the river, for names were hard to learn, but appellations related to appearance were easy. He had redone the loose knot of hair so that it was a little tidier, and with the rose threaded through it, it stayed through all his work. The rose stayed perfect and lovely. His fellow workers wondered at it, and thought it must be a false flower, for where could he get a fresh rose every day at that time of year? They joked about glass houses that kept summer longer than it should stay, and of ladies stitching velvet petals around wooden shafts. When they flirted with him, some teasingly and some seriously, he responded in kind; but no one apart from him was allowed to touch the rose.

He found he did not mind the nickname now, though it had caused him so much consternation as a child.

There were fewer vessels than there had been in the spring, but he didn't despair of the one he wanted. He listened to the other dockworkers and bargehands talking of how the river had begun its transformation. The river wandered and shifted as it swelled with winter rain and snow. Parts of it would change dramatically, especially in the low, flat south. It took an excellent and slightly reckless captain and crew to manage the river in those unsettled times, but the reward was correspondingly high. In light of these comments, Darragh pegged Earrin for one who would be out longer, and earlier, than anyone else.

He wasn't disappointed. A week after he came to Varrun, he saw the *Celestino* arrive, midafternoon on a dreary, cold day. Even the oar-pulls were wearing hoods to keep their ears warm while they rowed, and Earrin wore a fur stole around her neck. He waited with the other laborers until she came to choose a few; she spotted him right away. Her eyes widened; then she smiled, but said nothing until she had made her selections. Darragh was not among them. The unselected dispersed to other vessels, but Darragh remained, and Earrin opened her arms in an invitation to embrace. Darragh readily accepted. Again, her enfolding of him felt familiar, enough that, when combined with the thoughts of his childhood home churning in his mind, it brought forth in a hot rush all the nervousness and fear he had held at bay, waiting for her. She squeezed him tighter, as if she felt that heat, and said, "Come! We were so loaded down we had not even the space for my liquor, and I've been dreaming of a dram."

She took him to the very river tavern where he was staying, which made her laugh when he told her. "We will close your account when we finish, then, for you'll not be here much longer," she said. "You do want passage south, don't you?"

"Yes," he replied.

She nodded. "I will not ask you if you found em, for I can see that you did. I am sorry that it wasn't what you hoped, though."

"What makes you say that?" Darragh asked.

"You seem so sad," she replied. "Sadder than before."

Darragh shook his head, and when he smiled, it *was* sad. "It was what I hoped—it was more—I hardly know what my hopes were, or what they are, and that is why I am sad. I cannot, dare not, name them, but still I feel them. They clamor for my attention and commitment, and I fear them."

"Then are you going south to avoid them, or to face them?" Earrin asked.

"Both," Darragh said. "My hopes have always been divided, it seems. Between the past and the future."

"Between home and adventure?"

"In a way, perhaps, yes."

"And which one lies to the south?"

"Home. Or at least, where I grew up."

Earrin nodded. "In Cathal?"

"No, east of it. An old house outside the village of Maro. Do you know it?" Darragh asked, for her demeanor had shifted. She sat across from him with a rigidity deeply at odds with the river swagger he was accustomed to seeing in her. He could not tell whether it was the tension of excitement or fear.

"Yes. I spent some years there, a long time ago," Earrin said, striving for an easy tone and failing. "But I do not remember you."

Darragh stared at her, and she held his gaze, but said no more and did not relax. The longer he looked, the surer he was that there was some fear for her associated with his home village, and by extension, with him. He saw distrust creeping into her eyes and his heart stuttered. He did not know what the source of her fear was, but he was sure it could have no relation to him; he signaled for another round of liquor. The only way to reassure her was to tell his history.

"I grew up there, but I was not as I am now," he said. He untied his shirt neck and pulled it to the side to expose the tattoo below his collarbone, the triple-faced bust that identified him as one whose gender was different from the one he was raised under. Earrin's eyes widened. "That is what the Enchanter helped me with when I was a child, and that is why my father exiled me from that house when I was fifteen, and that is how I became a sailor."

"When you were fifteen," Earrin said quietly. The suspicion had faded, replaced by a distant focus, as if she was solving a problem in her mind. "From that old house. And your mother? What did she do?"

Darragh shook his head. "She had been gone some ten years by then."

Earrin's mouth fell open, and Darragh almost thought he could see his old name on her tongue. Now it was he who sat rigid in his chair, tense with excitement or fear; he still could not tell which. She did not say that name, though, as Vesta had. She did not need to.

"Can it be?" she whispered.

Darragh excused himself with a promise to return. He went up to his room and pulled the little packet of letters out of his bag. It seemed to him, as he descended the stairs to the tavern floor, that the letters shook in his hands, that the trembling came from them like some sign that they were near to the hand that had penned them. But of course, the shaking came from him.

He did not make it to the table before Earrin saw the letters and let out a sob. She jumped up and crushed him in an embrace that he now knew was familiar because he remembered it.

HIS PARENTS HAD MET on the river.

She had come down from the north in a little skiff, just another one of the youths leaving the backwater towns beyond Varrun, so inaccessible to new technologies that they seemed to exist only in the past. She wanted a future away from the shadow of the forest, where the generations of her family clung to the dark, dank rot of history. So she fled to the water. She went south, all the way to Cathal. She didn't find what she wanted there, but to go north again, she needed someone to row with her. He was desperate for any work that didn't involve woodcutting, which she could very much relate to.

Her appetite for men was small—she preferred women—but he charmed and pushed and promised, and they worked and worked and worked on the river, which she had grown to love. But when the time came to purchase a new vessel, a good vessel, it was the sea to which he turned. By then she was pregnant, and he charmed and pushed and promised until she said yes. They married. He bought a three-masted carrack, and his ruthless persistence soon became a profitable trade company.

In the early years of their marriage he was often gone, captaining his flagship himself. Six years was enough for him, though, and as soon as he could manage it, he elevated himself from merchant captain to gentleman merchant, even hiring a shipping manager to handle his Cathal offices so that he could spend his days in the country with his wife and, soon enough, two children.

Darragh had few clear memories of the first five years of his life. Speaking of his mother had been forbidden after she left, which was why his father's erasure of him from the family history was truly no surprise. Even portraits of her had been taken down and presumably burned. If he thought hard enough, he could remember the horrible smell of flaming paint. If he had stayed, if he had not left himself, perhaps he and Vesta would have pooled their memories somehow, to form some kind of picture of her, and he would have recognized Earrin—but he would not have even known her name.

She left because the power his father accrued outside their home dissolved the partnership they had once shared. Once she lost her position on the vessel, on the river, she became subordinate in his mind. He was more old-fashioned the older he got, hearkening not only back to his childhood but beyond, to the days when only those born and raised men could be heads of household. She argued and was met with violence. So she waited long enough to be confident he would never raise his voice or his hand to their children, and then she fled to the water.

"He never found you," Darragh said. "Then Earrin is not your real name?"

She laughed, wiping away the tears that had fallen like spring rain while she sat in his room, telling him all of this. "It is, actually. When we met I told him my name was Faustine. I wanted to reinvent myself. I was young. Or perhaps it was a stroke of wisdom, because I hadn't decided until that moment to become someone else. Perhaps part of me always knew I would have to flee him."

She reached over and took his hand. "And now, Darragh, please. Tell me your story."

Then, it was his turn to weep.

IT WAS DARK WHEN they went back to the *Celestino*. Earrin's second mate was waiting, as was Amon, on watch. Eir smile at seeing Darragh was hesitant, for the barge's lantern cast their resolute faces in a sinister glow.

"We set off at first light," Earrin said to her mate. "I will be debarking at Vicus with Darragh. There is some personal business I must attend to. You will be in command."

When Amon's watch ended, e slipped under Darragh's blanket, where e was welcomed. Darragh nestled his tense, trembling body against Amon's and let the youth's steady breath and warm arms unfurl the knot inside him.

42

WHERE LOVE IS FITTING

THERE WERE HALF AS many crew as there had been on Darragh's journey north, for the river's current was strong, and the wind going south was always good as autumn pushed out of the mountains. The single sail was out, and Darragh's hair and rose were well buffeted. Still it was secure, though, and the rose did not lose a single petal. He leaned onto the rail and let the air slide around him.

Amon, next to him, waited for an answer to eir question. E had asked for Darragh's story, and when he did not answer right away, changed eir question to simply: "What happened?"

Darragh watched the water shearing away from the side of the boat. "I think I fell in love."

Amon's eyes widened, and then e said, "What makes you think so?"

"I have been asking myself that since I left—since I left the forest," Darragh said. "It is still confusing and complicated to me, but it seems to me that all love is made up of component parts that can be reconfigured in endless ways, to form kinship, friendship, romance. So I think I fell into romantic love, because

I am full of an affection that is familiar, that which I have felt for you and for my dearest friends—a fondness for their nature, their moods, their minds, for all that makes them special. It is joined by the loyalty that I happily give those friends and that I even now feel for my family, though our bonds are strained. There is a physical attraction that twines itself in with the affection so that they feed on each other and make each other grow, getting larger and more powerful every moment, like a storm-tossed sea, a hurricane. I feel a . . . binding, of my heart to eirs, so sensitive am I to the shifts in eir mood; this sensitivity thrills and terrifies me, fills me with apprehension. And yet, when e is joyful, *I* am more joyful than I have ever been, as if it is doubled by this joining. And there is devotion. I am devoted to preserving and growing my relationship with this person, because I want em in my life forever."

He sighed. "I have felt each of these things before, individually and in combination, but never all together this way, so focused on a single person. And that is why this feels, to me, like I am in love."

"Oh, Darragh!" Amon embraced him from behind and squeezed. "That was beautiful. Thank you so much for sharing that with me."

Darragh smiled through the tears in his eyes and patted the thick forearms banded around his shoulders. "Thank you for listening. It felt good to say that all aloud."

Amon nodded; Darragh felt it against his head. He leaned against eir chest as the words he had just spoken echoed in his mind, demanding attention. He could not get his body to relax. There were too many truths, too heavy, too sticky for the wind to take away from him. He must remain surrounded by them. He could hardly remember having a mother; he had no fondness for having a father. He did not know how to have parents as an adult. How should he treat her? How did he want her to treat him? They had not spoken since embarking last night. He looked forward to and dreaded their ride to Maro, and what lay at the end for them.

He tried to practice what he would say—to Vesta, to his father—but the words slipped away from him, pushed out of the weakened and trembling grasp of his mind by all that he was leaving behind him, so much closer and more keen. He had fallen in love with Merrigan. Perhaps he had always been in love with em, in a way. Perhaps there was an instinct between them, as Earrin believed love was. He wanted to believe that, if only for the implication that Merrigan loved him too—but how could e? How could one such as e fall in love with a poor, rough sailor? What had he to offer em? Nothing but kindness and devotion.

"Which tale will be yours, I wonder?" Amon said.

"Hm?"

"Your book of tales. My story is like that of the woodcarver's apprentice, but since you have fallen in love, yours is different," Amon explained. "We should consult your books, and find one for you to see yourself in."

"I am not sure I could find one like that," Darragh said. "In any case, I left them behind."

"You didn't want them?"

He shook his head. "It was more . . . like a promise. To come back."

"Does that mean you found your home? A place to stay?"

Darragh's throat clenched. "I don't know. I don't know anything anymore."

Amon pressed a friendly, sympathetic kiss to Darragh's temple. "You'll find your way. I am sure of it."

DARRAGH AND EARRIN TOOK horses at Vicus. They both sat them unsteadily, though Darragh's seat was slightly more secure. Earrin was tense and grumbling as they set out, out of rhythm with the horse. At least the horse, an old, reliable mail carrier, did not seem bothered by her lack of skill. It followed the pace Darragh set, and let Earrin thump along its back with her out-of-sync posting.

"I was never one for the saddle. One of things your father came to loathe about me," she said as they trotted the path, balancing the need for haste with their rusty skills. "He—"

"Thought horseback riding was a sign of gentility," Darragh finished.

Earrin laughed. "Precisely. But I was never genteel enough for him. That was my mistake: I thought that no matter how ambitious he was, a woodcutter's son would be humble enough for an innkeeper's daughter."

"At least he has had Vesta," Darragh said, struggling to keep the bitterness out of his voice.

Earrin turned serious, the weather-and-laugh lines in her face drawing down. "The last time you saw her, she seemed . . . well?"

"It seems she has thrived," he said. "Though I admit to not knowing whether it is because she wanted the same things as he, or whether it was, at least in part, to survive alone with him."

"He was so doting," Earrin said. "I truly thought—I am so sorry for leaving you, and Vesta, behind. For not giving you even the choice."

Darragh looked at her, letting his horse follow the road; he nodded and smiled at her. "Thank you. I will not say it was not hard to be without you, but I understand why you left the way you did. I am glad we found each other again."

She returned his look quickly, then returned her focus to the road and her mount. "Still, I wish I could have been there to help you with your transition, though your father was so determined to be some kind of feudal lord, I am not sure what help I would have been. Would that I had told you where to find me, and you could have come to my barge ten years ago."

Darragh sighed. "I would say that I do not want to dwell in the past, yet it is exactly the past into which we ride."

"What is it you hope to gain from this, Darragh?"

"I want . . . to be free from his tyranny," he said. He had spent his nights since leaving the forest lying awake, trying to suss this very thing out from all the tumult inside him. "Whether that means regaining his love, or losing the sense of being bound to him through either loyalty or fear. If he can learn to love me again, or I him, let us try. If not, then I wish to live without his shadow always over me, darkening all my bonds with others, poisoning my estimation of my worth, trapping me in this uncertainty that prevents my ever moving forward in life."

They spent a few breaths in thoughtful silence, and then Earrin lifted a hand from her reins—the other clenched tightly still, though the horse had no need of her guidance—and reached for Darragh's. He took it, and she squeezed.

"That was very well said, my son," she said. "You have grown up so wise, and so good, all on your own, and I am so proud of you."

Darragh was stunned for half a heartbeat; then he reined up his horse so that both stopped, close to each other. He leaned over in his saddle and wrapped his arms around Earrin's waist, hiding his face in her chest. Breath came fast and harsh into his throat, and he could not quite get all of it into his lungs—until his mother embraced him, and he sobbed in her arms, right there in the middle of the road.

This was what he wanted. He wanted to fill his life with the people who saw him and loved him, whom he loved, each love as rich and unique and valuable as any treasure he could quest for. The dread he felt for this reunion with his father melted away, ran out of him with every tear. He knew at last what to do, what to say. More importantly, he knew how he would feel if it all went wrong, and therefore had nothing left to fear.

He and Earrin rode on, the hesitance between them broken; he called her mother without stumbling, and she called him son, as if they had no other names, at least not with each other. She was nervous the closer they got to Maro, afraid of being recognized. But she had more tattoos, and a shaved head, far more lines in her sun-browned face and far more patches on her boater's garb, so no one guessed she was the same reclusive merchant's wife who'd floated into town with her housekeeper scarcely more than twice a year over twenty years ago. If they were recognized, it was as sailors only, and only by a slightly suspicious look while they perused the autumn market stalls.

At last they reached the house, just as the sky began to turn orange with sunset. Earrin took time to observe the changes in it, just as Darragh had.

"I remember adding the second floor to the cottage," she said. "When Vesta was a baby. We felt so extravagant." She shook her head, and they approached the door of the larger building.

Their knock was answered not by Vesta, but by an elderly person who identified themself as Goodwoman Digna and peered at them through squinted eyes. Darragh could not tell whether the squint was suspicion or poor vision.

"Digna the cartwright?" Earrin said.

Then Digna laughed. "Not for a long time. How should you know me? Have you been to Maro before?"

Darragh and Earrin looked at each other. "Yes. We've come to visit Jovan. We heard he's been ill," Earrin said.

Digna nodded. "Aye, he has. But your timing is good, for he is awake now. You can say your goodbyes. He'll be glad to see you, he has been alone since his daughter rushed off."

"Vesta isn't here?" Darragh asked as they followed Digna inside.

"She asked me to take up her post here, said she had some emergency to handle. This was before he woke; I suppose the alchemist's potion wore off without Vesta administering it, I could find none in the house. I wrote the news to her at the city office, so I expect her home tomorrow," Digna said. "She has been in charge of all Sir Jovan's fleet since he fell ill. The letters between here and Cathal, you could pave a road with them. But of course you probably know that better than I do. Have you any idea of the emergency? No, don't answer that. I'm no gossip."

They looked at each other again and realized simultaneously that she thought they were two of Jovan's sailors—an easy mistake to make. With two tiny shrugs, they agreed not to correct her.

"Would you like tea?" Digna asked.

"I will help you with that," Earrin said. "Son, you go on upstairs. Better not to overwhelm a sick man. Unless you'd rather I go with you?"

Darragh shook his head. "That's all right. I don't mind. Is he awake now?"

"Yes. I just took his broth up," Digna said.

Darragh smiled and took his leave of them, and went to the stairs. It occurred to him that he didn't know which room was his father's in this part of the house, but he was relieved to see only one room with light shining from beyond the door. He approached it carefully, his boots—new at Varrun—finally worn in enough to match his soft steps, and put a hand to a brass knob that seemed ridiculous indoors, and a bedroom door at that. Then, without knocking, he opened the door and stepped inside.

The room was huge. It must have run the entire back length of the new wing. There was an open dressing room of sorts, with a full-length triple mirror that would have cost a fortune without the gold leaf on its frame; in the middle was a sort of miniature parlor, two fine chairs and a table in front of a fireplace, though Darragh couldn't imagine whom his father might entertain in such a place; and then the massive four-poster bed, large enough that Frederick in his beast form could have comfortably curled up on it, hung with thick curtains that obscured the interior of the bed from the door. Darragh walked cautiously around until he could see the far side: open, providing access to a small table upon which there sat a vase with dying flowers, a lit oil lamp, and a bowl.

His father was propped up on a mass of pillows, the linen colored various shades of gold by the light in the room. His body was covered by a dark quilt; he wore a nightshirt pleated at the neck and at the wrists, where his arms lay slack on either side of him. His head was tilted back and his eyes were closed, his mouth slightly open. He looked as if he could have expired just a moment before, or was only resting. Darragh started to reach for him.

Jovan jerked slightly and turned watery eyes on Darragh. His gaze narrowed, obviously suspicious, clear enough as he looked Darragh up and down. Darragh struggled not to hold his breath.

"How dare you?" wheezed Jovan. "Come here in such a state?"

Darragh strove to keep his voice even as he replied, "I have only just arrived."

"That is no excuse! Where is your belt? My officers are impeccably dressed at all times! Am I to understand from this that you no longer wish to be an officer of my fleet?" Jovan demanded.

He didn't recognize Darragh. Why should he? Ten years would do much to a person's appearance even without Merrigan's magic, and ten years at sea? Darragh should hardly recognize himself, if he looked in that beautiful huge mirror whose golden edges winked at him from the dark corner. He looked down at his father's frowning face and formed the words to reveal himself, to correct the misapprehension. *It's me, Father*, he had thought to say. He had thought to borrow from Vesta: *I am no Beauty now, but it is me.*

But he was Beauty again. The beauty simply did not come from this house, from outside him. The beauty was not in how others saw him or in what they expected of him. He felt beautiful, and it had nothing to do with how he looked.

And it had nothing to do with the man who had first called him by that name.

"Well?" said Jovan. "Speak up, boy."

Darragh laughed to himself. "You are correct. I no longer wish to be subordinate to you. Fair winds with your recovery."

Jovan continued to speak. Darragh did not hear him. He turned to go, and felt the soft weight of the rose in his hair, and remembered Merrigan instructing him to gift it to his father. He was reluctant to part with it, especially knowing that the hedge would undoubtedly be dead when he returned. Still, Darragh would not deny a request of Merrigan's. So, he reached up and tugged slightly on the rose. His hair fell smoothly away from it, freeing it more easily than anticipated. He gathered the dying bouquet out of the vase and dropped the rose into it, then left the room.

DIGNA HAD RETIRED, BUT Earrin waited below for him, a stack of linens on the table next to her, the teapot swaddled in a cloth to keep it warm. She handed him a cup and filled it, and they drank together quietly in the steady glow of the oil lamp.

"Perhaps it's for the best," Darragh said at last. "Even where love is fitting, it cannot be forced."

Earrin chuckled ruefully. "Hear, hear."

"Will you go to him?"

She drained her teacup, made a face at the bitterness of the dregs, and shook her head. "I made my peace with leaving him ages ago. Besides, Digna says the doctor believes he will die within the week. He and I became enemies, but I have no wish to kill him with shock."

"Shall we stay until he dies?"

"At least until Vesta returns," Earrin said. "I do want to see her."

Darragh nodded, then yawned.

Earrin patted the linens. "Shall we to bed? Digna warned the old cottage would be cold, but . . ."

"What is a little cold to a sailor?" Darragh said.

Earrin laughed and nodded, and handed him a sheet and a blanket. Together they went into the old cottage, one to the parents' room, one to the children's. Separately they pulled the dust covers off the old frames with their sagging ropes and flat straw sacks, and bedded down for the night.

43
FREEDOM

DARRAGH WOKE THAT NIGHT to the sound of weeping, not realizing for a moment that it was his own. But he did not weep for sorrow. He wept out of relief, the same relief he had felt when he realized the thorn was performing as promised and shaping his body after his hopes. *At last*, he thought. *At last, I am free.*

44

THE BALM OF KIN

DARRAGH STIRRED THE PORRIDGE and tried in vain to convince Digna to let him cook the eggs as well. He could not very well counter her insistence that he was a guest with the truth; nor could Earrin, who sat at the table with the fresh coffee, smirking at them. He was about to relent to the old cartwright's assessment of him as "a good dear boy" when thunderous shouting rumbled down to them from upstairs. The three of them froze, and then all of them headed to the upper hallway. The roars distilled, upon closer proximity, into calls for servants of various names and positions, as well as Vesta.

"Wait here; I'll call you if I should have need," Digna said.

Darragh and Earrin were only too happy to agree, and waited while she went into the room. She came back out a moment later shaking her head and holding a vase with a withered black flower in it.

"Amazing! Sitting up straight with his face all ruddy! You'd think he'd never been ill!" Digna cried. "He wants sausages, and we haven't a single link, I am sure. Darragh, run to the butcher's, will you?"

"Darragh?" Earrin nudged.

He hadn't heard; he had been staring at the rose in the vase, which had for nearly two weeks been unerringly perfect.

EARRIN WENT WITH HIM into Maro, and it was she who went to the butcher. She told Darragh to inquire about Vesta with the postmaster, who could confirm whether she had indeed gone to Cathal. With Jovan miraculously recovered, Earrin thought it dangerous to remain in the house, for though the townspeople did not recognize her, he surely would, and Darragh agreed. Likewise, she did not want to risk someone making the connection to her if she asked about Vesta, whereas Darragh would have no such problem.

So he went to the postmaster's office, which was also the inn, as well as the general store, to speak to the clerk-postmaster-innkeep. Earrin needn't have worried. The clerk was a jolly person not much older than Darragh, and unlikely to recognize a woman gone twenty years.

"Hello, there! How is the old master, then?" the clerk asked.

Darragh smiled. Maro was larger than Iarom, but not large enough to prevent the comings and goings of a stranger from becoming general news. "On the mend," he said. "I've come to ask about Mistress Vesta's letters. Are they here, or did she have them forwarded?"

"Oh, I'm holding them here. She said she wasn't sure of her final destination or where would be best to meet them, so I've kept them," they said. "Shall I get them for you, sir?"

Darragh nodded. When the clerk returned with a large stack, he said, "She's not gone to Cathal then? I wanted to fetch her back for Master Jovan, or at least write to her, to ease her mind."

"Not Cathal," agreed the clerk. "Somewhere north. My brother runs her stables; you'll have seen him. He got her horse back day before yesterday, brought down from Vicus with the mail. The carrier knew no more than that she was to bring the horse to the big house at Maro."

Darragh nodded again, thoughtfully. He thanked the clerk and went outside to find Earrin, who was still haggling at the butcher's. Seeing Darragh come in, she acquiesced to whatever their final deal had been, and together they began the walk out of town and up the hill to the old house.

"North," Earrin said. "Why would she go north?"

"I have no idea," Darragh replied.

"Do you think . . . did she know that *you* were going north?" Earrin asked.

Darragh frowned but thought through his last conversation with Vesta. He had not said anything about the north or the Enchanter, not that he remembered, and the horse he had borrowed had been returned from Cathal. As far as Vesta knew, that was where he had gone. He had left his sister quite abruptly, he now realized, making snide remarks about change but sharing nothing of his plans. He doubted that she would have had any sympathy for or interest in his quest for the Enchanter; she would have called him irrational, even as he stood as proof that the Enchanter and eir magic were real. But perhaps that was why he kept it from her. If he had said his hopes aloud at that point, perhaps they would have sounded impossible to his own ears.

"No," he said in answer to Earrin's question. "Even if she did, it is doubtful she would travel to find me."

"She came to find you when it looked like he was dying."

"And that homecoming went so well that she desired another when he woke?" Darragh said.

Earrin did not rise to his sarcasm. "The faith and hope we have in our families often lasts longer than what seems right or good. Sometimes it is a hinderance to us, as it was for us with Jovan. But not always. Sometimes our kin are the balm we need for what pains us."

She reached for his hand, and he took it, unable to summon words either of agreement or of trepidation. A horrible frail hope did rise in him, that Vesta, having found him again, did not want to let him go. Regaining his mother had made him hungry for, as she put it, the balm of kin.

"Then let us go north and find her, as quick as we can," he said.

Earrin smiled. "I think our horses can make Vicus by tomorrow."

Interlude
WELCOME

THE WAY SOUTH LOOKED so different, but the trees helped Merrigan find eir path. E had tried, and failed, to walk on without their assistance, and had gotten lost. Everything was darker and denser than e remembered. Though e held eir limbs close, e was beset by the constant caress of shrubs and the small plants that thrived in the shadow of the canopy, regularly obliged to step over branches fallen into the narrow way that had once been a wide path. And though e had not touched the trunks, though e stepped carefully around the roots, e felt the forest reaching out with such forgiveness and love and joy that e wept and at last gave in. E stepped from trunk to trunk, directed by their gentle guidance, south, south to the labyrinth.

At last Merrigan came to the part of the forest that was unchanged, that could not change, preserved as it was by eir young notion of sanctuary. As e stood and gazed at the dead rose hedge, e felt the full force of eir folly. The walls of the labyrinth, the thorns of the rose hedge, had never been able to protect em from the miseries of life. Only love could do that, the love e felt for emself, for eir family, for eir friends. Instead, the labyrinth had become a place to hide, like the whole of the forest before it, until it, too, became insufficient to distract em from all eir failures and faults and e had no choice but to withdraw entirely from time and thus, from life. Merrigan had taken the beauty of the labyrinth and wrapped it around emself like a shell, calcifying it into layers, when e should have watched its cycles of bloom and wither, of birth and death, of light and dark, and let the good and bad emotions likewise cycle by the day, the hour, the year, the century. E had done that once, had found a rabbit's corpse and wept, for the rabbit and for the illness down south e had not been able to cure; or watched a flower open to the daylight and thought of one of eir gender-kin, likewise blooming, with satisfaction and pride. Once, e had been able to let out eir poisons, at least a little, enough that e was not hiding from joy as well as from pain.

Merrigan did not know why things had changed, why e had started to store up all that bile until it incapacitated em; but as e looked now upon eir home e felt a gentle self-awareness that had been lacking before.

It was no comfort. For now e must face the dead rose hedge and all it represented. The brittle branches of the hedge pulled stutteringly and weakly apart so that e could pass, and Merrigan went between them carefully, fresh tears rolling silently down eir stinging cheeks.

"I am so sorry," e whispered, before e reached the end of the hedge. E repeated this without direction, apologizing for a multitude of mistakes e could not name, could not address in any form but this persistent and universal regret.

But the rose petals were soft under eir feet, and Frederick was there on the other side of the rose hedge. Merrigan saw him and said, again, "I am so, so sorry."

And Frederick pulled em into his arms and said, "Welcome home."

PART IV

45

DUST

DUST SWIRLED IN THE air, hung for a moment like the mist that caressed the edge of the woods in the liminal hours of the liminal seasons. Vesta's fingers clenched hard upon the sheet she had just pulled off the chair. She had snapped it with the sharpness of a sudden gust of wind slapping a sail into extension, had set this cloud of time free, hoped some breeze would carry it away—but instead, the dust clung to the air, and then to her skin and hair and clothes, and the chair that had been so close and yet so inaccessible under its protective sheet.

Vesta dropped the sheet and hurried out of the old house in disgust, returning to the new wing, which, if not spotless, was at least too young to be covered in memories.

She went to the kitchen, the place where she spent much of her time. It was rustic by the standards of the family's acquaintances in town, merely by virtue of being one of the front rooms, instead of hidden at the back of the house, or even in the basement. Her town friends thought it quaint that her country house had no servant's quarters or staircases. Vesta had not mentioned that it had been years since she had had any servant in the house other than her father's clerks, a constantly rotating set of young people hieing to and from the town offices. She listened to their reports and gave them their orders while she attended to the small duties she and her father required. There was never more than a handful of dishes, never much in the way of laundry; it was simply easier to do these things herself, and she was glad to have something to occupy her. Even before her father fell ill, he had kept to his room or his study when at home.

Vesta loved the kitchen. She loved the heat from the great iron stove; she loved her great broad wooden counter stretching the whole length of the wall; she loved her cool stone basins, two of them, so large she could bathe in them if she wished. She loved the pantry, with its door tucked into a corner, like a secret. She loved the sconces and the chandeliers, and the shelves where all their fine dishes were displayed. And she loved the table, which was the only thing in the house that remained of her mother. It had been made by Vesta's grandmother, her mother's mother, as a wedding gift for the innkeeper she married, and served for years as the gathering table of that inn. Vesta's mother said she had sent for it when *she* married, because she associated it so much with a sense of home and amiability and togetherness. Vesta's father had wanted to leave it in the old house with all the other furniture, but she had insisted on bringing it over, even if it must be demoted from formal dining table to kitchen bench.

Darragh had been in that kitchen—he had sat at that table. Vesta put her hands on it, reaching, by habit, for the notch in the smooth wood surface where their father's cutlass had bounced in its ineffectual arc toward Darragh's chest. She dug her nail into the wedge, but it had gone smooth in ten years of her worrying it. Her fingers had long since pulled all the splinters out.

It had been some five months since she'd gone to find him at the docks, since he'd come home and set off again so quickly that it almost seemed that he had never been at all—that she had dreamed it, again. But she knew she had not, because the Darragh who had appeared before her had been so unlike any imagined version of him she could have conjured. Somehow, she had not expected him to look different from his teenage self. She had expected a lean, petite man with bounteous golden hair, an elegant man not unlike the ones who asked to escort her into and out of the fashionable parties in Cathal. There were enough commissioned captains who maintained their gentlemanly softness; she was well acquainted with them. But Darragh was not a captain, had only become an officer through years before the mast; he had not been able to purchase privilege. What power he had gained in his seagoing career had been scraped, peeled, carved from his sun-and-wind-burned skin, not inherited like hers.

His letters lay before her in a musty, crumpled pile, the paper velvety with constant handling. She had read them often enough in the ten years since he'd gone, but the last few months, alone in that house with no living thing near her—only a half-living father—they had been an ever-present comfort and torment. They embodied the contradiction of the true Darragh. The oldest of them, written in rough pencil on cheap paper in the most elegant penmanship; and the last, from some four or five years ago, on good paper and written with good ink and quill, but in a scrawled print that had no time or inclination to flourish. That letter had told of his posting to the *Augustina*. When she'd used that information to find him, she had not expected to succeed, for that was a powerful long time for even an officer to stick to a single ship.

Vesta had teased him, called him rough, but he was so much more pensive than he had been—that had been clear, even in their two brief interviews. He looked as gnarled as any other sailor, but he moved and spoke with an unexpected gentleness, and his voice had not the harsh, rasping accent of so many seahands. But more than anything, he had seemed lonely. That was what had struck Vesta to her core, and left her shaking even months later: how very tired, and lonely, and heartbroken her little brother had seemed.

She blamed herself. She had been eighteen when he and their father had had their final confrontation, old enough to be some protection, old enough to know what was needed. Old enough, savvy enough, to have left with him and helped him survive. Yet she had stayed. She thought Darragh would come back soon enough—he had run away before, never for more than a few hours, never missed by anyone but her—she thought Jovan would look for him and bring him back. But he never spoke of Darragh again, not until he fell ill. All physical remnant of his presence was destroyed, just as their mother's had been. Still Vesta had stayed, imagining herself as a bridge between her father and the other members of the family. In the end, she was nothing but a tower, the solid perch from which Jovan watched the others vanish over the horizon.

The clock chimed. Vesta rose and slowly, slowly climbed the stairs, walked the hall to Jovan's bedchambers. The room was warm with the last of summer's heat, trapped by the glass windows Jovan never suffered to be opened. Vesta kept them closed even now, though he could not protest, because the longer the room collected heat, the longer she could put off firing the hearth. A fire in the room would necessitate her visiting more often.

Her father looked so powerless, there in his absurd four-poster bed. He hardly looked real; he could have been a wax doll if not for the clamminess of his skin. It was becoming hard to recall the times when it felt as though he towered over all of them. He had puffed himself up in so many ways—made his voice always louder than anyone else's, wore clothes that made him wider and taller than he naturally was, chose colors of fabric and wigs that drew the attention of a room like a bird crying desperately to be seen by the object of its affection. But affection was never Jovan's desire. Vesta might charitably say that loyalty was the thing he wanted most. Loyalty first, and silence second. She had learned to provide both. In the silence of his death-like sleep, she had taken to producing noise to amuse herself—first whispers, then conversations held with herself. She began to sing; finally she began to scream, at the top of her lungs, until the stablehand came rushing in with a whip in hand looking for some threat. But Vesta had only laughed and asked him to scream with her. Her father would not, could not wake. Not until she bade him.

She took now the two tablets provided by the alchemists, one to maintain the sleep, the other to provide some nutrients to his body, and mashed them in her small mortar with a little lard to produce a paste. She opened his jaw roughly—her delicate ministrations of his early days of sleep long since dispensed with—and smeared this paste on his tongue with a flat wooden spatula. She placed a conical cup with a hole in its base into his mouth next, and slowly poured water into it. She did these things twice a day; had done these things twice a day for months.

Is it better that he should die? Darragh had asked. At first, the idea had seemed blasphemous to Vesta. But the longer Jovan slept, the more Vesta wondered. Not whether he should die, necessarily—that is, she did not wish him dead—but rather at the fact that his being asleep brought her no sorrow any more than his being awake had brought her joy. Oh, she had wept tears for him. But she had been expected to do so. And she had been inspired in no small part by the guilty realization that no one else would cry for him at all.

Her last ministration was to take a large brush she had once used for her cosmetic powders, and brush the gathering dust from her father's face.

THIS WAS HOW GABIN found her: a wan, drained thing slumped amid the dust.

Darragh had not misjudged the ancient sorcerers' tower; it was an abandoned, useless thing, and so it only made sense that that was where Gabin lived, where her former colleagues, former subordinates, were content to let her convalesce. Periodically they came and asked her if she wouldn't give them permission to end the spell on her immortal tree for her. She did not give an answer to such absurd inquiries. She was more grateful than ever for the spell that kept her alive, because it gave her time to get her magic back.

This had been her consuming drive for several decades; but she knew that her best hope was to convince Merrigan to undo what e had done. Only e could. The guild, though much advanced, could still only scratch the surface of what Merrigan could do, especially when it came to magics on living things more complex than a worm. The guild was in major competition with the alchemists for medical precedence, and it was losing, for alchemical processes were more similar to and therefore more easily integrated with the workings of animal flesh. Gabin had studied it eagerly—for no spark of magic was required for most alchemy—until she realized that it was not advanced enough to help her.

Only Merrigan could.

Yet she had seen the forest after the cataclysm at Iarom. She had wondered then whether it was possible that Merrigan had met the limits of eir power. She imagined Merrigan shrunken and extinguished in a puff of smoky light, like the sprites upon which the guild had experimented for years; for em to be so reduced seemed impossible. Still, the forest had been painfully, unnaturally frozen even to her diminished senses. Over time, she began to believe that Merrigan had in fact died.

Until Darragh, and his thorn.

He couldn't have been more than thirty, and claimed to have received the magical gift as a child, which meant that Merrigan was not only still alive, but still had power. But the boy disliked something in Gabin; she felt that immediately, and knew he would not partner with her—she had been rejected that way so many times since losing her magic. So she followed him, by means of a cloak charmed to obscure the wearer from notice, for she could still make use of items that were permanently or independently magicked. She accompanied Darragh all the way north, to the very edge of Merrigan's forest.

She could not step foot in it, though. Merrigan would know her immediately, and even if e were somehow weakened, she was no match for Merrigan's fairy blood—had never been, even at the height of her power. So she went south again and nestled in to make her plans.

It seemed so simple, so obvious, when it came to her. Why Merrigan's power had seemed so limitless. Why e had been so furious at the increased logging. Gabin had had the pieces all along, from all the long talks of magic she and Merrigan had had, when they still loved each other. Merrigan's power came *from the forest*. E surely had some power of eir own, in eir flesh, but e could also channel that of the flora and fauna of that great woody wilderness, and it was this which made em seem so omnipotent.

This felt like a breakthrough. The more Gabin thought, though, the more she realized there was no argument she could make with Merrigan to regain her power. Merrigan was nothing if not stubborn and self-righteous; as the long years had embittered Gabin, so they must have done with Merrigan. The evidence was in the steely trees that guarded eir realm. E had grown pitiless. But how could Gabin force eir hand?

A plan formed; Gabin dusted off an old artifact.

It was not difficult to learn who Darragh was, where he was from, the circumstances of his family. She overhead all this while shadowing him on his journey north, and she saw, even if Earrin, and later Berin, did not, the family connection between them. So she was not surprised when she got to the town of Maro and saw Vesta at the post office with a little leaf-shaped birthmark on her wrist. It was the same mark that Fionn, grandmother of Berin, had passed on to the firstborn in every generation of her descendants.

Gabin watched the girl for several weeks. It was not at all uncomfortable to spend so long swathed in the obscuring cloak, for Gabin had long ago grown used to being ignored, overlooked. So she haunted the big house, tracing Vesta's steps from the kitchen to her father's deathbed and back again. For all the luxury of her own chambers, Vesta slept more often in a rocking chair by the kitchen hearth than she did in the great feather bed. The more time that passed since Darragh's visit, the more Vesta seemed to pull away from the corner of the house where her father lay in the horrible death-like sleep. Gabin watched Jovan, too, though more out of professional interest. She was sure a sorcerer could have produced a sleep with a more gentle appearance, and one that needed no constant refreshing. But that made no difference here.

At last, feeling the time ripe, Gabin tucked away her charmed cloak and knocked on the door of the big house.

Vesta answered, with the strained expression of someone who thought they ought to smile but could not quite remember how. "Can I help you?" she asked.

"I have come to help you, cousin," Gabin said.

That roused Vesta—or at least, her suspicion. "Cousin?"

Gabin raised her right arm to show her own leaf-shaped birthmark. It was not natural, she had begun work on it weeks ago; nor was it proof, but it was enough to widen Vesta's eyes. "Distantly," Gabin said. "I have news of your brother, Darragh."

And thus, her welcome was sealed: for few enough knew that the sailor called Darragh Thorn belonged in any way to this house. Vesta ushered her in and showed her to the kitchen—Gabin put on a great show of hesitation, though she had walked those boards often enough. When Vesta's shaking hands reached for the teapot, Gabin calmly pried them away and guided her to a chair.

"Let me, please; I know I have delivered a shock," she said.

"All right," Vesta said. "The tea is—"

"Here," Gabin replied, smiling. "Your kitchen is so well organized, I feel I must know it already."

Vesta did not linger on the pleasantry. "You've seen Darragh? Where is he?"

"Patience; let us have tea first," Gabin said. "For I'm afraid the story has more shocks yet."

"You cannot say such a thing and then keep me in suspense!"

"Yet I beg your trust, for you will be grateful of a hot drink while I tell you all that has passed," Gabin said.

She was immovable, and Vesta was forced to wait for talk of Darragh. But she could say, "You are from my mother's family."

"Indeed. Far away in the north. My branch split off several generations ago, but up there we prize family so that all connections are treated in the same way; though, to be fair, all the northern families are so old that you would be hard pressed to find a stranger who was *not* your cousin." Gabin laughed. "Do you know the old script of introduction, when you included your eldest parent's name and your place of birth? That was to help keep track of cousins."

"And do you know her? My mother?" Vesta asked.

"No, I have not had the pleasure of meeting her. I left the north before she did, as I understand it, and went back after she had left."

"Then she's not been back."

"Not to my knowledge," Gabin said mildly. The teapot whistled, and she poured it gently into two porcelain cups decorated with, of all things, a rose pattern. "Now. You know of course that your brother is . . . much changed, from his childhood?"

"Of course," Vesta said, her voice sharp with impatience.

"But did you never wonder how it was accomplished?"

Vesta frowned. "He told me about the stranger in the meadow; I thought he dreamt it, or conjured it up out of some childish fantasy. When he left home he was still . . . unformed enough that it was hard to discern any shift in him."

"And when you saw him as an adult?"

"I know the doctors and alchemists have the means to effect such changes," Vesta said. "He went to them, I'm sure. What do you mean by all this? Do you mean to say the stranger in the meadow was real?"

"I do. And this stranger is the very person to whom he ran in search of a cure for your father," Gabin said.

Vesta's frown deepened. "How do you know this? How—why should I believe you?"

Gabin sighed, and leaned onto her elbows on the solid old table. "Did your mother tell you many stories of the north? Any fairy tales?"

"A few," Vesta growled with exasperation.

"Of the Enchanter?"

At that, the shrewd young woman laughed. "Oh! So the Enchanter from my mother's stories was the stranger in the meadow, who gave my brother a magic twig that made him the man he is today, and to whom he ran as a grown adult in order to seek some miracle cure for his dying father so that he can rail at an old man for an old man's prejudices? This is a fairy tale indeed."

"Now you understand," Gabin said. "But the Enchanter is no benevolent fairy, and your brother has thrown himself into danger."

Vesta took a deep breath and stared with narrowed eyes at Gabin. The sorcerer could almost see the indecision and frustration in her, the skepticism mixing with the fear and worry and longing and the frenetic restlessness writhing just beneath her skin. It was this fever pitch for which Gabin had waited; it was this moment, when all Vesta's sense and intelligence were threaded with the thinnest cracks, waiting for pressure on just the right point to shatter and make room for the fantastic that her brother had long since embraced.

"What do you mean?" she asked tightly.

"The Enchanter's power comes from a hedge of the most beautiful roses in the world," Gabin said. "It was a thorn from these roses which e gave to your brother, and which made his transition possible. He went north, into the dark forest, and cut one of these roses, believing that if he brought it home, it would heal your father. But the Enchanter caught him, and is now holding him prisoner for the crime of stealing the rose."

"Why are you telling me this?" Vesta asked.

"Because I believe you can save him," Gabin said. She pulled the artifact from a pocket of her coat: a smooth black stone and an antique steel flint striker, formed into the shape of a fox, with etchings in the metal for the eyes and fur patterns. "These have been charmed to burn anything, even something protected by magic. Take them, and set fire to the rose hedge, and you will free your brother."

Vesta eyed the items, but did not move her hands from her teacup. "Why cannot you do this?"

Gabin shook her head. "I do not look it, but I am old. I could not survive the forest, to make it to the hedge. But you are young and strong and brave. That is why I have come to find you."

"And I suppose I can take one of the roses and save my father too," Vesta muttered.

"No—it will not kill the Enchanter if even one of the roses survives," Gabin said. "With the magic of the flint, you could likely escape the Enchanter with a rose; but your brother would remain in eir power. You must choose, I'm afraid. Your father, or your brother."

Vesta said nothing, only stared at the flint and striker. Gabin stood.

"I will leave these items with you. I will be at the inn for a few more days, if you should like to speak more on this subject," she said. "Thank you for the tea."

Gabin let herself out.

THE NEXT DAY, VESTA went into town. She hired old Digna to come and care for her father. She told the post office to hold her letters. And she bought a week's provisions.

46

WANDERER

VESTA RODE HARD AS far north as she could, pushing her best horse to his full speed along the smooth paved roads cutting through swaths of ripening fields until she reached Vicus, and the end of the paving. She had her horse re-shod and left instructions for his return to Maro, then went to the docks for passage north.

There were plenty of passenger ferries, but upon learning that they stopped at all the little towns between Vicus and Varrun, Vesta passed them over, and negotiated instead to be carried by a merchant barge that had only stopped at little Vicus to replace an injured oarhand. She sat in the bows of the barge, watching the green flow of the river, disorienting as the current rushed toward her and the oars pushed forward, and at last let her feelings return to her conscious mind.

Had her father died yet? She had not left instructions for Digna to administer the alchemist's tablets. Would he wake, when the materials inducing the death-like sleep had been all used up by his body, or would he slip into a true death—and would it be noticeable? Or would poor Digna continue to dribble water onto his lips until he began to smell like a corpse? It was too late to do anything about it now, yet Vesta reproached herself for cowardice. To hide the tablets was tantamount to a death sentence; she knew that, though simply doing so and then leaving had allowed her to feel the decision still unmade. Had her control of herself been weaker, she might have laughed, for the circumstance showed how little she had learned. Was she not in this position because of all the decisions she had made by inaction? Had not her inaction led to the ten-year estrangement between her and Darragh? At least she could not blame herself for their father's being put under the death-like sleep to begin with, because it was stipulated in the legal documents surrounding life-threatening events in the family that all possible—*all* possible means be taken to ensure Jovan's survival. Would he be proud, then, to know that Darragh had gone to the ends of the continent, had thrown himself into danger to find a cure?

Darragh—how fared her brother? Vesta imagined him trans-figured, in the form of a beast, or a bird, or even a vulnerable and voiceless plant. She saw him in cages of stone, of flashing silver trees with knives for leaves. She recalled tales and myths of victims dismembered but alive, their limbs carried to the far corners of the world, waiting in vain for someone to collect all the pieces and join them together again. She would do it, if that was what was needed. She had made her choice. Her brother had shown her more compassion and love in two brief, tense interviews than her father had in nearly the entire duration of Darragh's absence.

Jovan had been kind at first, as kind as he ever was. Given the sudden singular daughter where before there had been two, Vesta became the recipient of all her father's affections. But she became an adult and was no longer content to be a beautiful prop, a living testament to Jovan's status and success. He took her under his wing at his company, and all was well while she was still learning. Once she amassed some experience, though, and began to show a mastery of the material, friction emerged between them, for she did not always agree with her father's ideas and plans. Rather she thought him old-fashioned, ill-prepared for new routes and new technologies. He proved as conservative in business as he was socially, and their ships began to be outdone by their more proactive competitors. Jovan laughed, too, at Vesta's ideas for improving conditions aboard their ships in an effort to reduce crew turnover. Crews who had worked together for months, years, improved the efficiency of a vessel, and preserved both lives and assets in emergencies. Crews bonded in experience and love were less likely to abandon ship, less likely to mutiny; they were less likely to be reckless in bad weather or to steal for their own profit. There was less fighting and higher morale, better relationships between hands and officers—long, long lists of evidence, corroborated by competitors and by their own captains.

But the company was no democracy, and Jovan had flatly refused. Young and naive, being yet only twenty-two years old, Vesta had persisted, believing it to be merely a difference of opinion that impassioned debate could sway. In some other office, perhaps. In Jovan's, however, the other managers were sent away so they would not see Jovan slap Vesta across the face.

That was the first time, and it was so unprecedented, such a shock, that it took several more years of similar arguments for her to learn that her influence was not . . . valued. Jovan resorted to violence sooner and sooner, with greater and greater enthusiasm, until Vesta desisted in any reforming agendas. She was, to all appearances, an important part of the company, its much-loved heir; but she was simply a living figurehead, a prop in Jovan's performance, as she had been in her youth.

She thought of marrying, but Jovan made it clear that any partner of hers would be expected to marry *into* the company, rather than removing her from it. In any case, she was so at her father's beck and call that there was little time for courting.

Her eyes burned with the wind of the barge's passage, and with tears, at her cowardice and dishonesty when seeking Darragh. She had placed Jovan in the death-like sleep before seeking the *Augustina*. Truthfully she had never thought that they should see each other, or speak to each other. She had only wanted to see Darragh again, and to justify her place at Jovan's side. Someday, she would have told Darragh the truth, someday disclosed the years of suffering—first, though, she had to find the words. She had to wean herself off the imposed ignorance and silence. Surely, he would understand. He would forgive her.

But first, she had to save him.

SHE HIRED A HORSE from Varrun and followed the river north, keeping as straight a line as possible over the rolling hills while the Erastus slithered along the western horizon. The merchants in the city had told her where to find Iarom, though the directions were all hearsay, memories from the old ones who used to go up there with their carts twice a year. Now they no longer made the journey; it was not worth their effort. Sometimes a person would come down from the village, but as far as anyone knew, the few remaining families there eked out a quiet subsistence. They all assured her that Iarom was the only village on the river north of Varrun. So she found it without much trouble.

It was indeed a desolate, deserted little town whose abandoned foundations outnumbered the houses still standing; grass grew through the cobblestones, and Vesta was forever tugging on her horse's reins to stop him eating it. But there was a fire's glow through the mottled glass windows of what she took to be the inn, and so she dismounted and knocked on the door.

As it was the end of summer, Berin answered the door not with a smile but with surprise—eir fellow villagers never knocked—which feeling was only increased at the sight of the beautiful woman on eir step, dressed in high-quality and fashionable traveling clothes, holding the reins of a sweating horse that eagerly trimmed the cobblestone weeds. Vesta waited while the innkeeper's gaze wandered over her, but the appraisal was halted when Berin noticed the leaf-shaped birthmark on the wrist that shortened the horse's reins to stop his lunching.

"Welcome to Iarom. I am Dom Berin, proprietor," said the

innkeeper in a breathy, distant voice, eir wide eyes moving from Vesta's wrist to her face.

"I am Mistress Vesta she Lucanus," Vesta replied.

"I invite her into my house," said Berin, stepping aside.

"I accept eir hospitality," Vesta said. "Do you have a stable?"

"Oh, of course. Let me." Berin shook emself, came outside and took the horse's reins, then waved Vesta through the inn's door. "Please, seat yourself by the hearth while I take care of your horse."

Vesta smiled and followed Berin's instruction, a little shaken herself by the oddness of the innkeeper. But the hearth room was pleasant and warm, and Vesta relaxed into a chair a little off to the side of the fire. She put her feet up on another chair. As she let go the tension of her ride, her hands idly found themselves tracing the carvings on the chair, on the table; she noticed too the roses carved into the mantel above the fire, and admired the workmanship. The table back home, the one she had had put in the kitchen, was of a similar style.

A very similar style. A table made to celebrate a marriage to an innkeeper, away in the north.

When Berin entered, carrying a tray with a tea service, it was Vesta's turn to look wide-eyed upon em. She remembered her mother's face very little, and Berin was quite a bit darker than she remembered her mother being; but there was the same familiarity in Berin's face as in the carvings of the wood in the room.

Berin seemed to sense her question. E put down eir tray, and pulled back eir sleeve, holding eir wrist to the light so that Vesta could see the same dark leaf-shape on eir wrist.

For a moment, neither of them said anything. Then Vesta asked, "Have you seen my mother?"

Berin nodded. "She visits sometimes. Sometimes she'll come to stay for the winter. She captains a river barge."

Immediately Vesta tried to recall all the faces on the barge she had taken north; none of them matched her memories, or Berin. But she put aside thoughts of her mother for now. She at least was not in any danger. "And my brother?"

Berin wrinkled eir brow, and did not answer. Vesta thought it could not be that complicated a question—how many people came to this backwater inn? But it occurred to her that her mother still believed she had two daughters, and that Berin should only have that information, and that one might not immediately connect dark-haired, cream-skinned Vesta to the blond and bronzed Darragh.

"He—he is about my height, with short hair lightened by the sun," she said. "He would have come in spring, looking for—"

"The Enchanter. Yes. Your brother? Yes . . . yes, I understand now," said Berin, coming slowly around the table. Vesta put her feet to the floor and Berin sat in the chair they had just occupied. "He was here in the spring, for one night. He left before dawn, for the forest, I assume. I have not seen him since. Have you come to find him?" Berin looked mournfully at Vesta, making it clear what e thought: that Darragh was long dead.

No, he is a prisoner, Vesta thought. "I have come to kill the Enchanter," she said.

Berin's eyes widened. "And have you some plan to accomplish it?"

Vesta pulled the flint and striker from a small bag she wore on a string around her neck. "This was given to me by a cousin, Gabin—do you know her?"

"Yes. She is a sorcerer; if she gave it to you, then it must be magic in some way," Berin said.

Vesta nodded. "She said it will set fire to anything, even if it is protected by magic."

Berin reached toward the items, but did not touch them, and withdrew eir hand. "Do you believe he lives? Darragh?"

"I have to." She hesitated. She had been about to say that he was the only family she had left—but that wasn't true, was it?

Again, Berin seemed to sense her thoughts. E sighed and said, "Your mother . . ."

But Vesta shook her head and stood. "I do have questions, but

I must think of my brother first. I will leave for the forest at first light. Thank you for the tea. Please deliver supper to my room."

"Of course," Berin said softly. E rose and led Vesta to a room upstairs, where a fire had been lit and her saddlebags placed on the chest at the foot of the bed. A tense awkwardness seized them, and Vesta longed to be left alone. Ever intuitive, Berin did not linger in the room, except to pause on the threshold. "Darragh left a drawing of a shark on his pillow, the morning he left. Do you know why?"

Vesta gave a mirthless huff of laughter. "It's a sailor symbol. It means he is a wanderer."

"I see," Berin replied. "He did not seem like a wanderer, not at heart. Not like my daughter."

"No. He was forced to be one," Vesta said.

They locked eyes with one another, and Vesta felt a great pulling on her heart, the same as she had felt with Darragh, the powerful urge to show her most vulnerable self. But the rope that coiled around that much abused organ was threaded through a wall built between her and all others, the wall of her patriarchal tower. That tug of feeling only served to bruise her against those cold, unfeeling stones.

She looked down and said, "Good night . . . Gran."

Berin nodded, though Vesta saw neither that nor the tears in eir eyes, as e said, "Good night."

VESTA DECIDED TO FOLLOW the river. She knew to look for the roses, for both Gabin and Berin had said so, but the forest was vast and, if the mist was any guide, hostile. She was no navigator, but at least the river would help her to find her way out if necessary. In anticipation of being required to abandon the river at some point, she had begged an old white bath sheet from Berin, which she would cut into strips and tie to branches to mark her progress. She was as prepared as she could be.

In the morning, Vesta and Berin stood in the meadow before

the forest, at the edge of the thick, curling mist that obscured the trees Vesta knew to be there. She frowned and shook her head, handing the reins of her horse to Berin, who wordlessly took them. She would have to go by foot. The beast would only be at risk of injury and would not increase her speed. She took some necessary things from her saddlebags and put them in a sack Berin had thought to bring, checked again that the flint and striker were safe in the bag resting against her breastbone, and faced Berin with a determined nod.

Berin embraced her, and she set off into the mist.

47

SMOKE

IT WAS COLD IN the forest—a haunting, unnatural cold, pervaded by a clammy moisture that seemed only to grow more frigid as Vesta pressed on. She shivered and knew not whether it was the temperature or the fear. She longed for a fire, but superstitiously, she felt that she could start no fires until the one she would set on the rose hedge. She would bear the cold.

She walked on, carefully, unwilling to touch the trees even after she made it through the iron-barked sentinels. They stood so close together, closer than she'd ever seen trees stand, as if they were closing ranks against her. Anywhere else, such a thought would have been absurd, but in that place Vesta wouldn't have been surprised to see the trees actually move.

All around her was silence, broken only by her own steps. Even the river made no sound. If not for the rustle of humus under her feet, Vesta might have thought some damage had been done to her ears. At first she took comfort in the fact that there at least seemed to be no creatures in the forest that could attack her; then she wondered if they, too, were gifted with this preternatural silence, such that she could die before she ever heard them coming.

Seeking distraction, she tried to recall all the fairy tales she'd ever heard. Her mother had been full of them. She'd said . . . yes, hadn't she said that one of them was about their family? But which one?

"There's the one with the gnomes," Vesta said softly. "And the prince . . . but there are a lot of princes, aren't there? Always princes. Or tailors. What's so special about a tailor?"

Here she began to really believe, at last, in Darragh's Enchanter. Accepting a thing and believing it were different, she realized. She had accepted the notion of his Enchanter being real, accepted it with enough fervor to make this trip; but the Enchanter and eir magic had been an abstract concept, a dark cloud in the sky that had not yet broken into a storm. She believed now. More than belief, she felt in her bones the press of magic in the air, running through her, as if her skeleton were a bell, and the magic the hammer that set it ringing. It was not unpleasant. Rather, in the chill, Vesta felt flush. There was a warmth and an excitement in her that she could not attribute to any sensible feeling. She wondered—now knowing where her family came from, its long relationship to the forest—if it was an ancestral familiarity.

She had expected to be more afraid than she was.

How long she walked, she couldn't have said. The light never changed, and any fatigue she felt was confused in the jumble of other sensations. She walked and walked, with determination that thought little of the time that must be passing, until at last her determination began to falter, for she had seen no sign of roses, no sign of anything but purple-dark tree trunks and greenery gone sallow with approaching winter. She stopped and pulled out her compass in some effort to get her bearings. Beside her, the river oozed on, looking normal to her eyes but making not a sound.

The compass proved useless. It spun like a dancer at the height of a solo. Vesta tucked it away and observed the trees around her, wondering if it would be any use to climb one. No, there could be no hope of spotting roses through even the thinning canopy. But what was that story of the baker's daughter, something involving trees made of precious metals? That, Vesta could see from the top of a tree. Assuming such a thing was real, which she thought was rather an ambitious assumption. She sighed. "This is about the time in a tale when some creature or sprite would appear to offer me assistance," she muttered.

She decided to rest a moment, and sat upon a mossy rock at the edge of the river. She removed the flint and striker from the bag about her neck and held them flat in her palm, half expecting them to point her in the right direction.

It was this innocuous action which saved her from grievous injury at the beast's claws. For she happened to look up just in time to see him stalking her, his eyes luminous and red, his coat bronze in the dim light. And she managed, thoughtlessly, instinctually, to have the good sense to use the flint and striker already in her hand. Frederick leapt at her; she struck the stone; and the sparks landed in Frederick's fur and caught, turning him into a huge torch.

He howled, angrily, piteously; he tried to douse the flames in the river, rolling and sending up great plumes of steam. But as soon as the dampened part of him was exposed again to air, the magical flames returned. Vesta watched in horror and relief until at last Frederick gave up trying to fight the fire with conventional means.

He fled into the forest, and Vesta followed him.

He outpaced her at first, but the flames along his back were easy enough to follow even through the closeness of the trees; and even if they hadn't been, sparks jumped from him and caught in the forest, leaving a trail of bright beacons for her to follow. Soon a wide path opened, and Vesta could see the great glowing beast easily. She began to gain on him as he weakened and slowed. But still he pressed on, deeper and deeper, and she followed even as smoke began to gather and swirl just below the canopy above her.

This was how she found the rose hedge. She watched it slowly, laboriously peel itself apart for the beast. He dragged himself through, and Vesta caught just one glimpse, a tiny, momentary glimpse, of a beautiful shining person with dark skin and green robes that stood out against the orange-red glow of everything around her, before the hedge closed up again, just as she came close to it.

She had not seen Darragh. She squeezed the flint and striker in her hand and contemplated the rising brightness of fire around her, the smoke that began to burn her nose and eyes, the pitiful howling of the beast just beyond the hedge and his tormenting flames, reflecting off the stone and, somehow, the bright leaves of the trees beyond the hedge.

The hedge did not look powerful. The few blooms were dark and drooping. The thorns looked dull. The branches were tangled, and the overall effect was of self-strangulation. But Vesta had found the roses, and the Enchanter, and all had been as Gabin said; so she set striker to stone again, and sent sparks into the hedge. She prayed that once the Enchanter was dead, the flames would go out, and she would find Darragh in the ashes, whole and unharmed.

GABIN SAT ON THE roof of the inn, swathed in her obscuring cloak, a broomstick clutched in her thin white hands. From that perch she saw the dark smoke begin to overtake the white mist. She threw off the cloak, mounted the broomstick, and flew in a direct line for the plumes.

DARRAGH AND EARRIN DID not stop in Iarom, for as they crested the hill just above the town, they too saw the ominous, iron-gray smoke.

They had easily traced Vesta from Vicus, for she was memorable on the docks, and indeed the barge that had taken her north was known to Earrin. They did not bother to ask around in Varrun, for by then it seemed clear that Vesta knew exactly where to go; they hired new horses, for they had been obliged to ride from Vicus to Varrun, and set off for little Iarom-by-the-Barrow.

Little was said, both for the haste of their journey and for the fact that they hardly knew what to say. What was Vesta doing? How had she known to go north? Was she looking for him, or was it some entirely unrelated quest? Why had she suddenly left their father after her years of devotion? Darragh crushed his questions, his hopes, his fears, into a small part of himself and pushed it deep into the darkness of his mind so that they would not plague him until such time as the answers were made available; he could not think of these things until he had found Vesta.

Still, he allowed himself to take comfort in his mother riding by his side with equal haste and an equally closed and fierce expression. For the first time, he did not feel like a changeling, like a stranger, an orphan. For the first time since he was a very young child, he thought he understood what it felt like, what it meant, to share blood with someone, to *belong* to the same lineage as someone else. He wept into the headwind as he had done aboard ship so many times, but on this occasion, his tears were happy ones.

The kinship was so strong that he and Earrin did not stop to discuss what they would do; they rode right into the mist. They took blankets from their packs, and they went into the forest, following the river, with only a few nods to each other to communicate while they caught their breath and left their heaving horses in the meadow.

Soon they were forced to walk in the river itself, because there was fire everywhere. Darragh looked about in anguish as all Frederick's fears bloomed to cruel reality around him. It should not have been possible. The climate below the canopy was as humid as ever, the litter moist and fungal. But the fire creeping steadily through the humus, crowning the trees, winked occasionally a bright white amid the reds and oranges and yellows, and Darragh realized it must have some magical origin. He thought, with sudden horror, of the sorcerer back in Cathal—Gabin—the one who had looked with such hunger at his thorn. But how could they have come here, how could they have found the forest without the thorn?

Could it be that Vesta—?

"Darragh! We have to go back. This is too dangerous," Earrin said behind him, coughing.

"No, I have to find Merrigan and Frederick!" he shouted back. The fire filled the forest with sound, whooshing wind, breaking branches, the crackle that was so pleasant in a fireplace sounding more like the body of a person being ground under a millstone.

"What if they're already out?" Earrin asked. "What if they're safe in the mountains?"

Darragh had no response. He thought of Merrigan's cave; maybe it was deep enough to protect em, and Frederick too, or maybe it was only deep enough to cook em alive while the fire raged at the entrance. He knew his limitations. He knew the danger, the likelihood of finding them, the odds that he could get them all out. He simply could not bring himself to care.

At last he saw what he was looking for: a huge old alder that was entirely aflame but still standing, as if it were waiting for him. This alder was the signpost for the way to the labyrinth. Darragh stopped and squatted in the water, lying back, rolling in it, saturating his clothes and hair and coating himself in river mud.

"What are you doing?" Earrin shrieked as he soaked his blanket in the water.

Darragh stood and seized her, squeezing her tightly. She was rigid, indignant for a moment; and then she returned his embrace, and he felt her kissing his head.

"My foolish boy," she said, through gritted teeth. "My foolish, wonderful boy."

He smiled ruefully at her, as if she had caught him in some youthful mischief. Then he draped the heavy, sodden blanket over his head and shoulders and plunged into the raging fire.

48

ASH

THE LABYRINTH SEEMED SMALLER than Merrigan remembered. Or perhaps e had finally outgrown it.

The first few days of eir return were blissful. The animals all flocked to em, and Frederick proudly showed em all that he, and later Darragh, had done to make it a home. He showed em Darragh's attempts at a bread oven, the clay pots he had made, where he was attempting to age a rose wine. He showed em the books of folk tales Darragh had left behind. They hardly slept while Merrigan listened to Frederick describing the forest over the last hundred years; when they did feel tired, they climbed to the upper forest and dozed under the glittering leaves.

It had been Merrigan's home, and e had been happy there. It had become Frederick's home, and together they had had so many wonderful decades, despite his curse crawling closer and closer to their doorstep. They had both been content to hide away from the world.

But Darragh . . . oh, he had adapted to the forest so very well.

"He was never going to stay," Merrigan said.

"He wanted to," Frederick replied. "He loved this place."

"Yes. But he still has people to love in the world."

Frederick nodded. "Sidra."

"Yes," Merrigan said again. E closed eir eyes and leaned back against one of the black-trunked trees of the upper forest. "It was so nice to have him here, though, even for a little while."

"He'll come back," Frederick said.

Merrigan made a small noise that could have been skeptical or agreeing.

"Would you go to him?" Frederick asked after a moment.

Merrigan opened eir eyes and frowned. "How could I?"

But Frederick never answered; he stiffened, and looked out over the forest. Then he stood and said, "Wait here."

MERRIGAN FELT THE SPARK of flame touch Frederick's skin, and e screamed. The air around em filled with birds and butterflies and bees, anything that could take flight; below em the rumble of stampeding footfalls shook the earth as the animals heeded eir warning and fled. But e could neither fly nor run. E tumbled clumsily down to the floor of the labyrinth, to the rose hedge; but it was burning too.

THIS WAS HOW GABIN found em.

She touched down between the stone of the labyrinth and the burning rose hedge, where Merrigan stood screaming over the hulking body of Frederick, who moaned piteously while the flames scorched his back without consuming him. Perhaps it was her old apprentice's curse that preserved him, ironically protecting him from death because he must be a beast until true love set him free; but the curse was made a thousand times more cruel by Vesta's attack, because the magical flames could not be quenched. He would spend the rest of his life on fire.

The heat was powerful, oppressive, but Gabin felt no fear of it; her tree was protected in the cool Immortal Gardens of the Sorcerers' Guild. She needed only avoid the sparks; otherwise she would find herself in the same unenviable position as poor

Frederick. She kept close to the stone, and edged closer to the distraught pair.

"Merrigan!" Gabin cried, uncertain whether even her loudest voice could catch the attention of the Enchanter, who alternately clutched at Frederick and tore at eir own hair, trembling and weeping.

But e heard her, and turned eyes huge and white with fury upon her.

"*You,*" e said, eir voice both quiet and deafening.

"Me," Gabin replied. "I can end the fire, but you must restore my magic."

Merrigan began to cackle, a horrible noise such as Gabin had never heard em make before—an incredulous, heartbroken noise, an evil noise, which shook eir whole body and convulsed em as if it were a poison being vomited out; a rasping, hysterical hail of devastation, half laughter, half sob.

"Oh, cousin," the Enchanter said at last. "If I had the power to restore your magic, don't you think I would put out the fire myself?"

E stood and advanced on her, and Gabin for the first time felt afraid of em. Even when e had taken her magic, she had not felt this twisting inside, because she knew Merrigan would never wound her. But this being, this Enchanter coming closer to her, bore so little resemblance to the cousin she admired and loved and hated.

"Merrigan, you—you do have the power," Gabin said, her voice trembling. "Remember? It's in you like instinct, it's just like breathing to you! Just—just ask the forest like you used to—"

"This forest? This one burning alive around us?" Merrigan cackled again, and stepped forward. "It knows what you've done. Perhaps it would give its last ounce of power to me—and with it I would tease apart every minuscule part of you, I would unravel you like cloth, I would erase you from existence."

Cold fell upon Gabin like ice water, there even at the center of the conflagration. She backed hastily away from Merrigan, who took step after steady step toward her. E raised eir hands, as if e were about to summon that terrible power.

"You've gone mad," she said. "I never believed it. I heard all those stories, I *saw* what you did to the trees, but even so I believed you could never . . ."

Merrigan's top lip curled into a sneer, and e dropped eir hands heavily to eir sides. "Never use magic in such a deliberately cruel way? As always, you push me to my limits, cousin. But, though I have done things I regret, and made mistakes, I was never a crucial instrument in your punishments. I was a tool to you, like anyone else you ever cared for. *You* will always be the architect of your own destruction. Now begone and let me die in peace."

E turned eir back on her and returned to Frederick's side. It took a few moments for breath to return to Gabin's lungs; but when it did, she stumbled backward in relief.

Right into the burning rose hedge.

FAR AWAY SOUTH, THE Immortal Gardens suddenly exploded with firelight. Sorcerers rushed in and wove their spells, but they could not save the tree from whence the fire came. It burned to charcoal and kept burning until it collapsed into a dusty mound of ash.

"Whose tree was that?" asked one of the sorcerers.

"I think it belonged to that archivist," said another. "The one who lost her magic ages ago."

"Hmph. About time," said a third.

VESTA WAITED OUTSIDE THE burning hedge as long as she could, but soon she knew she could wait no longer. Her eyes felt as though they were boiling in her head, such was the pain; she could see nothing. Her lungs were so seared she wondered if she had inhaled a spark, if the magical fire was consuming her from the inside out. She turned away from the hedge and ran, as best she could, seeking spots of coolness inside an ever-increasing tempest of fire.

What a fool I have been, she thought, somewhat disconnectedly, as she ran. She ran, but there was no question of her surviving. *What a lifetime of foolishness is my legacy.*

She was about to stop, and give herself over to the heat, when something heavy and wet crushed her; suddenly she was being dragged, and then there was splashing, more water, not cold exactly but so different from the fire around her that it shocked her and she began to tremble.

Someone was speaking.

"I've got you, Vesta, I'm here," said the voice. It sounded familiar. She trusted it.

"Darragh?" she asked. No, that wasn't right.

"He went after Merrigan," the voice said. Who was Merrigan? Who was the voice?

"Oh oh oh, okay, it's all right," said the voice, for Vesta's knees had buckled and splashed down into the water. A river? The river. The one in the forest.

"Here now. This won't be comfortable. Can you grip the blanket? Go on, girl, grip it. Here now. Mother's got you," said the voice.

Vesta had a vague sense of being slung, like a yoke, across a pair of broad shoulders. The blanket, freshly wet, was smothering, but she held its corners in her hands anyway, as if her hands agreed with the voice that doing so was in their best interest. But Vesta was not thinking about the blanket. She was thinking only of that word, *mother*.

49

THE BURNING OF
THE LABYRINTH

THE ROSE HEDGE WAS little more than wisps of ash held in place by memory when Darragh reached it, yet still it dragged itself apart for him. If there had been any spare moisture in him, he would have wept as he passed through it, still draped in his blanket, though it had long since gone steamy and then dry.

He could see them before he made it through: Frederick, sides aflame and heaving with his pained, shortened breath, and Merrigan, curled upon the ground next to him, so still Darragh feared for a moment that e was dead. He pushed through the rest of the hedge, the branches crumbling around him, the blanket catching fire; he dropped it and tripped down to his knees at Merrigan's side.

He rolled em over and saw that e still lived; eir slack face twitched, slowly coming back to itself, and eir eyes narrowed at him. "Darragh?" e said.

"I'm here," he said, pulling em up, pulling em into his arms.

"You came back," Merrigan said absently.

"Come on. Get into the labyrinth. Get away from the flames," Darragh said. He lifted em with ease and pulled em toward the entrance, pushed em through it, then went back to Frederick. How could he be burning and still living? Was it his curse? Darragh looked back for the blanket, but it was consumed, gone; he ripped his shirt off instead and tried to smother the flames on Frederick's back.

Frederick growled and snapped at him; Darragh yelled back, leaned away, continued his efforts to tamp the flames. But soon his shirt caught fire, and he was forced by the flames and by Frederick's teeth to stagger away. Frederick snarled and looked at Merrigan, standing as though mystified in the entrance to the labyrinth. Darragh gave a frustrated growl of his own, but he took Frederick's meaning. He left the beast there and took Merrigan instead, pulling em along deep, deep into the labyrinth.

It was marginally cooler, and Darragh felt hope for the first time that if they could wait out the fire in the labyrinth, they would survive. That was what Frederick had said; that a forest fire would always burn itself out eventually. The smoke had curled into the outermost corridors of the labyrinth, but the deeper in they went, the clearer the air.

Now out of immediate danger, Darragh became aware of the livid heat all over his limbs, of the burning in his eyes, of the wheezing of his breath. But he walked on, pulling Merrigan with him until he reached the tower at the center, the room Frederick had used. Merrigan didn't resist. When they stopped at last, and Darragh guided em to sit on the moss mattress, e obliged, all the while staring at him with bewilderment.

"What are you doing here?" e asked at last.

Darragh went to the large cask Frederick kept filled with water. He ladled it into a bowl and found a spare cloth, then joined Merrigan on the bed. Dipping the cloth into the water, he began to dab at the soot on Merrigan's face. The only answer he gave was to raise his eyebrows; his purpose was obvious.

"The labyrinth will burn too. This is no ordinary fire,"

Merrigan said. "You should leave while you still can, go north, to the mountains."

"Are you strong enough?" Darragh asked.

Merrigan's eyes flashed with frustration, and e said, "Leave!"

Darragh only gave em a crooked smile. "That was the first thing you said to me, when I found you."

"Oh, if only you would listen to it," Merrigan moaned.

Smoke swirled around them, and the temperature began to rise; as Merrigan had said, even the stone of the labyrinth began to fall before the magical flame. Darragh set aside the bowl and cloth, then took Merrigan's hands in his. Gently, he laid himself down, stretching along the bed, and he guided Merrigan down with him. E allowed this, despite the swelling pressure in eir chest, the tightness in eir heart so painful e was sure it would rupture. Darragh laid on his side, his whole aspect turned toward Merrigan. Merrigan laid on eir back with only eir head turned toward him, as if that would be enough to save em.

"Why, Darragh?" e asked.

Darragh reached out, and caressed eir face. "Because I am too late to save you."

It was enough; they understood each other; and in that moment it did not seem strange to them that they should feel relieved. The tension went out of them. They breathed together, relaxing into the intimate proximity, and they were content. Merrigan lifted eir fingers and let them fall lightly onto Darragh's lips.

"Do you regret coming to the forest?" e asked.

Darragh smiled then. "No, for I found you here. If I were not here with you, even now, I think my heart would break; because it never felt more full of contentment and joy and hope than when I have been your friend. And so I am here, willingly, happily, and here I will remain until you send me away or until you draw your last breath, or I do, because there is no person more wonderful to me in all the world than you."

Merrigan laughed, or sobbed, and said, "You have the most beautiful soul I have ever known."

Darragh came closer to em; he pressed his body against eirs, moved on top of em as if to shield em from the flames now eating even this inner labyrinth wall, and his lips were next to Merrigan's ear when he said, "I love you, more than anything."

"I love you," Merrigan sighed into his hair. "I love you, I love you."

Darragh kissed eir cheek, gently, slowly, almost fearfully though they were at the gates of death and had nothing to fear anymore. E trembled beneath him. He felt it, and lifted his head. They gazed into each other's eyes. A question formed between them but could not make it past their lips, unsure whether it could even be heard over the roar of the fire that had found them. But as the question passed between them, so too did the answer.

And then their lips met at last, quick and hard as they seized the moment before it was too late — but they had time yet, to soften against each other, to open their mouths and taste of each other while the world burned around them. They did; though they both should have tasted like smoke, Merrigan would have sworn that Darragh's mouth had just been full of strawberries. Later, he would say that Merrigan must have been eating lavender. But the sweetness could not distract long from the wonderful weight of Darragh, of his hips against Merrigan's; eir legs spread to accommodate him, eir back arched so that his arm fit under it to hold em tight against his body, his hand cupped eir head to keep it within reach of his kisses. They could not tell the heat of the flames from that of their bodies.

50
DEATH

IT WAS A GOOD way to die.

IT WAS *NOT* HOW they died.

51

RAIN

THE MOMENT DARRAGH AND Merrigan kissed, a great light rose up in the forest, blotting out even the glow of the flames.

In Iarom, the villagers had gathered to see the smoke and wonder at what had happened. One of the elders had suggested making preparations, but no one had moved to do so; if the fire burned Iarom, so be it. Their fate had always been tied to the forest, and they were weary enough not to mind it.

But the light came, and the villagers watched in awe as the smoke from the fire turned pure white, then gray with rain. A roll of thunder passed over them and the clouds loosed their precious moisture onto the forest. The sun had long since set, but the rain seemed to sparkle, as if the stars themselves were falling from the sky. The flames were extinguished, and still it rained; it rained on and on until green erupted from trees that had been rotted and dead and charred. The forest turned once more lush and golden. The armor fell from the sentinel trees, and the villagers wept.

They watched the rain pour for hours; and when at last the

clouds were spent, they sank and shrouded the forest in mist. This, too, the villagers watched. They stood, as if transfixed, until dawn came and, for the first time in more than a hundred years, burned the mist away.

52

WARMTH

IT WAS THE EVENNESS of the warmth that first stirred Merrigan to wakefulness; the space of difference between this strong but diffuse sensation and the flickering unpredictable lashes of fire was wide enough for eir senses to register. Eir body tensed and relaxed, testing its bounds, its responsiveness. E opened eir eyes and saw nothing but open sky, a clear and undisturbed blue. It was the sun e felt on eir skin, not flame. E curled eir fingers, extended them. In this way, tendon by tendon, limb by limb, Merrigan realized that e was alive.

And not alone. Beside em, skin-to-skin with em lay a warmth that pulsed with life. Darragh. Merrigan lifted emself gently so as not to disturb the sleeping sailor, on his side in the soft, fragrant, brown-gray humus. There was no sign of the fire upon him. His hair fanned around his head; the scars on his bare upper body were all known to Merrigan, all attached to stories of cruelty, of bravery, of luck. The three-faced bust on his chest rose and fell with a steadiness Merrigan craved. E placed eir hand on that tattoo, let Darragh's breathing flow into eir own lungs' rhythm, timed the beating of eir heart with his. Then, e looked around.

The labyrinth was gone. Only the barest outline, the faintest shape of the walls could be detected, and only because Merrigan knew them so well; the walls had functioned as a kind of bark for Merrigan for so long, protecting eir soft vulnerabilities. Yet it had apparently vanished, without even the smallest bit of rubble. The rooms and storehouses and gardens maintained by Darragh and Frederick were present, visible in the huge new gap, spaced oddly far away from each other without the labyrinth to separate them. They were like stubborn camps, as if pioneers were determined to find their way alone but knew that safety lies in numbers. All told, the only sign of Merrigan's former sanctuary was the scattering of silver leaves on the moist earth.

Merrigan picked one up. It was thin, pliable, but undamaged by—what had happened? Fire—a confession of love before it was too late—and then what?

E stood, leaving Darragh to sleep, and walked to the edge of the gap left by the labyrinth's absence, through the boundary of ashes that had once been the most beautiful roses in the world. E looked out into the forest and saw green, endless green. E put a hand to the nearest trunk and felt the moss on it still damp with water. Rain—had rain extinguished those flames? But they had been cursed, unquenchable, they had—

Merrigan turned back to the gap and hurried to where e thought the entrance to the labyrinth had been, and fell to eir knees, sweeping eir hands through the loose humus until e found him. Frederick, sleeping as soundly as Darragh, naked and whole and human and perfect. Merrigan cried out, and the sound seemed to echo in that great new openness. Frederick stirred, and opened his eyes. He seemed to remember more, faster, than Merrigan had, for his eyes widened at the absence of stone. He leapt up and pawed at his body until he seemed convinced it was his. He locked eyes with Merrigan.

"What happened?" he asked.

"I hardly know," Merrigan answered.

"Darragh—I made him leave me," Frederick said.

"We hid in the labyrinth. The fire reached us eventually, but . . ."

Merrigan shrugged helplessly, gesturing around, wondering if this was after all a dream, or some vision of an afterlife where e and Frederick and Darragh could be together and be happy.

"The beast is gone," Frederick said. He was grinning, and before Merrigan could react, he had knelt before em. The look on his face was just shy of ecstatic joy, and it was contagious; Merrigan's heart quickened threefold, joy and fear and confusion all stealing eir borrowed calm.

"You told him how you felt," Frederick continued.

Merrigan nodded.

"And he told you."

"Yes," Merrigan said. "But I don't see how—"

Frederick laughed, and all at once, Merrigan did see; e remembered, and flushed with the memory and eir own naiveté. E remembered clutching Darragh to em in the unbearable heat, hardly registering the physical pain because of the sorrow, the injustice of such a person dying with a grace Merrigan had aspired to but never achieved. E had been content in numbness but never in pain, and never, ever in joy. All the world had been at arm's length until Darragh extended his hand, and Merrigan fell in love. Passionate, consuming, selfish love.

And that love could not let Darragh go. It roused the parts of Merrigan that had been strained and torn by eir pain and anger, and e found that e had healed—and so had eir magic. Eir magic had quenched the fire, restored the forest, and shattered Frederick's curse.

"I am so happy for you," Frederick said.

"And for yourself," Merrigan said, laughing.

"And for myself," he agreed, "and for Darragh."

Merrigan rose, and helped Frederick up, and they went together to where Darragh somehow still slept. While Frederick clothed himself from his special chest, Merrigan sat down by Darragh and caressed his face.

Darragh—awake after all, waiting—caught eir wrist, and

pulled em down, and rolled em into his arms, covering eir face with kisses while e laughed with a giddy ease that surprised em. At last he stopped, and looked at Merrigan with a hungry, roguish smile. He said nothing; nothing needed to be said. Not just then.

DARRAGH WAS A PRACTICAL man, and while some concerns had been allayed, others remained. And so, though his hands in Merrigan's, in Frederick's, remained relaxed and gentle, his face grew serious as he asked whether there were others yet in the forest. Merrigan, flexing eir long-dormant senses, could find none. So the three of them trekked with all haste for the forest's edge. Merrigan led, to find the easiest and most direct path, with Darragh matching eir steps as best he could, and Frederick coming behind.

They emerged under a high noon sun in a meadow yellow with autumn grasses and full of people—the whole village of Iarom, standing bewildered in land that had been a place of horror and mist for more than a lifetime.

A shout went up when the foresters were spotted, and the crowd parted for Earrin, who ran forward calling for her son. Darragh met her; their eager hands and relieved sighs communicated, better than words, their mutual health. But then Earrin tugged his hand and led him into the gathering, and Vesta's name was on their lips.

She was laid out in the grass, badly burned and barely breathing, having been carried too far from the rain to share in its rejuvenation. Darragh looked down at her, his breathing sympathetically short. He still knew not how she had come to be there, nor why—but there she was, come in search of him for good or ill. He turned and looked at Merrigan, where e and Frederick lingered, uncertain, within reach of the trees.

Darragh jogged to em, slid his hands around eir waist, pulled em to him and raised his face to em. Merrigan rested eir forehead against his. Darragh did not need to voice his thoughts, his wish; Merrigan kissed him, and slipped free of him, and walked toward the villagers.

They knew who e was. How could they not? Confusion and hesitance held each villager in place as Merrigan knelt beside Vesta. Here was the one they had been taught to fear, who had caused the ruination of their village. Here, the one who had caused the Barrow. But this Enchanter was no hunched, scowling figure, reveling in human devastation. E was nothing like they'd imagined. Some of them even then—especially then—thought they were dreaming, and simply watched. The others, they looked to Berin; and Berin looked on with cautious hope while Merrigan laid hands on eir newly met granddaughter.

There was little to see. Darragh and Frederick drew closer, stood by Earrin while Merrigan sat, cross-legged and silent at Vesta's side, her hand held loosely in eirs, resting in eir lap. At length, almost imperceptibly, Vesta's burns flaked away from clear, creamy brown skin. Her dark hair was loose and long. Her clothes were as fine and clean as they'd been the day she'd struck north; and her breath was as deep and as even as the most peaceful sleep.

When Merrigan opened eir eyes, they were full of tears. Darragh smiled and cupped eir face, and bent, and kissed em. The villagers began to breathe again. Some of them even smiled.

53

COME SAILING WITH ME

VESTA EMERGED FROM THEIR father's offices, and Darragh held his breath; then she grinned at him, opening her jacket to show the bundle of papers peeking from the top of her inner pocket. She crossed the road to join him, and together they began the long walk down the Cathal hill road. She handed him the papers, which he read with equal parts amazement and excitement. Such a sum of money as he'd never heard of before, never dreamed of—there, all below Vesta's name.

"I can't believe he allowed it," he said.

"He had no legal means to stop it," Vesta replied. "My inheritance and my rank in the company, my shares, were always separate things. I don't think he ever conceived of a situation in which my independence would matter more to me than his legacy."

So he had done it; their father had bought Vesta's shares in his company. She had been in the building for over an hour, and Darragh was sure she had spent most of that time under a barrage of verbal abuse. But perhaps she had given some in return. Her cheek was flush and her step was light, and when he handed the papers back, she tucked them away with a triumphant smile.

"Now all we need is a ship," Darragh said.

"This will get us a solid carrack," Vesta agreed. "But oughtn't we wait for Sidra? Will she even agree?"

"Oh, she will agree. She thinks as highly of our current owner as you do," Darragh said. "As to choosing a ship, leave that to Janne and me. We know what Sidra will look for."

Vesta nodded. She slipped her hand into the crook of Darragh's elbow. He smiled and bent the arm, the better to escort her.

IT HAD BEEN EARRIN'S idea. They had all been gathered in the inn at Iarom: Berin and Earrin, Vesta, Darragh, Merrigan, and Frederick. Upon learning that Jovan lived, Vesta had burst into tears, crying that she couldn't go back to him. Berin said immediately that she could stay as long in Iarom as she wished. Earrin had assured her that there was a place on the river barge for her. Then, she tapped her chin and asked Vesta whether she had full control of some trust or allowance. After hearing how things stood with Vesta's shares in Jovan's shipping empire, Earrin suggested she seize that capital.

"And do what with it?" Vesta had cried.

"Anything," Earrin said. "Anything you want."

Vesta frowned into the fire for a moment. Then she lifted her head and looked at Darragh, her expression hard and bright.

"I love the merchant marine," she said firmly.

"You could buy a ship," Earrin said. "You need not forsake a shipping legacy to spite him."

"I'd need a captain," Vesta said, eyes still on Darragh.

He smiled and said, "I know a good one."

Vesta returned the smile, her gaze already gone distant, gone south, imagining the available ships, totaling costs for refurbishments and cargo. Darragh took Merrigan's hand and kissed it softly. He leaned in to em, kissed eir cheek; then said gently in eir ear, "Come sailing with me."

Merrigan shivered, and clutched his hand tightly.

There followed a few nervous days of contemplation, when

each of them explored their possibilities, wandering between the village and the forest dazed with imagination.

Frederick found the statue of the shepherd; he slammed himself against it. Bereft of his bestial strength, it took him days to topple it. In those days the villagers watched him, whispering and questioning Merrigan and each other until they pieced together his origins. They thought he attacked the statue for vengeance. But once it had fallen, he got a spade, and he built the shepherd a burial mound. There he knelt, when his labor was over, until the remnants of his family—a cousin not yet born when he was cursed, now a wizened elder of the village, supported by her descendants—came and sat his vigil with him. Frederick wept and clasped their hands; they welcomed him into their house and he went with them. Yet the mornings always found him in the forest. Later, his cousins would go with him; later he would live in a cabin of his own at the forest's edge, and teach what he knew to young people who struck north to find themselves. Under his instruction, the responsible management of the forest eventually became the business of the entire village, and it became thoroughly revitalized.

But first he visited the forest alone, and reassured himself that his human senses still knew the trees as well as ever.

Vesta and Darragh sat side by side on the roof of the inn, as they used to do on the roof of the cottage down south. Vesta faced that same direction, jaw set and eyes flashing while she made her plans. Darragh, meanwhile, faced north, so he could clearly see, at last, the forest where he had spent so much time; and so he could watch Merrigan.

E had asked him once whether he could go back to sailing, and Darragh had said he had little choice. He no longer felt that way. He watched the upper branches of the distant trees ripple gently in the breeze, and he longed for the open water. He and Vesta had talked of it. How they could make the ocean their own; how it already was their own, their parent, their teacher, their home.

She was ready before he was, to hurry south and press their reconciliation into partnership. She sighed at him; then he would raise his eyebrows and she would follow his gaze to where Merrigan stood alone in the meadow. Then Vesta would soften beside him, and look south again. Darragh watched Merrigan, and waited.

Merrigan could not bring emself to enter the forest again. E slipped out of the bed e shared with Darragh in the cold before the sun rose; e found Frederick behind the inn and together they entered the meadow. But halfway to the tree line, Merrigan stopped, and stood, and watched from a distance as Frederick became another green shadow below the trees.

At first e thought it must be fear that made em hesitate before that place e loved so well; fear that once e entered e would become trapped again; but that notion was quickly set aside. The forest was eir family, one that had always supported em in the ways e requested, if not the ways e needed. No, it was guilt that stopped em, because e had, in eir anger, punished the forest as much as e had the village. E had not even asked the forest what it thought, how it wanted to deal with the lumberers, what help it wanted from em. E had forgotten, as Darragh reminded em later, the great longevity of the mighty organism so incompletely called by that word, *forest*. It was so much older and stronger than em. Had e only asked, how much pain and suffering could have been avoided?

One day Frederick came back out, and tugged gently on Merrigan's hand. "Just come listen," he said.

So, slowly, trepidatiously, Merrigan went with Frederick back into the forest. Long before e crossed the tree line, though, e heard the trees singing to em—of freedom and joy and forgiveness.

"WHAT SHOULD I DO at sea?" Merrigan asked.

"What would you like to do at sea?" Darragh countered.

They were on the inn roof, alone. The sun was bright and clear above them, the breeze strong, the countryside rolling all around them. Merrigan said, "I just want this. This openness."

Darragh nodded, and counted one heartbeat, then two, before he spoke; he did not want to seem too eager, to overwhelm

Merrigan with his idea. "Can you speak to the wind, the way you do the trees?" he asked, when the timing felt right.

"And say what to it?"

He shrugged. "To blow harder. Or not so hard. Or in a different direction."

He smiled slowly; he could not help it. He was found out. Merrigan considered him, eir eyes dancing over his face. Then e looked out across the landscape again.

"You think I could be a . . . what did you call them? A wind-singer?"

Darragh kissed eir bare shoulder. "I think you could be the best wind-singer the world has ever seen."

54

BESTIA

A SHIP WAS FOUND, and by Frederick's suggestion, they named it the *Bestia*, so that they might think of him often though he would not sail with them. He came south long enough to carve their figurehead. When he was finished, he patted the beast fondly, feeling it to be fully exorcised at last.

Now it was only for them to await Sidra's return. Darragh and Merrigan passed the time in his preferred tattoo shop. Merrigan got upon eir upper shoulder a perfect circle, the usual sailing tattoo for genderlessness; and they both of them got matching roses vining up their forearms.

Janne begged and was given the pleasure of delivering the news to Sidra. She and the *Augustina* returned battered and stressed from a particularly bad voyage; but all evaporated when Sidra learned that not only was Darragh alive, well, and reconciled with his sister, but that an offer of captaincy was extended with benefits she had never dreamed of. A fine salary, to be sure, but degrees of power and access and influence in the management of the ship such as few ship owners were willing to allow. One of these new powers was a part in the hiring of crew, including officers—which meant, Janne said with a sly, teasing sweetness, that if Sidra would have em, e could now sail with her; their long separations would be over.

Thus was the final piece slotted into place, and soon the *Bestia* was underway on its maiden voyage. Sidra, captain, Darragh, first officer, and Janne, second officer, stood all together on the deck as the helmer guided them into the open sea. They could not stop grinning at one another.

There was some small skepticism among the seahands about their new wind-singer at first, for e was clearly not guild trained. E seemed to use no tools at all, and hardly made a sound when e called the winds, and did not even wear green. But e was undeniably skilled; the best any of this crew had ever known, for eir summoned winds did not fight em as they often did others. They came smoothly and easily; and sometimes the seahands thought they heard the wind-singer laughing while e worked, and swore the wind laughed back.

But what really warmed the hands' hearts to Merrigan was eir interest in sailing beyond eir duties. E bustled all around the ship, learning each duty, lending eir strength and assistance when it was needed, admiring when it was not. And there were plenty of unexpected benefits to shipping with Merrigan. The *Bestia* was free of rats, weevils, and fleas. The hold stayed amazingly dry. The ropes never frayed and the sails never tore. The food stayed fresh, the wounds stayed clean, and the mood stayed high.

Darragh and Merrigan stood together in the bows one evening, watching the water turn red with sunset, holding each other in the cool buffeting air from the driving wind behind them and the brisk forward motion of the ship. Merrigan had shorn eir locs, too heavy for ship life; but Darragh had kept his long hair, which he wore securely braided. Merrigan toyed with the end of this braid, and found emself gazing at Darragh rather than the great beauty of the sunset.

Darragh, feeling eir eyes, turned and smiled up at em. "Are you enjoying yourself, my love?" he asked.

"Yes," Merrigan replied. "More than I thought possible."

The sun dipped below the horizon. Under a glittering canopy, the stars winking like silver leaves fluttering in the breeze, Darragh and Merrigan kissed and called each other beautiful; and all was well.

PHOTO BY KITTA BODMER

ABOUT THE AUTHOR

NEIL COCHRANE IS A queer, trans author and artist living and working in Portland, Oregon. He writes speculative fiction that centers queer characters overcoming obstacles and building families. He has worked in and around the publishing industry since 2012, in such various roles as editor, literary agent assistant, marketing director, and bookseller.

ACKNOWLEDGEMENTS

ALL THE THANKS IN the world go first and foremost to my husband Matt, whose unwavering emotional and material support of my creative work has helped me make my dreams a reality I get to inhabit on a daily basis. I love you more than I can say.

Thank you to my writing group, Orion Rodriguez, Lydia Rogue, Elisabeth Moore, and Bree Wolf, who shepherded this concept through its early manifestations and into the form it takes in these pages. The friendship and tenderness I've striven to capture in this story, I learned from you; this book would not exist without you.

Thank you to my publisher and editor Laura Stanfill, for taking a chance on a book outside the usual scope of Forest Avenue's offerings, for seeing the soul of this book as clearly as I do. I couldn't have asked for a better home for this story. Your enthusiasm for and belief in this novel is a gift that I will always treasure.

Thank you to Gina, Gigi, and everyone else at Forest Avenue Press who have helped this book find its voice, its face, and its place in the world; your efforts are most appreciated.

Thank you to the community of authors and publishing friends who have supported me and my work over the years—it is impossible to name all of you, but know that I am grateful for you all the time.

Thank you to my friends and family, for celebrating every milestone along the way with me.

If I've forgotten to address you directly, know that I am both grateful for your support and sorry that my brain let that particular bit of information slip.

And finally, thanks, of course, to you, the reader; may your path be smooth, and naught but kindness meet your ear.

THE STORY OF THE HUNDRED PROMISES

a novel

READERS' GUIDE

SAILORS' TATTOOS
AND SYMBOLS

triangle: the bearer is a woman

nested triangles: a woman who pairs with other women

mermaid's purse tangled with a harpoon: the bearer is a man

triple-faced head: the bearer is a different gender than the one given at birth

shark: represents wandering, a wanderer

length of rope with knots: shows the number of ships on which one has been stationed, one knot for each ship

glacier [upper chest]: denotes how far north one has gone

tropical plants [lower abdomen]: denotes how far south

whale: represents family

circle: represents genderlessness

TITLES

Dom, Homin, Goodhom: gender-neutral titles
Sir, Mister, Goodman: masculine titles
Madam, Mistress, Goodwoman: feminine titles

BLESSINGS AND RITUALS

"May your path be smooth, and naught but kindness meet your ears, and your belly full, and all the skies above you clear."

"For you I wish a life of light, though we now must part; what joy is yours, shall be mine too, for you are in my heart."

For welcome: "I invite [guest's pronoun] into my house"; "I accept [host's pronoun] hospitality."

BOOK CLUB QUESTIONS

1. Author Neil Cochrane calls his aesthetic "queer optimism." What do you think he means by that? Can you think of specific examples of queer optimism within the text?

2. Consider the title. What are some of the promises the characters make to each other?

3. This novel isn't a coming-out story. As author Neil Cochrane said, "It's a book about living in queerness, and it's a book about what happens when 'coming out' doesn't lead to instant or complete fulfillment. Queer people come out and still have to think about what brings them joy in their work, in their homes, in their friendships and love lives. We still get lonely, we still work dead-end jobs we're not sure we love. Even when queerness makes up a big part of someone's identity, it doesn't overtake everything." Name some plot points or characters that match Neil's intentions. What are some other books that explore living in queerness?

4. Think about the embedded fairy tales. How did your understanding of those stories shift by the end of the novel? If you haven't gone back to read them, do so now for deeper understanding. What do you think Neil is saying about bias with Gabin of Iarom and, more generally, about the people who claim to speak for history?

5. How does the book challenge or overturn traditional ideas about what kind of love is most valued? How about what relationships should look like?

6. Neil's book is a loose retelling of *Beauty and the Beast*. What are some other modern novels that turn old stories into modern works of literature?

7. Why do you think Merrigan removed emself from the world? What does the cave represent? Have you ever wanted to hide away from people, and if so, were you able to find a way to do it? Why or why not?

8. Does the story challenge your understanding of gender? Why or why not? Can you find specific examples in the text?

9. What does Darragh really want? The story begins with his urgent need to confront his father, but becomes a quest for contentment and security and love. How are those two threads of the story intertwined? Do you think Darragh finds what he's seeking? Name a time in your life when you wanted something desperately, and in trying to achieve it, you found yourself on an unexpected path.

10. What would society be like if we all introduced ourselves with pronouns instead of assuming or guessing each other's gender identity? Where and when do you regularly share your pronouns? Are there opportunities to share them that you haven't considered yet?

11. Vesta is a character with privilege. She has wealth and power, thanks to her close relationship with her father. But she must exist within her father's expectations, not her own. How does her character change through the novel? Do you think she and Darragh understand each other more by the end of the novel than when they were children? Why or why not?

12. Consider the relationship between Sidra and Janne. Is it an example of the ideal love? Why or why not? Do you think Darragh wishes for a relationship like that when he visits them early in the novel? Or is he content to appreciate their affection for each other?

13. Speaking of love, consider Darragh's response to Amon on page 70-71. Do you agree or disagree with his description? Do some of the concepts resonate more than others?

14. The Enchanter's role changes within eir community over the years. How has e changed? How has society changed during those same years? How do those two trajectories intersect or mirror each other?

15. This novel has a strong environmental thread. Where do you see this most strongly?